under southern stars

code blue hearts
book one

Cari Blake

Twilight Republic Publishing

For the emergency services providers who find light in twelve-hour shifts, who laugh to keep from crying, and who somehow keep showing up. This one's for you. The real heroes who inspired these fictional ones.

Preface

The *Code Blue Hearts* series reflects the emotional reality of working in emergency medicine. Each book contains intense medical situations that may be challenging for some readers. Nothing is shown in graphic detail, and all scenes are grounded in compassion and realism.

This novel contains scenes involving an emergency birth and a life-saving surgical procedure (cricothyrotomy). These moments reflect real clinical urgency and may be intense for some readers.

chapter
one

THE PHONE RINGS at the charge nurses' desk; it's an EMS squad calling report. I grab it, already eyeing the Starbucks cup I'd nearly inhaled on the drive here. Grande Sumatra red-eye, no cream, no sugar. The barista at the drive-through had looked horrified when I'd explained a red-eye was an espresso shot dunked in black coffee.

Amateur, I'd thought, but kept my mouth shut. She was working for a living, just like me. Honestly, some days a red-eye felt like the bare minimum to face the ER, especially when the barista looked at you like you'd ordered a cup of pure jet fuel.

My ritual morning coffee had cost nearly seven dollars—practically highway robbery compared to what it cost a decade ago—but it was non-negotiable. Like my carefully organized parking routine: teal section only, thank you very much. I'd learned that lesson my first week here, when security had wheezed their way into the ER to inform me I'd parked in the sacred yellow section. Three years later, they'd still asked if I remembered where to park.

"Emergency department," I answer, putting on my charge nurse voice.

"*Kia ora*, Metro General." That honey-warm Kiwi accent flows over the line. "Got a transport for you."

My stomach does something I refuse to acknowledge. We've been doing this dance over the phone for months, but hearing Jack's voice first thing in the morning still catches me off guard.

"Go ahead with report," I manage, glancing at the digital grease-board. Nine patients in a 45-bed ER. The night shift is practically whistling with relief. Easy for them; they're leaving to go home. The ER gods are definitely going to make us pay for this.

"Fifty-eight-year-old male, chronic back pain, demanding transport after his GP wouldn't refill his oxy script. Vitals stable, ambulating without assistance. He's...not pleased with the wait time."

I roll my eyes. "Sounds like a real emergency."

He chuckles, low and rich. "Threatened to call his lawyer when we suggested urgent care instead."

"Lucky us." I check my staffing sheet while he talks. Nathan's on today—solid. Tasha too—less solid. That girl has the skills, but the attitude..."ETA?"

"About eight minutes out."

"Copy that. Plan on taking our friend to triage."

"Ooh, brutal," he says, but I can hear the smile in his voice. "Though I'd expect nothing less from the legendary Sophia Bentley."

"Mitchell," I correct automatically, then wince. "It's Mitchell. The paperwork's still catching up."

Silence stretches across the line. I shouldn't have said that. Too personal. Too much information for a professional EMS report.

"Right. Sorry." His voice softens. "Mitchell. I'll remember that."

The line goes dead. I stand there for a second, clutching the phone. Behind me, Jen clears her throat.

"Morning, Sophia. Ready for report?"

I spin around, hoping my face isn't as flushed as it feels. Jen's got that knowing look night shifters get when they're about to escape a quiet shift. Nine patients. Christ.

"Don't even think about saying it," I warn her. "You know what happens when someone says the Q word."

Jen mimes zipping her lips. "Wouldn't dream of it. Though honestly, after the week you've had, you deserve an easy day."

I raise an eyebrow. "The week I've had?"

"You changed your badge back to Mitchell. And you've been ordering extra shots of espresso in your coffee. Plus," she lowers her voice, "I hear you didn't take any calls during your break yesterday. You always take calls from Madison."

Damn. Nurses notice everything.

"She's with her dad this week," I say carefully. "And the name change paperwork finally went through officially, that's all."

Jen gives me a look that says she's not buying it, but she's too professional to push. "Mmm*hmm*. Well, anyway, ready for report?"

"Please." I pull up a chair, grateful for the subject change.

"By the way," Jen adds as she pulls up the patient list, "that paramedic's been asking about you. The one with the accent? Wanted to know if you were working today."

I keep my expression neutral. "Jack asks about everyone's schedule. He likes to know who's on for trauma alerts."

"Mmhmm. *Sure* he does. That's why he only asked about you, specifically."

My face heats. "Can we just do report?"

Jen grins and launches into her rundown. Kidney stone in room 8. Chest pain in 15; probably anxiety but awaiting troponin. Drunk in 22 sleeping it off. As she talks, I scan the staffing sheet again. Nathan in trauma. Tasha in fast track—better to keep her with the minor stuff until she learns to control that mouth. God knows I don't need her telling some frequent flyer what she really thinks.

I fiddle with my stethoscope, a $5 disposable special crammed in the pocket of my scrubs. It isn't as nice as the $150 Littmann I'd bought myself as a present for successfully graduating from nursing school, but that one had been stolen after I set it down momentarily and one of the residents apparently decided no nurse would have a stethoscope that nice. Its $50 replacement had been destroyed when a psych patient boarding in the emergency department attempted to strangle me with it. So now, I make do with the el-cheapo model.

"...and that's it. Nine total. It's been dead since about three."

"Jen," I hiss. "What did I just say about—"

The radio crackles to life. "Medic 220 to Metro General, priority one traffic."

Jen grins sheepishly. "My bad."

I grab the radio. "Go ahead, 220."

"Metro, we've got a cardiac arrest inbound. Sixty-year-old male, witnessed collapse at home, CPR in progress, multiple shocks delivered. We have not achieved ROSC. Patient is intubated, 7.5 ETT, secured at 23 at the lip. Last rhythm check showed fine V-fib. Two rounds of epi given. ETA four minutes."

After I take the EMS report, I start to scan the assignment board, but Nathan appears from nowhere, already gloving up. "On it, boss."

I check the board quickly. Nathan and Priya in trauma; solid team. Carlos and Derek covering acute care. Tasha in fast track. Jan, not due in until eight for triage, which means I'll have to cover until then.

Tasha slouches past, heading for the break room. "Great. Just when I was hoping for an easy—"

"Don't," Nathan and I say in unison.

She rolls her eyes. "Whatever. You people and your superstitions."

The ambulance phone rings again. I sigh internally and grab it, knowing it's already bad news.

"Metro?" Jack's voice, professional now. "Heads up. MVA coming your way. Three vehicles, multiple patients. We're staging for additional units."

Of course. The ER gods don't do anything by halves.

"Copy that. How many are we looking at?"

"At least six, maybe more. Going to be a busy morning after all."

In the background, I hear sirens. Multiple units. The quiet morning is officially over.

"Tasha!" I call out. "Fast track's about to become trauma overflow. Set up rooms twelve through fifteen."

She pokes her head out of the break room, mouth full of what looks like someone's leftover birthday cake. "Seriously? I just—"

"Now, Tasha."

I grab the desk phone and page overhead. "Dr. Kowalski, Dr. Lee to the charge desk please. Dr. Kowalski, Dr. Lee to the charge desk."

Melissa arrives first, coffee in hand. "What's up, Sophia?"

"Just to add to our morning, the arrest is being followed by a multi-vehicle accident, at least six patients. Unknown acuity. ETA about seven minutes."

"Fantastic," she mutters, then louder: "I'll take bay one with Nathan."

Cameron strides up, already in fresh scrubs. Of course he is. "I heard MVC?"

"Multiple patients incoming," I confirm, trying to keep my tone neutral. Cameron's an excellent trauma attending, but his ego barely fits through the ambulance bay doors.

"I'll run bay two." He flashes that TV-doctor smile. "Morning, by the way. Looking lovely as always, Sophia."

I ignore the comment. "Priya will assist you. Dr. Kowalski here yet?"

"Saw him in the lounge," Melissa says, already heading toward trauma. "I'll grab him."

"And someone wake up Jeffries," I add. "We'll need all hands."

Cameron lingers. "You know, if you ever want to grab coffee—"

"We have multiple traumas incoming, Dr. Lee."

"Right. Of course." He winks and heads off.

Nathan catches my eye and shakes his head slightly. We both know Cameron hits on anything in scrubs, but it's especially annoying this early in the morning.

Nathan's already moving, directing staff with quiet efficiency. This is what we do. This is who we are when the chaos hits.

I check the time. 0700. My phone buzzes—a text from my daughter.

> Dad's being weird about the pickup
> schedule again. Can we talk later?

I type back quickly.

> Of course, baby. After school. Love you.

Another text appears below it. From my ex-husband.

> Need to discuss Madison's nutrition plan.
> She's not following the meal prep I
> designed.

I involuntarily clench my fist, and then delete it without reading the rest. The man who never had health insurance when we were married suddenly thinks he's a wellness guru. Classic.

"Sophia?" Jen hovers by the door. "I'm gonna clock out before—"

The overhead speaker blares. "Trauma team to bay one. Trauma team to bay one."

Jen practically sprints for the time clock. "Good luck!"

I drain the last of my red-eye and crack my neck. Nine patients. I should have known better.

The radio crackles again. "Memorial, Medic 402..."

My day has officially begun.

chapter
two

"I'M DYIN' here! You people don't understand, I need my medication!"

Mr. Henderson hasn't stopped complaining since we loaded him. Fifty-eight years old, chronic back pain, and mad as hell his primary care provider won't refill his oxy script. Currently thrashing on our gurney like we're torturing him, despite waiting for us at his door and walking just fine to the ambulance.

"Nearly there, Mr. Henderson," I tell him for the tenth time. "Just a few more minutes."

"This is medical negligence! I'll sue every last one of you!"

Baz catches my eye in the rearview mirror, fighting a smirk. "Guy's a real piece of work, Kiwi. Says the bumps are aggravating his 'delicate condition.'"

"Delicate as a concrete slab, more like," I mutter, checking the monitor. Vitals rock steady, of course. "Bloke's got lawyers on speed dial, apparently."

As Metro General comes into view, my mind shifts to what's waiting for us. Or rather, who. Mitchell.

Sophia *Mitchell*. Not Bentley anymore.

We punch in the EMS door code and wheel Mr. Henderson

through the automatic doors, the ER humming with its usual controlled chaos. I've seen her dozens of times before—quick hand-offs, professional nods, the occasional shared eye roll over difficult patients. But today, after that radio correction, I'm actually looking. Trying to reconcile the voice with the person I thought I knew.

She's at the charge nurse's station, on the phone, one hand gesturing decisively. Dark hair pulled back severely, all sharp angles and intense focus. Then she looks up, and I catch her eyes properly; startling blue under the fluorescent lights, scanning everything, missing nothing.

Something's different. Same competent charge nurse, but there's new armor there. Weight on her shoulders that wasn't there before.

"Medic 405," I announce as we approach. "Got your fifty-eight-year-old male, chronic back pain, demanding transport."

She nods, gaze direct. "Mr. Henderson, I presume?" Her voice is exactly as it was on the radio, just without the electronic distortion. That hint of warmth still there, buried under layers of professionalism.

"That's the one. Vitals are still stable, though he'd have you believe he's at death's door."

A flicker of what might be amusement crosses her lips before it vanishes. "We'll find him a nice comfortable chair in triage, then. Thanks, Jack."

She uses my first name. Just like I'd used hers—Soph—on the radio. The thought sends an unexpected jolt through me.

Before I can respond, Dr. Lee appears—tall, dark-haired, looking like he's stepped off a medical drama. "Everything alright here, Sophia? Need me to charm this gentleman into compliance?" He winks at her, then turns to me with casual disinterest. "Nice accent, by the way. You from Down Under?"

I manage not to wince visibly. "Otago, actually, Doctor. New Zealand."

"Oh, same thing, right?" He grins. "I've been to Sydney once. Loved seeing all the Sheilas on Bondi Beach." He pronounces it

"BOO-ahndy BAY-ch," drawing out the syllables like he's auditioning for a Crocodile Dundee reboot.

Baz gives me his familiar smirk. Nothing worse than being mistaken for an Aussie when you're a Kiwi—it'd be like confusing a Canadian for an American, only with a few hundred more years of rivalry packed in.

Sophia doesn't react to Lee's comment, just raises one perfectly sculpted eyebrow. "I've got it, Dr. Lee. Perhaps you could check and make sure Bay One is ready for the trauma inbound?"

Her tone is polite, but the dismissal is crystal clear. Lee grins, unbothered, and wanders off.

She turns back to us. "Alright, bring Mr. Henderson to triage bay three." Her blue eyes linger on me for a fraction of a second. "Thanks again, Medic 405."

"Anytime, Miss Mitchell." I let warmth creep into my tone, acknowledging the name change with slight emphasis. "Happy to help. *Chur.*"

Her eyes flicker at the Kiwi slang—"chur" being our catch-all expression of thanks, agreement, or general goodwill. A recognition that I've noticed the name change? Then she's turning away, directing a passing nurse, all business again.

Back in the rig, Baz lets out a low whistle. "Man, Mitchell doesn't mess around, does she? And she totally shut down Dr. Pretty Boy. Heard he'll try to charm anything in scrubs now that he's finally got that attending money rolling in."

"She knows her stuff," I agree, but I'm thinking about those blue eyes, the new weight in them.

"Too bad we don't hit Metro more," Baz stretches as he drives. "All the crazy stuff happens there or downtown at University. Station 5's getting to be a real snooze-fest, you know? Not enough action."

He's right. Station 5 is relatively cushy. Routine transports, nursing home calls. Meanwhile, the crews from Station 2—like Medic 402—they're here constantly. Real emergencies, actual challenges.

The kind of runs where you'd see Mitchell regularly. See her enough to maybe understand what changed. What put that armor up.

"Yeah," I say, mostly to myself. "Might be time for a bit of a change."

"What's that?"

"Nothing, mate. Just thinking."

As we pull away, I catch a glimpse of her through the glass doors. Same competent charge nurse, handling everything thrown at her. But now I'm noticing something else—a weariness, maybe, or something heavier she's carrying that I hadn't seen before.

Sophia Mitchell. Brilliant blue eyes, runs a tight ship, and definitely not from Australia. All great attributes.

Might be worth taking a tiki-tour through those transfer policies after all. Station 2 runs to Metro daily.

For professional development, obviously. Wouldn't want to get too bored or out of practice.

Nothing to do with wanting to understand what put that weight on her shoulders.

Nothing at all.

chapter
three

A FEW WEEKS had somehow evaporated since the morning of the I-95 pile-up. That MVA had been the chaotic mess everyone predicted, a blur of critical patients, barking doctors, and the metallic tang of blood that never quite left your nostrils until your shift ended.

We'd saved some, lost some. The usual brutal ER math. Life, as it always did in the trenches of Metro General, had rolled on. I'd handled it. Madison had started soccer practice, Troy was still being Troy via passive-aggressive co-parenting texts, and I was still main-lining caffeine like it was my lifeblood.

I'd heard Jack McKenzie's voice—Medic 405, Station 5—a handful of times on the radio since our brief in-person encounter when he'd brought in Mr. Henderson. The usual professional reports, always with that warm cadence that snagged my attention every time, sometimes a hint of the easy banter we'd had before.

No significant follow-up, though. Just another competent para-medic in a city full of them.

Right.

The ER is currently simmering at a low boil. Not dead quiet (*never, ever* say the Q-word) but manageable. I'm reviewing staffing for the next shift change when Maria, our unflappable unit secretary who has the uncanny ability to simultaneously answer three phones and know everyone's coffee order, glances up. "Heads up, Sophia, sounds like 402's got one for us. Might be interesting."

Medic 402. One of the busiest units, straight out of the city's roughest district. They usually patched criticals straight through on the hospital phone line; their primary response area actually had decent cell coverage, unlike some of the outlying districts. Better for detailed reports, less chance of radio interference.

So when the main radio channel crackles, it catches my attention. "Metro General, Medic 402 with a priority one patient, ETA five minutes. Adult male, approximately forties, found down, unresponsive by PD. Bystanders report PD administered Narcan without effect. On our arrival, patient remained unresponsive, GCS 3. Finger stick blood glucose was 18. IV established, D50 administered. Patient is now awake, alert, and conversing. Vitals stable."

Hypoglycemia masquerading as an OD. Classic. At least this crew had a glucometer and knew how to use it. My hand reaches for my own radio mic, ready to acknowledge.

"...McKenzie reporting."

My hand freezes. *McKenzie? On 402?* My brain does a quick, stuttering reboot. Medic 402 is a meat grinder, a burn-out assignment for even seasoned medics. Why in God's name would a Station 5, "Cushy Suburbs" medic be on *that* rig? Is he just covering a shift?

Flustered, and a beat too late, I key the mic. "Medic 402, uh... Jack? Understood on the D50. Glad he woke up for you. We'll have Trauma One ready. Any other immediate concerns en route?"

The second his name leaves my lips, I cringe internally. *Jack?* Over the open channel? Professional, Sophia. Real smooth. Across the charge desk, Maria, who truly hears *everything*, slowly, deliberately, raises one perfectly sculpted eyebrow at me over the top of her computer monitor. I can feel the heat creeping up my neck.

Jack's voice comes back, all business, but perhaps with the faintest hint of extra warmth layered beneath the professionalism that only I, having listened to him for months, might detect. "None at present, Metro. Patient is stable and conversant. We'll give a full bedside report on arrival."

My brain snaps back into ER mode, though my cheeks still feel warm. "Copy that, Medic 402. See you in five."

Internally, though, I'm still replaying my idiotic slip that had just broadcast to every emergency department, ambulance, fire truck, and scanner nerd in a thirty-mile radius.

I'll be hearing about this for *years*.

And as if to bookmark my dismay, the radio channel—momentarily quiet—crackles to life again. An unidentified unit, voice tinny and amused, pipes up, "Sounding friendly there, Metro! He buy you dinner first?"

"Channel clear for priority traffic!" I snap, my voice sharper than I intend, cheeks flaming. Then, more calmly, "Metro General, *out* and *clear* at 1305."

The implications hit me as I start assigning the incoming patient to a room and alerting Nathan. If McKenzie was on 402 regularly, that meant...more. More of him in my ER. More of that voice, those observant eyes. More chances for me to make an idiot of myself. My stomach does a complicated, unwelcome flip.

The bay doors hiss open, and they roll in—Jack and a paramedic I vaguely recognize as one of 402's regulars; Rodriguez, I think. The patient, a man looking to be in his forties and decidedly sheepish now that he was wide awake, is perched on the gurney. Jack looks different than I remember from his brief stint with Mr. Henderson. He still has that underlying calm, but there is a new intensity in his stance, a focused energy that comes from running in a high-volume area.

He gives a quick, efficient handover to Nathan, who meets them at the door. "This is Arthur Smith, forty-two. As per my radio report, he was found down, unresponsive. Discovered to have a finger stick blood glucose of 18, and woke right up with one amp of dextrose. States he hasn't eaten all day, had a couple of beers earlier. Denies any drug use, no significant medical history he's admitting to right now.

Said he woke up wondering where the biscuits were." Jack delivers the last bit with a completely straight face, but his eyes flicker to mine for a microsecond, a glint of shared amusement there.

They transfer Mr. Smith to our bed. I'm already thinking about labs, a full workup for the hypoglycemia, maybe a social work consult. In the organized flow, I am peripherally aware of Jack, not just hovering but seamlessly assisting where needed. Helping Mr. Smith sit up, ensuring his equipment is clear. He moves with a quiet competence that is…impressive. Annoyingly so.

Once Mr. Smith is settled and Nathan is drawing blood, Jack steps back, stripping off his gloves. Our eyes meet for a split second across the room. His are serious as he glances at the patient, but as they flicker back to me, there is something else there too, a directness that makes my skin prickle, and maybe, just maybe, that knowing smile is back in their depths.

Later, after Mr. Smith is munching on a turkey sandwich and awaiting a consult, I see Jack by the EMS supply closet, restocking. I need to know.

"McKenzie."

He turns, a faint smudge of something—pen ink?—on his cheekbone. "Why, Charge Nurse Mitchell. To what do I owe the pleasure?"

"Didn't realize you'd transferred to 402," I say, aiming for casual, professional curiosity. My heart, annoyingly, is not cooperating with the "casual" part.

A slow smile spreads across his face, crinkling the corners of those blue eyes. It is a surprisingly potent expression. "Figured it was time for a bit more… action." He holds my gaze for a beat longer than necessary. "Needed the challenge."

I just nod, not trusting my voice. *Challenge, right.* My internal bullshit meter is pinging, but another part of me, the part I've been trying to ignore for weeks, feels a ridiculous, treacherous flutter.

The rest of the shift is a blur of the usual ER madness, but under it all is a new, thrumming awareness. Jack McKenzie, the Kiwi paramedic with the warm voice and the surprisingly intense eyes, isn't just a pleasant radio interlude anymore. He is on Medic 402. He is going to be *here*. A lot. And I'd just broadcast my unprofessional, first-name-basis slip-up to half the city's emergency services.

Maria catches my eye as I'm doing chart checks. "So, 'Jack,' huh?" she murmurs, not even looking up from her screen.

I just shoot her a glare.

My phone buzzes. Madison.

> Dad's being a nightmare about this
> weekend. Says I can't go to the game.
> Can you fix it??? Pls mom!

Right. Real life. My actual, complicated, messy life that has no room for charming Kiwi paramedics who'd just decided to upend their careers, possibly just to get a bit more "action" in my ER.

Or so I tell myself.

chapter **four**

THE SECOND I push through the bay door into Station 2, I know it is coming. The silence is the first clue. It isn't the usual quiet of a crew checking their rigs; it is the predatory stillness of hyenas waiting for the wounded wildebeest to walk into the clearing.

Rodriguez, walking beside me, is grinning like he'd just won the lottery.

"You texted them, didn't you?" I mutter.

"I don't know what you could be talking about," Rodriguez says, albeit without trying to look the slightest bit innocent.

We round the corner, and the station erupts into catcalls and howls. The entire day shift crew materializes from various corners of the bay like they'd been lying in wait. Which, I realize, they probably have been. Some are pretending to check equipment, others have clearly abandoned whatever they'd been doing to witness this moment.

"JAAAAAACK!" O'Malley's voice echoes off the concrete walls.

"Oh, *Jaaaaaaaack*!" Martinez calls in a terrible falsetto that would have made a drag queen weep.

"*Uhhhh... Jack??*" Thompson adds, his impression of Sophia's radio voice surprisingly accurate.

"Well, well, well," says Kowalski, emerging from behind Engine 18 with a shit-eating grin. "Look what the Kiwi dragged in."

I surveyed the scene, taking inventory of the damage. The apparatus board now displays "Medic 402—Romeo Unit" in neat block letters. My gear locker is "decorated" with heart stickers that look suspiciously like they've been liberated from the pediatric trauma kit, along with what appears to be gas station roses with a note reading "From your secret admirer at Metro General."

Someone has even written "McKenzie ♥ Metro" in pink dry-erase marker on Engine 18's bumper.

"You lot have been busy," I observe.

"We're dedicated to excellence in all our endeavors," Martinez says solemnly, then immediately ruins the effect by snickering.

O'Malley cups his hands around his mouth like a megaphone. "Attention Station 2! McKenzie's girlfriend is on the radio!"

"She's not—" I start, then stop. There is no point. "Right, well, this is happening then."

The chant starts somewhere near the back of the group and quickly spreads: "He buy you dinner first? He buy you dinner first?"

The rhythm is getting more elaborate, like some kind of demented marching cadence. Thompson is starting to add percussion by banging on a clipboard.

Rodriguez leans against the ambulance, arms crossed, watching the spectacle with obvious satisfaction. "You should see your face right now, *hermano*."

"Traitor," I mutter.

"Professional development," Rodriguez corrects. "Character building. Very important for crew cohesion."

The bay door to the station offices opens with a sharp bang that cuts through the chaos like a fire axe through drywall. Lieutenant Isabela Delgado steps out, clipboard in hand, her expression carved from granite.

The catcalls and laughter die so abruptly it is almost louder than the noise had been.

"Martinez," she says, her voice carries the kind of quiet authority that makes grown men reconsider their life choices. "O'Malley. Don't you have rig checks to finish?"

"Yes, Lieutenant," they mumble in unison, suddenly fascinated by their boots.

"Thompson, I believe you're on inventory duty this week. That supply closet isn't going to organize itself."

"On it, El-tee."

"Kowalski, wasn't there something about the hose bed needing attention?"

The crew scatters like roaches under a sudden light, leaving me standing alone in the middle of the bay with Rodriguez, who is trying very hard to look like he hadn't been the ringleader of this particular circus.

Izzy's gaze sweeps over the decorated locker, the apparatus board, and finally lands on me. For just a moment, I could have sworn I see the corner of her mouth twitch.

"McKenzie," she says. "My office. Now."

As I follow her toward the small administrative office, Rodriguez whispers loudly, "Don't forget to use protection!"

Izzy stops dead in her tracks. Slowly, deliberately, she turns around.

"Rodriguez," she says, her voice sweet but simultaneously terrifying. "Toilet duty. All week. With a toothbrush."

Rodriguez's face falls. "Aww, come on, El-tee—"

"Two weeks."

Rodriguez's mouth snaps shut.

Izzy gestures for me to continue into her office, closing the door behind us with a soft click that somehow manages to sound ominous. The small space suddenly feels charged with tension, though whether it is disapproval or something else, I can't quite tell.

Lieutenant Delgado doesn't sit down. She just leans against her desk, arms crossed, studying me like I'm a *particularly* interesting species of insect.

"I don't care what you do on your own time," she begins, her voice low and controlled. "I don't care who you date. I don't care if you have a whirlwind romance with the entire nursing staff at Metro General."

She pauses, letting the words land.

"But when your flirtations are broadcast over the entire county's emergency radio network, it becomes my problem. When one of our crew members decides to make jokes over a recorded, public channel, it becomes a professionalism issue for this entire station. Do you understand?"

"Crystal, Lieutenant," I confirm, making sure to match her serious tone. "I'm sure it was a slip on her part, not intentional. And I had nothing to do with Rodriguez's commentary."

"I know. I know." Her expression softens almost imperceptibly. "I already wrote Rodriguez up for the radio comment. He'll be cleaning those toilets with his tears."

Despite the tension, I feel my mouth twitch. "Bit harsh, don't you think?"

"Was it funny? Yes. My abuela probably heard it on that ancient police scanner she's had since the Carter administration." Izzy shakes her head. "But this station—my crew—has a reputation for being the best. That means we're held to a higher standard. No more providing entertainment for the entire county's gossip network. We clear?"

I study her for a moment, recognizing something in her tone I've heard before—the careful control of someone who knows they are being watched more closely than others. She is having to have this conversation because she's a woman, I realize. If this was Captain Murphy's crew acting up, the brass would just chalk it up to 'boys being boys.' But when it's her station, every screw-up gets magnified. She has to work twice as hard to get half the credit.

"We're clear, Lieutenant."

"Good." She straightens, all business again. "Now get out of my office and go check your rig. And McKenzie? Try to keep the romantic declarations off the public airwaves. Some of us have professional reputations to maintain."

As I turn to leave, I hear her add, so quietly I almost miss it, "And for what it's worth...she could do a lot worse than you."

I glance back, but she is already focused on her paperwork, the moment of vulnerability gone as quickly as it had appeared.

Back in the bay, Rodriguez is very deliberately inventorying medical supplies, his earlier smugness is replaced by the resigned expression of a man facing two weeks of intimate toilet acquaintanceship.

"So," Rodriguez says without looking up from his clipboard. "Scale of one to ten, how dead am I?"

"Toothbrush dead," I confirm, unable to keep the grin out of my voice.

"Worth it," Rodriguez says firmly. "Totally worth it. You should have seen your face when you walked in here."

O'Malley appears from around the side of the engine, still chuckling. "Don't worry, Romeo. We'll make sure to answer all your calls from Metro General with appropriate...enthusiasm."

"Professional enthusiasm only," I warn, but can't swallow the smile I'm fighting now.

The truth is, as mortifying as the whole thing is, there is something oddly warming about it. In the weird, twisted logic of firehouse culture, this level of elaborate harassment means acceptance. They care enough about me to put genuine effort into making my life miserable.

It is, in its own strange way, a kind of love.

Suddenly, the station PA comes to life with what sounds like a basketball buzzer, just as our radios crackle to life. "Chest pain, 57-year-old male, 3616 Michigan Avenue, cross street Maple, Medic 402 respond."

I key my radio with deliberate professionalism. "Medic 402, responding."

The timing is perfect—it gives us an escape route from the

ongoing harassment. But as Rodriguez and I head for the rig, a chorus of voices follows us: "Tell Sophia we say hiiiiii!" "Ask her if she has any single friends!"

I wave them off without turning around, but he is grinning now. Rodriguez climbs into the driver's seat, still chuckling.

"You know this is never going away, right?" Rodriguez says as they pull out of the bay. "Twenty years from now, they'll still be calling you Romeo."

"Could be worse," I say, settling back in his seat. "Could be 'McKenzie's girlfriend is on the radio.'"

"Oh, that's definitely sticking too."

As Rodriguez hits the lights and sirens, I find myself wondering if Sophia finds the station's reception party as mortifying as I do, or if maybe—just maybe—she is a little amused by it all.

Rodriguez glances over at his partner's thoughtful expression. "You're thinking about her, aren't you?"

"Just wondering what she'd think about all that," I admit, nodding in the general direction of the station.

"Oh, you'll find out. I guarantee she'll hear about it. Trust me. Hospital gossip travels faster than light." Rodriguez grins. "Question is, what are you gonna do about it?"

I consider this seriously as we weave through traffic, sirens wailing. What am I going to do about it?

Maybe it is time to stop pretending this is just casual radio banter.

"We'll see," I say finally.

"That's what I thought," Rodriguez says, satisfaction clear in his voice.

chapter **five**

Sophia

"MOM, YOU'RE BURNING THE GARLIC."

Madison's voice cuts through my distraction, and I quickly turn down the heat under the pan, stirring the suddenly too-brown bits with more force than necessary.

"It's *caramelized*," I say defensively, though we both know better.

"Uh-huh." Madison looks up from her chemistry homework spread across the kitchen counter. "That's what we're calling it?"

I shoot her a look, but she is already back to balancing equations, her pencil tapping against her lip in concentration. The kitchen fills with the smell of garlic that has definitely crossed the line from golden to bitter.

"How is school?" I ask, salvaging what I can of the pasta sauce.

"Fine. Mrs. Patterson assigns our final projects for AP Bio. I'm thinking about doing something on cardiac electrophysiology." She glances up hopefully. "Maybe you could help? You know, professional insight?"

"Of course." I smile, genuinely pleased. Madison has been showing more interest in medicine lately, asking thoughtful questions about my work instead of just tolerating my ER stories. "What's your angle?"

"Maybe something about how electrical conduction abnormalities can mimic other conditions? Like, how you can't always trust what the monitor shows you?"

I pause in my stirring. That is remarkably sophisticated thinking for a fifteen-year-old. "That's...actually brilliant. Very advanced."

"I have a good teacher," she says with a grin, then returns to her homework.

As I add tomatoes to the pan, I find myself humming softly... nothing specific, just a tune that has been stuck in my head for days. The kitchen feels warm and comfortable, the kind of domestic peace I've been craving for years.

"Ooookay, what's up with you?" Madison asks suddenly.

"What do you mean?"

"You're humming. You never hum." She sets down her pencil and studies me with the intense focus she usually reserves for particularly challenging homework problems. "And you've been doing it a lot lately."

"I hum!" I protest, though even as I say it, I can't remember the last time I have.

"Mom. You whistle sometimes when you're really concentrating. You sing along with the radio in the car. But you don't just... *hum*." She tilts her head. "It's nice! Different, but nice."

I consider this, stirring the sauce more slowly. "Different how?"

"I don't know. Lighter? Like..." She searches for the right words. "Like you're not carrying something heavy all the time."

The observation hits me unexpectedly. Out of the mouths of babes. "I don't carry anything heavy."

"Mom." Madison's voice carries that particular teenage inflection that manages to convey both affection and gentle exasperation. "You carry everything heavy. Work stress, money stress, Dad stress, me stress—"

"You're not stress," I interrupt quickly.

"I'm *teenager* stress, which is totally different but definitely still stress." She grins. "But you just seem...I don't know. Happier? More relaxed?"

I turn to face her fully, leaning against the counter. "You notice all that?"

"I live here too, Mom. Kind of hard to miss when the general atmospheric tension decreases." She returns to her chemistry equations. "Not complaining, by the way. It's nice."

For a moment, I just watch her work—this remarkable person I've somehow managed to raise despite all my mistakes and uncertainties. When has she become so perceptive? So emotionally intelligent?

"Madison?"

"Mmm?"

"Do you remember Dad ever noticing when I was happy or sad?"

She looks up, her expression suddenly serious. "...honestly? No. Dad notices when you disagree with him or when you are not doing what he wanted you to do. But just...your moods? Whether you are okay?" She shakes her head. "I don't think he pays attention to that stuff."

The casual honesty of it stings, even though I'd known it was true. Troy was excellent at cataloging my failures but utterly blind to my emotional state unless it directly affected him.

"But you notice," I say.

"Of course I notice. You're my mom." Madison's tone suggests this is the most obvious thing in the world. "Plus, you take care of everyone else all the time. Someone should take care of you too."

I feel an unexpected tightness in my throat. "I'm fine, baby. I don't need—"

"Everyone needs someone to notice when they're happy," Madison interrupts gently. "Even moms."

I turn back to the stove, ostensibly to check the pasta but really to compose myself. When has my daughter become so wise?

"So," Madison says, clearly sensing the need for a subject change. "What's making you happy? New coffee blend? Finally get decent residents who don't try to kill patients?"

I laugh despite myself. "Something like that."

"Good. You deserve to be happy, Mom. You know that, right?"

The simple statement hits me harder than it should have. "I...yes. Of course."

"I'm not sure you do know that," Madison says thoughtfully. "Sometimes I think you believe you have to earn happiness instead of just... having it."

I stare at her, wondering when my fifteen-year-old has become a therapist. "Where did that come from?"

"AP Psychology. Also, living with you for fifteen years." She grins. "You're not as mysterious as you think you are."

The timer for the pasta chooses that moment to go off, saving me from having to respond. As I drain the noodles and combine everything in the pan, I find myself thinking about Madison's observations.

Have I been carrying everything heavy? Is it really that noticeable when I'm not?

And if so, what exactly has changed?

"Dinner's ready," I call, plating the pasta with the slightly-burned-but-still-edible sauce.

Madison clears her homework from the counter, making space for our plates. As we settle in to eat, she looks at me with that same thoughtful expression.

"Mom?"

"Yes?"

"Whatever's making you hum? I hope it sticks around."

I smile, twirling pasta around my fork. "Me too, baby. Me too."

As we eat, the conversation drifts to safer topics—Madison's upcoming chemistry test, weekend plans, whether we should finally replace the broken garbage disposal. Normal, domestic, comfortable topics that fill the kitchen with the kind of easy contentment I'd forgotten is possible.

But underneath it all, Madison's words echo: *You deserve to be happy.*

Maybe she's right.

Maybe I do.

chapter
six

"NO, Mum, I'm not 'playing paramedic.'" I wedge the phone between my shoulder and ear while measuring coffee grounds. "I *am* a paramedic. Have been for three years now."

"Such a waste, Jackson. Nearly thirty-three years old and still running around in an ambulance." Her voice carries that particular mix of disappointment and affection that only mothers can manage. "You could be running the Wanaka vineyard by now. Your father's been managing both properties, and the new Pinot harvest—"

"Dad's doing fine without me." I dump the grounds into my ancient coffee maker. "How's the weather in Otago?"

"Don't change the subject. If you must insist on this healthcare... *phase*...you could at least work for Te Whatu Ora back home. They're always looking for flight medics at Milford Sound for all the tourists. Then you'd still be doing your 'real work' but be where you *belong*."

"Mum—"

"Your sister Lily's getting married soon. To Oliver Ashford. You remember him? The cardiac surgeon from Dunedin Hospital? Lovely boy. Perhaps you could—"

"Perhaps I could what? Bring a date?" I think of sharp blue eyes and a voice like good whiskey. "Working on it."

"Oh?" Her tone perks up immediately. "Who is she? What does she do?"

"She's in healthcare." True enough. "Listen, Mum, I've got shift in an hour. Give Dad my best, yeah?"

"The charity auction is next month. In Queenstown. You could at least—"

"Love you too. *Chur.*"

I end the call before she can mention the family's private jet or the new villa overlooking Lake Wakatipu. Three years, and she still thinks this is some kind of rebellion phase. Maybe it started that way —the black sheep of the McKenzie family choosing sirens over vineyards and sheep stations.

But somewhere between my first life saved and watching real people do real work for real reasons, it became who I am.

The coffee tastes like burnt rubber, but it's mine. No imported beans, no family crest on the mug. Just me and my modest apartment and the job I actually love.

My phone buzzes. Rodriguez.

Ready for another shift in paradise, Kiwi?

Paradise. Right. Medic 402 runs through some of the roughest neighborhoods in the city. Gang violence, overdoses, domestics gone wrong. Yesterday alone we had two stabbings and a jumper from the bridge.

Still better than sitting in a boardroom, pretending to care about profit margins.

I grab my gear and head out. Two days since Sophia Mitchell said my name over the public radio channel. Two days of replaying that "*Uhh ... Jack?*" and the way her voice caught on it.

Time to see if she's still blushing about it.

Rodriguez is already at the station, checking the rig. "Alright, Romeo McKenzie, you ready to get back out there? Maybe get to see Sophiaaaaa?"

I tried to stifle a grin, unsuccessfully. "She was just being polite. You know. Professional courtesy."

"Right. That's why you transferred to 402, huh? 'Professional courtesy'?"

I don't answer, but Rodriguez laughs anyway. "Well, did she shut you down? Mitchell doesn't exactly have a reputation for being... approachable."

"Haven't asked anything to be shut down from."

"Yet."

Fair point.

Our first three calls are routine—elderly fall, anxiety attack, minor MVA. But the fourth...

"Medic 402, respond to 1542 Oak Street, apartment 3B. Thirty-four-year-old male, reports severe abdominal pain, states pain medication isn't working."

Rodriguez groans. "That's Thompson. Third time this week."

I know the type. Chronic pain patient, probably legitimate originally, now caught in the cycle of seeking stronger meds. Doctors won't prescribe, so they call 911 hoping the ER will cave.

"Sweet as," I say, flipping on the lights. "Let's go help Mr. Thompson."

"Help him find a new dealer, maybe," Rodriguez mutters.

But when we arrive, Thompson's genuinely in distress. Sweating, clutching his stomach, rocking back and forth on his couch.

"G'morning, Mr. Thompson." I kneel beside him, voice calm. "Tell me about this pain."

"It's...different. Not like usual. Sharp. Here." He points to his belly, right lower quadrant.

Rodriguez rolls his eyes, but I'm already doing the assessment. Rebound tenderness. Guarding. Slight fever.

"When did you last eat?"

"Two days ago? Maybe three? The pain..."

"Right. Let's get you to hospital, yeah? This might be more than your usual."

We load him up, and I'm thinking appendicitis, maybe early perforation. Rodriguez drives while I establish IV access.

I pull out my phone to call in the report, and despite myself, I'm hoping Sophia's working the desk today. Her voice over the radio is one thing, but an actual phone conversation...

I dial Metro General's direct line, pulse quickening slightly as I wait for someone to pick up.

Thompson moans. "They think I'm drug seeking. They always think..."

"Not today, mate," I assure him while the phone rings. "Today you've got something real, and they'll see that."

chapter
seven

THE PHONE RINGS at the charge desk; EMS calling report again. I grab it, already juggling three other things.

"Emergency department."

"*Kia ora*, Sophia." Once again, that honey-warm Kiwi accent flows over the line. "Got a transport for you."

My brain stutters for half a second. Jack. Of course it's Jack.

"Go ahead with report," I manage, keeping my voice professional.

"Thirty-four-year-old male, chronic pain patient, presenting with acute right lower quadrant pain, fever of 101.2, positive rebound tenderness. Vitals stable, IV established. Patient's convinced you'll think he's drug seeking."

"Roger that." I'm updating the computer, but his accent is doing things to my concentration. "ETA?"

"About ten minutes out."

"Copy that. And you can call back anytime with that accent."

The words are out before I can stop them. My hand flies to my mouth. Did I just—? *Oh my God.*

Silence stretches across the line. My face burns. I'm the charge nurse. I don't flirt with paramedics. I especially don't accidentally proposition them over recorded hospital lines.

"I mean—to give report. You can call to give report. About patients. That's what I—"

"Sophia." The way he says my name stops my babbling. I can hear the smile in his voice. "I'll hold you to that."

The line goes dead. I stand there, clutching the phone, wondering if anyone else heard that trainwreck.

Manny, one of our techs, walks by with a knowing smirk. "Smooth, boss. Real smooth."

Great. Just fantastic.

chapter
eight

METRO GENERAL'S afternoon shift is in full swing when we arrive. I spot Sophia immediately—she's at the nurses' station, managing three conversations at once while typing. That dark hair's escaping its tie again, wisps framing her face.

She hasn't looked up yet, probably still mortified from our phone call earlier. I can't help but smile remembering her flustered backtracking: "*I mean—to give report. You can call to give report. About patients.*"

An idea strikes. Probably stupid. Definitely risky. But Rodriguez's words echo: "Haven't asked anything to be shut down from."

"Room twelve," Priya directs us. "Dr. Ward's waiting."

We transfer Thompson, and I give report to Delaney Ward. She agrees; it looks surgical. Thompson nearly cries with relief when she says she'll order a CT.

"See?" I tell him. "Sometimes the pain is real."

After cleanup, I make my move. The coffee shop in the hospital lobby knows me now—one of the perks of running to Metro constantly.

I ordered a flat white. The Metro General café gave it a decent crack, all things considered. Then, casual as I can manage: "Actually, quick question. The charge nurse from the ER—dark hair, always looks like she needs more caffeine?"

The barista grins. "Sophia? Oh yeah, she's a regular. Why?"

"Thought I'd bring her one. Been a rough shift." I lean on the counter, friendly but not creepy. "What's her usual?"

"Red-eye, no cream, no sugar." She shakes her head. "That woman drinks jet fuel, I swear. Sometimes asks for an extra shot when it's really bad."

"Better make it with the extra shot then." I slide a twenty across the counter for a six-dollar coffee. "Keep the change, eh? Appreciate the help."

"Trying to impress the ice queen?" She winks as she adds the extra shot. "Good luck with that."

Ice queen. Not the first time I've heard that. But I remember her voice on the phone: flustered, warm, but *definitely* not frozen.

I carry both coffees back to the ER. She's still at the nurses' station, now frowning at what looks like a staffing grid. Her cheeks are slightly pink—still thinking about our phone call, maybe? I set the red-eye on the desk next to her.

"Figured you might need this, Charge Nurse." I keep my tone light, testing the waters after our earlier... moment. "Heard it's been a busy one."

She stares at the cup like it might explode. "How did you..."

"The barista was very helpful." I sip my flat white innocently. "Apparently you're famous for your coffee orders. Something about jet fuel?"

Her eyes narrow. "You bribed the barista for my coffee order?"

"Bribed is such a strong word. I prefer 'tipped generously for information.'"

The tiniest smile tugs at her mouth before she suppresses it. "That's...thank you." She picks up the cup carefully, inhales the aroma. "Extra shot?"

"Barista's recommendation for rough shifts."

She takes a sip, and her eyes close for just a second. Worth every penny of that twenty.

"Well, well." Dr. Cameron Lee materializes like smoke. Always does have terrible timing. "Mitchell, about that dinner we discussed..."

Sophia's eyes snap open. "We've never discussed dinner, Dr. Lee."

"We should rectify that." He leans on the counter, completely ignoring me. "Tonight? That new French place downtown? I've got reservations."

"I don't—"

"Come on." His smile would probably work on someone who hadn't been dealing with him for years. "One dinner. What's the harm?"

Before I can step back, before I can make a graceful exit, Sophia's hand lands on my forearm. Her fingers are cool through my uniform sleeve.

"Actually, I already have dinner plans." Her voice is steady, but I feel the slight tremor in her grip.

Cameron's eyebrows rise. "Oh? With who?"

Her fingers tighten almost imperceptibly. Here it comes.

"Jack here just asked me out on a date." She glances at me, and something in her eyes is half challenge, half plea. "Didn't you, Jack?"

The ER seems to pause. Even the monitors sound quieter. I can feel everyone within earshot holding their breath.

"That's right." I set down my coffee, turn to face her fully. If we're doing this, we're doing it properly. "Tonight, actually. Hope you haven't changed your mind?"

Her eyes widen slightly—surprise that I'm playing along? Relief? Something else?

"Wouldn't dream of it." Her voice has that charge nurse authority, but underneath...

Cameron's face cycles through several expressions before landing on skeptical. "Really. The paramedic."

"'*The paramedic*' has a name," I say mildly. "And a reservation."

"Since when—"

"Since now." Sophia's voice could cut glass. "Was there something medical you needed, Dr. Lee?"

Tasha chooses that moment to appear, because of *course* she does. I've handed off enough patients to her in fast track to know her timing is always impeccable... and usually unfortunate. "Did I just hear right? Mitchell's got a date with the Kiwi?"

The look Sophia gives her could freeze hell, but before she can respond, my phone buzzes. Rodriguez, texting from the rig, wanting to know my status.

"I should go." I touch Sophia's hand where it still rests on my arm. "So, tonight? Giuseppe's downtown?"

She hesitates, calculating. "Eight-thirty? I need to drop Madison at her friend's house first."

"Eight-thirty it is." I squeeze her hand gently. "I'll meet you there."

"Meet me?" Her eyebrows raise slightly.

"Figured you'd want your own car." I lower my voice, just for her. "In case you need an escape route."

Something softens in her eyes. "Eight-thirty, then."

Cameron makes a sound like he's choking. Tasha's mouth actually falls open.

"Italian sounds perfect." Sophia's voice is steady now, decided. "Giuseppe's has that nice corner booth."

"The one with the view." I grab my coffee, grin at the audience. "See you tonight, Mitchell."

As I head for the exit, I hear Tasha's voice: "Did that really just happen?"

And Sophia's response, dry as dust: "Don't you have patients in fast track?"

Rodriguez is leaning against the rig when I get outside, grinning like a loon. "Friday night date with the ice queen. Better pray we don't get held over."

"Don't even say it." I climb into the passenger seat, reality setting in. "Christ. I've got an actual date tonight."

"Better hope dispatch is quiet after seven." He starts the engine. "Nothing worse than showing up late, covered in someone else's blood."

Eight-thirty. That gives me...I check my watch. Just over six hours to get through shift without a late call, get home, shower, find something decent to wear, and figure out how to turn a fake date into something real.

The tones drop. "Medic 402," dispatch crackles. "Respond to..."

Back to work. But now I've got something to think about besides the next call. Something real.

Someone real.

The afternoon suddenly looks a lot more terrifying.

And interesting.

chapter
nine

Sophia

"MOM, seriously, *which* friend's house am I going to again?"
Madison scrolls through her phone from the passenger seat, sneakers
propped against my dashboard despite my hundred warnings not to.

"Feet down," I say automatically. "And it's Chloe's. The sleep-
over, remember? You've been planning this all week."

"Ohhh, right." She drops her feet but keeps scrolling. "I thought
that was tomorrow night."

"It's...both, now."

Madison slowly looks up from her phone, one eyebrow raised.
"Both nights? Since when?"

"Since...this afternoon. I called Rachel and asked if you could
stay tonight too."

"Mmm-hmm." She drags out the sound, eyes narrowing with
teenage suspicion. "And this has nothing to do with the fact that you
suddenly needed to run home and change into your good dress?"

My face heats. "That's just... being tidy."

"Sure." She grins. "So where are you going? Hot date with a
medical journal?"

"I told you. Book club."

"Right. Book club. That's why you smell like your expensive

perfume and not like the ER." She goes back to scrolling, but I can see her smirking.

"Madison—"

"Dad's being weird about tomorrow's soccer game again," Madison says, quickly changing the subject. "Says he might have a work thing."

Translation: Troy's new girlfriend probably wants to do something else. I bite back what I want to say. "We'll figure it out, baby. One thing at a time."

It's 7:57. I managed to get home, shower, and somehow squeeze into the one nice dress that still fits post-divorce stress eating. The black one that made Troy say I looked "too intense" and "intimidating"—words he wielded like weapons during our marriage. Words that, with every utterance, made me fold in on myself just a little more. Now, I think as I smooth the fabric over my hips, *intense* and *intimidating* sound like compliments. Perfect for tonight, then.

"So." Madison's voice goes carefully casual. "This date. Is it the paramedic with the accent?"

I nearly rear-end the Honda in front of us. "What? How did you—"

"Mom. Everyone knows. Literally everyone. Aisha's mom works in radiology and she said you claimed some hot New Zealand guy in front of Dr. Lee." She grins. "About time someone shut him down."

"Madison Grace."

"What? He's gross. Remember when he hit on the student nurse at the Christmas party? She was like, nineteen."

Christ. Nothing's sacred in that hospital. "It's just dinner. And how do you even know about—never mind."

"Is it the same guy you said could call you anytime?"

My face burns. "You heard about that too?"

"Mom, give me a little credit." She actually looks up from her phone to study me. "You really like him, huh?"

"It's complicated."

"You always say that." She's quiet for a moment, then: "You know it's okay, right? To like someone who isn't Dad?"

My throat tightens. When did my fifteen-year-old get so wise? And when did she start seeing through me so easily? Here was my daughter, understanding what I couldn't say aloud: that I was afraid. Afraid of wanting. Afraid of hoping. Afraid of getting it wrong again.

The radio fills the silence, and suddenly a familiar beat comes on. Chappell Roan's "The Giver" starts playing.

"Oh my God, I love this song!" Madison cranks up the volume.

Without thinking, I start singing along, word for word.

Madison whips her head around so fast I worry about whiplash. "MOM. You know this song?"

"What? I like Chappell Roan!"

"But do you know what it's ABOUT?" She's looking at me like I just announced I speak fluent Klingon.

Just to mess with her—but also because it's an amazing song—I lock eyes with Madison and belt out the chorus to "The Giver" at full volume.

"Oh my God. Oh my GOD." Madison covers her face. "Please tell me you don't actually know what—"

"Madison, I'm thirty-eight, not dead. Also, I was in college once."

"MOOOOOM!" She's practically climbing out the window. "Ew ew ew ew ew!"

I turn the volume down slightly, grinning at her mortification. There's something unexpectedly liberating about shocking my teenager, about being seen as something more than just "Mom."

"Okay, changing the subject forever," Madison says. She studies me as I pull into Chloe's driveway. "So. You really like this guy, huh?"

"It's complicated."

"You always say that." She grabs her bag but doesn't get out yet. "Just...try to have fun tonight? Without overthinking everything?"

"I don't overthink—"

She gives me a look that's pure fifteen-year-old superiority. "Mom. You pre-plan your grocery lists. In order of store layout."

"That's being efficient."

"That's overthinking." She opens the door. "Don't be efficient tonight. Just be...you. The you who knows all the words to 'The Giver'."

"Madison—"

"Love you! Have fun! Don't do anything I wouldn't do!" She practically runs to Chloe's door, leaving me sitting there with my face burning.

My fifteen-year-old just gave me dating advice.

And used Chappell Roan to do it.

God help me.

8:24. Six minutes to get to Giuseppe's. Six minutes to figure out what the hell I'm doing. Six minutes to talk myself into—or out of—whatever is happening between Jack and me.

My phone buzzes. Jack:

> Running few minutes late. Got caught
> with a late call. Be there by 8:40. Sorry!

> No problem. I'll grab us a table.

Another buzz. From Troy. Of *course*.

> Madison says you have plans tonight.
> Must be nice to have free time. We need
> to discuss her college fund. Ethereum is
> up and I have thoughts.

Delete.

The passive-aggressive jab is typical Troy. During our marriage, he'd mastered the art of making me feel guilty for every moment not devoted to him or Madison. A girls' night out? Selfish. A professional conference? Unnecessary. His free time was essential; mine was indulgent.

I check my reflection in the rearview mirror. The dress is prob-ably too much. The heels definitely are. What was I thinking? This isn't even a real date. It's just two coworkers grabbing dinner after I used him as a human shield against Cameron.

My phone buzzes again. Maria this time:

> I bet that boy cleans up NICE. Have fun tonight!

Great. The entire hospital's probably betting on how this goes.

I arrive at Giuseppe's fifteen minutes early, suddenly self-conscious about everything—my dress, my hair, the fact that I'm here at all. The hostess gives me a knowing smile when I ask for "a nice table for two, please." She leads me to a corner booth with a small candle flickering in the center.

"Date night?" she asks, setting down menus.

"Just dinner," I reply automatically, then catch myself. "I mean, yes. I suppose it is."

"I'll bring water for both of you," she says with a wink. "And our wine list?"

"Please."

8:39. I'm sitting in Giuseppe's at a corner table, watching the door like a teenager. The waiter's already asked twice if I'm ready to order.

I ask him to give me a minute, I'm waiting for one more. Madi-son's words echo as I fiddle with the menu. Maybe she's right. Maybe it's time to stop being so careful, so controlled, so calculated, so...

chapter
ten

I'M STANDING outside Giuseppe's like a complete muppet, checking my reflection in the dark window for the tenth bloody time. The shirt's wrong. Everything's wrong. Should've worn the blue one. Or maybe the jacket. Christ, I don't even own a proper jacket anymore.

Rodriguez would be taking the piss right now if he could see me. "Smooth operator" my arse.

The restaurant glows warm through the windows—candlelit tables, exposed brick, the kind of place that knows what it's doing with both wine and pasta. I can see the corner booth from here. Can see her.

And that's when everything stops.

I am, just... fucking *speechless*.

Sophia Mitchell is sitting alone at a table for two, and she's absolutely *devastating*.

Gone are the scrubs, the severe ponytail, the charge nurse armor. Her dark hair falls in waves past her shoulders. The black dress— Christ Almighty, that dress—shows off shoulders I've never seen before, the elegant line of her throat. She's fidgeting with her menu, checking her phone, looking toward the door every few seconds.

She's...*nervous*?! Sophia "Ice Queen" Mitchell is nervous about *our* date?!

There's just no way.

I take an involuntary step backward. What the hell am I doing? I'm punching so far above my weight, I'm in orbit. She's brilliant, beautiful, raises a teenager, runs an entire emergency department without breaking a sweat. And I'm... what? Some rich boy playing at being working class? A thirty-two-year-old who disappointed his entire family to ride around in an ambulance?

She deserves someone established. Someone who hasn't spent years hiding from his real life. Someone who doesn't have to borrow Rodriguez's decent shirt, which is at *least* a full size too small, because all his *own* shirts are either uniforms or ancient band tees.

My phone buzzes. Message from her:

No rush. Got us the good table.

The good table. Like this is something she's thought about. Like it matters.

I'm about to turn around, text some excuse about being held over after all, when she looks toward the door again. Can't see me through the glass, but something in her expression stops me cold.

She looks...hopeful. Vulnerable. Like maybe she's fighting her own doubts too.

Don't be a tosser, McKenzie. You transferred stations for this woman. You convinced her to say yes. You don't get to bottle it now.

I take a deep breath, push through the door before I can think too hard about it.

The hostess starts toward me, but I'm already moving. Sophia hasn't seen me yet—she's looking down at her phone again. Gives me a moment to really see her. The curve of her neck. The way the candlelight catches in her hair. How she bites her lip when she's thinking.

"Sophia?"

She looks up, and those blue eyes go wide. For a second, neither of us says anything. Just...look.

"Sorry I'm late." My voice comes out rougher than intended. "Had to beg Morrison to cover the last hour. Cost me three shift trades and my dignity."

"You look..." She stops herself, color rising in her cheeks.

"Like I own real clothes?" I manage a grin, slide into the seat across from her. "You look..."

Incredible. Stunning. Like every fantasy I've had about you since that first radio call, only better.

"Yeah," is what comes out. "That dress is...yeah."

Smooth, McKenzie. Real smooth, mate.

She's still staring at me like she's seeing me for the first time. Like maybe she had her own moment of doubt waiting here. Like maybe we're both in over our heads.

"So," I say finally. "This is weird."

"Extremely weird."

"Want to get wine and pretend it's not?"

"*God,* yes."

And just like that, the spell breaks. She laughs, I laugh, and suddenly we're just Sophia and Jack, figuring it out as we go.

But that image of her waiting at the table, beautiful and nervous and real, is burned into my brain forever.

Way out of your league. But here you are anyway.

Sometimes that's all you need.

chapter
eleven

"SOPHIA?"

I look up.

Jesus Christ.

Jack's standing there in dark jeans and a button-down that makes his shoulders look broader. His hair's still damp from a shower, and there's a tiny shaving cut on his jaw that makes him impossibly human.

But it's the shirt that catches my attention. Unlike the loose EMS uniform that usually hides everything, this button-down is definitely a size too small, pulling across his chest, outlining muscles I've been pretending not to notice for weeks. The fabric stretches just enough to hint at abs underneath.

He had to have done that on purpose.

I feel heat creeping up my neck.

"Sorry I'm late." He slides into the seat across from me, and I catch a hint of soap and something woodsy. "Had to beg Morrison to cover the last hour. Cost me three shift trades and my dignity."

"You look..." I stop myself before I say something stupid. Like commenting on how that shirt is doing things to my concentration.

"Like I own real clothes?" He grins, tugging at the collar self-consciously. Maybe he knows it's too small. "You look incredible. That dress is... yeah."

We stare at each other for a moment, the reality of this hitting us both.

"So," he says finally. "This is weird."

"Extremely weird."

"Want to get wine and pretend it's not?"

"*God*, yes."

He signals the waiter. "Do you have a..." He peruses the wine list briefly. "2019 McKenzie Estate Otago Pinot?"

The waiter's eyebrows rise almost imperceptibly. "Excellent choice, sir. That's a particularly good vintage."

"My thoughts exactly," Jack says casually, then glances at me. "If that's alright? Or would you prefer something else?"

"Sounds perfect," I say, wondering briefly at the coincidence of the name.

When the waiter leaves, Jack leans back, studying me.

"For what it's worth," he says quietly, "I was going to ask you anyway. Been trying to for ages now. Just, ahh... hadn't worked up the nerve yet."

"Really?"

"Really. Though Dr. Lee's face was a bonus."

I laugh despite myself. "Tasha's probably started a betting pool by now."

"Rodriguez already tried to get me to put twenty on whether we make it to dessert."

"Did you?"

His eyes crinkle at the corners. "Fifty on us closing the place down."

The wine arrives. The waiter presents the bottle with particular care, and I notice the elegant label, with what looks like mountains in the background. Jack examines it briefly, nods approval.

"Beautiful label," I comment as the waiter pours.

"Central Otago does produce some stunners," Jack says neutrally.

He raises his glass. "To fake dates that aren't actually fake?"

"To taking chances," I counter, thinking of Madison's words.

We clink glasses. The wine is incredible—rich, complex, probably costs more than I want to know.

"So, Jack McKenzie." I set down my glass. "Tell me something that's not in your personnel file."

"What do you want to know?"

Everything, I think. But I start simple. "Why paramedicine? Really?"

Something flickers across his face. "You want the real answer or the interview answer?"

"Real. Always real."

He's quiet for a moment, turning his wine glass. "My family owns...businesses. Back home. The kind where you're expected to take over." He looks up. "I was supposed to run things. Had the degree, the training. Then I watched my dad save a tourist who was choking at a restaurant. Grabbed him, did the Heimlich, kept going like it was nothing."

"And?"

"And I realized I'd spent my life never doing anything that mattered. Never saved anyone. Never even tried." He shrugs. "So I left. Came here. Became a paramedic. My mother still thinks it's a phase."

"How long has this 'phase' lasted?"

"Had my license for three years and counting." His smile's self-deprecating. "What about you? Always wanted to be a nurse?"

"God, no. I wanted to be a marine biologist. Saw dolphins at SeaWorld when I was seven and that was it. Dreams mapped out."

"What changed?"

"Got pregnant at twenty-two. Married at twenty-three. Needed a real job with real benefits." I trace the rim of my glass. "Turns out

I'm good at it. The controlled chaos, the adrenaline. Making order out of disasters."

"Like your life?"

I look up sharply, but his eyes are kind.

"Maybe," I admit. "Troy—my ex—he was supposed to be the stable one. Finance degree, big dreams. Turned out his dreams kept shifting. Day trader, cryptocurrency, life coaching. Whatever his podcasts told him was the path to millions."

"While you held down the fort."

"Somebody had to." I take another sip. "Madison needed consistency. Health insurance. Food."

"And now?"

"Now she's fifteen and wise beyond her years, and I'm thirty-eight and having dinner with a man I told to 'call me anytime with that accent.'"

His grin is immediate. "Still standing by that invitation."

"It was a slip of the tongue!"

"Freudian, maybe? And I'm thirty-two. Since we're sharing ages and embarrassing moments."

I do the math. Six years younger. "Your mother must love that you're dating older women along with playing paramedic."

"Haven't told her yet." He grins. "Want to make sure you'll stick around through appetizers first."

The waiter appears. We haven't even looked at the menus. Jack orders for us both in Italian that definitely didn't come from Duolingo.

"Hidden talents?" I ask.

"Spent a summer in Rome during uni. Family business." He makes quote marks. "Learned the important things. Wine, food, how to apologize for being a tourist."

"What else don't I know?"

"Let's see. Can't sing at all. I play rugby badly, not like my sisters."

"You seem pretty good at chaos management too, though," I say, "or else you're in the wrong line of business."

He smiles, taking a sip of his wine. "I was thinking the same about you. Though you were built for chaos too, in your way," he says, circling back to my earlier comment. "Tell me more about that."

I take another sip of my wine, considering how much to share. "Three years into nursing, I was working this quiet Tuesday morning shift in triage. I was taking the blood pressure of a sweet little blue-haired lady who probably had a UTI, when we heard the crash."

Jack leans forward, his food momentarily forgotten.

"Almost right outside our ambulance bay, a driver had a seizure, lost control, and plowed into a farmers market. Bystanders started loading victims into their cars, ambulances were scrambling. We had maybe a thirty-second warning before seventeen people arrived. Simultaneously."

"Jesus," Jack murmurs.

"Our manager—" I shake my head, "nice guy, but he'd come from a medsurg unit, wanted to try his hand at the ER. God knows why administration thought that was a good idea. But anyway, he just...froze. Complete deer-in-headlights. And I knew we had seconds to get organized."

I find myself gesturing with my hands, the memory vivid even years later. "So I started barking orders. Pulled every available nurse, called in the off-duty docs who were sleeping in the lounge, commandeered the hallways for overflow. Told transport to clear the CT scanner, redirected elective cases. Started tagging patients—red, yellow, green."

"Mass casualty protocol," Jack nods approvingly.

"We had three critical head traumas, two pneumothoraxes, a near-amputation, and a pregnant woman in premature labor. But we saved them. Every single one." I pause, then add more quietly, "I never got any recognition beyond being made a permanent charge nurse after that. But you don't get 'attagirls' for doing your job, right?"

Jack's looking at me with something that feels like respect mixed with admiration. It's different from Troy's dismissive tolerance of my work, or Cameron's performative praise that always felt like a prelude to asking me out.

"That's...incredible, Sophia," he says finally. "You probably saved half those people before the doctors even touched them. Just by organizing the chaos."

I feel a flush of pleasure at the genuine appreciation in his voice. "It's what we do, right? You see it on the streets, I see it in the department."

"Still," he says, "that's not *just* doing your job. That's leadership under fire."

"Sounds like something you'd see plenty of in paramedicine," I deflect, not used to this kind of attention.

"Different kind of chaos," he acknowledges. "But I think I get it now. Why you're so good at being charge. It's not only experience. You're naturally wired for it."

"My dad was military," I hear myself saying, surprised at the disclosure. "We moved constantly. Maybe I learned to adapt quickly from that. To take control where I could."

"Is he still around?"

"Passed a couple years ago. Heart attack." I swallow against the sudden tightness in my throat. "He was my rock when my marriage was ending. Used to drive four hours just to take Madison for a weekend so I could have a break."

Jack reaches across the table, his fingers brushing mine in a gesture so natural it doesn't feel intrusive. "He sounds like a good man."

"He was." I smile, pushing back the melancholy. "Would have liked you, I think. He appreciated competence and had no patience for BS."

"Man after my own heart. What about your mom?"

"Retired teacher, lives in Florida now. Calls Madison twice a week for 'girl chats' and sends me articles about how I work too much."

"She's not wrong," Jack teases gently.

"Probably not," I concede. "Though having a fifteen-year-old doesn't leave much downtime. Madison's great, but—" I laugh, "— she has strong opinions about everything. Last month she made this ridiculous PowerPoint presentation titled 'Why Mom Needs a Social Life' with actual pie charts about my work-to-fun ratio."

Jack laughs, that warm sound that seems to vibrate through me. "Smart kid."

"Too smart sometimes," I agree. "So. We got a little sidetracked. Your sisters?"

"Right! My sisters," Jack says, leaning back. "I have three of them, and they'd eat you alive but in the nicest way." He grins at the memory. "Emma—my middle sister—actually had a shot at making it on the Black Ferns."

"The Black Ferns?"

"New Zealand women's national rugby team. Absolute legends. She broke her arm in a scrimmage but walked around with it broken for a week so she wouldn't miss the tryout." He shakes his head. "Mum nearly had a coronary when she found out."

"Did she make the team?"

"Probably would have, if the medics hadn't spotted the fracture during physicals. Although I don't think they held that against her. She coaches youth rugby now. Says it's less painful." He takes a sip of wine. "My youngest sister, Lily, is finishing her PhD in marine biology—living your dream, actually. And the oldest, Charlotte, she runs the business side of things back home with my dad."

"And you became a paramedic."

"Black sheep of the family. Though Lily backs me up. Says at least I'm doing something useful instead of 'perpetuating the global network of capital.'"

I laugh. "She sounds fun."

"She's a terror. You'd love her." He pauses. "Hmm. Think American coffee's basically dishwater—present company's red-eyes excluded. Oh, and I make a mean pavlova."

"Pavlova?"

"Meringue dessert. National treasure back home. I'll make you one sometime."

The casual future tense makes my stomach flip.

"Your turn," he says. "Secret talents?"

"I could put an IV in the back of a rock if I had to. Uhm. I can quote 'The Princess Bride' entirely. Once I delivered a baby in a casino bathroom stall."

"Story there?"

"Lady thought it was heartburn from the buffet. Turned out to be labor. Security helped me carry her out while she was still attached to her newborn by the umbilical cord."

"Brilliant." He's laughing, really laughing. "What else?"

"I read romance novels voraciously. The smuttier, the better. Have a secret Instagram for plant photos. I have to buy the 50% off flowers at Lowe's; can't keep any of them alive, but I do it anyway. Oh, and I might have a tiny crush on the new paramedic who's been calling on the radio and keeps bringing me coffee."

The words are out before I can stop them. Wine on an empty stomach—rookie mistake.

"Tiny?" His voice drops half an octave.

"Microscopic."

"That's why you announced I'd asked you out in front of half the ER?"

"Pure self-defense."

"*Right*. And the accent comment?"

"Temporary insanity."

"Which makes this the second occurrence."

I throw my napkin at him. He catches it, grinning.

"For what it's worth," he says, handing it back, "I transferred to 402 because of you."

I freeze. "What?"

"Not in a creepy way. It's just... Station 5 was too quiet. Not enough challenges. Not enough opportunities."

"Opportunities?"

"To bring you coffee. Hear your voice. Watch you orchestrate controlled chaos like you're conducting a symphony."

"*Jack.*"

"I know. Workplace dynamics. Recent divorce. Single mum. Complications everywhere." He reaches across the table, touches my hand lightly. "But maybe complicated's worth it?"

I turn my hand over, let our fingers tangle briefly. "Maybe it is."

The food arrives, breaking the moment. But something's shifted. This isn't pretend anymore.

Maybe it never was.

We eat, we talk, we laugh. He tells me about a sheep farmer who thought he was having a heart attack but had actually been kicked by a ram in a very sensitive area.

"Wait, wait," I'm crying with laughter. "He called 911 for that?"

"111 in New Zealand, but yeah. Thought his chest pain was cardiac. Turns out the ram got him in the wedding tackle and the pain radiated up." Jack's accent gets thicker when he's storytelling. "Poor bloke was mortified when we worked it out."

"What gave it away?"

"The hoof-shaped bruise on his nethers." He's laughing too now. "He made us promise not to tell his wife. Apparently, she'd warned him about that particular ram."

I tell him about the time Madison tried to set me up with her soccer coach, not realizing he was married to the assistant coach— who was also a man.

"She was so embarrassed. Kept apologizing to both of them for weeks."

"Smart kid, though. Good instincts about you needing to date."

"She's too smart. Tonight she basically told me to stop overthinking and just *feel* things. Used Chappell Roan lyrics as a therapy session."

"The youth of today," he says solemnly. "Wise beyond their years."

"She likes you, by the way. Or at least the idea of you."

His eyes light up. "Yeah?"

"Don't let it go to your head."

"Too late. Fifteen-year-old approval is the gold standard."

The waiter clears our plates, offers dessert. We order tiramisu to share, more wine. The restaurant's emptying around us.

"Rodriguez is going to win that bet," I say.

"Good. He'll be insufferable otherwise."

"This is nice," I say, surprised by my own honesty. "I forgot what this felt like."

"What?"

"Just talking to someone. Not about patients or schedules or custody arrangements. Just... talking."

His thumb brushes over my knuckles. "We can do more of this. If you want."

"I'd like that."

The tiramisu arrives. We share it, trading bites and stories. He teaches me how to swear in Māori ("But only for emergencies," he warns), and I teach him the proper way to handle Tasha ("Agree with her, then do whatever you were going to do anyway").

"Jack?" I say as the waiter brings our check. "This doesn't have to be complicated."

"No?"

"No. It can be... this. Whatever this is."

"And what is this?"

I think about Madison's words, about feelings and letting things be real.

"I don't know yet," I admit. "But I want to find out."

He smiles, that slow, warm thing that made me notice his accent in the first place. "Me too."

We close the place down. He walks me to my car, hands in his pockets like he's keeping them from reaching for me. The night air is cool, and I shiver slightly in my dress.

"Cold?" He's already shrugging out of his jacket.

"I'm fine—"

But he's draping it over my shoulders, and it smells like him, and I'm definitely not fine in the best possible way.

"This was…" I start.

"Yeah," he agrees. "It was."

"Same time next week?"

"Tomorrow, if you want. I'm on call 'till three, but as long as…" He shrugs.

"I've got Madison tomorrow. Soccer game."

"Sunday?"

"Sunday works."

He steps closer, and I think he's going to kiss me. Want him to so badly. But he just reaches up, tucks a strand of hair behind my ear.

"Goodnight, Sophia."

"Night, Jack."

I drive home in a daze, wearing his jacket, face warm where his fingers brushed. My phone's lighting up with texts—Maria, Nathan, probably half the ER—but I ignore them all.

Madison's right. Some things are worth feeling, even if they're terrifying.

Especially then.

I pull into my driveway, sit in the dark for a moment. Tomorrow I'll have to face the gossip, the knowing looks, the complications.

But tonight?

Tonight I went on a date with a kind man who makes me laugh. Who brings me coffee. Who transferred to a busier station just for more chances to see me. Who orders excellent wine and tells stories that make me forget I'm supposed to be careful.

Who looks at me like I'm more than just someone's ex-wife, someone's mother, someone's nurse.

Like I'm just Sophia.
And that's terrifying.
And perfect.
And real.

chapter
twelve

Jack

THAT WAS BLOODY *AMAZING*.

I sit in my car outside Giuseppe's for a full ten minutes after Sophia has driven away, grinning like an absolute fool. My face actually hurts from smiling, but I can't seem to stop. The ghost of her hair between my fingers lingers, that soft strand I'd tucked behind her ear instead of kissing her like every instinct had screamed at me to do.

God, the restraint that had taken. She'd looked up at me with those incredible blue eyes, lips slightly parted, and I'd wanted nothing more than to close that last inch of distance between us. But something had held me back—maybe the newness of it all, maybe the knowledge that when I finally kiss Sophia Mitchell, I want it to be perfect.

The way she'd shivered in the night air, how natural it had felt to drape my jacket around her shoulders. She'd practically melted into the warmth, and the sight of her wrapped in something of mine had done dangerous things to my composure. And then she'd driven away still wearing it, taking a piece of me with her.

"This was..."

"Yeah. It was."

Christ, if that wasn't the understatement of the century.
My phone buzzes. Emma, of course.

> How'd it go, Romeo? Did you cock it up?

I type back:

> Definitely didn't cock it up. She's...bloody
> hell, Em. She's incredible.

> That good, eh? When's the next one?

> Sunday.

> Moving fast. You lot who see people die
> for a living don't waste time, do you? 🩶 I
> like her already.

Sunday. Two days away. It feels like forever.

I finally start the car, my mind replaying every moment of the evening. The way she'd laughed when I'd told her about the ram incident, how she'd opened up about that mass casualty event, the quiet confidence she carries. How she'd made me feel both completely comfortable and utterly off-balance.

"I don't know yet, but I want to find out."

Her words echo in my head as I drive home. That honesty, that willingness to step into something uncertain together. No games, no pretense. Just Sophia being brave enough to admit she doesn't have all the answers.

Back in my apartment, I pace restlessly, too wired to sleep. I keep thinking about the way she'd defended her work, how she'd made that crack about having a tiny crush on "the new paramedic who keeps bringing me coffee." The flush on her cheeks when she'd realized what she'd said.

My phone rings. Charlotte, calling from New Zealand.

"Well?" she says without preamble. "How was the mysterious date?"

"How did you—Emma," I answer myself.

"Obviously. She said you were properly smitten. True?"

I lean back on my couch, still grinning. "Char, I think I'm in serious trouble."

"Good trouble or bad trouble?"

"The best kind," I admit. "She's...I don't even have words. Smart, funny, gorgeous. Doesn't take any shit, but she's got this incredible warmth underneath all that competence."

"And you're seeing her again?"

"Sunday."

Charlotte is quiet for a moment. "Jack, this is the first time I've heard you talk about a woman like this. Ever."

"I know."

"So when do we meet her?"

The question hits me like a physical blow. When do they meet her? When do I tell Sophia about the estate, the money, the family expectations? When do I risk everything I'd just found by revealing how much I'd been hiding?

"Jack? You still there?"

"Yeah, sorry. Just...it's complicated, Char."

"It's always complicated with you." Her tone softens. "But if she's as special as you seem to think, maybe it's worth the complication."

After we hang up, I sit in the dark, the high from the evening slowly giving way to a familiar anxiety. How long can I keep this up? How long before Sophia starts asking more pointed questions about my background, my family, my life before America?

"It can just be...this. Whatever this is."

She is right. It doesn't have to be complicated. Not yet. Not when we are just figuring out what this is between us.

I have to tell her eventually. Soon. Because whatever this is, it is too important to build on a foundation of half-truths.

But not yet. Not when everything is so new, so fragile. A few more dates. A few more chances to show her who I really am before revealing what I come from.

A little more time to be just Jack.

chapter
thirteen

THE SUN STREAMING through my kitchen window feels accusatory. I'm on my third cup of coffee, still wearing Jack's jacket from last night—it smells of cedar and something uniquely him—and I've checked my phone approximately eight thousand times

Last night feels like a fever dream. Chloe's mom, Rachel, had given me this knowing little smile when she dropped Madison off to get ready for soccer. "Have fun at book club?" she'd asked, winking. "That's what Madison said you were doing."

Book club. Right. I should have known something was up then.

"Mom, you're being weird." Madison emerges from her room, already in her soccer uniform. "Also, is that a man's jacket?"

"It got cold last night."

She grins, sliding into a chair. "Uh-huh. Sure. And you always look like you just had the best night of your life the morning after 'book club'?

My face heats. "Madison *Grace*—"

"Don't worry, I only told Chloe's mom you had a date. Not who with. Yet." She steals a piece of my toast. "So how was Mr. New Zealand?"

"His name is Jack."

"Ooh, first name basis already?" She steals a piece of my toast. "Did he kiss you goodnight?"

"Madison—"

"He didn't?" She looks horrified. "Mom, no. *Nooooo*. Please tell me you didn't do the awkward car door shuffle."

"I don't know what that means."

"It means you sat in your car for like five minutes wondering if you should kiss him first." She shakes her head. "Classic over-thinking."

The accuracy stings. "Shouldn't you be warming up for your game?"

"Dad's picking me up in twenty." She checks her phone, frowns. "Of course, he's already fifteen minutes late."

"And Chloe's mom is bringing you back to their house?"

"Yeah, she—" Madison stops mid-bite. "Wait. You're coming to my game, right?"

"Of course."

"Even though Dad will be there with Tiffany?" She watches me carefully.

Right. Troy's new girlfriend. The wellness influencer who's convinced Madison needs to cut out gluten and dairy and joy. As if my daughter needs some Instagram-inspired 'optimization.' Just another way Troy tries to assert control.

"I'll be there," I promise. "Want me to grab breakfast after?"

"Can Jack come?"

My coffee goes down wrong. "What? No. Madison, we've had one date—"

"But if he wanted to?"

"He has to work." I think. Maybe. I didn't actually ask about his weekend schedule.

My phone buzzes. My heart does something ridiculous.

But it's just Maria:

DETAILS. NOW!!!! THE WHOLE ER IS
DYING.

Madison leans over, reads it. "See? Everyone's invested. You have to make this work."

"That's not how relationships—"

"Mom." She puts on her serious face. "You know what Brené Brown says about vulnerability?"

"What?! Since when do you read Brené Brown?"

"Since Dad started dating someone who quotes her incorrectly on Instagram." She scrolls through her phone. "Here. 'Vulnerability is the birthplace of love, belonging, joy, courage, empathy, and creativity.' Maybe stop armor-ing up?"

A car honks outside. Troy, in his new Tesla that he definitely can't afford.

"That's my ride." Madison grabs her gear, then pauses. "Mom? I'm glad you went out last night. You looked...happy when you got home."

She's gone before I can respond, leaving me alone with my coffee and a teenager's wisdom.

I wander into the living room, drawn to the bookshelf where our photo albums live. There's one from our early marriage—Troy and me at some finance company party, both trying so hard to look successful.

Next to it, Madison's baby album. Then nothing for the last five years. Like our life stopped being worth documenting when things got hard.

Maybe it's time for new pictures. Maybe it's time to start documenting what comes next—whatever that might be.

My phone buzzes again. This time, my stupid heart wins. It's Jack:

> Morning. Hope you slept well. Still on for
> Sunday? Thinking coffee and a walk if the
> weather holds.

I stare at the text for an embarrassingly long time. Three sentences. Perfectly normal. Casual. Friendly.

> Sounds perfect. Marina Park? 10am?

His response is immediate:

> It's a date. Hey, random question, does
> Madison's team need any help today?
> Rodriguez's kid plays in the same league.
> Could swing by if you need an extra
> parent for drills or something.

I reread it twice. He's offering to come to Madison's game. To meet my ex. To insert himself into the complicated reality of my life.

My thumb hovers over the keyboard. This is a line. Cross it, and there's no pretending this is just casual.

> Game's at Field 3, 11am. But you really
> don't have to!

> Want to! If that's okay?

Want to. Not "happy to" or "sure, why not." Want to. With an exclamation point!

> My ex, Troy, will be there. Fair warning.

> No worries. I can handle Troy.

Something about his confidence makes me smile. Troy with his

Tesla and his wellness girlfriend and his cryptocurrency portfolio. Jack with his paramedic salary and his easy smile.

> Okay. Field 3. 11am. I'll bring real coffee. For, y'know. Medicinal purposes.

> See you then.

I set my phone down, heart racing. This is happening. Jack McKenzie is coming to my daughter's soccer game. He's going to meet my ex. He's stepping into my real life, not just the after-hours version.

My phone rings. Maria.

"Do *NOT* 'hey' me, Sophia Mitchell. I need every detail from last night or I'm coming over there with wine and a lie detector."

I slump into a chair. "It was perfect."

"Define perfect."

"He remembered how I like my coffee. He speaks Italian. He told me about his sisters and their rugby careers. He makes pavlova."

"What's pavlova?"

"Some New Zealand dessert. The point is, he was...wonderful."

"But?" Maria knows me too well.

"But nothing. That's the problem. It was too perfect. Like there has to be a catch somewhere."

"Maybe there isn't. Maybe he's just a good guy who brings you coffee and saves lives."

"Nobody's that simple."

"Honey, you're looking for problems that might not exist. Just enjoy it."

After we hang up, I stare at my phone. In two hours, I'll see him at Madison's game. I'll watch him meet Troy, navigate my complicated life, probably handle it all with that easy grace.

My phone buzzes. Another text.

> Looking forward to seeing you!

My heart does a backflip.

He's coming with his partner. His partner's kid. Building connections between our lives already. And *he's looking forward to seeing me.*

> Me too! See you there!!

I remove the exclamation points. Put them back. Take them back out, and only put one in, but add a smiley face. Then delete it. Add it again.

God, I really am acting like a lovesick teenager.

Time to armor up, as Madison would say. Or maybe—*just maybe*—time to let the armor crack a little and let vulnerability be the birthplace of something new.

chapter
fourteen

"YOU'RE FIDGETING," Rodriguez observes, pulling into the sports complex parking lot. "Since when do you fidget?"

"Since when do you care?" I scan the fields, looking for the right one. It's a circus out here—kids in uniforms everywhere, parents hauling coolers and folding chairs, coaches with clipboards barking orders.

His son Diego bounces in the backseat. "Is this your girlfriend's kid's game? Mom says you have a girlfriend now."

"She's not my—" I catch Rodriguez's amused look in the mirror. "It's complicated."

"Everything's complicated with you." He parks next to a Tesla with vanity plates reading 'CRYPTO1'. "Bet that belongs to the ex."

I spot Field 3, see a familiar figure setting up a folding chair. Sophia's in jeans and a Metro General Fun Run t-shirt, hair in a ponytail, looking absolutely perfect.

"There she is," Rodriguez says, following my gaze. "My man, you've got it *bad*."

A man joins her—tall, artificially white teeth, carefully styled hair. The Tesla owner, I'm guessing. Troy. He's got his arm around a blonde woman who looks like she stepped out of a yoga Instagram ad.

"That the ex?" Rodriguez asks.

"Yeah."

"He looks like he sells NFTs to elderly people."

Despite my nerves, I laugh. "Crypto, actually. According to his license plate."

"Even worse." Rodriguez grabs the coffee carrier from the back. "Come on, Romeo. Time to meet the family."

We cross the field, and I try not to overthink how Sophia's shoulders stiffen when she spots us. Or how her smile seems forced.

"Jack." She stands, and there's something in her eyes I can't read. "You came."

"Said I would." I hold out the coffee. "Red-eye, blonde roast, extra caffeine. Figured you might need it."

Her fingers brush mine as she takes it. "You remember my coffee order?"

"I remember everything about you."

Rodriguez coughs dramatically. "Hi, I'm Luis Rodriguez, the wingman. And you are the famous Sophia Mitchell. Lovely to meet you outside the hospital."

"Famous?" She shakes his hand, glancing between us.

"Oh yeah. Kiwi here hasn't shut up about—"

"And that's enough from you." I turn to the Tesla couple. "Jack McKenzie. I work with Sophia."

Troy looks me up and down like he's calculating my net worth. "Troy Bentley. This is Tiffany." He doesn't offer his hand.

The blonde—Tiffany—smiles vaguely. "Are you Madison's coach? Troy says she needs more focused training to reach her potential."

"He's a paramedic," Sophia says, something sharp in her tone. "A friend."

Friend. Right.

"Paramedic?" Troy's expression shifts to barely concealed disdain. "That's...nice. Important work, I'm sure."

"Speaking of work," Tiffany chirps, "Troy's latest investment in wellness tech is absolutely exploding. We're disrupting the entire supplement industry. As Martin Luther King Jr. said, 'Even the smallest person can change the course of the future.'"

I bite my tongue so hard, I can almost taste blood.

"That's...that's from *Lord of the Rings*," Rodriguez says slowly. "Galadriel. Not...not MLK."

Tiffany blinks vapidly. "Oh, well, the sentiment still applies to our wellness journey!"

Troy's face has gone slightly red, but he doubles down. "Tiffany's very well-read. She's always finding inspiration in unexpected places."

"There's Madison!" Sophia interrupts, pointing to the field. A teen with Sophia's dark hair is juggling a soccer ball, laughing with teammates.

She's good. Really good. The kind of natural athlete that makes it look effortless. The thought hits me before I can stop it: she'd be a *phenomenal* wing in rugby. That explosive speed, the footwork, the spatial awareness. Emma would spot her potential in seconds. I make a mental note to mention it someday, if things ever...progress.

"She gets that from me," Troy says. "Played in college."

Rodriguez snorts. "Intramural doesn't count as Division II, bro."

I bite back a laugh as Troy's face reddens. "I'm sorry, who are you again?"

"Luis Rodriguez. Paramedic. My kid's on the other team. That's Diego, number 12, right next to that absolute *fox* of a coach." He points to a smaller kid doing keepie-uppies. "Diego got a scholarship to the academy program. They're already scouting him for the national youth team."

He grins. "The other one lets me scout her every night."

Troy deflates slightly. Tiffany fills the silence with something about the crystal healing properties of athletic wear. I'm not really listening—Sophia's standing close enough that I can smell her shampoo, something citrusy and clean—and she keeps glancing at me with that unreadable expression, like she's waiting to see what I'll do.

The ref blows the whistle. Madison looks up from the field and spots me, her brow furrowing. She glances at her mom, who gives her the tiniest nod.

Madison's eyes widen. She waves, tentative at first, then more confidently when I return it, and shoots Sophia a discreet thumbs-up before jogging back into position.

"So," Troy says, apparently unable to help himself, "what station do you work out of, Jake?"

"Jack," I correct. "And Station 2. Downtown."

"Tough area," he muses. "But I suppose someone has to do it. The pay must be...adequate."

"Troy," Sophia warns.

"What? I'm just making conversation. Tiffany's brother is a doctor. Now that's a career with growth potential."

"Her brother's a chiropractor," Sophia mutters. "Who lost his license in two states."

A burst of movement pulls my attention. Madison jogs over from the sidelines, slightly out of breath and still in her shin guards. "Mom, Coach says I can sub out for five. I saw you talking and I just wanted to say hi."

She turns to me with a quick, curious smile. "You're Jack, right?"

I nod. "And you're Madison. Good to meet you, superstar."

Her eyes brighten. "You remembered my name."

"Hard to forget when your mom talks about you like she's your agent."

She laughs, then glances at Sophia. "I'll be back in ten." She waves to Tiffany and Troy, then darts off again.

I turn to Sophia, about to comment on Madison's whirlwind energy, when my phone buzzes. Emergency alert from dispatch. Mass casualty incident on I-95. All available units.

Rodriguez's phone goes off simultaneously. We exchange looks.

"Multi-vehicle accident," he reads. "Gotta be a pileup. They're calling everyone in."

My eyes meet Sophia's immediately. A silent *oh, fuck* understanding passes between us. An all-units call means casualties. Multiple. Serious. The kind of scene that sticks with you for years.

As if on cue, Sophia's phone buzzes too. She glances at it with a pained wince.

"Go," she says immediately to us. "Both of you." She's already pulling out her phone, hitting a speed dial. "Hey, it's Sophia. I saw the alert. Do you need me to..." She pauses, listening. "Okay. Okay, but if that changes...Yeah, I can be there in twenty."

She hangs up, looks at us. "They've got full staffing right now, but I'm on standby. Now go. People need you."

"You sure?" But I'm already backing toward the parking lot. This is the job. This is why we both do this.

"Of course. Be safe." She turns to Troy. "Can you take Madison to Chloe's after the game if I get called in?"

Troy makes a smug noise. "See, this is why stability matters. You can't just—"

"They're going to save lives, Troy," Sophia says calmly. "And I might need to help with the aftermath. So yes or no on Madison?"

"Fine," he grumbles. "But this is exactly what I mean about—"

"Shut up, Troy," Sophia says evenly. A surprising thrill runs through me at her directness. No drama, no raising her voice...just calm authority. "Jack, go. Both of you."

I catch her eye, see something fierce and proud there. It makes my chest tight.

"I'll call you later," I promise.

"You better."

Rodriguez waves and blows his wife a kiss, then he and I run for his car. As we peel out of the parking lot, he glances at me. "That ex is a real piece of work."

"Yeah."

"Mitchell handled it well, though. You see her face when the alert came through? Looked damn proud of you. That's no fancy feat, my man."

I had seen it. That fierce expression, the immediate understanding. No complaints about leaving, no guilt trips. Just "be safe."

"Drive faster," I tell him. "People need us."

But I'm already thinking about after. About calling Sophia. About explaining...well, not the money. Not yet. But about us. About what this is becoming.

About why she matters more than anything else.

chapter
fifteen

I'VE BEEN CHECKING my phone every three minutes since Jack left. The I-95 accident is all over the news—fifteen vehicles, multiple fatalities, absolute chaos. Every ambulance in the city responded.

Madison's team won 3-1. She scored twice, but I barely registered it. Too busy watching news updates and trying not to think about twisted metal and broken glass.

"Mom, you're doing it again," Madison says, stealing a fry from my plate. We're at her favorite post-game diner, the one with sticky vinyl booths and a waitress who calls everyone "hon."

"Doing what?"

"The worried face. He's fine. They're trained for this stuff."

Troy left with Tiffany right after the game, of course. Something about a crypto emergency, which probably meant the market was tanking again. Madison didn't seem surprised or disappointed.

"I liked Jack," she says suddenly. "He seemed...real. Not like Dad's new friends who are always talking about their portfolios."

"You talked to him for thirty seconds."

"Yeah, but he remembered my name. Plus, did you see Dad's face when Jack had to leave for an actual emergency? Priceless. And," she grins, "I *loved* his accent."

My phone buzzes. Relief floods through me until I see it's from Maria, not Jack.

Turn on Channel 7. NOW.

I flag down our waitress. "Excuse me, could you turn on Channel 7, please? Something about the accident."

She grabs the remote from behind the counter and changes the channel. The anchor is mid-sentence: "...remarkable rescue by Summit County Fire Rescue paramedics. We have exclusive footage from the scene."

Shaky phone video fills the screen. The accident is worse than I imagined—cars crushed and scattered across the highway like toys. In the center, a silver minivan is wedged under a semi-trailer, the roof partially collapsed.

And there's Jack.

He's half-inside the van through the passenger window, working on someone trapped inside. Even from the amateur footage, I can see the focused intensity in his movements.

"—paramedic risked his own safety to reach the trapped family," the reporter continues. "With the vehicle unstable and leaking fuel—"

"Oh my God," Madison breathes beside me.

The video shows Jack emerging from the van, carefully extracting a small child. He passes her to Rodriguez, then immediately dives back in. The van shifts visibly, metal groaning.

"Emergency crews report the paramedic refused to wait for extraction equipment, stating the patient's condition was critical—"

A horrible grinding sound from the TV. The van lurches. People start shouting. The camera shakes as the person filming backs away.

But Jack doesn't come out.

Ten seconds. Twenty. My heart hammers against my ribs.

Finally, he emerges, pulling an unconscious woman through the window just as firefighters arrive with support equipment. He and

Rodriguez work on her right there on the asphalt, CPR compressions visible even in the grainy footage.

"The victim, identified as 34-year-old Margaret Le, was successfully resuscitated at the scene. She's currently in critical but stable condition at Metro General, along with her three children, all of whom survived thanks to the quick actions of—"

I don't hear the rest. Jack's alive. Jack's safe. Jack saved an entire family while I was sitting here eating fries and angsting over his text response time.

"Mom." Madison's hand covers mine. "You're crushing your phone."

I realize I'm gripping it hard enough to nearly crack the screen. "Sorry. I just—"

"You really like him." It's not a question.

"It's complicated."

"No," she says, stealing another fry. "It's really not."

My phone rings. Unknown number.

"Hello?"

"Sophia?" Jack's voice, exhausted but warm. "Sorry for the weird number. My phone's somewhere in the back of the rig. Borrowed Rodriguez's."

"I saw the news." My voice sounds steadier than I feel. "That was incredibly stupid and brave."

He laughs, the sound rough. "Mostly stupid, according to the fire captain. How was the rest of the game?"

"Madison scored twice." I move away from the counter, needing privacy. "Are you okay? Really okay?"

"Few bruises. Might've torn my uniform. Morrison's going to kill me." A pause. "I'm sorry I had to leave like that."

"Don't apologize for saving lives, Jack."

"Your ex seemed thrilled."

"My ex is an ass. I'm sorry about him."

"Don't apologize for things that aren't your fault either." His voice softens. "Still on for tomorrow?"

Tomorrow. Coffee. Our second date.

"Actually," I say, making a decision, "what are you doing right now?"

"Sitting in the rig, just heading back to the station. Guess we're covering until midnight. Why?"

"Just wondering." I catch Madison's eye. She's grinning, making shooing motions. "Be safe out there."

"Always am. Well, mostly."

After we hang up, Madison's practically bouncing. "You're going to see him tonight."

"I didn't say—"

"Mom. Your face says everything." She slides out of the booth. "Chloe's mom is picking me up here in ten minutes anyway. You should go home and change into something cute."

"Madison—"

"Something that says 'I'm incredibly attracted to your heroic acts.'"

Forty minutes later, I'm standing outside Station 2 holding a bag of takeout from the good Thai place and wondering what the hell I'm doing. It's 8:47 PM. I'm a charge nurse at Metro General. I don't bring food to paramedics like some kind of...

The bay door opens. Rodriguez appears, grinning. "Well, well. Special delivery?"

"I thought you guys might be hungry." I hold up the bag lamely. "Tough shift."

"Uh-huh." His grin widens. "Kiwi's in the day room. Through there, second door on the right. I'll be...literally anywhere else."

The station smells like diesel and disinfectant and coffee. I follow Rodriguez's directions, finding a small break room with mismatched furniture and a TV playing quietly.

Jack's on a battered couch, head tipped back, eyes closed. His uniform shirt is indeed torn at the shoulder, revealing a nasty bruise underneath. He looks exhausted and heroic and absolutely beautiful.

"Hey," I say softly.

His eyes open, focusing on me with surprise that shifts quickly to something warmer. "Sophia? What are you—"

"Brought dinner." I hold up the bag. "Figured you earned it today."

He sits up straighter, wincing slightly. "You saw the news?"

"Everyone saw the news. You're probably trending." I sit beside him, careful not to jostle his injured shoulder. "That was an incredibly stupid thing to do."

"Had to. The mom was losing consciousness. Kids were screaming." He runs a hand through his hair. "Couldn't wait for the heavy rescue guys."

"I know." I unpack the food, noting how he favors his left arm. "Let me see that shoulder."

"It's fine—"

"Jack." I use my charge nurse voice. "Let me see."

He sighs but pulls the torn fabric aside. The bruise is spectacular —deep purple blooming across his shoulder and down his chest. I probe it gently, feeling for breaks or separations.

"Just bruising," I conclude. "But you should ice it."

"Yes, ma'am." He's smiling now. "This is good. You taking care of me."

"Someone has to." I hand him pad Thai. "Since you clearly have no self-preservation instincts."

We eat in comfortable silence for a few minutes. The station is quiet—no calls, just the distant sound of someone watching TV in another room.

"So," he says finally. "This is unexpected."

"Good unexpected or bad unexpected?"

"Good. Definitely good." He sets down his spoon and fork. "I was sitting here thinking about you. About how you just...understood. When the call came."

"It's what we do," I say simply.

"Yeah, but Troy didn't get it. Most people don't."

"Trust me, Troy doesn't get much." I shift closer. "How bad was it? The accident?"

"I've seen worse, but not by much." His voice goes distant. "Kids were trapped in the back. Kept trying to get Mom to wake up, but she was unconscious..." He stops. "The fuel leak was getting worse. Could smell it. Battalion Chief kept yelling at me to wait, but those kids..."

"You saved them."

"*We* saved them. Rodriguez was right there. So was Medic 5, Medic 16, Engine 18, Engine 4. Hell, the staties were even directing traffic. It was a whole team effort."

"The news made it sound like you were Captain America."

He laughs softly. "Hardly. Just saw what needed doing and did it."

"Jack." I put my hand on his, gently. "C'mon. I saw you on TV. And I've seen a lot in the ER. You're a hero."

He shakes his head. "I'm not a hero, Sophia. Just a guy who—"

I lean in and kiss him. Can't help it. He tastes like Thai food and exhaustion and something uniquely Jack. After a moment of surprise, he kisses me back, gentle despite everything.

When we break apart, we're both breathing differently.

"That was—" he starts.

"Overdue," I finish.

He grins. "Was going to say brilliant, but overdue works too."

An alarm blares through the station. "Medic 402, Medic 402. Respond to cardiac arrest..."

Jack starts to move, but Rodriguez's voice booms from the hallway. "McKENZIE! You were called in! So you're technically off duty as of—" he checks his watch dramatically "—an hour ago. I've got Kollman. Go home, hero."

"But—"

"That's an order. You've done enough today." Rodriguez appears in the doorway, already in his gear, grinning at us both. "Besides, I'm not cockblocking the charge nurse. The entire emergency department would murder me."

He's gone before either of us can respond. We hear him jogging down the hall, then the bay doors opening.

Jack and I stare at each other in the sudden silence.

"So," he says softly. "I'm officially off duty."

"And Madison's at her friend Chloe's for the night." My voice sounds breathier than I intended.

"Your place?"

"My car's outside."

He stands, favoring his bruised shoulder. I grab the leftover Thai food, and we walk through the empty station. The energy between us has shifted—charged, inevitable.

In the parking lot, he catches my hand. "Sophia, are you sure? We can just—"

I turn, pressing him not-so-gently against my car. "Jack. I've been sure since you first said '*Kia ora*' over the phone."

His eyes darken. "That was months ago."

"I know." I kiss him again, deeper this time. When we break apart, we're both breathing hard. "My place. *Now.*"

The drive to my house is charged with anticipation. Jack's hand rests on my thigh, his thumb tracing small circles through my jeans. Every red light feels eternal. I can feel a warmth and wetness spreading between my thighs.

"Nice neighborhood," he comments as I pull into my driveway, and aggressively shift the car into park.

"Divorce settlement." I fumble with my keys at the front door, hyperaware of him behind me. "Troy got the investment accounts. I got the house."

"His loss."

Inside, I barely get the door closed before he's pressing me against it, kissing me like he's been thinking about it for months. Maybe he has. God knows I have.

"Bedroom?" he asks against my lips.

"Upstairs. But your shoulder—"

"Shoulder's fine." He proves it by lifting me easily, making me gasp. "Which way?"

"Second door on the right."

He carries me up the stairs like I weigh nothing, despite the bruising. The bedroom door closes behind us with a soft click.

"Jack," I breathe as he sets me down beside the bed. "Are you sure you're okay to—"

"Sophia." He cups my face in his hands. "I've wanted this since the first time I heard your voice. I'm more than okay."

Jack's mouth finds mine again, urgent this time, a low sound of relief and desire vibrating against my lips. His hands slide down my back, pulling me against him, his warmth soaking through me. Even exhausted, bruised, and battered, he feels strong and steady—exactly what I didn't know I needed.

"Careful," I whisper, conscious of his injured shoulder.

"I've been careful all day," he murmurs, his lips tracing a hot path down my throat. "I'm done with careful."

A shiver races through me. I tug his torn uniform shirt off, exposing lean muscle, the vivid bruises marring his skin. My fingers trace each bruise softly, reverently. He watches me, the intensity in his eyes almost overwhelming.

"I'm fine, Soph," he says softly, sensing my hesitation. "Really."

"You're better than fine," I whisper back. "You're perfect."

His fingers find the hem of my shirt, and I lift my arms, letting him pull it off. The cool air hits my skin, quickly replaced by the heat of his mouth on my collarbone, the gentle scrape of his teeth sending sparks through me. He trails slow, careful kisses downward, each touch like a quiet promise of more to come.

When he reaches my chest, he pauses, eyes meeting mine, silently asking permission. My breath hitches, and I nod, incapable of speech. The brush of his lips over my nipples send heat pooling deep in my core. He's slow, tender, yet with an undercurrent of tightly leashed hunger. Every touch feels like he's savoring something precious.

He traces a line with his mouth down to my navel, and then- *ohhh*- lower. Oh, my God. *Oh my GOD.*

"Jack," I breathe, my fingers threading into his hair, holding him to me. He tastes me—God, I thought I was wet before—lightning bolts cross my eyes. It's electric. *Fuck*, his tongue. He traces it around my clit, then darts it inside me, over and over. I can feel my toes curl involuntarily. A noise escapes my mouth that I cannot describe.

He rises just enough to meet my gaze again, his blue eyes blazing, darkened with desire and something softer, more vulnerable. "Tell me what you want."

"You," I say simply. "All of you."

He kisses me again, hard and deep, and then we're moving toward the bed, clothes falling away piece by piece, the room fading to nothing but our tangled breath, the heat of his skin against mine. He lays me back, gently, carefully despite his words, eyes never leaving mine. His hands roam over me like he's memorizing every curve, every reaction, each gasp and sigh I make.

"You're beautiful," he whispers into my skin, the words more sensation than sound. My body arches into his touch, every nerve alive and thrumming with anticipation. He's slow and thorough, making me shiver, making me ache.

When he finally moves over me, his weight settling gently between my thighs, he pauses again, breathing heavy, forehead resting against mine. "Sophia—"

"Jack." My voice is pleading, urgent now. "*Please.*"

He moves slowly, deliberately, eyes locked on mine as he sinks into me inch by exquisite inch. My breath catches at the fullness, the perfect, aching rightness of it. His jaw clenches, holding himself still for a moment, allowing us both to adjust to the sudden, perfect intimacy.

"God," he whispers raggedly. "You feel...this is..."

"Exactly right," I finish, wrapping my legs around him, drawing him deeper. "Don't stop."

He doesn't. He moves again, slow at first, careful to read my reactions, until the gentleness gives way to something stronger, something raw and desperate. Our rhythm builds, driven by weeks of carefully suppressed desire, months of casual flirtation, every stolen glance and secret smile leading us here, now.

The bruises on his shoulder make me cautious, but Jack guides my touch away from them gently, murmuring reassurances into my neck, his lips finding the sensitive skin behind my ear, making me gasp his name. His voice, whispering my name in response, is low and reverent, filled with awe and need.

"Sophia," he breathes, our pace quickening now, urgency building. I cling to him, nails digging lightly into his back, and he groans, the sound sending heat spiraling through me.

"Jack, please," I gasp, feeling the edge drawing closer, that exquisite tension coiling tightly inside me.

He shifts slightly, deepening his thrusts, and suddenly the tension snaps. Pleasure explodes through me, bright and blinding, washing away every coherent thought. Jack's movements falter as he follows, gasping my name as he shudders against me, every muscle taut, every breath harsh and ragged.

We lie tangled together afterward, breathing slowly returning to normal, our bodies pressed close, skin slick and heated. He brushes hair away from my face, his fingers gentle, lingering.

"Worth the wait?" he asks softly, his voice thick with exhaustion and satisfaction.

I smile, shifting closer, feeling strangely shy after everything we've just shared. "More than worth it."

"Better than I imagined." He presses a kiss to my shoulder. "And I've imagined it. A *lot*."

"Just how long have you been thinking about this?"

"Truthfully?" His voice is sleepy, content. "Since you told me I could call anytime with my accent. Nearly drove off the road."

I laugh, turning in his arms to face him. "We should have done this sooner."

"No." He's serious now, those blue eyes finding mine in the darkness. "It happened exactly when it should have. When we were both ready."

He's right. A few months ago, I was still too raw from the divorce, too guarded. Now...

"What happens tomorrow?" I ask.

"Tomorrow, we have coffee at Marina Park. Take a walk. Maybe hold hands in public." He grins. "Scandalous stuff."

"The hospital gossip mill is going to explode."

"Let them talk." He pulls me closer. "I'm not hiding this. You?"

"No." I trace the edge of his bruise gently. "No more hiding."

He plants feather kisses on my forehead tenderly, over and over again, his arm tightening around me. "Good. Because I'm not planning on going anywhere."

"Good," I echo, closing my eyes, letting myself sink into the warmth and safety of his embrace. For once, I don't think about tomorrow or complications or what could go wrong.

We fall asleep like that, wrapped around each other, the future uncertain but somehow less frightening than it's been in years.

Because tonight, right here, is exactly enough.

chapter
sixteen

I **WAKE** to sunlight streaming through unfamiliar curtains and the scent of Sophia's shampoo on the pillow beside me. For a moment, I just lie there, taking it in. Her bedroom in daylight—photos of Madison on the dresser, a stack of romance novels on the nightstand, scrubs thrown over a chair.

Real life. Her real life. And I'm in it now.

The shower's running in the en suite. I check my phone—8:47 AM. We said ten o'clock for coffee, but that was before...this.

The bathroom door opens, and Sophia emerges in a towel, hair damp. She freezes when she sees me awake.

"Morning," I say, voice rough with sleep.

"Hi." That shyness from last night returns. "I didn't want to wake you. Thought you needed sleep after yesterday."

"Best sleep I've had in months." I sit up, wincing slightly as my shoulder protests. "Even with this."

She moves closer, studying the bruise in daylight. It's properly spectacular now—deep purple spreading across my chest.

"Jack, that looks—"

"Worse than it feels." I catch her hand. "Promise."

She stands at the bed's edge, fingers ghosting over the bruise. "You saved a whole family."

"We saved them. Team effort."

"Well, the *news* didn't make it sound like a team effort." Her fingers trail lower, and my breath catches. "*They* made it sound like you were Superman."

"Clark Kent was a journalist, not a paramedic." I pull her closer. "And I don't look that good in tights."

"I don't know..." Her eyes darken.

"Now, you?" I tell her very seriously, "I think you'd look good in anything. I mean, the towel looks great..."

The towel slips slightly. My hand finds her hip, thumb stroking bare skin.

"...but it'd look even better on the floor."

The towel drops all the way to the ground, and I take in the most beautiful sight in the whole *fucking* world.

Sophia leans in, kisses me soft and sweet, morning breath and all. She moves to sit on my lap. I forget about my shoulder, forget about coffee, forget about everything except her warm weight settling onto my lap.

"Gorgeous, *gorgeous*," I murmur against her throat. "How are you real?"

She makes a sound that goes straight through me. I'm barely hanging on now, and—

My phone buzzes. Dispatch.

"Ignore it," she breathes.

It buzzes again. And again.

"Shit." I fumble for it one-handed, not letting her go. "McKenzie."

"Morning, Kiwi!" Morrison's voice is unnecessarily cheerful. "Need you to swing by and fill out incident reports from yesterday. Insurance needs them ASAP."

"Now?"

"Within the hour. Hero paperwork waits for no one."

I hang up, groaning. "Bloody bureaucracy."

Sophia laughs, climbing off my lap. I become painfully aware of my erection, which is throbbing like it was the star feature in one of Sophie's smutty novels. I spend a moment just admiring her beautiful body, speechless.

"I need clothes anyway," I say when I can speak again. "Can't keep borrowing your t-shirts."

"That's too bad." She disappears back into the bathroom. "There's coffee downstairs. Help yourself."

Twenty minutes later, we're both dressed—me in yesterday's uniform pants and a Metro General shirt that's slightly too small, Sophia in jeans and a soft blue sweater that makes her eyes impossible to look away from.

She's making eggs when her phone rings. "It's Maria. I should—" She answers. "Hey, what's—"

I can hear Maria's excited voice from across the kitchen. Something about the news, viral video, the whole hospital talking.

"No, I haven't seen—yes, he's—Maria!" Sophia's blushing. "I'm hanging up now."

She sets the phone down, shaking her head. "The video's gone viral. You're internet famous."

"Brilliant." I steal a piece of toast. "Just what every paramedic dreams of."

We're eating in comfortable silence when the front door slams open.

"Sophia? I know you're home. We need to talk about Madison's nutrition—"

Troy. Fucking Troy.

"Ain't this a pisser," I mutter, standing quickly.

Troy rounds the corner into the kitchen, stopping dead when he sees me. His eyes narrow, taking in my obvious bed head, bare feet, the borrowed shirt.

"What's he doing here?" Troy demands.

"Having coffee," Sophia says calmly. "In *my* house. Which you no longer have keys to, by the way."

"I still have keys. You never changed the locks." He puffs up like an angry peacock. "And Madison's nutrition is a serious concern. Tiffany says processed foods are affecting her athletic performance—"

"Madison's fine." Sophia's voice could freeze hell. "And give me those keys. Now."

"I have a right to—"

"You have a right to scheduled visitation. Not to barge into my house on Sunday morning." She holds out her hand. "Keys."

Troy's face reddens, but he spots my uniform pants, the Metro General shirt. "Stayed the night, did you?" His voice drips disdain. "How professional. What kind of example is this for Madison?"

"A better one than you set," I say mildly. "Least I have a job."

"I'm an entrepreneur—"

"You're unemployed," Sophia cuts in. "Living off Tiffany's trust fund while playing with imaginary internet money."

"Cryptocurrency is the future—"

"Keys." Her hand doesn't waver. "Now."

He slams them on the counter. "This isn't over. My lawyer—"

"Your lawyer who you pay in Dogecoin?" I ask innocently.

Troy's face turns purple. He storms toward the door, pausing to throw back: "It's Solana, you idiot. Do your research. Doge is a joke. Sol's up 40% this quarter. You think real men meme-trade?"

The door slams behind him.

"Charming bloke," I say into the silence. "Really can't imagine why you divorced him."

Sophia laughs, but it's shaky. "Sorry. He's not usually that... actually, yes, he is."

"Hey." I pull her into my arms. "You alright?"

"Yeah. Just...embarrassed. You shouldn't have to deal with my ex-husband drama."

"Part of the package, yeah? You get my interfering mum, I get your tosser ex." I check the time. "Shit. Morrison's waiting. But we're still on for the park?"

"Ten o'clock." She stretches up to kiss me. "I'll bring coffee."

"Want me to bring pastries from that French place?"

"Perfect." She grabs her keys. "C'mon, I'll drop you at the station."

The ride is comfortable, her hand occasionally brushing mine on the gear shift. When we pull up to Station 2, she turns to me.

"Ten o'clock, Marina Park?"

"Wouldn't miss it." I lean over, kiss her softly. "Thanks for the ride."

"Thanks for...last night. This morning. Everything."

I grin. "Anytime, Nurse Mitchell."

***

An hour later, paperwork completed and wearing fresh clothes from my locker, I'm waiting at Marina Park with a box of croissants when Sophia pulls up. She emerges from her car with two coffees, looking like sunshine in that blue sweater.

"Flat white for you, red-eye for me." She hands over my cup. "How was the paperwork?"

"Thrilling. Described the incident in triplicate." I offer her a chocolate croissant. "Morrison says I'm trending on TikTok."

"My daughter already texted me three different edits of the rescue footage set to dramatic music."

We walk along the harbor path, easy conversation flowing. The park's busy—joggers, dog walkers, families out enjoying the morning. Normal people doing normal things. It feels surreal after yesterday's chaos.

I can't help watching Sophia as she walks slightly ahead, the way those jeans fit perfectly. Without thinking, I reach out and squeeze her oh *so* perfect ass.

She jumps. "Jack! People are looking!"

"Sorry." I grin, not sorry at *all*. "It's just so perfect. Can't help myself."

She tries to look stern but her eyes are dancing. "Oh, you're a *butt* guy, huh?"

"Listen, *tāku ipo*," I pull her closer, squeezing again. "On you, I'm not picky. You're perfect everywhere, but this—" another squeeze "—is *heaven*."

"You're insufferable."

"Is that a complaint?"

"Definitely not." She threads her fingers through mine. "What's that thing you called me? Tāku..."

"*Tāku ipo*. Maori. Means 'my darling' or 'my beloved.'" I bring her hand to my lips. "Too much?"

"No." Her voice is soft. "I like it."

We find a bench overlooking the water. Time to bring up good old Aotearoa.

"Actually," I say, aiming for casual, "I need to go back home for a bit before long. Family thing."

Her face falls slightly. "Oh. When?"

"Three weeks. It's autumn there—harvest season. Family needs all hands on deck at the property." I take a breath. "I know it's sort-of late notice, but, ahh...thing is...that's Madison's spring break, yeah? You both have passports?"

"We do, actually. Troy was going to take her to Costa Rica last year, but the memecoin he'd been hyping got pump and dumped. He lost everything he'd invested." She rolls her eyes. "ShibaMoonRocket or something equally stupid."

"So...want to come with me? You and Madison? I've got Air New Zealand points saved up. Could cover the flights."

"Jack, that's...are you sure? Meeting your family, that's a big step."

"Already told them about you." At her surprised look, I add quickly, "Just that I'm seeing someone. Someone special."

"What exactly did you tell them?"

"That you're brilliant. Beautiful. Raise an amazing daughter. Run an entire ER without breaking a sweat." I pause. "Left out the bit about you making me walk into walls when you wear that black dress."

She laughs. "Smooth."

"So? What do you think? Week and a half in New Zealand? Show Madison some sheep, let her try proper fish and chips, maybe do some wine tasting?"

"Wine tasting?" She raises an eyebrow. "At your family's 'property'?"

My stomach drops slightly. "Well, the whole region's known for wine. Lots of places to visit."

"Uh-huh." But she's smiling. "Madison would love it. She's been dying to travel somewhere since the Costa Rica thing fell through."

"Is that a yes?"

"I need to check work schedules...I might have to have someone pick up a couple shifts from me, but...yes. God, yes. Time away from Troy and his lectures sounds like heaven."

"Speaking of Troy..." I hesitate. "Can I ask something? You don't have to answer."

"About the marriage?"

"About how he...treated you."

She's quiet for a moment, watching a sailboat glide past. "It wasn't always bad. At first, he was charming. Ambitious. I thought his confidence was attractive."

"What changed?"

"He discovered podcasts." She says it so dryly I almost laugh. "Started listening to all these 'alpha male' influencers. Suddenly everything was about dominance and traditional gender roles and how feminism was destroying society."

"Christ."

"He decided that since I made more money, I was emasculating him. But *also* that I should do all the housework because that was 'women's work.' The mental gymnastics were impressive."

"How very modern of him."

"The worst part was the bedroom stuff," she says quietly, looking out at the water. "He... he refused to go down on me. Said it'd 'make him gay.'"

I nearly choke on my coffee. "He *what*?"

"Yeah. Receiving was fine, of course. But giving? That was 'submissive' and 'emasculating.'" She shakes her head. "I spent years thinking I was asking for too much."

"What a fucking cunt."

Sophia gasps, hand flying to her mouth. "Jack!"

"Sorry, I—" I ran a hand through my hair. "Cultural thing. We use that word more casually in New Zealand. Like calling someone a right bastard."

"It's just... that word here is..." She's actually blushing.

"Did you know it's one of the oldest words in the English language? Goes all the way back to Chaucer and Middle English. 'Queynte,' they called it." I grin at her surprised expression. "Four years of literature courses at uni. Had to be good for something."

"I never thought I'd get an etymology lesson on that particular word in the middle of the park," she says, but she's fighting a smile.

"It's only shocking because people made it that way. In Kiwi, it's practically a term of endearment. Over the ditch, the Aussies use it as a comma." I pull her closer. "But seriously, Soph. Any man who thinks pleasuring his partner makes him less of a man is a bloody idiot. And definitely, historically, a cunt."

She laughs despite herself. "I'm still getting used to Kiwi cursing. You make it sound almost... scholarly."

"Wait till you meet my sisters. Charlotte *definitely* uses it as a comma. She could make a sailor blush. Keep telling her she'll have to clean it up before she becomes Prime Minister." I kiss her temple. "For what it's worth, last night was... you tasted incredible. Could've stayed down there for hours."

Her cheeks flame again, but her eyes darken. "Very scholarly observation, Professor McKenzie."

"I'm a thorough researcher," I murmur against her ear. "Always happy to conduct more field studies."

Now she's definitely blushing. "Jack!"

"What? It's true. Troy's loss." I grin wickedly. "Though I suppose I should thank him for being such a tosser. Led you straight to me."

"Silver lining," she agrees, then more seriously: "You really want us to come to New Zealand? It's not too fast?"

"Nothing about us has been normal speed," I point out. "Why start now?"

She leans against my shoulder. "Fair point. When would we leave?"

"I'm thinking the Saturday of spring break? Direct flight to Auckland, then connect to Queenstown. Back the following Sunday."

"Nine days away with you." She smiles. "Madison's going to flip out. She's already obsessed with your accent."

"She'd better be prepared. Whole family of accents. My sister Lily's is thick as thieves, she's been living in Dunedin for her PhD."

"The marine biologist?"

"That's the one. She'll love Madison. Probably drag her to look at tide pools and lecture about ocean conservation."

"Madison would actually love that." Sophia turns to face me fully. "This is really happening? We're going to New Zealand?"

"If you want to."

"I want to." She kisses me softly. "I want to see where you grew up. Meet your family. Watch Madison experience something besides Troy's broken promises."

"Brilliant. I'll sort the flights this week." I pull out my phone. "What's your middle name? For the booking."

"Rose. Sophia Rose Mitchell."

"Beautiful name for a beautiful woman." I type it in. "Madison's?"

"Madison Grace *Bently*," she sighed. "Though she's been going by Mitchell at school. We haven't done the legal change yet on the passport."

I save the information. "I'll send you the flight details once they're booked."

"Let me pay for—"

"Already told you, got points saved up. EMS conferences, went back and forth a couple times to move here."

She eyes me suspiciously but doesn't press. "Thank you. This is... this is amazing."

"You're amazing." I check the time. "Shit. Promised Rodriguez I'd cover his afternoon shift."

"I should get home anyway. Madison will be back soon and she'll want every detail about last night." She blushes. "Well, not EVERY detail."

"Probably wise." I stand, pulling her up with me. "Dinner tomorrow? After shift?"

"Ahh, can't tomorrow. Tuesday?"

"Perfect. I'll cook for you both. Madison likes Italian?"

"She likes everything except Troy's green smoothies." Sophia stretches up to kiss me. "Thank you for this morning. For dealing with Troy. For...everything."

"*Tāku ipo,*" I murmur against her lips. "This is just the beginning."

We walk back through the park hand in hand. The future suddenly seems full of possibility—New Zealand, meeting families, building something real together.

Three weeks until we fly. Three weeks until she sees the estate, meets my family, discovers exactly what I walked away from.

But watching her laugh as a dog chases a frisbee past us, feeling her hand warm in mine, I'm not worried. Sophia sees me—really sees me—not my family's money or expectations.

Just Jack.

And that's exactly who I want to be.

chapter
seventeen

MID-SHIFT CHAOS. That's what I call Tuesday afternoons, when the weekend warriors have finally decided their injuries need attention, and the lunch-break heart attacks start rolling in. I'm reviewing the board—twenty-three patients in various stages of treatment—when my phone buzzes.

> Thinking about you. Can't wait for NZ.
> How's your day?

I smile despite the controlled mayhem around me. Three weeks until New Zealand. Three weeks until I meet his family, see where he grew up. The anticipation mingles with something that feels dangerously close to hope.

I type back quickly:

> Typical Tuesday. Missing my coffee
> delivery service.

His response is immediate:

> Service can resume anytime. Just say
> when.

"Get a room," Maria mutters mischievously, fluttering her eyebrows suggestively as she passes by with lab results. "Some of us are trying to work here."

"Some of us ARE working," I counter, pocketing my phone. "Where's Tasha?"

"Fast track. And before you ask, yes, she's behaving. Mostly." Maria pauses. "Though she did ask if 'getting railed by a hot paramedic' improves your complexion because, and I quote, 'Sophia's practically glowing.'"

My face heats. "She did not—"

"Bay 3 needs orders," Maria says innocently, floating away before I can respond.

The afternoon flows in its usual rhythm: controlled chaos punctuated by moments of pure adrenaline. Nathan's running triage with his typical quiet efficiency, Melissa's handling a complex cardiac case, and Cameron Lee is...being Cameron.

"Sophia." He materializes beside me at the nurses' station, leaning against the counter in what he probably thinks is a casual pose. "Heard you're heading to New Zealand."

"News travels fast."

"With the paramedic." His tone suggests I've announced plans to join a cult. "Interesting choice."

"Was there something medical you needed, Dr. Lee?"

"Just concerned about a colleague." He lowers his voice conspiratorially. "You know, if you wanted someone more...established, the offer still stands."

"What offer would that be?"

"Dinner. Somewhere that doesn't serve its wine from boxes." He winks. "I know a place that has an excellent New Zealand collection, actually. The McKenzie Estate makes a particularly nice—"

I almost laugh. "I've actually had that. It's quite good." The memory of dinner with Jack warms me for a moment.

"Oh?" His eyebrows raise. "Their 2019 Pinot is exceptional. Three hundred a bottle, but worth it for the right company."

My stomach drops. *Three hundred dollars!? Jack spent three hundred dollars on wine for our first date?*

"That's..." I can't finish the sentence. That's almost a car payment. That's more than some people's weekly grocery budget. That's what a paramedic—someone who probably makes less than I do—spent on one bottle of wine to impress me.

Cameron misreads my shock. "I know, pricey. But some things are worth the investment." He leans closer. "The offer stands, Sophia. Whenever you're ready for something more...substantial."

I barely hear him leave. Three hundred dollars. I feel simultaneously touched and furious. How could he spend that much? Why would he spend that much? And why do I feel so guilty about it now?

"Sophia!" Tasha's voice, usually edged with boredom or complaint, crackled with genuine alarm over the radio. "I need you in Fast Track 3. *Now.*"

I was halfway there before she finished. Tasha didn't panic easily unless it was about her break being delayed. I push through the curtain to find her standing beside a young man—late teens, maybe early twenties—who was bolt upright on the stretcher, leaning forward, his eyes wide with a terror I recognized instantly. Stridor. That high-pitched, desperate sound of an airway closing. He was drooling, unable to swallow, his color a dusky gray.

"Came in for a sore throat about twenty minutes ago," Tasha said, her voice tight but controlled. "Said it started this morning, got rapidly worse. Temp's 102. Looked like bad strep, but then this." She gestured to the patient's tripoding posture. "It was so fast."

My mind races. Epiglottitis. Rare in adults and older teens since the HiB vaccine, but the classic signs were all there—the tripod, the drool, the stridor, the toxic appearance. This wasn't just a sore throat; this was an airway about to slam shut.

"Get him to Trauma One!" I barked, my charge nurse voice kicking in, overriding the knot of ice in my own stomach. "Nate, I need you! Maria, call Anesthesia and ENT! Page them overhead if you have to. Someone grab the difficult airway cart and the cric kit!"

"On it!" Nathan appeared from nowhere, already in motion. That's what I love about him—no questions, just action.

We moved as a unit—me, Tasha, Nathan, and two techs—wheeling the patient down the hall while I called out orders.

"Get respiratory here now! Set up for emergency cric! Where's anesthesia?"

"Dr. Singh is coming," someone called back.

"And ENT?"

"Dr. Williams is in surgery. Twenty minutes minimum."

"We don't have twenty minutes," I mutter, watching the patient's oxygen saturation plummet. "We've got seconds."

Trauma One erupted into controlled chaos as we transferred the patient to the resuscitation bed. Dr. Singh, our on-call anesthesiologist, arrives, takes one look, and starts prepping for intubation. "Can't see a damn thing," he muttered after his first attempt, the laryngoscope blade useless against the massive swelling. "Cords are buried. Someone hand me the Glidescope."

The high-tech video laryngoscope didn't help. Second attempt. Failed.

The patient's sats hit the seventies. His lips are turning blue.

"Can't visualize," Singh said, frustration bleeding through his usual calm. "Everything's swollen shut. We need a surgical airway! Where's ENT?"

"Still in surgery," I report. "We need—"

"We need to cric him." Dr. Cameron Lee's voice cuts through the tension, surprisingly calm and decisive. He'd appeared at the foot of the bed at some point, drawn by the overhead page for a difficult airway, his usual preening arrogance stripped away, replaced by a laser focus.

My eyes meet his. No time for ego, no time for our usual dance of polite antagonism. Just the patient. "Sophia, where's the cric tray?" he asked, his voice devoid of any of its usual flirtatious lilt.

"Mayo stand, right corner!" I was already anticipating, had made sure it was there.

He moves with a speed and focus that momentarily stuns me. He grabs the kit, his hands steady. "Scalpel. Trach hook. Bougie." He barked the requests, and Nate was there, slapping instruments into his palm. In a move that was both shocking and brutally efficient, Lee literally jumps from the floor onto the bed with both feet in one smooth motion, straddling the patient's chest to get the angle and leverage he needed.

Damn the man, but he can move when a life is on the line. Hands of a surgeon, alright.

I was coordinating, calling out vitals, "Sats are 72 and falling!" making sure suction was ready, trying to keep Tasha, who was white-faced and trembling but still managing to bag the patient under Nate's guidance, from completely losing it. "Focus, Tasha, I need you," I said, my voice sharp but, I hoped, not unkind. She nodded, her eyes huge.

Lee made a swift, decisive incision. There was a horrifying, wet, tearing sound, then a gush of dark blood that Nate was instantly suctioning. "Tube," Lee grunted. He threaded it in. "Ambu to the tube."

Nate connected the bag. Squeezed. We all held our breath. A faint mist in the tube. A slight rise in the chest. "I'm in," Lee said, his voice tight. "Sats coming up. 82...85..." The collective exhale in Trauma One was almost a physical force. The kid wasn't out of the woods, not by a long shot, but he had an airway. He had a chance.

Dr. Lee slid off the bed, his movements economical. He gave a few curt post-procedure orders to the respiratory therapist who had just arrived, then stripped off his bloody gloves and walked out of the trauma bay without a backward glance. As he passes me, I catch a glimpse of his face. It's pale, almost grey, a stark contrast to his usual confident flush. He looked like he was about to be sick.

Our eyes meet briefly. He knows I've seen it. I give the slightest nod—acknowledgment, not judgment—and he's gone.

The aftermath was a flurry of activity—securing the new airway, getting lines, drawing labs, calling report to the ICU. I checked on the patient, then my team. Tasha was leaning against a wall, tears streaming down her face.

"I should have seen it sooner," she whispered, her voice choked. "He just said his throat was sore..."

Nate put a steadying hand on her shoulder. "You did good, Tasha. You recognized he was in trouble, and you got Sophia. That's what matters. Epiglottitis is a zebra, especially in an older kid or young adult. Most of us will go years without seeing one."

I nodded, adding my own reassurance. "Nate's right. You escalated appropriately. That's the job." She still looked unconvinced, but the raw panic was easing from her eyes. She needed more experience, more confidence, but she hadn't frozen. She'd called for help. That was a start.

"But—"

"No buts." Nathan appears at her other side, solid and reassuring. "You did good, Tasha. The patient's alive because you acted fast."

She looks between us, tears threatening. "I've never seen...I didn't know..."

"And now you have," I say. "Next time, you'll recognize it faster. That's how we learn."

"Come on," Nathan says gently. "Let's get some water. You did good today."

He leads her away, and I see her lean into him slightly—not romantic, just seeking comfort from someone steady. There's something there, something that could grow. I file it away for later consideration.

The trauma bay slowly returns to normal as the patient is wheeled up to surgery. I'm updating the computer when my phone buzzes.

Rodriguez says evening shift is slow.
Coffee delivery in 20?

I text back:

Just cric'd someone. Today was special
kind of hell. Counting minutes to NZ.

On my way with caffeine and
inappropriate jokes. No worries, love.
She'll be right.

Despite everything, I smile. Three weeks. Three weeks until I can breathe again, can be just Sophia instead of Charge Nurse Mitchell.

I catch Dr. Ward approvingly surveying the scene. "That was impressive," Dr. Ward says when she sees I've noticed. "Lee handled that well."

"He did," I agree, thinking of that grey face, that trembling hand. "He really did."

The rest of the shift blurs together—post-procedure paperwork, checking on Tasha (she's better, Nathan's still with her), fielding questions about the dramatic save. The ER never stops, just shifts into different gears.

By the time Jack arrives with coffee, I'm exhausted but wired, that particular post-adrenaline state unique to emergency medicine.

"Heard you had some excitement," he says, handing me a red-eye with an extra shot.

"Acute epiglottitis." Jack whistled appreciatively.

"Cameron Lee, of all people." The gossip network clearly never rests. "Heard he went full action hero."

"He did what needed doing," I say carefully, protective of Cameron's moment of vulnerability. "Saved a life."

Jack studies me, reading something in my expression. "Good on him, then."

We sit in the break room, sharing war stories and planning New

Zealand. He shows me pictures of the places he wants to take us—beaches, mountains, something called a "glow worm cave" that makes Madison squeal with delight when she FaceTimes us during her lunch break.

"Mom, you look tired," she observes with teenage bluntness.

"Rough case today, baby. But I'm good."

"Is Jack taking care of you?"

I glance at him, see the genuine concern in those blue eyes. "Yeah. He is."

After we hang up, Jack pulls me closer. "Three weeks, *tāku ipo*. Then you get a proper break."

"Three weeks," I agree, letting myself lean into his warmth.

As I gather my things, I spot Cameron in the hallway. He's back to his usual self—confident stride, perfect hair—but there's something different. Sharper, maybe. More performative.

"Good work today," I call out.

He pauses, turns, that practiced smile sliding into place a beat too quickly. "Not bad for a Tuesday. Though I have to say, bed gymnastics weren't exactly covered in residency." The joke sounds forced, like he's trying too hard to make light of it. "Just another save at Metro General."

The gratitude I expected isn't there. Instead, there's something defensive in his posture, like he's already building walls around what happened in that trauma bay.

Sigh.

Three weeks. Three weeks until Jack's family, until Kiwi coffee, and until Madison gets to see somewhere beyond her father's broken promises.

chapter
eighteen

"RIGHT, SO THE TRICK WITH CARBONARA," I tell Madison as she hovers beside me in their kitchen, "is getting the eggs to cook without scrambling them."

"That sounds impossible." She's got Sophia's eyes but none of her mother's caution. Curious about everything, unafraid to ask questions. "How do you not scramble eggs when you cook them?"

"Patience and temperature control." I hand her the wooden spoon. "Want to try stirring while I add the eggs?"

"What if I mess it up?"

"Then we order pizza and try again next time."

She grins. "Mom says you're teaching her Māori swear words."

"Did she now?" I glance toward the living room where Sophia's pretending to read a magazine but really watching us. "Only the educational ones."

Madison laughs. "Is it true you saved a whole family over the weekend? Mom showed me the video."

"Team effort. Your mum saves people every day at the hospital."

"Yeah, but she doesn't crawl into crashed cars." Madison keeps stirring as I slowly add the egg mixture. "That looked terrifying."

"Bit scary, yeah. But that's the job sometimes."

"Is that why you became a paramedic? To save people?"

The question catches me off guard. So simple, so direct. "Something like that."

"Mom says you could be doing other things. Like, with your family's business?"

I freeze for a moment, and consider how to respond.

"My family has their thing, I have mine," I say carefully. "Perfect temperature—see how it's coating the pasta but not clumping?"

"It's working!" Madison sounds delighted. "This is actually easier than I thought."

"Most things are once you understand the technique." I add the pancetta. "I didn't get to see the end of your soccer game, but I heard you did a great job."

"Yeah. Dad thinks I should focus more on training, but I just like playing." She makes a face. "His girlfriend keeps trying to get me to drink these gross green smoothies for 'athletic performance.'"

"What's your favorite position?"

"Midfielder. I like being where the action is." She glances at me sideways. "Do you play any sports?"

"Rugby, badly. My sisters were the real athletes in the family."

"Mom said one of them almost made the national team?"

"Emma. Broke her arm right before tryouts but kept playing for a week so she wouldn't miss them."

Madison's eyes widen. "That's hardcore."

"Soccer's great," I say, "but women's rugby players? There's tough and then there's TOUGH. My dad always used to tell me, 'Son, men get into fights to impress women, but women get into fights to WIN.' Watch a women's rugby match and you'll know it's true."

Madison laughs. "Your sister sounds badass."

"All my sisters are. You'd fit right in."

Madison blushes, for a moment, and then reaches out to add the final touch of pepper. "Is this done? It smells amazing."

"Let's see." I taste it, nod. "Perfect. You're a natural."

"Jack!" She bounces slightly. "Can you teach me to make that pavlova thing Mom talked about?"

"'Course. But that's a whole project. Meringue takes patience."

"Unlike pasta, which takes temperature control." She grins, clearly proud of remembering. "I'll set the table."

As she bustles off with plates, Sophia appears in the doorway. She's changed from her scrubs into jeans and a soft sweater, hair down, looking absolutely beautiful.

"You're good with her," she says softly.

"She's a great kid." I pull her closer. "Smart like her mum."

"She really likes you." There's something vulnerable in her voice. "She doesn't warm up to people quickly."

"Well, I did bribe her with pasta."

"Jack." She's serious now. "This is...this is a big deal. Having you here. Cooking for us. Being..."

"Part of your life?"

She nods, not trusting her voice.

"Soph." I cup her face gently. "I'm exactly where I want to be."

She kisses me, soft and sweet, until—

"Gross! I'm trying to eat here!" Madison calls from the dining room.

Sophia pulls back, laughing. "The joys of parenting."

"Ready!" Madison announces.

The table looks perfect—she's even lit candles. We settle in, passing dishes, and for a moment it feels so normal, so right, that my chest tightens.

"So," Madison says, twirling her fork expertly, "when do we leave for New Zealand?"

"Two and a half weeks," Sophia answers. "The Saturday you get off school."

"And we're really flying all the way there? Like, over the ocean?"

"All the way," I confirm. "Sixteen hours to Auckland, then another couple to Queenstown."

"I've never been on a plane that long." Her excitement is infectious. "Do they really have beds in first class?"

"Some planes do indeed," I say carefully. "Still an adventure no matter what, though—movies, meals, maybe spot some islands out the window."

"Cool! Will we all sit together?"

"Nah, we're putting you on the wing." I catch Sophia's eye. "Thought you might enjoy the fresh air."

Madison rolls her eyes dramatically. "Ha ha. Very funny." She points her fork at me. "At least come up with original dad jokes if you're going to try."

I clutch my chest in mock offense. "Original dad jokes? That's a high standard. I'll have to up my game."

"You'd better," she grins, then turns thoughtful. "Sixteen hours though. That's, like, forever."

"It goes faster than you think," I assure her. "Especially with good movies and real food."

"This is going to be amazing." Madison takes another bite. "Oh! Can we see those glow worms Mom mentioned?"

"Waitomo Caves? Probably! They're about two hours from Auckland."

"And we'll meet your whole family?"

"If that's alright. They're pretty keen to meet you both."

"What are they like?"

"Loud," I say immediately. "My sister Charlotte runs the family business, very organized. Emma, as you know, is the rugby coach—she'll probably try to recruit you. And Lily's the baby, doing her PhD in marine biology."

"The one living Mom's dream," Madison says with a grin.

"Exactly."

"And your parents?"

"Dad's...traditional. Mum's lovely but has opinions about everything." I pause. "Fair warning—she'll probably try to feed you constantly. It's her love language."

"I can handle that." Madison looks thoughtful. "Do they know about us? Like, that Mom and I are coming?"

"They know I'm bringing two very special people to meet them."

"Smooth," Madison says approvingly. "You're good at this."

"At what?"

"The boyfriend thing. Way better than Dad's girlfriends." She makes a face. "Tiffany kept calling me 'sweetie' and trying to bond over 'girl stuff.' Like, I just met you, lady."

"Madison," Sophia warns.

"What? It's true. She tried to give me a crystal for 'positive athletic energy.'" She looks at me. "You don't believe in crystal healing, right?"

"Only if the crystal's been properly prescribed by a medical professional."

Madison laughs. "See? Normal. Mom, he's normal."

"Mostly," Sophia agrees, catching my eye.

We finish dinner with easy conversation—Madison telling stories about school, asking about New Zealand wildlife, wondering if she'll be able to understand our accents.

"Right," I say once we're done. "Who wants to learn about pavlova?"

"Me!" Madison jumps up. "Is it really the national dessert?"

"There's some debate. Aussies claim they invented it, but they're wrong." I start gathering ingredients. "It's named after a Russian ballerina, Anna Pavlova, who toured both countries in the 1920s."

"Food history! I love this." Madison watches as I separate eggs. "Mom, are you helping?"

"I'll supervise," Sophia says, settling onto a bar stool.

"Now," I tell Madison, "the secret to good meringue is making sure no yolk gets in the whites. Even a tiny bit will ruin it."

She watches intently as I demonstrate. "Why?"

"Fat prevents the proteins from binding properly. It's all chemistry."

"Like the pasta temperature thing. Science cooking!"

We work together, Madison asking constant questions, Sophia occasionally offering commentary. When we get to the whipping stage, Madison's fascinated by the transformation.

"It's like magic! How does liquid become solid?"

"Air bubbles trapped in protein networks." I show her how to test for stiff peaks. "See? Perfect."

"This is the coolest thing ever." She carefully spoons meringue onto the parchment. "How long does it bake?"

"Hour and a half, very low temperature. Then it cools in the oven overnight."

"Overnight?" She looks disappointed. "So we can't eat it tonight?"

"Afraid not. But I'll make another one before we leave for New Zealand. Deal?"

"Deal." She high-fives me with a slightly sticky hand.

As I slide the pavlova into the oven, Madison starts cleaning up without being asked. Sophia joins her, and I watch them work together, comfortable in their rhythm.

"Mom, can Jack stay for movie night?" Madison asks suddenly.

Sophia glances at me. "I'm sure Jack has things to—"

"I'd love to," I interrupt. "If that's okay?"

"Yes!" Madison pumps her fist. "We're watching '*The Princess Bride*'. Mom can quote the whole thing."

"As you wish," Sophia says in a perfect Westley impression.

Madison groans. "See? Every. Single. Line."

We settle in the living room, Madison claiming the middle of the couch. As the movie starts, she provides running commentary.

"Okay, so this is the best sword fight ever filmed. The guy actually learned to fence left-handed for it."

"Inconceivable!" Sophia and Madison shout in unison at the screen.

I'm not really watching the movie. I'm watching them—the way they mouth the dialogue, Madison's head gradually dropping onto

Sophia's shoulder, Sophia's fingers absently playing with her daughter's hair.

This. This is what I want. Not the estate, not the business meetings, not the charity galas. This cozy living room with these two amazing people.

"You okay?" Sophia whispers.

I realize I've been staring. "Perfect."

By the time Westley mostly-dies, Madison's mostly asleep.

"Should I carry her up?" I offer quietly.

"She's fifteen," Sophia smiles. "And would be mortified. But thank you." She gently shakes Madison's shoulder. "Bed time, baby."

"Mm'already asleep," Madison mumbles.

"Come on. School tomorrow."

Madison sits up, blinking. "Oh. Hi, Jack. Did I fall asleep?"

"Right about the time they entered the Fire Swamp."

"Classic." She stretches. "Thanks for dinner. And the science lesson."

"Anytime."

She hugs her mom, then, surprising me, gives me a quick hug too. "Night, Jack. Thanks for being normal."

After she heads upstairs, Sophia walks me to the door.

"Thank you," she says softly. "For tonight. For being so good with her."

"I meant what I said. I want to be part of your life. Both your lives."

She kisses me, slow and deep. When we break apart, her eyes are bright.

"Two and a half weeks," she murmurs.

"Two and a half weeks," I agree. "Then you meet my slightly abnormal family."

"Can't be worse than Troy."

"Famous last words." I kiss her once more. "Breakfast tomorrow? Before shift?"

"The place with the good pastries?"

"Six thirty? I know it's early, but—"

"It's perfect. I'll already be up anyway."

"It's a date."

I drive home with the ghost of her kiss on my lips and the echo of Madison's laughter in my ears. Six-thirty tomorrow morning—just the two of us, good coffee, her smile across the table.

Two and a half weeks until New Zealand. Until I have to navigate introducing the woman I love to a world I walked away from. Not because I'm ashamed—fuck no. My family worked hard for what they have. But that's just it—it's theirs, not mine.

I chose ambulances over board meetings. Chose saving lives over stock portfolios. Chose to matter in ways that can't be measured in profit margins.

The weight of not telling Sophia sits heavy in my chest. It's not about trust—Christ, I'd trust her with my life. But once people know about the money, everything changes. Every gesture gets questioned. Every gift becomes suspect.

I just want more time being Jack-the-paramedic, not Jack-the-heir-who-disappointed-his-family. More dinners where we argue about pasta techniques. More movie nights where I'm just the guy Madison calls "normal."

Tomorrow at breakfast, I'll probably chicken out again. Order her coffee, watch her review staffing schedules, and convince myself that waiting until New Zealand is better. That showing her is better than telling her.

My phone buzzes. Emma.

> Mum's beside herself with excitement. She's already planning menus for your 'special friend.' Fair warning, she's assuming wedding bells.

I groan. My family's going to scare Sophia off before she even processes the estate situation.

But then I remember Madison's hug. Sophia's trust. The way they both just accepted me into their lives.

Maybe they'll accept all of me too.

Even the parts I've spent years running from.

chapter
nineteen

"UGH, THIS MAN!" I slam my laptop shut, the legalese from the IRS publication blurring before my eyes.

It's Wednesday afternoon. Madison's at school. It's been a week since movie night, a week of stolen kisses and quick coffees and anticipation building for New Zealand. Ten days until we fly.

Troy is being particularly insufferable today, demanding I unearth three years' worth of school expense receipts for some obscure tax deduction he's trying to claim. Now he's insisting on a Zoom call in twenty minutes to "ensure compliance." The implication, as always, is that I'm too incompetent to handle it myself.

Jack, who'd been lounging on my couch watching rugby highlights on his phone, looks up. "Troy still giving you grief, *tāku ipo*?"

"Grief doesn't even begin to cover it." I pace my small home office—really just a corner of the living room with a desk. I'm wearing my "work from home but might have to look presentable" uniform: a silk blouse I'd thrown on for a hospital admin call earlier, paired with my oldest, softest college sweatpants. Professional on top, utter chaos below. Much like my current mental state.

Jack unfolds himself from the couch and walks over, his presence instantly both calming and distracting. He starts rubbing my shoulders, thumbs finding the knots of tension. "Want me to run interference? I can be surprisingly intimidating when I use my 'official paramedic' voice."

I lean back into his touch, a small sigh escaping. "As tempting as that is, it would just give him more ammunition. '*Sophia can't even handle her own paperwork without her new boyfriend stepping in.*'" I mimic Troy's pompous tone. "No, I just need to get through this. But honestly, Jack, if you don't leave soon, I'll never get this done. You're far too distracting in the best possible way."

A slow, wicked grin spreads across his face. The kind that usually precedes him doing something utterly unexpected and thoroughly delightful. "'*Distracting*', am I?" He kneels, his hands sliding from my shoulders down my arms, eyes sparkling with mischief.

"Intensely," I admit, my breath already hitching. "And I have a Zoom call with who-know-who in—" I glance at the clock, "—eighteen minutes."

"Plenty of time for some…inter-departmental stress management," he murmurs, his gaze dropping pointedly to the hem of my sweatpants. He tugs gently at the drawstring.

My eyes widen. "Jack McKenzie, you wouldn't dare."

His grin widens. "Wouldn't I, Charge Nurse Mitchell?" He's already easing my sweatpants down, warm hands brushing against my thighs. He presses a kiss to my hipbone, then another, his movements deliberate and slow.

"Jack, the call…" I whisper, but my protest is weak, already undermined by the shiver his touch sends through me.

He looks up, blue eyes alight with playful fire. "You just focus on your important paperwork, Soph. Let me handle the stress relief." He winks, then disappears beneath my desk.

My office chair suddenly feels like a throne of impending doom and exquisite torture. I can hear him settling, the rustle of movement. My heart hammers against my ribs.

"What are you—" I start, trying to peer under the desk, but his hand on my knee stops me.

"Focus on your work, Charge Nurse Mitchell," his voice comes from below, muffled but vibrating with amusement. "Wouldn't want Troy to think you're not giving his demands your full attention."

I take a deep breath, smooth my blouse, and open the Zoom link, still breathless, forcing every neuron to snap into clinical efficiency. My best war face.

Troy's video flickers on. "Sophia. Finally." His face fills the screen, his expression already set to 'condescending prick.' He's in his chrome-and-white home office, that new Rolex visible on his wrist. "Glad you could make it. Do you have the 1098-T forms I asked for?"

"Yes, Troy," I say, my voice impressively steady considering Jack's fingers are now tracing patterns on my inner thigh. "I have them right here." I hold one up to the camera.

"Good. Now, on line three, subsection B..."

He drones on about deductions and dependents, completely oblivious. Under the desk, Jack begins his ministrations. Slowly. Methodically. His warm breath ghosts over my dampening core, and I have to grip the desk edge to stifle a gasp.

Jack's tongue flicks out—a delicate, teasing touch—and lightning bolts shoot through me once again. I clear my throat. "Line three, subsection B. Crystal clear."

Jack's mouth seals over my clit like he's got all the time in the world. I clench my jaw. "I'm reviewing it now."

"You're late going over this, you know. If the school doesn't get this by Friday—"

"I'm aware of the deadline." My voice is steady. A miracle.

"And for the dependent care credits," Troy continues, "I'll need copies of all Madison's after-school program invoices. You did keep those, didn't you? Or was that too much 'adulting' for one year?"

Deep breath. Don't murder him. Don't moan. Jack is now fully engaged, his mouth working with focused intensity, teasing but respectful, somehow knowing my limits exactly. I can feel my orgasm building like a storm on the horizon.

"Of *course* I kept them," I manage, voice slightly higher. "I'll scan them after this call."

"Also," Troy leans forward, and I spot Tiffany doing yoga in the background, "about that New Zealand trip... seems extravagant for a paramedic's salary. Have you considered the tax implications? International travel with a minor? My accountant says—"

Jack groans softly into me, a low, muffled "*fuuuccckkkk*". The vibration makes my whole body clench. I disguise it as a cough.

Troy cocks his head, and glances at the screen. "You alright? You look flushed."

"*Fine*," I say tightly. "Air conditioning's off."

"Right." He keeps talking. Something about not claiming the dependent credit two years in a row.

I feel heat build low in my belly, blooming outward, a slow-burn ache I've been holding at bay all week. Jack's tongue flicks in tight, perfect patterns... he's learned me too well.

"Well, make sure they're legible this time. Your last scans were atrocious. And Sophia? Maybe consider Costa Rica instead. More... appropriate."

Jack's rhythm intensifies. He knows I'm close. The wonderful, terrible bastard.

The pressure coils tighter, a spark snapping along every nerve. My thighs tremble. My toes curl inside my socks. I taste actual blood. I've bitten the inside of my lip so hard trying not to scream. If I come now, it'll be a full-body blackout.

One more second. Just one more—

"Got it, Troy. Legible scans. Withinthehour, *bye*."

I slam the laptop shut just as the orgasm crashes over me like a dam breaking, sudden and uncontrollable. I throw my head back, biting down a scream, one hand slamming against the desk for balance. Jack doesn't let up. He rides it out with me, coaxing every last tremor until I'm breathless and boneless, collapsed into the chair like I've run a marathon.

"fffffFFFFFUUUUUCCCCCKKKKKKKKKK!"

There's a beat of silence. Then he emerges from under the desk, looking smug and completely unrepentant.

"Still mad I didn't leave?" he asks innocently, wiping the corner of his mouth with the back of his hand.

I stare at him, panting, then a wicked smile spreads across my face. "Almost, McKenzie. Almost." I slide from the chair. "But now it's my turn."

His eyes darken as I stare at him evilly. "Soph—"

"Quiet," I command, already working at his jeans. "You made me keep composure for Troy. Let's see how you handle reciprocal stress relief."

He looks at me, confused. I grab him by the collar of his stupidly soft t-shirt and march us both toward the couch like I'm triaging a trauma patient—decisive, focused, clinically aroused.

"Couch. Now."

His grin is full wattage. "Yes, ma'am. Should I be worried?"

"Deeply."

He drops onto the couch with a thump, legs spread, arms wide, watching me with a mixture of anticipation and open admiration. Still a little breathless from earlier, but cocky as hell.

Not for long.

I straddle him without preamble, knees on either side of his hips, pressing my weight down until I feel him—*already hard*, of course—underneath me.

"You've been smug since you brought that coffee," I say, my hands sliding under his shirt. "So you tell me, Mr. McKenzie. Do smug paramedics deserve rewards?"

His breath hitches slightly. "I think they deserve...further evaluation."

I lean in close, lips brushing his ear. "You want to be quiet under the table and test my composure? Let's see how *you* do."

I slide off his lap, kneel between his legs, and tug at his sweatpants. He lifts his hips without hesitation, no protest, no instructions. Just trust. And hunger.

God, I love this man.

He's thick and warm in my hand, twitching slightly as I stroke him once, slow and deliberate. Jack's head tips back against the couch, and I watch the way his throat works as he swallows. Still trying to play it cool.

I swirl my tongue around the head of his cock, feather-light, teasing. He grunts, hips twitching. Then I take him into my mouth fully, slow and unhurried. He groans again—louder this time, hips bucking just a fraction before I flatten my hands against his thighs.

"Stay still," I murmur, letting him slide free for just a moment. "You made me have to keep a straight face for Troy. Let's see how good *your* poker face is."

"Jesus Christ, Sophia—"

I take him again, deeper this time, one hand wrapped around the base, the other bracing myself on his knee. I let my lips and tongue work in sync, building rhythm, suction, pressure. He gasps, tries to muffle the sound, one hand gripping the back of the couch like it's the only thing anchoring him to earth.

"Soph—fuck—Sophia—"

"Quiet!" I whisper intensely, eyes locked on his. "You wanted this."

He lets out this noise—half-moan, half-prayer—and it hits me somewhere deep, carnal, the way his voice roughens when he's right on the edge but doesn't want to fall. Not yet. Not without me.

I increase the pace, flicking my tongue in just the way I know will drive him wild, hollowing my cheeks as I take him deeper. His breathing turns ragged. His thighs tense beneath my hands. I can feel him unraveling, losing control one heartbeat at a time.

When I feel him throb, close, I slow—pulling back, letting cool air hit him before easing off entirely.

His eyes fly open. "What the—"

I crawl up his body slowly, straddling him again, kissing him until he tastes himself on my tongue. "Oh, no. I'm not done with you yet."

He growls, low in his throat, and flips us, pinning me against the cushions. His lips crash into mine, his hands everywhere—rough with need, reverent with restraint.

"Still think I should've left?" he breathes against my mouth.

"I think," I pant, wrapping my legs around his waist, "you should shut up and fuck me already."

He thrusts into me with a growl that vibrates through my entire body. No teasing now—just raw, rolling need. I moan into his mouth, hands scrambling for purchase on his back, his arms bracketing me like steel.

The stretch hits hard—deep, perfect, greedy. My back arches instinctively. It's not polite. It's not slow. It's full-body, toe-curling, mess-up-your-insides kind of sex. The kind you feel for hours. The kind I haven't felt for *years*.

It is *perfect*.

"Don't stop," I gasp. "Don't you dare stop—"

He doesn't. He drives into me like he can't bear to leave, like he wants to etch himself into my skin. I come apart again, this time with sound, with shudders that won't stop. He follows with a broken curse and my name like it's a benediction.

The second time comes faster. For both of us. He buries his face in my neck as he groans my name, hips stuttering, and I follow, biting his shoulder to muffle the sounds spilling from my throat. It's not elegant. It's not planned. It's *real*.

When we finally collapse, sweaty and tangled and boneless, I can't stop laughing. He bubbles out of me like champagne.

Jack grins against my collarbone. "That good, huh?"

"You," I gasp, "are banned from ever bringing coffee and smug grins into my kitchen again."

"Noted. Counteroffer: I bring coffee and smug grins, but also flowers and foot rubs."

"Deal."

He lifts his head, brushing hair back from my damp forehead. "You okay?"

I nod, sobering slightly. "Actually...yeah. I really, really am."

Outside, a delivery truck rumbles past. Inside, the world is soft and slow, our bodies still wrapped around each other like we've got all the time in the world.

"Ten days," Jack murmurs against my neck, his accent thicker in his post-orgasmic haze.

"Ten days," I agree, then remember Troy's dig about the trip. "Jack? The flights—how exactly did you manage—"

"Points," he says quickly. "Lot of miles between here and there. They add up real quick." His eyes briefly shift away, a tell I'm starting to recognize. "Between flights home, medical conferences, even that All Blacks match in San Diego last year against Fiji—sixteen hours to Auckland or four to California still counts the same to the airline."

"That's a lot of flying."

His hand traces circles on my hip, too casual. "Plus there's routing bonuses. Stopover in LA adds miles. Premium credit card multipliers." He's explaining too much now. "Amazing what you can accumulate if you're strategic."

Something in his tone makes me want to push. But then he's kissing me again, slow and deep, and Troy's paperwork can definitely wait another hour.

Or three.

chapter
twenty

THE PHONE RINGS at 6 AM, which means it's 11 PM in New Zealand. I know who it is before I even check the screen.

"*Kia ora*, Mum."

"Jackson! Finally! I was beginning to think you'd forgotten you had a family." Her voice carries that particular mix of guilt and affection that only mothers can manage. "Charlotte says you haven't returned her calls either."

"Been busy, Mum. Work's been—"

"Yes, yes, playing paramedic." She dismisses a few years of my life with casual efficiency. "Now, about this Sophia..."

I groan internally. Here we go. "What about her?"

"When do we meet her? And her daughter? Madison, isn't it? Emma's already planning activities for a teenager. She's got some daft idea about a rugby clinic."

"Mum, they're coming for a holiday, not boot camp."

"Oh, don't be dramatic. Emma just wants to share her passion. Like your father with the vineyard tours he's planning."

My stomach drops. "Vineyard tours?"

"Well, of course! Can't have them staying at the estate without showing them the operation. Your father's already selected the vintages for the tasting. The '15 Pinot is drinking beautifully right now."

I pinch the bridge of my nose. "Mum, I told you, we don't need anything fancy—"

"Nonsense. It's not every day my son brings home a woman. The staff are beside themselves. Mrs. Petersen is planning a proper welcome feast, and Tane's already preparing the guest wing."

"The guest wing?" My voice cracks slightly. "Mum, no. We don't need the guest wing. The pool house would be—"

"The pool house? For your girlfriend and her daughter? Absolutely not. They'll have the blue suite. Best views of the mountains and the lake."

I can see it now—Sophia's face when she realizes the "family property" has a guest wing. And staff. And multiple suites with mountain views.

"Mum, listen. Sophia doesn't know about...everything."

Silence. Then: "What do you mean she doesn't know?"

"She thinks I'm just a paramedic."

"You ARE just a paramedic, darling. That doesn't mean you have to live like one. Honestly, this martyrdom is exhausting." I can hear her frowning through the phone. "Jackson Charles McKenzie, please tell me you haven't been lying to this poor woman. You're representing the McKenzie name, whether you like it or not."

"I haven't lied. I just...haven't mentioned certain things."

"Certain things? Like your inheritance? The estate? The family holdings? Four generations of McKenzies have built this legacy with grit and vision, Jackson. It's not something to hide away like it's shameful."

"Mum—"

"You can't keep doing this, Jack." Her voice drops, softens. "Not everyone is Vanessa."

The name hits me like a physical blow, even after all these years. "This has nothing to do with her."

"Doesn't it?" My mother's sigh carries across oceans. "Darling, what she did was awful, unforgivable even. But hiding who you are isn't the answer."

"I'm not hiding," I argue, but we both know it's a lie. The memory rises unbidden—Vanessa's voice, crystal clear through the cellar door I'd been about to open, carrying up from the tasting room. *"God, Melissa, don't be daft. Of course I don't love him. But have you seen that ring? His grandmother's, apparently. Worth a small fortune."* Her laugh, brittle as glass. *"I'm thinking: two kids, ten years, then Bali and Honolulu, baby."*

I'd stood there, grandmother's ring burning a hole in my pocket where I'd just retrieved it from the safe, plans for a vineyard proposal shattered at my feet.

"Jack?" My mother's voice pulls me back. "Are you still there?"

"Yeah." My voice is rougher than I intend. "Look, Sophia isn't Vanessa. She doesn't care about money or status."

"You didn't think Vanessa did either, if I recall."

"That's not fair."

"Life isn't fair, darling. If it were, that woman wouldn't have spent two years pretending to love you while planning how to cash in on our name."

The anger I thought I'd buried flares again. "You think I don't know that? You think I don't remember how she looked at me when I confronted her? Like I was nothing but a bank account with legs."

My mother's voice softens. "That's exactly my point, Jack. You ran away after that—to the other side of the world—to become 'just Jack.' But hiding your background from this new woman, this Sophia...it's no better than what Vanessa did. You're both creating false versions of yourselves."

The parallel hadn't occurred to me, and it lands like a punch to the gut. "That's different."

"Is it? Vanessa pretended to love you for your money. You're pretending not to have money for Sophia's love. Both are deceptions, darling."

"I'm not pretending—" But even as I say it, I know she's right.

Sins of omission are still sins. "She's different, Mum. She doesn't care about status or wealth. Her ex was all about that, and it destroyed their marriage."

"So you thought pretending to be poor was the solution? After what happened last time?"

"I'm not pretending to be poor. I live on my salary. I work my shifts. This is my life."

"In a one-bedroom flat when you could be living properly, upholding the family name. Your great-grandfather would be turning in his grave."

"This is exactly why I didn't tell her!" The words come out sharper than intended. "Because everyone thinks the money is who I am. It's not. It never was."

Mum sighs. "You're right. I'm sorry. It's just...we worry about you, darling. Living so far away, working such dangerous jobs...especially after everything with Vanessa. That woman nearly destroyed you."

"But she didn't," I say quietly. "And I learned a valuable lesson."

"That all women who show interest in you are after your money?"

"No. That I need to be loved for who I am, not what I have."

"Then why not be honest from the start? Find someone who knows everything and loves you anyway?"

"Because the minute people find out, they change. You've seen it, Mum. Even people who've known me for years look at me differently once they know."

"Your father was terrified to tell me about his family's money when we met," she says unexpectedly. "Thought I'd run for the hills."

"Did you?"

"Nearly. Not because of the money, but because he'd hidden it. Made me wonder what else he might hide." She pauses. "But then I realized he was just scared. Scared I'd see the money instead of him."

"That's exactly it."

"So I told him, 'Michael McKenzie, I don't give a rat's arse about your money. But if you ever keep something from me again, money or no money, I'll feed you to the sheep.'"

Despite everything, I smile. "And he believed you?"

"Darling, he'd seen me handle a ram at shearing time. He knew I meant it." Her voice warms. "Forty years later, here we are."

The parallel is clear, even if she doesn't hammer it home. If Sophia is worth keeping, she'll understand my deception. If not...

"Jackson." Her voice takes on that tone from when I was small and scared of disappointing her. "Love means being honest. All of yourself, not just the parts you think they'll like. What Vanessa did was cruel, but letting it make you hide who you are is giving her power she doesn't deserve."

"I know."

After we hang up, I pace my apartment, then grab my phone again. Dad answers on the second ring.

"Jack? Everything alright? Your mother said you're bringing someone home."

"Yeah, Dad. Actually, I wanted to ask you something. Could you...this might sound strange, but could you look into someone for me? Just basic stuff, nothing invasive."

"Who?"

"Troy Bentley. He's Sophia's ex-husband. He's being a right tosser about custody and finances, and I just want to make sure..." I trail off, not sure what I'm asking.

"You want to protect her."

"Yeah."

"Send me what you know. I'll have Rawiri make some inquiries. Nothing heavy-handed."

"Thanks, Dad."

"Jack? Your mother's right. You need to tell this woman the truth. Before you get here."

"I know."

But even as I hang up, I'm already finding excuses. Nine days left. Eight if you don't count travel time.

My phone buzzes. Madison.

> Hey Jack! Do you think Emma would
> teach me some rugby moves?

I smile, typing back:

> Emma would love that. We can stop by
> the All Blacks shop at Sky Tower in
> Auckland too, get you proper gear.

> OMG YES! Can we get Mom something
> too? She pretends she doesn't care
> about sports but she totally does.

This kid.

> Absolutely. Maybe a Black Ferns jersey?

> PERFECT. Mom will pretend she doesn't
> want it but she'll wear it all the time. Like
> that hoodie of yours she "borrowed."

My heart clenches. They've already made room for me in their lives, these two incredible women. And I'm about to risk it all because I was too scared to be honest from the start.

> Dad's being weird about the trip. Says we
> can't afford it. Mom told him it's none of
> his business. She's right, right?

> Your mum's always right. Don't worry
> about the cost.

> K! Can't wait! Mom's humming while
> doing paperwork. She NEVER hums. You
> make her happy!!!

Christ. The weight of what I'm risking sits heavier with each passing day. I think of Vanessa's cold calculation, the way she'd mapped out exactly how to extract maximum wealth from my family, and contrast it with Sophia's fierce independence, her dedication to a job that exhausts her but fulfills her.

No. Sophia is nothing like Vanessa. She deserves the truth.

I drive to meet Sophia, already knowing today won't be the day I tell her either. Tomorrow, maybe.

Or the next day.

Nine days to figure out how to say: "Remember that $300 I spent on wine? Well, about that..."

Nine days until she sees the estate and realizes just how much I've been hiding.

Nine days of being just Jack, before I have to be Jackson Charles McKenzie.

The countdown feels like a ticking bomb, and I'm the one who set the timer.

chapter
twenty-one

MY RADIO CRACKLES TO LIFE: "Sophia, can you come to triage? It's Nate."

I frown. Nathan Crawford doesn't call for backup unless it's serious, and he'd normally specify if it was a medical emergency. Must be an irate patient or family member—probably someone demanding to know why their stubbed toe isn't getting priority over the cardiac arrest.

"On my way," I respond, setting down the chart I was reviewing and heading toward the triage area.

What I find isn't an angry patient, but a petite woman in a tailored pantsuit standing beside Nate's desk. She's carrying a leather portfolio and wearing the kind of smile that screams "corporate."

"Sophia," Nate says, his expression professionally neutral but his eyes sending me a clear SOS. "This is Karen Scharenbroch from Workflow Management. She'd like to speak with me about some metrics."

"In the middle of triage?" I don't hide my incredulity.

"I understand you're busy," Karen says, not sounding like she understands at all, "but this will only take five minutes. It's about the department's patient flow inefficiencies."

I glance at the waiting room—nine patients, none looking immediately critical, and as I recall, we only had one ambulance inbound. Not our worst day by a long shot.

"Five minutes," I say firmly. I think for a moment, and then toggle my radio. "Tasha! I need you in triage."

Tasha shows up in triage thirty seconds later, surprised. "Yes?"

"Could you cover Nate in triage so he can have a chat with our, ahem...'*efficiency expert*'?"

Tasha doesn't even attempt to hide her surprise. "Me? In triage?"

"Just for five minutes." I give her a pointed look. "You've been saying you want more responsibility."

She approaches warily. "Sure, but—"

"If anything looks critical, come grab me immediately," Nate tells her quietly. "But don't worry. You've got this."

Tasha takes Nate's seat with a mix of determination and trepidation. It's a vote of confidence she clearly wasn't expecting, and despite her usual attitude, I can see she's trying not to look pleased.

"Five minutes," I remind Karen, who nods enthusiastically.

"That's all I need!"

Fifteen minutes later, my radio crackles again: "Sophia? It's Tasha. I've got five new walk-ins and you've sent two squads out here on top of that. Where the hell is Nate?"

I was in the middle of reviewing labs, but now my head snaps up. "What!? He's not back yet?"

"Would I be asking if he was?" Tasha's stress is evident even through the crackling connection.

I march to the charge desk. "Maria, where did they go? Conference Room B?"

"Last I heard." Maria doesn't look up from her computer. "Want me to page him?"

"I'll handle it."

I stride down the hallway, my irritation building with each step. Five minutes, she said. Five minutes during a relatively quiet period was manageable. But now we're picking up, and I need my most experienced triage nurse back where he belongs.

As I approach Conference Room B, I can hear Nate's voice—still professional but with an edge I rarely hear from him.

"—believe the data needs more context. You can't just look at raw wait times without considering—"

"The numbers are quite clear, Mr. Crawford."

I push the door open without knocking. Nate sits across from Karen, whose smile tightens when she sees me.

"What's going on?" I demand. "It's been fifteen minutes."

"Miss Mitchell," Karen says, maintaining her plastic smile. "We're discussing some concerning patterns in Mr. Crawford's triage metrics."

"What's she talking about?" I ask Nate directly.

"Apparently my wait times are too long," he says evenly. "I've been trying to explain that I often get assigned the busiest shifts, and I tend to be more thorough with certain high-risk populations."

"Nathan," I say, using my charge nurse voice, "you're needed back in triage. The department's picking up."

"Yes, ma'am." He starts to stand immediately, but a hand shoots out from across the table to grab his wrist and stop him.

"Excuse me," Karen interjects, "but we're in the middle of a productivity consultation. I just need a few more—"

"*Don't. Touch. My. Nurses.*" The words slipped out of me in a low, venomous tone that made both Karen and Nate freeze instantly. Everyone in the room could feel the temperature drop ten degrees.

Karen's eyes widen, her corporate smile faltering as she slowly withdrew her hand from Nate's wrist.

"The hospital is paying me to run this emergency department," I cut in. "If anything goes wrong, if anyone dies, that's on me. That's why they pay me that stunning extra dollar an hour to be a charge nurse."

"I understand your concern, but—"

"I'm short-staffed, we're getting busy, and you've just taken my most experienced triage nurse away for three times longer than you promised. If you want to pull my nurses for extended consultations, hire me more people."

Karen's smile doesn't waver. "I understand hiring more staff is frequently the only solution that employee focus groups can articulate to improve workflow efficiency," she says, her tone like she's explaining to a five-year-old why they can't have ice cream for dinner, "which isn't surprising as they are often too involved in the problem to understand that's an unreasonable expectation."

Nate's eyes widen almost comically. He shoots me a look that clearly says, "*Can I please leave, now?*" and then prudently edges toward the door.

"You're dismissed, Nate," I say, not taking my eyes off Karen. "Head on back to triage, please."

"Aye, aye, ma'am," he says quickly, literally sprinting for the exit.

As the door closes behind Nate, I feel my blood pressure rising. Great plan, Sophia. Now you have to shut this jackass down properly. I check my watch; we have multiple patients waiting, but I'm not letting this go.

Three minutes. I'll give myself three minutes to educate this woman.

I calmly take Nate's vacated chair and deliberately drag it closer to Karen, *juuuuust* this side of professionally acceptable, but close enough that she has to resist the urge to lean back.

"Let me *elucidate* something for you, Miss Scharenbroch," I say, not bothering to disguise the contempt in my voice, leaning slightly forward for emphasis. "This isn't Home Depot, where if you don't have enough people working in plumbing, someone doesn't get a faucet. Okay?" I jab a finger in the direction of the ER. "This isn't Applebee's, where the worst thing that happens is your food gets cold. If we screw up here, people *die*. Do you get that? Is there something inherently confusing about that?"

"Miss Mitchell—" she starts, her corporate smile finally faltering as she shifts uncomfortably in her chair. I cut her off immediately with a dismissive wave.

"Do you want to know about our staffing problems?" I flatten my palms on the table, invading her space even more. Karen inches her chair back slightly. "Corporate says we have to run understaffed for six months consecutively before they'll even consider hiring more people. Six months, understaffed, every. Single. *Day*." I punctuate each word with a tap on the table.

"But here's the *brilliant* catch-22: If we have two nurses quit without notice, and I—as charge nurse—manage to cobble together coverage by begging people to work doubles, shuffling assignments, and pulling staff from other areas, then guess what? According to your metrics, we weren't technically 'understaffed' that day." I throw my hands up. "So our six-month clock starts over! Because I did my job and kept patients safe despite the shortage. It's like congratulating a drunk driver for making it home without killing anyone!"

Karen starts to reply, but I hold up a hand so close to her face she actually flinches. "Wait, wait—it gets better!" I step forward, voice rising. "Your precious metrics? They don't even count the 'hold' patients. So when the upstairs units are full or short-staffed—don't worry, I know, silly me bringing up 'staffing' again"—I roll my eyes theatrically—"guess where those overflow patients go? They don't go anywhere! They stay *right here* in the ER."

I sweep my hand toward the department beyond the conference room. "So now my team's stuck boarding admitted patients for days. Cardiac patients. ICU-level patients. Psych patients. All of them. And we're still expected to handle the new ER patients coming through the door—trauma alerts, strokes, overdoses—because technically our census only reflects 'active' emergency cases. Not the ten or fifteen admitted patients we're babysitting because there's no room upstairs."

Karen's clipboard twitches in her hands like she wants to disappear behind it. I'm just getting started.

"That means an ER nurse might be caring for a suicidal teen, a septic dialysis patient, and someone in acute heart failure—all at the same time. But does that show up on your precious dashboard? Nope. According to you, we're not busy. According to your spreadsheet, we're not understaffed." I smile sweetly, venom in every syllable. "So when patients wait hours in triage, the blame falls on us. Not the broken system. Not the bottlenecks. Just the frontline staff. But hey, no problem! Just like you said, it's not a staffing issue, right?"

"I don't think—" Karen begins, finally frowning in earnest, her body language completely transformed from her initial confident pose; but before she can get anything else out, I swoop in, kneeling down to her eye level.

"Oh, I'm *sure* you don't, honey," I say, clapping my hands around hers congenially, my voice thick and sweet with sarcastic empathy. "I'm sure you don't. Listen, I'd love to sit here and talk to you about all of it, but I'm probably boring you to tears! Clearly, you already know all this, and I have to get out to triage and make sure our numbers don't keep making us look bad. Mmmkay? Mmmkay."

I straighten up, smoothing my scrubs, and head for the door without a backward glance. My heart is pounding, adrenaline coursing through my veins. I haven't laid into someone like that in far too long.

When I return to the charge desk, Maria gives me a knowing look. "Feel better?"

"Much." I grab the nearest chart, needing to focus on actual medicine now. That's when I spot it—a cup of coffee and a small paper bag from my favorite bakery sitting at my station. A sticky note in familiar handwriting:

For after your shift. Hope your day gets better. -J

My stomach sinks. Jack must have stopped by while I was

educating Ms. Workflow Management. He left this sweet gesture and I wasn't even here to see him.

"When did this get here?" I ask Maria, trying to keep my voice casual.

"About ten minutes ago. Your Kiwi dropped it off. Said he tried texting but figured you were busy." She raises an eyebrow. "I told him you were educating corporate on the realities of healthcare."

"And?"

"He laughed and said he'll call you later." She lowers her voice. "Left those flowers too."

I hadn't even noticed the small bouquet of daisies next to the coffee. Simple, cheerful, and thoughtful—just like him.

For a moment, I'm irrationally angry that Karen Scharenbroch's corporate bullshit made me miss seeing Jack. Then I'm just sad that I missed a bright spot in an otherwise frustrating day.

I sigh and begin typing an email to my manager, certain I'm going to have to explain this more in detail later, when Nate appears at my elbow. His expression is a mixture of gratitude and awe.

"Thank you," he says quietly. "For rescuing me back there."

"Just doing my job." I pause my typing and look up. "How bad was it before I arrived?"

"She had spreadsheets comparing my triage times with everyone else's." He shakes his head. "No consideration for acuity or patient complexity. Just raw numbers."

"Corporate," I mutter.

"I've never seen anyone shut someone down that thoroughly." There's a hint of admiration in his voice. "Everyone in the department's talking about it."

I narrow my eyes. "You were back in triage. How would *you* know?"

He winces, caught. "Okay, so...apparently a few folks were, uh, charting nearby and kind of...stayed to listen."

"Stayed to *eavesdrop*, you mean. And then bolted like roaches when I wrapped it up."

He shrugs noncommittally. "Who can really say?"

I sigh. Great. Just what I need: to be on administration's radar *and* the talk of the ER. "That's fine. Let them talk. I meant every word."

"I know you did." Nate hesitates. "By the way, I checked on Tasha. She's actually doing really well in triage."

That surprises me. "Really?"

He nods. "She's got good instincts when she bothers to use them. Caught an elderly sepsis presentation that was masquerading as 'just feeling weak.' Tagged it ESI 2 when most would have probably scored it a 3."

I glance over at Tasha, who's efficiently working through assessments with more focus than I've ever seen from her. "Huh."

"Maybe we should let her flex there more often," Nate suggests. "Under supervision, of course. But she could learn."

For a moment, I see something in his expression—a flicker of... not just professional interest. Interesting.

"We'll see," I say noncommittally. "One medical save doesn't erase a year of attitude."

"No," he agrees. "But everyone deserves a chance to grow." His eyes drift toward Tasha again, lingering a moment too long to be purely professional.

"Nathan Crawford," I say, keeping my voice light. "If I didn't know better, I'd say that almost sounded like optimism."

He looks startled, then a small smile forms. "Don't tell anyone. I have a reputation to maintain."

"Your secret's safe with me." I gather my charts. "Back to the trenches."

Nate's already moving toward his next patient. His reliability is comforting—a constant in the chaos of the ER. I make a mental note to remember this moment: Nate, defending Tasha. Seeing potential where others see only problems.

Maybe Karen was inadvertently useful after all. Not that I'd ever admit it.

I take another sip of Jack's coffee, drawing strength from the caffeine and the thoughtfulness behind it. Seven days until New Zealand. Seven days until we're far away from efficiency experts and metrics.

Seven days suddenly feels like forever.

chapter
twenty-two Jack

I'M deep into a game of Civilization, trying to guide my fledgling empire towards a cultural victory, a welcome distraction from the low hum of anxiety about the upcoming New Zealand trip. I've even named my two most prosperous cities 'Sophia's Landing' and 'Fort Madison'—a sentimental move I'd never admit to Rodriguez, but it makes me smile every time their banners pop up on screen. It's my go-to for relaxation these days; I've learned my lesson with Football Manager and those bloody rugby mods. I start a game at nine one night and the next thing I know, my alarm is going off for my six a.m. shift. Never again. Civ is safer. Usually.

Just as I'm about to research Pottery in 'Sophia's Landing,' my laptop pings—an encrypted file transfer from Dad's associate, Rawiri. He is ex-NZ Special Air Service, has spent time in Afghanistan, and now handles the less, ahh... savory aspects of McKenzie family security and information gathering. A good bloke, quiet, efficient. I've asked Dad to just do a light sweep on Troy Bentley after Sophia's stress over those tax forms, just to see if there is anything she should be aware of, anything that might cause her more grief down the line.

I'm expecting maybe some undeclared income, a few bad investments—the usual for a self-proclaimed "finance bro" who seems to live off his new girlfriend's money. But as I click the file open, a knot tightens in my gut. Rawiri is not one for fluff; if he sends something, it is usually significant.

"Too bloody easy," reads Rawiri's note. "No special access needed. All publicly available, unfortunately."

The first few documents are what I'd half-expected: some murky crypto transactions, a string of failed online ventures, nothing overtly illegal that jumps out, but definitely a pattern of financial instability and perhaps some creative accounting. Enough to make me understand why Sophia is always so tense when Troy brings up money.

Then I hit the social media deep dive.

It is not hard to find, not really. Troy, under a thinly veiled pseudonym—"AlphaTRex"—is clearly trying to build himself into some kind of online influencer. His profile picture is a gym selfie, all aggressive posture and sneer. The bio reads: "Unapologetic Male. Financial Dominance. Traditional Values. Escaping the Matrix."

My stomach turns. I've heard Sophia mention Troy had gone down some dark rabbit holes both before and after the divorce, something about the "manosphere." This looks like he'd not only gone down the hole but has set up shop and is trying to sell tickets.

I start clicking through his posts, his linked podcast clips, the videos. It's a cesspit. Standard "redpill" rhetoric at first—men are victims, women are manipulative, feminism is cancer. Vile, but depressingly common in certain corners of the internet.

Then it gets worse.

He has a whole series on "Female Nature" and "Navigating the Modern Dating Market." The language is demeaning, objectifying. Women are assets or liabilities, their value tied to their youth, their "purity," their willingness to be submissive. My blood starts to simmer. This is the man Sophia was married to, the father of her daughter.

In one particularly enlightening forum thread where he was "advising" other men, he'd stated, with absolute conviction, "Women can't get orgasms from sex with a man. I know this for a fact. No woman I've ever been with has had one. It's a biological impossibility, a myth perpetuated by..." He'd gone on some bizarre tangent about societal conditioning.

Jesus Christ, I think, a humorless laugh bubbling in my chest. *You couldn't have waterboarded that admission out of me. Surely couldn't be a skill issue, eh, mate?* The sheer, unadulterated arrogance mixed with profound ignorance is breathtaking. No wonder Sophia is so guarded.

The escalation comes when I find a section, a "thread" he'd done, specifically on raising daughters in the "current degenerate age." It is not directly about Madison, not by name, but the implications are chilling. Posts about how daughters are a "father's property until marriage," how their primary role is to "attract a high-value man," how a father needs to "instill obedience early" to prevent them from becoming "unmanageable shrews."

"Daughters as liabilities if not properly controlled." The phrase jumps out at me. Liabilities.

My hands clench into fists. I think of Madison—just last week, after her soccer game, she'd been excitedly telling me about a school project, her eyes bright with intelligence and enthusiasm. She'd high-fived me when I'd shown her how to properly fold a fitted sheet, laughing that infectious, uninhibited laugh of hers. That bright, funny fifteen-year-old, a liability? The idea is obscene.

The gut punch, the one that makes me physically ill, is a clip from his latest podcast appearance. His voice, smug and self-assured, fills my small apartment: "...and that's the bottom line, fellas. Your daughters? They need to understand their place. They need to be taught to obey men, to respect male authority unquestioningly. It's for their own good, their own protection. A daughter who doesn't know how to submit to a strong man is a danger to herself and a disgrace to her father..."

I slam the laptop shut so hard the plastic creaks, a choked sound catching in my throat. My stomach roils. I push back from the desk, hands shaking, and have to brace myself against the wall, breathing heavily into my palms, trying to quell the sudden wave of nausea.

Madison. He's talking about Madison. About Sophia's daughter. About *his* daughter. About this incredible young woman I'm already starting to care about like she's family. The thought of her ever hearing that, ever internalizing even a fraction of that poison... it makes me literally see red.

I feel a tremor run through me, a mixture of rage and a profound, aching sadness for what Sophia must have endured, for what Madison might be unknowingly exposed to. I actually feel my eyes prickle, the image of Madison's trusting smile when I'd talked about rugby with her flashing in my mind.

I need to talk to someone who understands righteous fury, someone who understands protecting family. My fingers fumble for my phone, scrolling until I find Emma's number. My middle sister, the rugby coach, the one who'd walked around with a broken arm for a week rather than miss a tryout.

She answers on the second ring, her voice booms even through the speaker. "Jack! You finally remember you have a sister! What's up, little bro? Need bail money?"

"Em," my voice is rougher than I intended. "Got a minute?"

"For you? Always. What's wrong? You sound like you've seen a taniwha."

I quickly, grimly, outline what I've found. I don't spare the details of Troy's rhetoric. Emma is quiet for a long moment after I finish, a silence so profound I think the call might have dropped.

Then, her voice comes back, low and dangerous, the voice she uses when one of her players is being unfairly targeted by a ref. "That absolute twat." The word is a vicious spit. "Sophia's ex? Madison's father?"

"Yeah."

"Right. Give us his address."

"Emma, no. What are you thinking?"

"Thinking I might need to have a chat with him about respecting women. Maybe demonstrate a proper rugby tackle. To his teeth. Headbutt's good too. Very efficient for getting your point across, I find."

Despite the sickness in my gut, a small, hysterical laugh escapes me. "As much as I appreciate the sentiment, and believe me, I really do, I don't think international incidents involving aggravated assault are going to help Sophia or Madison right now."

"Probably not," she concedes, though she sounds disappointed. "But Jack, this is... this is beyond awful. That poor girl. That poor woman. Does Sophia know he's spewing this filth online?"

"I don't think so. Not the extent of it, anyway. She knows he's gone down the manosphere rabbit hole, but this is...this is next level."

"And Madison?" Emma's voice is sharp with concern. "Has she seen any of this?"

"God, I hope not. That's what's eating me up, Em. If she stumbles across this, it could destroy her. Her own father saying things like that..."

"She's fifteen, Jack. She's online. If he's trying to be an influencer, she'll find it eventually, or one of her friends will." Emma is right, and the thought is like another punch. "You have to tell Sophia."

"I know. But when? How? We're supposed to be going to New Zealand in a few days. This will wreck her. And what if Troy uses it against her in some custody bullshit? 'She's turning Madison against me because she doesn't like my opinions!'"

"His opinions are that his daughter is property and women are scum," Emma says flatly. "That's not an opinion, that's a bloody character flaw the size of Mount Cook. Sophia needs to know so she can protect Madison. And mate, you need to protect them too."

"I want to. Christ, Em, I want to wring his bloody neck."

"Join the queue," Emma says darkly. "Look, little bro. You're a good man. You see this for what it is. You do what's right. Tell Sophia. Help her figure out how to shield Madison. And if you need someone to...'have a quiet word' with Mr. AlphaTRex about the potential downsides of public misogyny, you know who to call. I'm very persuasive. And I travel well."

I laugh again, a little less hysterically this time. "Thanks, Em. I needed that."

"Anytime. Now go sort it. And bring Sophia and Madison home. Mum's already planning enough kai to feed the entire All Blacks squad."

After we hang up, I sit there for a long time, the weight of it all pressing down. Emma is right. Sophia has to know. Madison has to be protected.

But how? When? The trip is supposed to be an escape, a chance for us to connect, for Madison to see a different world. Now it feels like I'm carrying a bomb.

The decision solidifies, hard and clear. I can't let him continue. I need to talk to Sophia, yes. But not yet. Not until after I've tried to deal with Troy myself.

Two text messages, a phone call to the station, and a small schedule swap later, I'm sitting in the back corner of a coffee shop at 4:45 PM the next day, positioned to see the entrance but partially hidden by a large fern. I know from Sophia that Troy picks Madison up here one afternoon a week for dinner—a neutral territory agreement from their custody arrangement.

Madison arrives first with her soccer bag, immediately gluing herself to her phone while she waits. She's ordered some frozen sugary concoction that's more dessert than coffee. The barista knows her by name.

At precisely 5:07 PM, Troy strolls in—twelve minutes late, not that I'm counting. He's wearing a tight black t-shirt with "ALPHA" emblazoned across the chest in gold letters. I think of the smug voice from the podcast, and my jaw clenches. Madison doesn't look up from her phone until he's standing over her.

"Hey, kiddo. Ready to go?"

She nods, gathering her things. They're heading for the door when I step out from behind the fern.

"Troy!?" I feign surprise. "Kia ora, mate, I thought that was you."

His eyes narrow slightly, passive-aggressively "trying" to place me. "Ohhh. Right. You're the Australian paramedic. John?"

"Close enough." I gesture to the counter. "Just grabbing coffee before shift. How are you?"

Madison brightens. "Jack! Mom said you were working today."

"Change of plans." I smile at her, then turn back to Troy. "Actually, could I have a quick word? Professional matter." To Madison, I add, "Medical confidentiality stuff. Super boring."

Troy hesitates, clearly irritated at the interruption. "Madison, wait by the car. I'll be right there."

She rolls her eyes but complies. "Bye, Jack. Tell Mom I'll be home by nine."

Once she's out of earshot, Troy's demeanor shifts. "What do you want? I've got dinner reservations."

"Just a friendly chat." I gesture to a corner table, away from the other customers. "About your online content."

His expression freezes for a microsecond, so brief I would have missed it if I wasn't looking for it. "My what?"

"Your Alpha Male Revolution podcast appearance was particularly interesting." I keep my voice conversational, non-threatening. "The one where you call daughters 'liabilities' unless they marry well. Where you say they need to 'obey men' to have value."

All the color drains from his face.

"I don't know what—"

"I've read the Discord comments too. The newsletter. The YouTube channel." I lean forward slightly. "The posts coaching men on how to hide assets during custody proceedings. The threads about how family courts are 'rigged against real men' and how to game the system."

"That's taken out of context," he hisses, looking around nervously. "It's a persona. For marketing. You have to be edgy to break through these days, the, the... the algorithm rewards controversial takes. Nobody gets followers being moderate."

"A persona." I let the word hang there. "So you don't actually *believe* daughters are liabilities, you just *say it* publicly for clicks because the algorithm told you to. That's your defense?"

He opens his mouth. Closes it.

"Well, that's an interesting marketing strategy." I open my phone to the screenshot. "Calling your own daughter a 'liability' seems like a bold choice either way."

"I *never* said—"

"You never used Madison's name, no. But you have exactly one daughter." I put the phone away. "She's fifteen now. Spends hours online. How long before she finds this content, Troy?"

Real fear flashes in his eyes, quickly replaced by anger. "Are you... *threatening* me?"

"Oh, no. Not at all. Trust me," I assure him, "you'd definitely know if I was. No, I'm giving you a chance to fix this before she sees it." I keep my tone calm, reasonable. "Because she will find it eventually. Kids always do."

"What do you want?" His voice has lost its alpha male confidence. "Money? Is that it?"

I physically recoil. "What? No. Christ, no."

"Then what?"

"Delete it. All of it. The podcast. The videos. The Discord messages. Everything that talks about women's 'value' or daughters being 'liabilities.' Everything that makes Madison sound like a fucking investment property instead of a human being."

"That's my livelihood!"

"Find another one." I stand, towering over him. "Madison loves you. God knows why, but she does. And if she ever finds those videos, that podcast, it'll destroy her."

"You can't—"

"*I'm* not doing anything, Troy. I'm just pointing out that your content exists forever unless you delete it. And Madison is getting older, more curious. One day, she'll Google you." I let that sink in. "What do you want her to find?"

I see conflict in his eyes, the financial incentive of his 'brand' wrestling with whatever parental instinct might still exist.

"How did you even find all this?" he asks finally.

I shrug. "Anyone with internet access could find it. It's all public."

That seems to hit him harder than anything else I've said. The color drains from his face again.

"There's more, too," I add casually. "I notice how you reply to Joe Rogan and Jordan Peterson tweets. Like, within seconds of them posting. Every. Single. Time."

His face reddens. "So what? They're thought leaders—"

"You're literally waiting by your phone to lick their arseholes the instant they post." I shake my head. "Maybe try touching grass sometime, mate."

Troy's jaw tightens. "Are we done here?"

"Almost." I keep my voice level, measured. "Look, I'm not going to force you to do anything. For the moment, anyway, freedom of speech is still the law in this country. But I want to be crystal clear about something: I'm not telling Madison about any of this. Because I know it would destroy her."

I let that hang for a moment between us.

"Take some time to think about what kind of father you want to be, Troy. What you want your daughter to find when she inevitably googles you. Because that day is coming."

"I'll... think about it."

"Do that, mate." I step away from the table. "And Troy? This conversation stays between us. For Madison's sake."

Outside, Madison is sitting in Troy's Tesla, head bowed over her phone. She looks up as I pass, waves cheerfully. I wave back, my heart breaking for this incredible kid who has no idea what her father really thinks of her.

I drive home in a daze, wondering if I've done the right thing. Should I have told Sophia immediately? Is confronting Troy directly a mistake? What if he retaliates by trying to limit Madison's time with Sophia?

At a red light, my phone buzzes with a text. Sophia.

> Just finishing up at work. Can't wait to
> see you. Madison will be back by 9pm so
> we have the place to ourselves for a little.
> ;) Decided to wear something interesting
> under my scrubs today. Here's something
> I took earlier to show you what you have
> to look forward to.

I open the message and nearly drop my phone. It's Sophia—my God, is it ever Sophia—in her bathroom mirror at home, wearing a lacy black bra that's doing God's work. Matching panties that barely qualify as clothing. Her hair's pinned up, tendrils falling loose against her collarbone, and her mouth is curved in a knowing, wicked little smirk that tells me she knows *exactly* what this picture is doing to me.

I stiffen instantly. There's not a prayer I'm shaking this off.

A second message pings through:

> We won't have long. You gonna make it
> worth my while, McKenzie? Or should I
> send this to someone else who knows
> how to use their hands? ;)

I groan aloud. Jesus Christ. She's *really* trying to kill me.

I fumble to type back with one hand, the other now useless thanks to the steel bar forming behind my zipper:

> You send that to anyone else and I will
> personally drag them into the bay and
> drown them with my bare hands.

A moment later, her reply:

That's the energy I like to see. Better
bring it. I shaved my legs for this.

A horn blares behind me. The light's green.

I toss my phone onto the passenger seat like it burned me,
shifting in my seat with a grimace. My jeans are now a prison. I need a
cold shower—or Sophia. Preferably both.

I quickly do the math in my head: Sophia gets off at 7. Madison's
with Troy until 9. Two hours. I had planned to head home first,
shower, change—I'm still in the clothes I wore to confront Troy. But
with traffic, I'll barely make it to Sophia's by 7:45. Maybe 8:00.

Fuck that.

Fuck that!

I make a hard right at the next intersection, ignoring a blaring
horn, and head directly for Sophia's house. I'll damn well wait in her
driveway if I have to. After the day I've had—after seeing what Troy
really thinks about his daughter, after worrying about telling Sophia
—I'm not wasting a single minute of our time together.

Six days until New Zealand. Six days until we're far away from
Troy's toxic bullshit and hateful ideology.

Six days to figure out if I should tell Sophia what I found.

But one thing I know with absolute certainty—I'll do whatever it
takes to make sure Madison never sees herself as just a "liability."
Never believes her value comes from "obeying" men.

Even if that means protecting her from her own father's poiso-
nous worldview.

For now, though, I'll have about ninety minutes alone with the
woman who just sent me that photo. And I plan to make *every single
one* of those minutes count.

chapter
twenty-three

I SIP MY FLAT WHITE, scrolling through the overnight report on my tablet. Jack has politely cajoled me into trying one last week, and I've initially refused on principle—I take a certain pride in drinking coffee strong enough to make grown men cry. But I've finally given in, and though I've played it off as "ehhhh, they're *okay*," the truth is I actually enjoy the velvety texture.

Not that I'd admit that to Jack. He'd never let me hear the end of it after all my stubborn resistance.

Of course... if he punishes me for that admission in the same way he did last night... maybe I wouldn't mind so much.

The thought sends a flicker of heat low in my belly, a phantom ache that makes me cross my legs unconsciously. Jack is significantly bigger than I'm used to. Bigger than Troy ever was, in every possible way... and I'm *still* adjusting.

In the *best* way.

I take another sip of coffee and try to focus on my shift report, not on the memory of him pinning my wrists to the head of my bed like I was the only thing that had ever mattered.

The break room hums with the usual shift-change energy. Day shift nurses huddle around the table and lean against counters, some still yawning, others already buzzing with caffeine. I've gotten the changeover brief from the night charge nurse, and am about to go over assignments and flag any troublesome patients, but I am waiting for one more person.

Nate Crawford, who punches in at precisely 6:45 AM every single day without fail. Military punctuality that's become so reliable we practically set our watches by it.

It's now 6:55, and he's still not here.

I check my phone. No messages. No calls. This is very unusual. I am about to text him when the break room door bursts open.

Nate rushes in, looking utterly harried...and he is not alone.

Tailing him, looking small and sleepy and utterly out of place, is a girl of about eleven, clutching a worn-looking backpack shaped like a cartoon cat and a well-worn paperback. Her dark hair is pulled into a messy ponytail, and she blinks owlishly against the harsh fluorescent lights. Paige, I realize with a start. I'd met her once at the department holiday party a couple years back, but she'd grown several inches since then and now sports blue braces that flash briefly when she nervously bites her lip. I'd heard Nate mention her a thousand times, his voice always softening, but seeing her here, in the hospital, is jarring.

The break room goes silent. Every eye turns to Nate and the child —his pristine professional image visibly cracks under the weight of what is clearly an emergency situation.

"I..." he starts, then falters, his usual calm completely shattered. The collective stares of his colleagues seem to make it worse, though several smile kindly at Paige.

I stand up immediately. "Nathan. The charge office, please?"

He nods gratefully, steering Paige toward the charge nurse office just off the main corridor. As they pass, Paige clutches her book tighter, like a shield.

Once inside, Nate closes the door and turns to me, his voice low and urgent.

"Soph—Miss Mitchell. Ma'am, I apologize for the breach of

protocol." He actually uses "ma'am". His eyes, usually so steady, dart around like he's expecting hospital administration to rappel in from the ceiling. "My babysitter didn't show, no warning, no communication. I had no alternative childcare options available on short notice. I have no excuse, ma'am."

I take in his stressed face, the way his shoulders are hunched. This is Nathan Crawford, my most reliable, unflappable nurse, looking like he is about to face a firing squad. I know the broad strokes of his story. Paige's mom had walked out when Paige was just a baby, maybe three months old, wanting a life free of responsibility. He never talks about it, not really, but the weight of it is there, in the way he pours everything into his daughter and his job. He's trying not just 100%, but 200% to make up for that absence, and I always got the heartbreaking sense that he feels like he's still not quite enough, even though he's absolutely a superdad by any measure.

"Nathan," I say quietly, "you could be on fire and you'd apologize for the smoke. Relax. It's okay."

He inhales sharply, a barely perceptible relaxation in his shoulders.

I smile at Paige. "Hi there. I'm Sophia. Your dad's told me a lot about you."

She gives a small, polite nod. "Nice to meet you."

"Okay, Nate," I say, keeping my voice even. "Deep breath. It happens." My own mind is already racing. A kid in the ER, even in a quiet corner, is against every policy imaginable. Safety, HIPAA, the sheer unpredictability of what might roll through those doors. But looking at Nate's desperate face, and little Paige trying to make herself invisible in the corner of my office...

"She can't go out there," I say, more gently, bringing us back to the immediate problem. "And you'll be worried sick if she's just tucked away somewhere." I glance at the schedule. We're adequately staffed for the moment, but that could change with one bad call. "Can you get someone to pick her up soon?"

He runs a hand over his face. "Working on it. My neighbor

usually helps in a pinch, but she's out of town until this afternoon. I'm calling everyone I know."

"You could call out," I offer, even though we both know what that means. "I can try to cover triage myself for a bit, or ask Maria to pull someone from the float pool, but..." I hesitate. "It'd count as an occurrence. And a late call-out."

We don't need to say the rest. HR's latest memo has been clear: calling out within thirty minutes of your shift means an automatic written warning. One more after that, and your job is on the line. And I can't fudge his timecard without putting both our necks on the block.

Nate just shakes his head, looking even more miserable.

A knock at the door interrupts us. Tasha Williams sticks her head in, holding her travel coffee mug.

"Oh my God, *hiiiii*, is this your daughter?" Tasha asks, her eyes lighting on Paige. "The one who drew that heart valves picture you showed everyone!?"

Paige looks startled. "You showed my picture to people?"

Nate's ears redden slightly. "It was exceptional work."

Tasha leans down slightly to Paige's level. "I thought it was soooooo cool how you included the interatrial septum. Most people forget that's technically a fifth distinct area."

Paige brightens visibly, sitting up straighter. "Dad helped me build a model!"

"If you need someone to watch her," Tasha says, turning to me, her usual sharp edge softened by a *very* uncharacteristic awkwardness, "I could stay with her in the break room. Just until Nate can sort something out." She shrugs, aiming for casual. "I'm good with kids. Got a bunch of younger cousins."

I stare at her. Nate looks equally stunned. This is Tasha Williams, queen of the eye-roll and the "not my patient" sigh, offering to babysit. The ER gods truly work in mysterious ways.

"Are you sure, Tasha?" I ask, keeping my voice neutral, appraising her. This can't be a half-hearted offer. "You'd be responsible for her. I'd need to pull you from the floor."

"I can handle it," Tasha says, a flicker of her usual defensiveness in her tone, but her eyes are fixed on Paige with something that looks surprisingly like... empathy? "For an hour or so. Give Nate time to make some calls."

I make a quick decision. It is not ideal, but it is the best bad option we have. "Okay, Tasha. Thank you. For an hour. Break room. I'll let Nathan and I handle Fast Track between us."

Nate looks like he could weep with relief. "Tasha, I... thank you. Seriously. I owe you big time."

"No worries, Nate," Tasha says, already turning to Paige. She gestures to the book in Paige's hands. "Is that 'The Giver'?"

Paige nods, holding it up. "For school."

"That's one of my favorites," Tasha says, her face lighting up with genuine enthusiasm. "The ending still makes me mad, though."

Paige's eyes widen. "You've read it?"

"Dystopian literature is kind of my thing," Tasha admits, then looks at me defensively. "What? I read!"

I raise my hands in surrender. "Never doubted it."

Nate hesitates, then unzips his backpack and hands Paige a smaller bag. "Your lunch. Protein bar for midmorning. Water bottle's full. Remember your inhaler's in the side pocket if you need it."

"*Dad*," Paige mutters, embarrassed. "I know."

"Want a juice box, Paige?" Tasha asks. "We've got apple, orange, and prune... mmmmm, we should probably skip that last one."

Once they're out of earshot, the door closing behind them, I turn back to Nate. The immediate crisis is averted, but the stress still clings to him.

"Are you okay, Nate?" I ask, lowering my voice. "Have you heard anything from... her?"

He knows who I mean. Paige's mom. His jaw tightens almost imperceptibly. "No. Last I heard, she was somewhere in Florida. 'Finding herself.'" He lets out a short, humorless breath. "I still email photos of Paige to her folks, her grandparents. Never hear anything back. It is what it is."

The casual dismissal doesn't hide the old hurt. He clearly feels Paige needs a mom, even if he has no romantic interest left in the woman who'd been her mother.

"Thank you, Sophia," Nate says then, his voice thick with gratitude, shifting the subject. "For trusting Tasha with her. I don't know what I would have done."

"Tasha stepped up. And you needed a solution," I say, giving him a small smile. "Go make your calls, Nate. Find a real babysitter. And Tasha just earned herself some serious good karma."

"I can have HR take an hour or two of my sick time or PTO to pay for her time," Nate says, his rigid sense of fairness asserts itself even in crisis.

I wave him off. "Nate, this is real life, and real life is messy. If we asked corporate or HR, they wouldn't have let this happen at all, but that's why they pay me to figure these things out." I smile at him. "You're an asset to our department. And you're our friend. You'd do the same for any of us."

He nods, a flicker of something like gratitude in his eyes, then pulls out his phone, a measure of the usual Nate-like efficiency returns to his movements. I watch him for a moment, then head back to the break room to distribute assignments. The ER is calm for the moment, but the day is young.

An hour later, just as things are starting to pick up, Nate finds me. "Got it sorted out. My neighbor, Mrs. Swanson—it turns out her flight got in earlier than she expected. She can take Paige. She's on her way now."

"Good," I say. "How was Paige with Tasha?"

A rare, genuine smile touches Nate's lips. "Actually... really good. When I went to check on them, Tasha was showing Paige how to make a butterfly out of a tongue depressor and some tape. Paige was actually laughing." He shakes his head, a hint of wonder in his voice. "Never would have pegged Tasha for a craft queen."

"People'll surprise you," I say, thinking of Jack, of his unexpected transfer, his quiet pursuit.

When Nate's neighbor, Mrs. Swanson, a kind-faced woman who looks like she bakes cookies for the entire street, arrives, Paige gives Tasha a quick, shy hug. Tasha, to her credit, looks almost as surprised as Paige, but she pats the girl's shoulder awkwardly.

"See you around, kiddo," Tasha says, trying for casual but her voice is a little softer than usual. "Let me know what you think about the ending of that book, okay?"

As Nate walks Paige out, I catch Tasha watching them go, a thoughtful, almost wistful expression on her face before her usual bored mask slips back into place.

Interesting.

Very interesting.

chapter
twenty-four

I **CLOSE** my laptop with more force than necessary, the image of Troy's whining face still burned into my retinas.

"Oh, fuck right off, you discount Andrew Tate," I mutter to the empty apartment.

The "AlphaTRex" content is gone; the vile posts about female "value," the disgusting rants about daughters being "liabilities," all of it scrubbed. But he'd replaced it with something almost as nauseating: a five-minute video of himself, looking appropriately somber in a black t-shirt, explaining how he is being "canceled by the woke mob" for "speaking truth to the feminized culture." He'd even set up a donation link to "help fight back against censorship."

Pathetic. But the primary goal is accomplished—Madison won't stumble across the worst of it now. That is what matters.

I check my watch. Five hours until I need to pick up Sophia and Madison. My bag sits by the door, already packed with what little I'll need. The rest—well, there is plenty waiting for me back home. My chest tightens at the thought.

Home. I am taking Sophia and Madison home.

I've been so careful. For three years, I've maintained the fiction that I'm just Jack McKenzie, paramedic, ordinary bloke who happens to have a Kiwi accent. The careful omissions. The strategic vagueness about my family's "businesses." The way I've casually deflected questions about my university days or why I'd really left New Zealand.

And for better or worse, it's about to all come crashing down.

I sit on the edge of my bed, head in my hands. This is supposed to be a simple holiday—showing Sophia and Madison my country, my favorite places. But nothing about the McKenzie Estate is simple. Nothing about my family's position in Otago is ordinary.

My phone buzzes. Sophia:

> Just finished packing Madison's "essentials" bag. How she needs three pairs of headphones for one flight is beyond me. I'm actually more nervous than she is!

I smile despite my churning thoughts.

> All part of teen travel protocol, apparently. Don't worry, I've handled enough post-party resuscitations to manage a 16-hour flight with a teenager.

> Rude. And accurate. Okay, compression socks packed, baby aspirin ready for DVT prevention, and I've created a schedule for getting up and stretching every 2-3 hours because those economy seats are going to be murder on your legs.

I wince at "economy seats." Another small lie of omission I've maintained, letting her believe we'd be cramped in the back of the plane.

> You've thought of everything. Charge Nurse on and off duty.

> Someone has to keep us alive on that
> metal tube of recycled air and jetlag.
> Madison won't stop talking about seeing
> a kiwi bird. I told her they're nocturnal but
> she doesn't care.

> We'll find her one, promise. Plenty at the
> wildlife centers.

What I don't mention is the private sanctuary on the estate, where kiwi are nesting, part of my family's conservation efforts. Just another detail I've conveniently avoided.

> Madison wants to know if we can eat
> Marmite in New Zealand too, or just
> Australia?

> That's VEGEMITE in Australia, you
> heathens. We have the superior Marmite.
> And yes, I'll introduce you both to proper
> breakfast. Fair warning though, Madison
> will hate it. You might too.

> Challenge accepted. See you at 2. xo

"XO." Those two little letters shouldn't make my heart lurch, but they do. Beneath all the anxiety about the wealth reveal, there is this—the simple, unexpected joy of Sophia Mitchell and her daughter entering my life. The growing certainty that I'd do anything to keep them there.

My phone rings. Charlotte, my oldest sister. Perfect timing, as always.

"Kia ora," I answer.

"Jack! Tell me you're actually on schedule for once in your life. Mum's driving everyone mental with preparations."

I could picture Charlotte in her Christchurch office, designer glasses perched on her nose, managing the McKenzie businesses with terrifying efficiency.

"Flight's still on time, Char. We are landing in Auckland tomorrow, overnight there, then down to Queenstown the next day."

"And you're sure they don't know? About...everything?"

I sigh. "Sophia thinks we're flying economy, if that answers your question."

"Jesus, Jack." I can practically hear her pinching the bridge of her nose. "This is going to be a disaster."

"Thanks for the vote of confidence."

"You know what I mean. You should have told her weeks ago. Not sprung it on her when she's standing in front of the bloody estate."

"I know," I admit. "I've tried. Every time, it just...the moment never seems right."

"When is the 'right moment' to tell someone you're heir to a wine empire and a couple hundred mil in assets?"

I wince. "That's not helping, Char."

She sighs. "Look, just...prepare her somehow, yeah? Don't let Mum's welcome committee be her first clue. You know how she gets."

Our mother's idea of a "casual welcome" involves staff lined up at the gates, vintage champagne, and usually some poor local official she'd strong-armed into making an appearance.

"I'm working on it," I promise. "The flight upgrades will be step one."

"Upgrades, plural? I thought you said economy?"

"That's what Sophia thinks. Madison's in Business Premier, we're in Premium Economy."

"Why not all in Business?"

"Because I'm trying not to terrify them, Char. Baby steps."

She makes a noise that somehow conveys generations of McKenzie skepticism. "You've got a night planned in Queenstown before heading to the estate, right? You're telling her then?"

"Well...yeah...probably."

"Jack." Her voice sharpens. "Listen. I understand what you're going through, but I reaaalllllyy think you need to think this one through. Showing up at the estate with her completely unprepared is asking for disaster."

"I will, I am, I'm going to," I insist, not sounding convincing even to myself.

"It's not just about the couple hundred million in assets, Jack." Charlotte sounds exasperated. Even converting from New Zealand dollars, that is a number I try not to think about too often.

"I know."

"I'm not talking about the stuff you've already told her—the sisters, the vineyard. I'm talking about the things that make them your family. The reputation in the community. The expectations."

"I get it, Char."

"Dad's already planning the vineyard tour, by the way."

"Of course he is."

"And Mum's invited the Wallaces for dinner your first night."

"She what?" I sit bolt upright. "No. Absolutely not. Charlotte, I swear to God—"

"Already handled it," she says smoothly. "Told her you'd all be jet-lagged. The Wallaces will come for Sunday lunch instead."

"You're evil."

"I'm efficient. There's a difference." She pauses. "They matter to you, don't they? This woman and her daughter?"

"Yeah," I say quietly. "They do."

"Then you better make sure it'll work out," Charlotte says with her usual certainty. "If it doesn't, Lily and Emma will help me hide your body in the vineyard. We've got plenty of space."

"Your support is overwhelming."

"That's what sisters are for. Safe travels, little brother. Text when you land."

After we hang up, I sit staring at my phone. My sister is right—this has disaster potential. But somehow, the alternative—not bringing Sophia and Madison home, not showing them this part of my life—feels even worse.

I spend the next few hours double-checking everything. Our tickets are confirmed. The Auckland hotel suite is booked. The car service is arranged. I've done everything to make this journey as smooth and comfortable as possible.

Everything except be honest from the start.

"You know, I can carry my own bag and Madison's," Sophia says as I load the last suitcase into my car. "I've been doing it for years."

"Humor me," I reply, closing the trunk. "I'm trying to be gallant here."

"It's working," Madison chirps from the back seat, not looking up from her phone. "Mom never lets anyone help with bags."

"That's because most men only offer so they can complain about how heavy they are," Sophia retorts. "Making a big production about the weight."

"Your bag could be filled with bricks and I wouldn't comment," I promise, sliding into the driver's seat.

"Yeah, but you're a paramedic," Madison points out. "You carry people on stretchers and stuff."

"True. Though technically I shouldn't lift more than 50 pounds without help."

"Well, my makeup bag alone is about 40," Madison says gravely.

Sophia rolls her eyes. "Says the girl who owns exactly one mascara and a tinted lip balm."

The drive to the airport is filled with this kind of easy banter. Sophia has her usual coffee in hand—the velvety flat white she's finally admitted to enjoying—and a folder with printed confirmations, passport copies, and a meticulous itinerary. Classic Sophia, prepared for any emergency from missed connections to spontaneous appendicitis.

Madison alternates between teenage excitement and studied nonchalance, the way only fifteen-year-olds can. One moment she is peppered with questions about New Zealand, the next pretending she is not remotely impressed by anything.

"So I can't get a kiwi as a pet, right?" she asks as we merge onto the highway.

"Absolutely not," I confirm. "They're endangered, nocturnal, and would hate your bedroom. Also, the smell-"

"But they're so cute! With their little beaks and fuzzy bodies."

"You can visit them at wildlife sanctuaries," I promise. "They're actually quite large—bigger than people expect."

"Like how big? Chicken size?"

"More like a small cat. And their eggs are enormous compared to their body size."

Madison's eyes widen. "Cool. What else should I know before we go? Any cultural things I might mess up?"

I consider this. "Don't call us Aussies. Don't say our accent sounds like Australia. In fact, just don't mention Australia at all unless you're prepared for a twenty-minute lecture."

"Got it. Australia is New Zealand's Canada."

I laugh. "Something like that. And don't worry about Māori pronunciation. Most Kiwis appreciate the effort even if you get it wrong."

"What about that thing you call mom sometimes? Ta-koo something?"

Heat creeps up my neck. "Tāku ipo. It means 'my darling' in Māori."

"That's sweet," Sophia says, her fingers finding mine across the console. "Though your accent makes everything sound sweet."

"Gross," Madison declares from the backseat. "But also kind of cute, I guess."

We arrive at the international terminal three hours before our flight, as Sophia has insisted. ("What if there's a security incident? Or a line? Or a global pandemic?") Check-in is mercifully quick.

"Can I have the window seat?" Madison asks as we head toward security. "I want to see everything during takeoff."

"Absolutely," I agree. "I'm an aisle man myself."

As we join the security line, Sophia leans close to me, her voice lowered. "I have no problem with Madison having the window, but between us, I'm a little jealous. I love window seats on planes."

"Don't worry, tāku ipo," I say, pressing a kiss to her temple. "It'll work out."

She looks up at me, brow furrowed slightly at my tone. "What does that mean?"

"That I'm looking forward to sixteen hours with you beside me."

She studies me a moment longer, then shakes her head with a small smile. "You're being mysterious."

"Just excited to show you my home."

Security is a breeze, and we make our way through the terminal toward our gate. Madison marvels at the duty-free shops, while Sophia keeps checking her watch and consulting her folder.

"We're fine for time," I assure her, guiding them through the international concourse. "The gate's just up ahead."

As we approach Gate 17, the Air New Zealand Koru logo makes my heart skip. It has been too long since I'd been home.

We find seats near the boarding area, and Madison immediately asks about the in-flight movies. "Will they have the new Marvel one? Or do they have different movies in New Zealand?"

"Same movies," I promise. "Air New Zealand actually has excellent entertainment systems."

"How do you know?" Sophia asks. "Fly with them often?"

Another moment where honesty battles with my carefully constructed narrative. "When I first moved here. I went back and forth a bit before settling."

Not exactly a lie, but not the whole truth either.

The gate agent's voice comes over the loudspeaker: "Air New Zealand Flight 1 to Auckland now welcoming our Business Premier passengers, Star Alliance Gold members, and Airpoints Elite customers for priority boarding."

"That's us," I say, standing and gathering our carry-ons. "Let's go."

Sophia stares at me. "What? Us? Jack, what are you talking about?"

I cannot help the smile that spreads across my face. "I had some points saved up. Thought I'd surprise you."

Her eyes narrow. "What kind of points get you boarded first?"

"From all those medical conferences before I transferred to 402. International flights rack up miles fast." The explanation is plausible enough. "Madison's in Business Premier—seat 5K. Full pod, it lies completely flat."

Madison's jaw drops. "I'm in first class?"

"Business Premier," I correct. "But yes, essentially."

"Oh my God!" Madison clutches her mother's arm. "Mom!"

Sophia looks stunned. "Jack, that's...that must have been a fortune in points. Are you sure?"

"Absolutely. Teenagers need proper sleep on long flights. Otherwise, they get cranky and overthrow the crew."

Madison is already bouncing on her toes. "Is it like the pods in the movies? Do I get pajamas? Is there a menu?"

"Yes, yes, and yes," I confirm, unable to resist her enthusiasm. "And we're in Premium Economy—24A and B. Window and aisle."

Sophia's expression cycles through surprise, gratitude, and something else—a fleeting moment of calculation, quickly dismissed.

"Jack, this is incredibly generous," she says softly.

"It's nothing," I reply, meaning it. If she only knew. "Come on, they're boarding."

Madison practically sprints to the gate, her boarding pass clutched like a golden ticket. The attendant scans it with a smile. "Business Premier, Miss Mitchell. Right this way."

Sophia and I follow more sedately. She keeps shooting me sideways glances.

"What?" I ask innocently.

"Medical conferences, huh?"

"Paramedic continuing education. Very important. Plus a few back-and-forth trips when I first moved."

She seems to accept this. "Well, thank you. Madison's over the moon."

"Wait till she sees the seat. It's quite something."

Once onboard, a flight attendant shows Madison to her pod in Business Premier. Her "Oh my God, MOM!" could probably be heard back in the terminal. We watch as she is presented with a substantial swag bag containing Bose noise-canceling headphones, luxury skincare products, and premium pajamas with the Air New Zealand logo. Madison looks like she might pass out from excitement.

Sophia and I continue to our Premium Economy seats—significantly more spacious than standard economy, with decent recline and legroom.

"Window's all yours," I say, gesturing for her to slide in first.

She settles into her seat with a small sigh of appreciation. "This is...not what I was expecting."

"Good surprise?"

"Very good." She squeezes my hand. "Though I did pack those compression socks for nothing."

"Still wouldn't hurt to wear them. And stick to the getting up and moving schedule. DVTs are no joke."

She laughs. "Says the man who just upgraded us."

"Medical professional," I remind her. "Safety first, luxury second."

As the plane fills around us, I watch Sophia. She runs her fingers over the amenity kit, examines the larger entertainment screen, tests the footrest. Small luxuries that are nothing compared to what waits for her in New Zealand, but her appreciation makes something warm unfurl in my chest.

This woman who works so hard, who carries so much, who deserves every comfort I can give her—she is genuinely pleased with

Premium Economy. What will she make of the estate? The staff? The McKenzie name that is known throughout the region?

I push the thought away. One step at a time.

Once we are airborne, the cabin crew begins the meal service. Madison appears briefly from Business Premier, still euphoric.

"Mom! They gave me REAL menus. And hot towels! And the seat goes completely flat!" She demonstrates with her hands. "The flight attendant says I can order whenever I want. And there's ice cream sundaes!"

"That's wonderful, sweetie," Sophia says, clearly enjoying her daughter's excitement. "Just don't overdo it, okay? Remember your stomach on the Springfield roller coaster."

Madison makes a face. "That was different. This is fancy food." She turns to me. "Thank you, Jack. This is the coolest thing ever."

"You're welcome, Madison. Glad you're enjoying it."

She leans closer, lowering her voice. "The guy across from me is, like, definitely someone important. He has monogrammed cufflinks."

"Very fancy," I agree solemnly.

"I'm going back to watch a movie on my gigantic screen." She practically skips back to Business.

"You've made her entire year," Sophia says, watching her go.

"Good. She deserves it."

The flight attendant brings our own Premium Economy meals—not quite Business Premier standard, but still quite good. Sophia opts for the wine, and I join her. The Air New Zealand Pinot Noir is not from the McKenzie Estate, thankfully, though I recognize it from a neighboring vineyard.

After dinner, we settle in to watch a movie together. The cabin lights dim, creating a cocoon of semi-privacy. I put my arm around Sophia's shoulders, and she nestles against me.

"This was thoughtful," she murmurs, halfway through the film. "All of it."

"Just the beginning," I reply, pressing a kiss to her hair.

"Madison's so excited to see New Zealand. Your home."

"I can't wait to show you both."

"Tell me more about your family," she says, looking up at me. "What makes them your family? Something you love about each of them."

The question catches me off guard, digging deeper than her previous inquiries. I think for a moment.

"Charlotte has this laugh," I say finally. "She's serious most of the time—all business and efficiency—but when something really gets her, she has this laugh that sounds exactly like she did when she was five. Completely unguarded. Makes everyone around her laugh too, even if they don't know what's funny."

Sophia smiles. "I can picture that."

"Emma collects vintage rugby jerseys. Not valuable ones, necessarily—just ones with stories. She has this ancient, moth-eaten Otago jersey that belonged to our great-grandfather. She wears it for good luck during important matches, even though Mum threatens to burn it every time she sees it."

"And Lily?"

"Lily talks to plants. Full conversations. She'll be taking measurements in her research garden, chatting away to the specimens about her day. She swears they grow better when she does. She even names them—her doctoral research subjects are all named after characters from The Lord of the Rings."

Sophia's expression has softened. "They sound wonderful. And your parents?"

"Dad keeps a journal. He has since he was a teenager. One entry every day, no matter what. When we were kids, he'd let us draw in the margins sometimes. And Mum..." I smile at the memory. "Mum can't sing to save her life, but she does it anyway. Loudest, most tone-deaf rendition of 'Happy Birthday' you've ever heard, every single year."

Sophia squeezes my hand. "Thank you for sharing that. It makes them feel more real to me."

If only you knew how real they're about to become.

As the movie ends, Sophia checks on Madison again. "Sound asleep," she reports, returning to her seat. "Flat on her back with three blankets and an eye mask. Living the dream."

"Good. She should get some proper rest."

The cabin is quiet now, most passengers either sleeping or watching their screens with headphones. Sophia leans her seat back and closes her eyes.

"You should sleep too," she tells me. "Long day tomorrow."

"I will," I promise, though sleep feels impossible with my thoughts racing.

Despite everything, I must have dozed off. The steady hum of the engines, Sophia's warmth beside me, the wine—it all conspires to pull me under. My head drifts toward her shoulder, consciousness slipping away.

I am vaguely aware of Sophia shifting beside me, then getting up. Bathroom, probably. I should rouse myself, but my limbs feel weighted, my eyes too heavy to open.

Just five more minutes...

Someone gently pokes my shoulder. I force my eyes open, blinking in the dim cabin.

Sophia stands in the aisle, her eyes glittering in the dark.

"Jack," she whispers, bending close. "Come with me."

Suddenly, I am very much awake.

chapter
twenty-five

THE GENTLE HUM of the engines and the subtle swaying of the cabin should have lulled me to sleep hours ago. Most passengers are already out cold, strange shapes in the dim blue lighting, wrapped in airline blankets and contorted into whatever passes for comfort at 35,000 feet. But my mind is wide awake, hyperaware of everything— the lingering taste of surprisingly decent New Zealand Pinot Noir, the quiet breathing of sleeping strangers, and most of all, Jack's warm weight against my shoulder.

He'd dozed off halfway through our second movie, his breathing deepening until his head tilts toward me, hair brushing my cheek. I don't mind. I like watching him like this—face relaxed, defenses down, the perpetual good humor in his expression softened into something more vulnerable.

A flight attendant passes silently through our cabin, checking on sleeping passengers, adjusting a blanket here and there. When she notices me awake, she offers a questioning thumbs-up toward Business Premier. I nod, understanding her silent question. She mouths "still sleeping" with a smile, confirming Madison is lost to the world in her pod, no doubt exhausted from the excitement and the three desserts she'd managed to consume before finally reclining her seat.

The night stretches ahead of us—hours of enforced stillness over the vast Pacific. Time suspended in this metal tube between our old life and whatever waits for us in New Zealand.

I study Jack's profile in the dim light. The faint stubble along his jaw. The slight furrow between his brows even in sleep. The curve of his mouth that always seems ready to smile. This man who'd transferred to Medic 402 just for more chances to see me. Who teaches Madison to make pasta. Who'd upgraded our flights with mysterious "points" and looked at me like I was something precious.

This man. This moment. The sheer audacity of it.

Why not?

The thought comes from nowhere... or, maybe, from somewhere deep inside me that had been dormant for too long. A part of me that hasn't been consulted during the careful, responsible years of single motherhood. The version of Sophia who exists before scrub caps and badge reels and divorce papers.

I slip from beneath Jack's head, carefully lowering him against the headrest. He makes a small sound of protest but doesn't wake. The cabin floor is cool beneath my sock-covered feet as I make my way forward, toward the galley where a flight attendant is quietly organizing breakfast trays for the morning service.

She looks up, surprised to see a passenger vertical. "Can I help you with something?" Her name tag reads Aroha, and her smile is kind beneath professional politeness.

"I hope so," I say, my voice low. "Ahh." I wince. "This is going to sound strange..."

I pull out my phone, scrolling quickly to the video I'd saved: Jack diving into that wrecked car, pulling the family to safety while metal groaned and gasoline leaked. The footage that had gone viral and made him briefly internet famous.

"That's him," I say, nodding back toward our row. "He's a paramedic. We're on our first real vacation since..." I hesitate. "Well, first one in forever. He upgraded us with his points. My daughter's in Business Premier, completely over the moon."

Aroha's eyes widen slightly as she watches the video. "I remember this. It was all over the news. He pulled that whole family out?"

"Every one of them," I confirm. "That's just who he is." I take a deep breath, then lean closer, dropping my voice further. "Listen, this is completely out of character for me, but... I was wondering if there might be a way I could... uhm... thank him properly." I feel my cheeks heat. "In private."

Understanding dawns in her eyes, followed by a spark of amusement. For a terrifying moment, I think she might laugh or, worse, report me to the captain for even suggesting it.

Instead, she glances each way down the aisle, then back at me with a conspirator's smile. "Forward lavatory in Premium Economy. Ten minutes, after I finish this inventory. I'll make sure it stays... unoccupied." She winks. "For the hero."

"Thank you," I whisper, equal parts mortified and thrilled. "Seriously."

"We Kiwis look after our own," she says. "And their partners."

I make my way back to our seats, heart hammering against my ribs. Am I really doing this? Responsible, careful Sophia Mitchell planning to sneak into an airplane bathroom with a man nearly six years her junior? My mother would faint. Madison would die of embarrassment. And Troy... Troy would *never* believe it.

That last thought strengthens my resolve. Troy, who'd made me feel like my desires were unimportant. Who'd never bothered to learn what I liked, what I needed. Who'd treated sex as a transaction rather than a connection.

Jack dozes on, oblivious to my racing thoughts and reckless plans. He looks impossibly young and peaceful in sleep, and for a moment I waver. Maybe I should just curl up beside him, enjoy the comfort of his warmth, and save the adventure for another time.

No. I am done with safer paths, with putting off joy, with saving things for someday. Someday is now, 35,000 feet above the Pacific, with this man who looks at me like I hung the moon.

I take a deep breath and gently poke his shoulder.

His eyes open immediately, blinking in the low light. I see the moment awareness returns—first recognition, then a drowsy warmth, then a flicker of question as he registers my posture, my expression.

"Jack," I whisper, bending close to his ear. "Come with me."

His eyebrows rise slightly, but he doesn't hesitate. He unbuckles his seatbelt and follows me into the aisle, moving with that quiet, controlled grace that had first caught my attention all those months ago.

I lead him toward the front of the Premium Economy cabin, conscious of every rustle, every shift of another passenger. The lavatory light shows green—unoccupied. Just as Aroha had promised. Jack's hand finds mine, his fingers warm and certain as they intertwine with my own.

"Sophia?" he whispers, question clear in his voice.

I don't answer, just pull him toward the lavatory door. His eyes widen as understanding dawns, that familiar smile spreading across his face—half amused, half hungry.

We slip inside, the automatic door closes behind us with a soft pneumatic hiss. The lock clicks into place, and suddenly we are alone, truly alone, in a space barely big enough for one person, let alone two adults with intentions.

Jack's eyes never leave mine as reality settles over us. "Are we really—"

"Yes," I say, and kiss him before he could finish.

The kiss ignites instantly. Urgent, fierce, and reckless—the pure thrill of knowing we were doing something forbidden surges between us. Jack's hands slide down my sides, settling possessively on my hips, pulling me closer until every inch of him presses tightly against me. My heart pounds at the unmistakable hardness pressing into my thigh.

His lips trace hot paths along my neck, and I shiver as his breath whispers against my skin. "Whose idea was this again? Because she's a bloody genius."

"Flight attendant helped," I whisper, already fumbling at his belt. "But we don't have long."

He chuckles softly, deep in his chest. "Then let's not waste a second."

His palms slip down further, cupping my buttocks firmly, squeezing gently. He murmurs against my ear, his accent thick with desire. "Heaven. Just like I thought."

My breath catches as I press tighter against him, reveling in the sensation of his hands gripping me. His fingers slide lower, guiding my pants and panties down just enough to make his intentions clear. The air in the tiny lavatory feels charged, electric with anticipation.

With practiced ease, he lifts me onto the narrow counter, porcelain cold beneath my thighs, and settles between them. We both gasp softly as he eases inside me, my body yielding to him in one smooth, deep thrust.

For a moment, there is only sensation—the way he fills me completely, stretching me, our breaths mingling as we adjust to each other. He begins to move slowly, carefully, conscious of the cramped space.

But the position quickly proves awkward, limited. I need more—I need him closer, deeper, harder. "Wait," I whisper breathlessly, pressing a hand against his chest.

He pulls back instantly, concern flickering briefly across his face. "Are you—?"

"Turn me around," I say, my voice husky and commanding in a way I'd forgotten I could be. "Bend me over. I want you deeper."

Jack's eyes darken further, desire flaring hotly at my words. Without hesitation, he helps me off the counter, turning me around gently but swiftly. My hands brace against the wall, and his body covers mine, his mouth finding the sensitive spot beneath my ear as he presses into me again from behind.

"Oh God," I breathe, arching instinctively, needing every inch of him buried deep within me. "Yes. Just like that."

His breath rasps against my neck as he begins to move with

powerful, purposeful thrusts, the awkwardness forgotten as pleasure overwhelms every other sensation. My hands press harder against the cool plastic wall, bracing myself as his hips surge forward again and again, each thrust deeper and more insistent than the last.

I am lost in the feel of him, the delicious friction, the heat and intensity that had built between us finally unleashed. Jack's hand slides around my hip, fingertips brushing teasingly against the sensitive spot between my legs, and I nearly cry out before catching myself.

"God, Jack," I gasp, pressing back into him, feeling every bit as reckless and free as the woman who'd marched up to a flight attendant to arrange this madness. "Don't stop. Don't you dare stop."

"Never," he groans softly, voice tight with pleasure and determination. "You feel incredible."

We move in perfect rhythm, desperation growing, our breathing shallow and rapid. He thrusts deeper still, pressing me closer against the wall, and a delicious pressure builds, coiling tighter with each movement. I tilt my head back against his shoulder, panting softly into his neck, aware we needed to remain quiet but nearly overwhelmed by the force of what he was making me feel.

"Sophia," Jack murmurs roughly, his voice thick with urgency. "I'm close."

My own climax is spiraling higher, dangerously close to shattering me. In a boldness I'd forgotten I possessed, I tilt my head slightly, whispering breathlessly into his ear:

"I want to feel all of you, Jack. Fill me completely. I want to feel you inside me, even when we land on the other side of the world."

My words break something in him. His hips surge forward urgently, powerfully, driving me to the edge and beyond. I bite down on my lip to hold back the cry of pure pleasure, my body trembling as wave after wave of release crashes through me. Moments later, Jack stills behind me, pressing deep as his body tenses, his breath catching harshly against my shoulder as he finds his own release, filling me just as I'd asked.

We stay like that, bodies locked together, breaths mingling softly, the absurdity of our situation finally catching up to us. Jack rests his forehead gently against my back, breathing heavily, a soft laugh escapes him.

"God," he murmurs, voice still rough. "When you said you liked the accent, I had no idea it would lead here."

I laugh breathlessly, still shaky and overwhelmed by sensation. "Neither did I."

Cleanup is quick but gentle, a quiet, intimate ritual as we redress, exchange sheepish smiles and quiet laughter. As Jack helps straighten my sweater, he catches my eyes in the mirror, his expression tender and warm.

"You're full of surprises, Sophia Mitchell," he whispers softly. "And I adore every one of them."

I press a lingering kiss to his lips, savoring the closeness one last moment before we face the world again. "Likewise, Jack McKenzie."

He slips out first, promising to check the coast was clear, and I take a moment alone to catch my breath. My cheeks are flushed, my hair a tousled mess, but something in my eyes is new. Alive, confident, radiant.

This is not the careful, cautious Sophia who plans meticulously, who weighs every choice. This is Sophia, the woman who'd just claimed what she wanted, unapologetically and passionately. Who doesn't just react to life, but seizes it.

And I like her very much.

When I emerge a minute later, the cabin is still dark and quiet. Aroha catches my eye from the galley and gives me a discreet thumbs-up. I nod my thanks, feeling my cheeks heat again, and make my way back to our seats.

Jack is waiting, looking unfairly composed except for the telltale darkness of his eyes and the slight flush along his cheekbones. He lifts the armrest between us as I settle in, pulling me against his side, his lips brushing my temple.

"That," he whispers, "was the best wake-up call I've ever had."

I snuggle closer, enjoying the solid warmth of him. "Better than a red-eye?"

"Much better." His fingers trace lazy patterns on my arm. "Though I wouldn't say no to coffee later."

We fall into comfortable silence, the plane humming around us, the miles passing beneath us in the darkness. I feel my eyelids growing heavy, the aftermath of wine and adrenaline and release finally catching up to me.

"Sleep, *tāku ipo,*" Jack murmurs, his voice a warm rumble against my ear. "You've earned it."

As I drift off, nestled against his shoulder, a fleeting thought surfaces—how many points did a paramedic really need to accumulate for premium seats?—before dissolving into the soft edges of sleep. It doesn't matter. Nothing matters except this moment, this man, this adventure we are on together.

New Zealand waits on the horizon, with all its mysteries and beauty.

And so does Jack's family.

But for now, in the liminal space between worlds, there is just us.

And that is more than enough.

chapter
twenty-six

"WELCOME HOME, MR. MCKENZIE."

The immigration officer's cheerful greeting sends a small ripple of anxiety through me as I glance quickly at Sophia, but she is busy helping Madison gather her things, oblivious to the subtle deference in the man's tone. He'd barely glanced at my passport before stamping it.

"Thanks, mate. Good to be back." I keep my voice casual, accepting the passport with a nod.

We'd landed in Auckland twenty minutes ago, the familiar sight of the Manukau Harbour spreading beneath us as we descended. The relief of being back on New Zealand soil is immediate and visceral—the quality of the light, the accents around me, even the particular scent of the airport terminal. *Home.*

But now, standing in the immigration hall with Sophia and Madison beside me, that sense of homecoming is tangled with a knot of anxiety. The familiar had suddenly become fraught with potential landmines. Every interaction could betray me.

Sophia moves to the officer next, Madison bouncing impatiently behind her. The teenager had practically floated off the plane, raving about her Business Premier experience to anyone who would listen.

The flight attendants had thoroughly spoiled her, and she'd slept for a solid eight hours in her pod. She looks refreshed and eager, while most of our fellow passengers shuffle through immigration with the glazed expressions of the truly jet-lagged.

Sophia, though...Sophia is different. There is a new softness to her expression, a private smile that surfaced whenever our eyes met. The memory of our mid-flight adventure hangs between us like a delicious secret, creating a bubble of intimacy even in this crowded immigration hall. Her hair is pulled back in a messy ponytail, and she's wearing the same clothes she'd boarded in... yet, somehow, she looks more beautiful than ever.

"First time in New Zealand?" the officer asks her.

"Yes," Sophia answers, handing over her and Madison's passports.

"Welcome to Aotearoa. Purpose of your visit?"

"Vacation," she says, with a glance toward me. "Visiting... friends."

The officer nods stamping their passports efficiently. "Enjoy your stay."

"Oh my God, the accents," Madison whispers loudly as we move away from the booth. "They're even better than yours, Jack."

I laugh. "Cheeky. That's because mine's gone a bit American on me, hasn't it? Two weeks here and I'll be sounding properly Kiwi again."

"Wow, it's still Sunday here too?" Madison asks, checking her phone as we head toward baggage claim.

"Actually, love, because we crossed the International Date Line, we skipped Sunday," I correct gently. "It's Monday morning here."

Madison's eyes widen. "Wait, so we, like...lost a day?"

"Not lost," Sophia says. "Just...condensed. We'll get it back on the return flight."

"That's so weird," Madison marvels. "We literally flew to tomorrow. We're in the future!"

"And yet the future looks suspiciously like an airport," I tease, spotting our bags on the carousel. "Here, let me grab those."

After collecting our luggage and clearing customs (where Madison had to be reassured that yes, her sneakers were clean enough to bring into the country), we head toward the exit.

"I've arranged a car service," I say casually, steering them toward the arrivals hall. "Easier than messing about with taxis when you're jet-lagged."

The car waiting for us is a sleek black Mercedes—nothing too ostentatious, but certainly nicer than your standard airport shuttle. Not exactly billionaire transportation, but definitely a step up from what a paramedic should logically afford. I'd specifically requested something understated from the family's usual service, but even this feels like pushing my luck.

"Fancy," Sophia comments, eyebrows slightly raised.

"Just part of the deal, nothing flash," I say vaguely, helping the driver load our bags. "Welcome to New Zealand, where the coffee's strong, the people are friendly, and the sheep outnumber humans."

"The essential facts," Sophia deadpans, but she is smiling.

The drive into Auckland is a blur of Madison's excited observations ("The steering wheel's on the wrong side!" "Look at those trees!" "Why are all the signs in two languages?") and my casual explanations of Māori place names and local landmarks. Sophia is quieter, gazing out the window with tired but interested eyes, her hand finding mine on the seat between us.

Our hotel, the QT Auckland, is in the central business district— modern, stylish, but not extravagantly luxurious. I'd booked a spacious suite with a separate bedroom, the kind of accommodation that wouldn't raise eyebrows given the special occasion but wouldn't scream 'family money' either.

"This is amazing!" Madison exclaims as she explores the room, opening every drawer and testing every switch. "Look, Mom, there's a little balcony! And the bathroom has those fancy toiletries!"

Sophia gives me a look that is equal parts gratitude and a question I'm not ready to answer. "This is lovely, Jack. Really lovely."

"Nothing but the best for my girls," I say lightly, then freeze slightly at my own words. *My girls.* It slipped out so naturally.

But Sophia's smile just widens, and she leans up to kiss me quickly. "Your girls appreciate it."

After a quick freshen-up, we decided to push through the jet lag and grab an early dinner before crashing. The Viaduct Harbour is just a short walk away, the early evening air crisp with autumn, the harbor lights beginning to twinkle against the dusk.

"Proper Kiwi fish and chips," I say proudly, tapping my fork against the golden-battered fillet on my plate.

"Wait," Madison says, "Say that again."

"Say what again?"

"What are you eating?"

"Fish and chips."

She grins. "That's not what you said. You said *'fush and chups.'*"

"I did not."

"You *so* did." She wrinkles her nose. "I'm not really a fish person."

I sigh dramatically, shaking my head. "Americans. Just like the Aussies, no appreciation for the classics." I flag down our server. "Excuse me, do you have chicken parmy on the menu? For the young visitor?"

The server grins. "Course we do. Coming right up."

"Chicken what?" Madison asks.

"Chicken parmigiana. Aussie pub classic that we've nicked. Basically a chicken schnitzel with tomato sauce and cheese on top. You'll love it, I promise."

Sophia, meanwhile, has gone straight for the local green-lipped mussels, looking blissful as she dips crusty bread into the garlic butter sauce. "Oh my God," she moans. "These are incredible."

"Told you New Zealand food would surprise you," I say, stealing a mussel from her plate and earning a playful slap on the hand.

The conversation flows easily—first impressions of New Zealand, plans for tomorrow, Madison's detailed review of every amenity in Business Premier ("They gave me real metal silverware, Mom. And the ice cream had actual chocolate chunks!") It is...normal. Beautifully, surprisingly normal. Just a man having dinner with his girlfriend and her daughter on vacation.

For a moment, I let myself forget what is coming. Forget that in less than forty-eight hours, I'll be driving them up to the estate. Forget that the life I'd built with Sophia is balanced on a lie of omission that could collapse with a single phone call from the wrong person.

"You okay?" Sophia's voice breaks through my thoughts, her hand warm on mine. "You drifted away for a second."

"Just jet lag," I lie, squeezing her hand. "And thinking how glad I am you're both here."

"Me too," she says softly.

By the time we get back to the hotel, Madison is yawning every thirty seconds, and even Sophia is fading fast. We all surrender to the jet lag, Madison falling asleep in her clothes on top of the covers, Sophia and I barely managing to change before collapsing into the king bed in the separate bedroom.

"Tomorrow," Sophia murmurs sleepily against my chest. "Show us your country tomorrow."

I press a kiss to her hair. "Promise."

"This is '*real*' coffee, huh?" Sophia stares at the flat white I'd handed her, skepticism written across her face.

"Just give it a go," I urge, watching her expectantly.

We are sitting at a small café in Britomart, the morning sunshine warming the outdoor tables. Madison is still working her way through a stack of pancakes, looking much more rested after a solid twelve hours of sleep.

Sophia is, as expected, deeply skeptical. She ordered one, takes a tentative sip, and then her eyes widen. She stares into the cup, then back at me, then back at the cup, a look of profound, almost religious shock on her face.

Madison, thankfully, is engrossed in trying to Instagram a picture of her elaborate hot chocolate.

"What the actual..." She looks up at me, bewildered. "This is... this is what coffee is supposed to taste like? All the time?"

I can't help the laugh that escapes me, nearly choking on my own drink. "Told you Kiwi coffee was different."

"Oh my God, Jack..." Sophia finally breathes, her voice hushed. "This is... this is like when I was sixteen and I figured out what else my electric toothbrush could do."

I choke noisily on my own flat white, coffee exploding from my nose in a less-than-dignified spray. Laughter, sharp and sudden, bursts from me as I grab a napkin. Sophia is already bright red, her hand flying to her mouth, but her eyes are dancing with unapologetic amusement.

"What's wrong with you two?" Madison asks, looking up from her phone, completely oblivious.

After breakfast, we make our way to the Sky Tower, Auckland's iconic landmark. Madison's excitement builds as we ride the elevator to the observation deck, her face pressed against the glass as the city spreads out beneath us.

"You can see everything!" she exclaims, pointing at the harbor, the volcanic cones, the distant islands. "Look, Mom, those are volcanoes! Actual volcanoes!"

"*Dormant* volcanoes," I clarify quickly, seeing Sophia's momentary alarm. "Auckland's built on a volcanic field, but no worries, love, they've been quiet for centuries."

"Less reassuring than you think," Sophia mutters, but she is smiling as she takes in the 360-degree views.

I play tour guide, pointing out landmarks and sharing stories. When Madison asks about the possibility of bungee jumping from the tower, it earns an emphatic "Absolutely not" from Sophia. Instead, we head down to the All Blacks Experience, an interactive exhibit celebrating New Zealand's national rugby team. Madison, to my surprise and delight, is immediately fascinated.

The exhibit leads us through rugby history, famous players, and iconic moments. I am careful to keep my comments general, steering clear of any references to the times my family had hosted All Blacks players at events or my father's position on various rugby boards.

"So it's like football but you can only throw it backward?" she asks, trying to pass a rugby ball the proper way in one of the interactive displays.

"And no pads," I add. "Just pure grit and good sense."

"That's insane," she says admiringly. "I want to try it."

Sophia shoots me an accusatory look. "Now you've done it. She'll be tackling people in the hotel lobby by dinner."

When we reach the haka display, Madison stops, completely captivated.

"This is amazing," she breathes, watching the video of the All Blacks performing the pre-match challenge, their faces fierce with concentration.

chapter
twenty-seven

WE SPEND the afternoon in Auckland Domain, the city's oldest park. We've found a quiet spot near the duck pond, the trees providing welcome shade as we rest our feet after a morning exploring the Sky Tower and the All Blacks Experience.

Jack, do you know how to do the haka?" Madison sits up, eyes bright.

He hesitates, aware of my curious gaze. "I learned one in school, yeah. Most Kiwi boys do, especially if they play footy."

"Can you show me?" Madison's eyes are bright with genuine interest.

He considers for a moment before answering. "I can show you a little bit. But first, I need you to understand something. The haka is not just a war dance or a sports ritual. It's a *taonga*, a cultural treasure. It tells a story, expresses mana—that's like personal power and pride—and connects to the history of Aotearoa."

He stands up, moving to a clear patch of grass. "The one I learned for school rugby was Ka Mate, probably the most famous one. Each movement has meaning—the slapping of hands on thighs to show strength, the wide eyes to show life, the outstretched tongue to show defiance."

Quietly, with respect, he demonstrates a few of the basic movements and calls, explaining each one's purpose. It is not a full performance—I understand that would have been inappropriate in this setting—but rather an educational demonstration.

"*That* was Ka Mate, the haka the All Blacks have used since the early 1900s. The words are hundreds of years old, originally by Te Rauparaha, a chief of the Ngāti Toa iwi. It was a chant of survival."

"I didn't realize..." I trail off. "That it would be that powerful."

"It's not just shouting," Jack says. "It's telling a story. It's a declaration. It says: I know who I am. I know where I come from. I'm not afraid of you."

He glances at Madison, his voice softening. "When we played schoolboy rugby, we had our own haka. All of us learned it. Our coaches made sure we understood the meaning. Not just the words, but the weight of it."

"You performed that?" Madison asks, eyes big. "Like, actually did a haka?"

Jack nods. "Yeah. Never just for show. Always as a team. Always with respect. Before big games, before facing schools we'd trained all year to beat. It wasn't just about the match. It was about belonging."

"Did you ever forget the words?" Madison whispers, awed.

Jack grins. "One time, I mixed up two lines and almost got flattened by a second-row forward who took haka very seriously. Never again."

She laughs, then grows serious. "Could you show me sometime?"

Jack hesitates.

"I mean, not like, perform it," Madison says quickly. "I just want to understand."

"I'd be honored," Jack says. "We'll ask Em if she still remembers ours. Might even make Lily join in. But only if we talk about what it means first. You don't just do the haka. You carry it."

I reach for his hand, lacing our fingers together. "You really are full of surprises."

"Wait till you see me in rugby shorts," he murmurs, earning a quiet snort from Madison.

"I heard that," she mutters.

"Emma pulled some strings," Jack says casually, as if his sister has not just produced what Madison informs me were "literally impossible to get" tickets to the Pacific Four Series opener. "Nothing special."

"Nothing special?" Madison's voice rises to a pitch I haven't heard since she was twelve. "Jack! These are INTERNATIONAL tickets! To the Pacific Four Series opener! For the RIVALRY match! Against AUSTRALIA!"

I smile despite myself. Our second day in New Zealand, and my daughter has apparently already become a rugby fanatic. She's wearing a Black Ferns jersey—a gift from Jack earlier in the day—and reciting player statistics with disturbing accuracy. I shouldn't have been surprised; she'd spent a good portion of our flight poring over rugby rules on her tablet, using the airliner's seat-to-seat messaging system to pepper Jack dozens of questions that he'd answered with infinite patience.

"Eden Park," Jack explains as we approach the imposing structure, New Zealand's largest and most revered sporting venue. "Hallowed ground for rugby in this country. The All Blacks haven't lost here since 1994."

As we find our seats, the stadium is already humming with anticipation, a sea of black jerseys punctuated by the occasional flash of color from visiting fans. The perfectly manicured pitch glows emerald green under the floodlights, the white boundary lines crisp and precise. The stadium begins to fill, the distinctive sound of the Kiwi accent rising and falling in excited conversation about line-ups and predictions.

"This is where history happens," Jack tells Madison, whose eyes widen as she takes in the scale of it all. "Where dreams are made or broken in eighty minutes of play."

Madison leans forward eagerly, pointing toward the players warming up. "Which one is Thompson? Jack, you said she's the fastest winger they've had in years, right?"

"That's her," Jack nods toward a player running drills near the sideline. "And, yep. Probably the best they've had in a decade. Faster than most of the men's team."

"I read she was scouted when she was only sixteen!" Madison's enthusiasm is infectious, her eyes bright with excitement. "Do you think she'll score today?"

"Against the Aussies? Sweet as."

The stadium atmosphere is unlike anything I've ever experienced —a sea of black and white, coordinated chants already echoing through the stands. Behind us, a group of men in matching Black Ferns scarves are passing around lyric sheets.

"What are they doing?" I ask Jack, nodding toward the group.

He follows my gaze and laughs. "Probably working on a new chant for the Australian captain. Last time she was here, they had a five-verse song about her controversial penalty in the World Cup quarterfinal."

"You're joking."

"Welcome to Kiwi rugby, *tāku ipo*." He guides us to our seats, hand at the small of my back. "During my very first All Blacks match, the blokes behind us performed a four-part harmony about the opposing fly-half's drunk driving charge. To the tune of 'Clair de Lune.'"

"Jesus," I laugh. "And I thought SEC football rivalries were intense."

"Americans chant 'Defense! Defense!'" Jack mimics in a deep, flat American monotone. "Kiwis compose operettas about your personal failures."

Madison's eyes are wide. "That's hardcore."

"That's rugby, love." Jack grins, then perks up as fans around us surge to their feet. "Here they come!"

The Black Ferns enter to deafening noise. Jack immediately joins in, his accent thickening as he shouts encouragement in what sounds like a mixture of English and Māori. Madison catches on quickly, mimicking his chants with surprising accuracy.

"So when they have the ball, that's good, right?" I ask, trying to follow the blur of motion on the field.

Jack and Madison exchange an amused glance.

"Yes, Mom, that's good," Madison says with the patient tone of someone explaining colors to a toddler.

"Just checking!" I hold up my hands defensively. "I'm learning!"

The intensity builds through the first half. I've never been much of a sports fan, but there is something about their shared enthusiasm that is utterly captivating. Jack is explaining something to Madison—hand gestures illustrating some complex play—when a roar goes up from the crowd.

"Wait, what just happened? Is that more points?"

"Australia's down to fourteen players," Jack explains, excitement edging his voice. "Yellow card for a high tackle on Wilson."

"Is that good for us?" Madison asks.

"Very good. Watch what happens next."

"Wait, is that like a power play in hockey?" I ask, searching for any familiar sports reference.

"Exactly!" Jack looks impressed. "One player down for ten minutes."

"I know some sports things," I say proudly.

The Black Ferns capitalize immediately. Their offensive line surges forward, passing the ball with lightning precision. The crowd noise builds like a gathering storm.

"There's Thompson!" Jack yells as a player breaks away. "GO GO GO!"

"GET THERE!" Madison screams beside him, on her feet now.

"GO TEAM!" I shout, caught up in their excitement despite

only vaguely understanding what is happening. "DO THE THING!"

The Australian defense converges, but Thompson somehow slips through, ball tucked under her arm.

"She's going to do it!" Jack's arm is around my shoulders, pulling me up. "WATCH THIS!"

"What's she doing?" I ask as Thompson suddenly kicks the ball forward.

"Chip kick!" Madison explains, eyes locked on the field. "Smart move!"

"Chip kick! Yes!" I echo, nodding as if I'd been expecting this all along. "Excellent chip...kicking!"

The ball bounces perfectly as Thompson races toward it. An Australian defender is closing in fast.

"She's not going to make it," I say, but Jack is shaking his head.

"Just watch!"

What happens next seems to unfold in slow motion. Thompson reaches the ball at the sideline, but her momentum is carrying her out of bounds. Somehow, impossibly, she plants her left foot and hops—actually hops—along the sideline, kicking the ball with her right foot while airborne.

The ball arcs perfectly into the try zone.

"SHE DID IT!" Jack roars, his voice lost in the thunderous crowd.

"DID YOU SEE THAT?" Madison screams, grabbing my arm. "SHE KICKED ON ONE LEG!"

"OH MY GOD!" I find myself jumping and screaming too, caught up in the electric atmosphere. "THAT WAS AMAZING! IS THAT WORTH POINTS?"

"Five points!" Jack shouts back. "If it's confirmed!"

The replay appears on the giant screen, and the stadium goes berserk. Thompson hopping on one foot, defying gravity and logic, the ball crossing the line just as she tumbles out of bounds.

"They're checking if it's a try," Jack explains, his voice hoarse. "Her foot might have touched the line—"

"TRY!" The referee's voice booms over the PA system, and the stadium erupts.

"IT'S GOOD!" Madison jumps up and down. "IT COUNTS!"

"YES!" I pump my fist in the air. "This is just like when we beat Alabama my sophomore year and everyone rushed the field! I've never heard a stadium this loud!"

Around us, fans break into a coordinated chant that sounds more like a military drill than a celebration. The men behind us launch into what appears to be a full-blown choreographed routine, complete with hand motions.

"What are they singing?" I ask Jack, barely able to hear myself over the noise.

He listens for a moment, then laughs. "Something very unflattering about the Australian fullback's dating history. Trust me, you don't want the translation."

Madison is still jumping, her face flushed with excitement. "That was INCREDIBLE! Did you see how she stayed inbounds? ONE LEG, Mom! ONE LEG!"

Jack turns to me, face flushed with excitement, eyes bright with joy. Without warning, he cups my face in his hands and kisses me—deeply, passionately, right there in the middle of the cheering crowd.

When he pulls back, there is something different in his eyes. Something I haven't seen before. Raw emotion, unfiltered by his usual careful restraint.

"What was that for?" I ask, breathless.

"For being here. For bringing Madison. For—" He gestures around us, at the stadium, at New Zealand. "For understanding why this matters to me."

Madison finally notices, raising her eyebrows. "Geez, get a room, you two."

Jack laughs, throwing an arm around her shoulders and pulling her into a half-hug. "You're just jealous you don't have my rugby knowledge, Madison McKenzie."

"McKenzie?" She looks startled, then grins. "I'm a Mitchell, thank you very much."

"For now," he says, so quietly I almost miss it.

The implications hit me like a physical force. For now. As if there might be a future where that changes. My heart does a complicated little stutter that has nothing to do with the game unfolding before us.

"Are those real flames?" I ask as fire shoots up from the corners of the field after another New Zealand score, desperate to distract myself from the sudden rush of emotion.

"Pyrotechnics," Jack confirms. "They do it for every try."

"Like touchdown flames! Awesome!" I cheer as the crowd roars again. "Wait, what happened this time?"

"Conversion!" Madison explains importantly. "Two more points after a try!"

"Look at you with all the rugby knowledge," I say, genuinely impressed by how quickly she'd picked it up.

She beams. "Jack explained it all. It's actually pretty easy once you understand the basic rules."

The rest of the match passes in a blur of shouting, cheering, and Jack patiently explaining rugby's Byzantine rules. The Black Ferns win 27-18, and the crowd is delirious with joy.

As we file out of the stadium, Madison chattering excitedly about Thompson's "impossible try," Jack's hand finds mine, fingers intertwining naturally.

"Thank you," I say quietly.

"For what?"

"For sharing this with us. For making Madison so happy."

His smile is like sunrise breaking over mountains. "This is what I wanted—to show you my home, my world."

"I like your world," I tell him, and mean it.

Despite the lingering questions and all the things we still need to discuss, in this moment, everything feels right. Jack's hand in mine, Madison bouncing ahead of us in her new jersey, surrounded by the joyful chaos of post-match celebration.

———————

Back at the hotel, Madison is still buzzing with excitement, scrolling through her phone to show us highlights that are already being shared online.

"Thompson's try is trending worldwide!" she announces. "Look, even ESPN posts it!"

"I'm going to grab a shower," Jack says, pressing a kiss to my temple. "Back in a few."

As soon as he disappears into the bathroom, Madison flops onto the couch beside me.

"So," she says, trying and failing to sound casual. "He called me Madison McKenzie."

"I heard," I reply, equally casual.

"And I think we can both agree that it was not accidental."

I raise an eyebrow. "Maybe he was just caught up in the moment."

"Mom. He said 'for now' when I corrected him." She gives me a significant look. "You heard that too. I saw your face."

"I did," I admit.

"So..." Madison draws out the word. "Is this, like, a serious thing?"

I consider my answer carefully. "It feels serious. But we're still figuring things out."

"You're happy, though," she says, not a question.

"I am." I smile at her. "Are you? With all this? With Jack?"

"Definitely." Madison pulls her legs up under her on the couch. "He's cool. Not trying too hard like Dad's girlfriends. And he actually listens when I talk." She hesitates. "Plus, he looks at you like you're...important. Like he actually sees you."

My throat tightens unexpectedly. "That's a pretty mature observation."

She rolls her eyes, teenage nonchalance returning. "Whatever. I'm just saying he's not terrible and I wouldn't, like, *die* of embarrassment if he stuck around."

"High praise."

"The highest." She grins, then grows serious again. "So when are we going to see his family tomorrow, right?"

I nod. "That's the plan. Flight to Queenstown in the morning, then to see his family the next day."

"Do you think they'll be nice?"

"I'm sure they will be," I say, though a small flutter of nervousness awakens in my stomach. "From everything Jack's told us, they sound lovely."

"I wonder if it's like a little family operation or something bigger," Madison muses. "Jack never really says much about it."

I'd wondered the same thing. Jack had been deliberately vague about most aspects of his family business, mentioning only that his sister Charlotte handles most of the operation now.

"We'll find out soon enough," I say, pushing away the nagging questions that had been accumulating. I have to admit, the discrepancies between paramedic Jack and New Zealand Jack are gnawing at me a little. The comfortable hotel, the car service, his sister's ability to secure "impossible" rugby tickets.

But then I remember his face during the match, the pure joy in his expression, the passionate kiss, the way he'd included Madison in everything. Whatever else is going on, that connection is real.

The shower shuts off, and moments later Jack emerges, hair damp, wearing a fresh t-shirt and jeans. He smiles at us both, and my heart does that ridiculous flip again.

"So," he says, dropping onto the couch beside me. "First time at a proper rugby match. Verdict?"

"AMAZING," Madison declares. "Can we go to another one before we leave?"

"I'll see what we can sort out," Jack says, his arm slides naturally around my shoulders. "What about you, Sophia? Did we convert you to the religion of rugby?"

"I'm a believer," I confirm, leaning into him. "Though I reserve the right to ask stupid questions for at least three more matches."

"Fair enough," he laughs.

As Madison launches into an enthusiastic recap of her favorite moments from the game, I watch Jack's face—the way his eyes crinkle at the corners when he smiles, the attentive nod when Madison speaks, the casual comfort of his body next to mine.

Whatever questions tomorrow might bring about vineyards and family businesses, tonight we are just three people enjoying each other's company. That feels like the most important thing of all.

For now, we're just a family, celebrating a victory.

chapter
twenty-eight

I WOKE to gray Auckland dawn light filtering through hotel curtains, Sophia's warm form curled against my side. For several precious moments, I simply watch her sleep, her face relaxed and peaceful in a way I rarely get to see. The charge nurse armor completely shed, no worry lines, just... *Sophia*.

Madison has been texting her friends half the night from her connecting room, thrilled with the Business Premier experience and her newfound status as international traveler. Her enthusiasm for everything—from the Auckland Sky Tower to meeting a real Black Fern at last night's match—has been absolutely contagious. Even Sophia, usually so carefully controlled, had shouted herself hoarse cheering for Thompson's impossible try.

I brush a strand of dark hair from Sophia's forehead, remembering how she'd looked in the stadium lights, face flushed with excitement, eyes bright with joy as she'd turned to me. That impulsive kiss we'd shared in the middle of thousands of cheering fans has felt more significant than I can explain, as if some invisible barrier has finally fallen. When Madison had corrected my slip of calling her "Madison McKenzie" and I'd whispered "for now," Sophia's expression had shifted in a way that makes my heart skip.

For one perfect moment, I'd let myself imagine a future where everything was simple: Sophia, Madison, me. A family.

Then reality comes crashing back.

We are heading to Queenstown today. To Central Otago tomorrow. To the estate.

To the truth.

A knot forms in my stomach that has nothing to do with the flat white I haven't yet consumed. Queenstown is the last buffer before everything changes. My last day of being just Jack, the paramedic with the accent, the man who brings Sophia coffee and teaches Madison to make pavlova. Tomorrow, I'll be Jackson Charles McKenzie, heir to McKenzie Estate Wines and all the complications that come with it.

Sophia stirs, her eyes fluttering open. "You're thinking too loudly," she murmurs, voice still rough with sleep.

I force a smile. "Just excited to show you my favorite city."

Her fingers trace my jawline, feather-light. "You're nervous about us meeting your family, aren't you?"

"A bit," I admit. Half-truth, half-lie. The story of the past few months.

"We'll be fine," she says, pressing a soft kiss to my shoulder. "Madison already loves you, and I..." She pauses, and my heart stutters. "I'm pretty fond of you too, McKenzie."

I pull her closer, burying my face in her hair to hide whatever emotions might be playing across my face. "Just pretty fond, then?"

She laughs softly against my chest. "Fishing for compliments before breakfast? Bold strategy."

A knock at the door interrupts us. "Mom? Jack? Are you guys up? Our flight's in like three hours and I'm starving!"

"We're up, sweetie!" Sophia calls back. "Give us ten minutes."

"I'm counting!" Madison's footsteps retreat.

Sophia stretches and sits up, the sheets pooling around her waist. Morning sunlight catches in her dark hair, illuminating the curves of her body, and desire jolts through me despite the anxiety churning in my gut.

"Like what you see, Kiwi?" she teases, catching my gaze.

I reach for her, pulling her back down for a kiss that quickly deepens. "Always," I murmur against her lips. "Every single time."

She pulls back, studying my face. "You're sure everything's okay? You seem... I don't know. Different this morning."

"Just want to make sure you enjoy the South Island," I say, forcing lightness into my tone. "It's even more beautiful than Auckland. You'll see."

———

"I think I'm going to die," Madison announces dramatically as our Air New Zealand 737 banks sharply. "Is this normal? Do pilots usually fly directly at mountains?"

"Perfectly normal," I assure her, enjoying both her wide eyes and Sophia's white-knuckled grip on the armrests. "Queenstown Airport has one of the more challenging approaches in the world. The Air Force doesn't have fighter jets anymore, so our commercial pilots like to pretend this approach is their Top Gun moment."

"Not helping," Sophia mutters, but a smile tugs at the corner of her mouth.

The 737 executes another steep turn, the mountains seeming close enough to touch through the windows. The larger aircraft makes the already dramatic descent feel even more intense, the wings tipping precariously as the pilot navigates between peaks.

"Look," I say, pointing past Madison toward the window. "The Remarkables. One of the most aptly named mountain ranges in the world."

Both of them lean toward the glass as the jagged peaks come into view, their snow-capped summits stark against the blue sky.

"Oh my God," Madison breathes. "It's like something from a movie."

"And there's Lake Wakatipu," I continue, watching their expressions. "Third largest lake in New Zealand. According to Māori legend, it was formed from the bed impression of a sleeping giant."

Sophia's eyes are wide with wonder as she takes in the scenery. "It's breathtaking," she whispers.

"Wait till you see it up close," I promise.

The plane descends rapidly, executing another sharp turn that has Madison clutching her armrests and Sophia closing her eyes briefly. We touch down with a slight bump, both of them exhaling audibly as we taxi toward the small but modern terminal.

"We survived!" Madison declares, unbuckling her seatbelt the second the sign turns off. "That was *terrifying* but also kind of awesome?"

"Welcome to Queenstown," I grin. "Adventure capital of the world."

As we disembark, I can't help scanning the tarmac out of habit. Three private jets are parked at the far end of the runway. Not unusual for Queenstown, especially during harvest season when wealthy vineyard owners often fly in from abroad. I guide Sophia and Madison quickly past the charter terminal, not wanting to run into any family acquaintances who might be arriving.

The terminal buzzes with the energy I remember: backpackers with oversized bags, wealthy tourists in cashmere, local guides holding signs for heli-skiing adventures. Queenstown exists in that unique space where extreme wealth and backpacker culture somehow coexist, united by the pursuit of adrenaline and natural beauty.

"So many accents," Madison observes, looking around with undisguised curiosity. "Is that German? And Chinese? And... Australian?"

"Queenstown draws people from everywhere," I explain as we collect our bags. "It's got world-class skiing in winter, tramping and adventure sports in summer, and—" I hesitate slightly "—wine tourism year-round."

"Because of the vineyards?" Sophia asks, catching my momentary pause.

"Right. Central Otago produces some of the world's best Pinot Noir," I say, steering the conversation to safer ground. "We'll definitely have to try some while we're here."

Outside the terminal, I guide them to the waiting car service I'd arranged. Nothing too flashy, just a comfortable SUV that would blend in among the tourist vehicles.

"Kamana Lakehouse first?" the driver confirms, loading our bags.

"Yes, thanks, mate," I reply, opening the door for Sophia and Madison.

Madison's eyes widen at the handful of brochures she'd nabbed as we pull away from the airport. "Are those hang gliders? And is that a BUNGY JUMPING PLATFORM?"

"Shotover Canyon," I confirm. "One of the original bungy sites." Seeing her expression, I quickly add, "But there's plenty of less terrifying ways to enjoy Queenstown too."

"I want to do it," she declares immediately.

"Absolutely not," Sophia replies with equal speed. "Not happening."

"*Moooooom*," Madison groans. "Jack, tell her it's safe!"

I catch Sophia's warning look. "It's...professionally managed," I offer diplomatically. "But maybe we start with something less extreme? The Skyline Gondola has amazing views, and there's jet boating on the lake if you want an adrenaline rush without hurling yourself off a bridge."

Madison considers this compromise. "Fine. Jet boating sounds cool."

The drive to Kamana Lakehouse takes us along Lake Wakatipu, the water impossibly blue against the backdrop of mountains. I'd chosen the boutique hotel carefully—luxurious enough to be special but not ostentatious enough to raise questions about my budget. Certainly not the penthouse suite at Eichardt's where my parents usually stayed, or the private villa outside town that Charlotte maintained for business trips.

As we drive, I point out the contrast that makes Queenstown unique: adventure outfitters nestled alongside high-end boutiques, backpackers with dreadlocks walking past women in designer ski wear, modest hostels sharing views with multi-million dollar alpine retreats.

"This place is like...if REI and Neiman Marcus had a baby," Sophia observes, watching a helicopter land on a pad adjacent to a luxury hotel.

"That's Queenstown," I agree. "Everyone comes for the same mountains, just with different budgets."

"This is where we're staying?" Sophia asks as we pull up to the modern lodge perched on a hillside overlooking the lake.

"Wait till you see the view from your suite," the driver smiles, retrieving our bags.

Inside, the check-in process is smooth and efficient, the staff professional without being obsequious. I'd made the reservation under just "McKenzie" without any additional details, wanting to avoid any special treatment that might raise Sophia's suspicions. The suite I'd booked had a spacious living area, a bedroom with floor-to-ceiling windows overlooking the lake, and a connecting room for Madison.

"Jack, this is gorgeous," Sophia breathes as we enter. "You really didn't have to—"

"Special occasion," I interrupt, not wanting to have the money conversation yet. "First time showing you my home country."

Madison is already exploring her connecting room, exclaiming over the heated bathroom floors and rainforest shower. "This is amazing! Can I FaceTime Chloe and show her?"

"After we get settled," Sophia calls back. "Let's figure out what we're doing today first."

I move to the windows, gesturing for Sophia to join me. "That's Cecil Peak," I say, pointing to the mountain dominating the view.

"And down there is Queenstown Gardens. We can walk through there to get to town."

She leans against me, warm and solid. "It's beautiful, Jack. Thank you for bringing us here."

The sincerity in her voice twists like a knife. I wrap an arm around her waist, pulling her closer. "Thank you for coming."

The afternoon unfolds in a blur of perfect moments.

Sophia and Madison gasp in unison as our jet boat executes a 360-degree spin on Lake Wakatipu, sending up a spray of crystal-clear water that momentarily obscures the mountains. Madison's laughter is infectious, her hair whipping in the wind as we zoom across the lake's surface. Sophia, initially tense, gradually relaxes into the experience, her face alight with the simple joy of speed and spectacular scenery.

"That was AWESOME!" Madison declares as we disembark, her face flushed with excitement. "Mom, admit it, you loved it too!"

"It was... exhilarating," Sophia concedes, smoothing her wind-blown hair. "Though I think my stomach is still halfway across the lake."

I guide them through Queenstown Gardens next, taking the scenic route toward the town center. The autumn colors are in full display, crisp golden leaves crunching underfoot as we stroll beneath towering trees.

"It's so strange to think it's fall here when it's spring back home," Sophia remarks, her hand warm in mine.

"Southern Hemisphere," I shrug. "Everything's upside down. Wait 'till you experience Christmas in summer."

She looks at me sharply, and I realize my slip—implying future holidays together, something we haven't discussed. But her expression softens, a small smile playing at her lips. "That'd be... interesting."

The Skyline Gondola carries us up Bob's Peak after lunch, offering panoramic views that make even Madison briefly forget her phone. I point out landmarks as the cable car climbs steadily upward —the historic steamship TSS *Earnslaw* plies the lake's waters, the distant Richardson Mountains, the small neighborhoods nestled along the shore.

"It's like a postcard," Sophia murmurs, pressed against the glass. "I can't believe people actually live with this view every day."

"Some lucky bastards," I agree, thinking of the estate we'll visit tomorrow, with its sweeping views of Lake Dunstan and the Central Otago mountains.

At the summit, we take obligatory photos with the spectacular backdrop, Madison insisting on several "family shots" that have Sophia and me exchanging surprised glances over her head. I play tour guide, sharing stories about the region but carefully sanitizing any that might hint at my family's prominence.

When Madison spots the luge track and begs to try it, I gladly purchase tickets, watching as she and Sophia race down the mountain on wheeled carts, their laughter echoing back up the hillside. For those few hours, I almost forget what is coming.

Almost.

By early afternoon, hunger drives us to Fergburger, Queenstown's famous burger joint where the line typically stretches down the block.

"Seriously? We're waiting in this?" Sophia asks skeptically, eyeing the queue.

"Trust me," I assure them. "This burger will change your lives."

Forty minutes later, seated at a small table with massive, sauce-dripping burgers in front of us, Madison takes her first bite and her eyes widen comically.

"Oh my *God*," she moans around a mouthful. "This is... this is..."

"Toldja," I grin, watching as Sophia closes her eyes in appreciation after her own first bite.

"Okay, you win," she admits. "Worth the wait."

As they finish their meals, I find myself cataloging these moments, storing them away: Madison's face smeared with aioli, Sophia's laughter as she tries to manage her unwieldy burger, the way the sunlight catches in both their dark hair. I am building a treasure trove of memories, just in case.

Throughout the day, I'd navigated us carefully through Queenstown, avoiding certain shops owned by family friends and restaurants where I might be recognized. When Sophia had suggested a particular winery for late lunch, I'd redirected to a craft brewery instead, mentioning the better views. When Madison had wanted to browse a specific boutique, I'd suggested a different one nearby first, saying we could check out both if we had time. It wasn't a lie exactly, but I steer us so thoroughly through the second shop that we "ran out of time" for the first... which happened to be owned by my father's oldest friend.

It is exhausting, this constant vigilance. The half-truths. The omissions.

And yet, seeing Sophia's face as she gazes out over the lake, stress melting from her shoulders with each passing hour; watching Madison embrace each new experience with unbridled enthusiasm— it only confirms what I already know. I would do anything to keep them in my life, even if it meant facing the music tomorrow.

"I'm exhausted," Madison announces dramatically. "I think the jet lag is still catching up with me."

"We've had a pretty full day," Sophia agrees, stifling a yawn behind her hand.

"Why don't you head back to the hotel?" I suggest to Madison. "Order room service, watch a movie. Your mom and I could have a quick drink somewhere nearby, then join you."

Madison's eyebrows rise suggestively. "Oh, I see. You two want *alone time.*"

"Madison *Grace*!" Sophia's cheeks flush.

"Whatever," Madison shrugs, grinning. "I'm cool with it. I wanted to FaceTime Chloe anyway, show her all my photos from today. Plus I'm literally about to pass out."

Twenty minutes later, we've walked Madison back to the hotel, making sure she is settled with access to room service and promises to text if she needed anything.

"Just us, then," Sophia says as Madison's door closes.

"I was thinking," I say, taking her hand. "There's this place by the lake, Little Blackwood? Nice cocktails, great view. Would you... would you care to dress up a bit? Have a proper date night?"

Her eyes light up. "Really? That sounds lovely."

"I'll give you some time to get ready?" I offer. "I can go check on a few things, be back in thirty minutes?"

"Perfect," she agrees with a smile.

I use the time to make a quick reservation, ensuring we'll get that perfect corner table overlooking the lake, then return to find the bedroom door still closed. I change quickly into dark slacks and a blue button-down shirt that Emma always says matches my eyes, adding a sports coat I had packed specifically for tonight.

When Sophia emerges from the bedroom, I actually forget to breathe for a moment.

She wears a deep burgundy dress that hugs her curves before flowing gently to just below her knees. Elegant, but comfortable enough for walking. Her dark hair falls in loose waves around her shoulders, and she'd added small gold earrings that catch the light when she moves. The dress is cut to show just enough of her collarbones and shoulders to make my mouth go dry, but it is practical enough that she can walk comfortably in the low heels she'd paired with it.

"You look..." I begin, then falter completely. "You...I...buh-buh—" I stop, swallow hard, and try again. "Beautiful. So beautiful."

A smile spreads across her face, part amusement, part pleasure at my reaction. "Did I just render Jack McKenzie speechless?"

I nod, still recovering. "First time for everything."

She crosses to me, straightening my collar with a gentle touch. "You clean up pretty well yourself, McKenzie."

I catch her hand, press a kiss to her palm. "Shall we? I can call a car if you prefer."

"It's a beautiful night," she says. "Let's walk. I packed these shoes specifically because they're comfortable enough for actually moving around."

I offer her my arm, ridiculously pleased when she takes it. As we make our way through the Queenstown Gardens, the setting sun bathes everything in golden light. Sophia draws admiring glances from passersby, and I can't help the surge of pride and possessiveness I feel with her on my arm.

"You're staring," she notes as we walk along the lake path.

"Can't help it," I admit. "You're stunning."

She squeezes my arm gently. "Sweet talker."

Little Blackwood is exactly as I remember, intimate but not pretentious, with a roaring fire and floor-to-ceiling windows overlooking the lake. The maître d' greets us warmly, guiding us to the corner table I'd reserved, angled perfectly to catch the lights of the TSS *Earnslaw* as it glides across the water.

"This is beautiful," Sophia says, settling into her seat. "Perfect way to end the day."

I order a Gibbston Valley Pinot Noir, carefully avoiding any McKenzie Estate offerings on the wine list. The sommelier raises an eyebrow but makes no comment.

"What a perfect spring night," Sophia remarks, gazing out at the clear, star-strewn sky above the lake.

"Perfect autumn night, *tāku ipo*," I correct gently. "Remember, we're upside down here."

She laughs. "Right. I keep forgetting." She takes a sip of wine, her expression appreciative. "This is excellent."

"Central Otago Pinot Noir," I explain, more comfortable on this topic than most. "The region's specialty. The combination of hot days, cool nights, and these rocky soils gives it a unique profile. Notes of dark cherry, a bit of spice."

"Listen to you," she teases. "Secret wine expert?"

I shrug, aiming for casual. "You pick things up, growing up around here."

"Tell me more about tomorrow," she says, leaning forward. "Your family's place. What should I expect?"

I take a generous swallow of wine, buying time. "It's...in a beautiful setting. The vineyard's been in the family for generations."

"Jack McKenzie, man of mystery," she says, but her smile is fond. "You always do this, you know. Deflect questions about your background."

"Do I?"

"Mmhmm." She traces the rim of her wineglass. "I've noticed. You'll tell me about your sisters, your childhood adventures, but whenever I ask about what your family actually does, you get vague. 'Family business.' 'Wine industry.' Never specifics."

My heart rate picks up. "I guess I'm just... used to keeping my worlds separate."

Her eyes meet mine, searching. "And which world am I? The paramedic one, or the mysterious New Zealand one?"

"Both," I say honestly. "That's what makes you special, Sophia. I want you in every part of my life."

She smiles, the candlelight catching in her eyes. "Good answer, McKenzie."

As the evening progresses, I can't help but notice how naturally she fits into this setting. There's no discomfort, no awkwardness as the waiter describes complex dishes or the sommelier discusses wine pairings. She moves through the world of fine dining with the same quiet confidence she shows in her ER—adaptable, intelligent, unintimidated. It only makes me fall deeper, even as it heightens my anxiety about tomorrow's reveal.

"I ordered us each a different entrée," I explain as the waiter sets down our meals. "Local venison for you, because you have to try it while you're here. South Island salmon for me."

"Sharing?" she asks, eyes twinkling.

"Of course," I grin. "Wouldn't have it any other way."

I reach across the table, taking her hand. "How about you? Any regrets so far about coming to New Zealand?"

"Are you kidding?" She looks at me incredulously. "Jack, this has been... I don't even have words. Madison is happier than I've seen her in years. I'm actually relaxed. Do you know how rare that is? And you..." She squeezes my hand. "You made this happen. Troy would have promised this trip and then canceled last minute because some cryptocurrency tanked."

"Low bar," I joke, though the comparison pleases me.

"No, it's not just that," she insists. "It's you. The way you are with Madison. The way you listen. The way you... see me." She takes a deep breath. "I haven't had that in a long time. Maybe ever."

The knot in my stomach tightens. She trusts me completely, and tomorrow I will show her just how much I'd kept from her.

"What are you thinking about?" she asks, noticing my expression. "You got serious all of a sudden."

"Just...how lucky I am," I say, forcing a smile. "To have found you."

Her expression softens. "Jack McKenzie, are you getting sentimental on me?"

"Maybe." I refill our glasses. "Is that allowed?"

"I'll permit it," she says solemnly, though her eyes dance. "Just this once."

We talk for hours, the wine flowing, the conversation wandering from Madison's sudden rugby obsession to Sophia's work stories to my childhood memories of Queenstown. I find myself sharing more than I'd planned—stories of summer hikes in the mountains, winter ski trips, the mischief my sisters and I would get up to during harvest season.

Watching her laugh, seeing her truly relaxed and happy, I wish desperately that tomorrow doesn't have to come. That we could stay here forever, just Sophia and Jack, uncomplicated and perfect. The weight of what I haven't yet said presses heavily on my chest. If I don't say it now, I might never have the chance.

As the restaurant begins to empty, I pay the bill and we step out into the crisp night air. The stars blaze above us, the Southern Cross clearly visible in the dark sky.

"Look," I say, pointing upward. "That constellation there? That's the Southern Cross. It's on our flag. Only visible in the Southern Hemisphere."

Sophia tilts her head back, her breath fogging in the cool air. "It's beautiful. Everything here is beautiful."

The soft lap of water against the lakeshore underscores the quiet between us, stars reflected like scattered diamonds on the surface. Sophia shivers slightly in the cool night air, and instinctively I wrap my arm tighter around her, pulling her close as we gaze into the heavens. "Cold?"

"A little," she admits, leaning back against me. "But I don't want to go in yet. It's too perfect out here."

I turn her in my arms, cradling her face in my hands. "You're perfect," I whisper, then kiss her under the vast southern sky.

The kiss deepens quickly, all the emotions I can't express pouring into it—my fear, my hope, my love. Her arms wrap around my neck, her body presses against mine as if she could absorb the unspoken words through her skin.

As our bodies move together, slow and deep and achingly tender, I try to convey everything I can't speak. Every gentle touch is an apology; every kiss a silent promise. Forgive me. I never wanted to hurt you. Please stay. Please love me still, tomorrow.

When we finally break apart, both breathing hard, she looks up at me with such trust, such openness, that my chest aches.

"What was that for?" she asks softly.

"Because I love you," I say, the words slipping out before I could stop them. The truth—the real truth—lodges painfully in my throat, threatening to choke me. I want to say it all now, confess everything, but the look in her eyes stops me.

She trusts me, and God, how I need one more night of her trust.

Her eyes widen, surprise quickly replaced by warmth and something deeper, something raw and real. Her voice trembles slightly as she rises onto her tiptoes, brushing a kiss across my lips. "Well, that's convenient," she murmurs softly, almost shyly. "Because I might be falling for you too, Jack McKenzie."

My name in her mouth—the name that is true but incomplete—sends a pang through me. Tomorrow, she will know the full truth. Tonight, I will hold her close and pretend that nothing has to change.

We check on Madison (sound asleep, phone still clutched in her hand) before retreating to our room. Sophia moves to the windows, gazing out at the moonlight on the lake, and I watch her silhouette against the glass. Strong, beautiful... utterly precious to me.

"C'mere," she says softly, not turning around.

I cross to her, wrapping my arms around her waist. She leans back against me, her head resting on my shoulder.

"Thank you for today," she whispers. "For all of this."

"Anything for you," I reply, meaning it completely.

She turns in my arms, her hands sliding up my chest. "Anything?" she asks, her voice dropping to that husky tone that never fails to send heat rushing through me.

In answer, I bend and capture her mouth with mine. She responds immediately, fingers tangling in my hair, pulling me closer. As the kiss deepens, her hands grow more urgent, tugging at my shirt.

"Madison—" I begin.

"Is sound asleep with her headphones in," Sophia finishes, already working on my buttons. "And if we're quiet..." She presses a kiss to my newly exposed collarbone. "Very, very quiet..."

I don't need further invitation, lifting her easily and carrying her to the bed. The moonlight spills through the windows, illuminating her skin as I slowly undress her, taking my time, memorizing every inch. Her body arches beneath my hands and mouth, her breathing quickening as I worship her.

When we finally come together, it is slow and deep and achingly tender. I try to pour everything I can't say into each touch, each kiss. I love you. I'm sorry. Please forgive me. Don't leave me. Her eyes, dark and luminous in the moonlight, hold mine as we move together, her hands fierce and possessive on my back.

Later, curled against each other in the tangled sheets, her head on my chest, I listen to her breathing slow and deepen as she drifts toward sleep.

"I could get used to this," she murmurs drowsily. "New Zealand. You. All of it."

I press a kiss to her hair, throat too tight to respond.

chapter
twenty-nine

THE MORNING SUN streams through our hotel room windows, painting golden stripes across the rumpled sheets. Jack has already slipped out for coffee, leaving a note on his pillow about grabbing "proper flat whites before our drive." I stretch, surprisingly well-rested despite the lingering jet lag.

My phone vibrates with a text from Maria back at Metro General.

> You won't believe this!!! Tasha stepped
> up BIG TIME. We have to talk soon! You
> are going to squeal!

I smile. The ER seems to be surviving without me, which is both reassuring and slightly deflating.

"Mom? You up?" Madison's voice comes through the connecting door, followed by her head poking in. "Jack says we're leaving in an hour."

"I'm up." I swing my legs over the side of the bed. "Did you pack your overnight bag like I asked?"

"Almost done." She flops onto the foot of my bed, scrolling through her phone. "Emma—Jack's sister—texted me a bunch of pictures of the vineyard. It looks so cool! There are actual mountains behind it."

"Let me see." I lean over as she holds up her phone, displaying photos of stunning mountain vistas behind neatly organized rows of grapevines. "Wow. That is beautiful."

"Jack says his other sister Lily has a collection of seashells from all over New Zealand that she wants to show me. And we might get to see kiwi birds!" Madison's excitement is palpable, her legs bouncing against the mattress.

"Someone's excited about meeting the family," I tease, though my own stomach flutters with anticipation.

"Well, yeah." Her tone suggests this is obvious. "They raised Jack, and he's pretty cool, so they must be awesome too."

The simple logic of teenagers. I hope she's right.

"Plus," she adds with studied casualness, "I told Chloe that if this trip goes well, we might be able to come back for Christmas or something. You know, since you and Jack are...whatever you are."

"Whatever we are?" I raise an eyebrow.

She rolls her eyes. "You know. Like, serious. He told you he loves you, Mom. I heard him say it last night when you guys came back from dinner."

Heat rushes to my cheeks. "Madison *Grace*—"

"I wasn't eavesdropping!" she protests. "The walls are thin, and you guys were right outside my door. Besides, I think it's nice." Her expression softens. "He looks at you like you're something special."

Something in my chest loosens, a knot I hadn't realized was there. "He is...special," I admit quietly. "But we're still figuring things out."

"Well, figure faster," she says, pushing herself off the bed. "Because Emma says their mom is already planning our Christmas visit, and I want to see what a Southern Hemisphere Christmas looks like."

After she bounces back to her room, I sit for a moment, letting her words sink in. *Jack told you he loves you.* Not just in a heat-of-the-moment whisper, but openly enough that Madison had heard. And I'd said it back, sort of. I might be falling for you too.

It still terrifies me, that vulnerability. But for the first time in years, the fear feels like excitement rather than dread.

Jack appears in the doorway twenty minutes later, carrying a cardboard tray with three cups. "Morning, gorgeous. Brought flat whites for us adults, and that chocolate monstrosity Madison claims is coffee."

I accept my cup with a kiss. "You're a saint."

"Practical, not saintly. The drive to Central Otago takes a bit, and I'd rather have you both properly caffeinated." His smile doesn't quite reach his eyes.

"Nervous about us meeting your family?" I ask gently.

He pauses, then nods, gaze dropping to his coffee. "A bit. My mum can be... intense. And it's been a while since I've brought anyone home."

"Well, Madison's already made Christmas plans with Emma, so I think we're stuck with you," I tease.

His head snaps up. "Christmas plans?"

"Apparently your sister and my daughter are already plotting a summer Christmas for us." I sip my coffee, watching him carefully. "Too presumptuous?"

"No," he says quickly. "No, that's... brilliant, actually. I'd love that." His smile warms, becoming more genuine. "The Southern Hemisphere Christmas is something to experience. Beach barbecues, swimming, sunburn. Not a snowflake in sight."

"Sounds perfect." I reach for his hand, giving it a squeeze. "Don't worry about today. We're going to be fine."

He squeezes back, but something flashes in his eyes—worry, guilt, I couldn't quite place it. Before I can ask, Madison bounds in, grabbing for her chocolate drink.

"So when do we leave? I want to see everything!"

The drive starts pleasantly enough, with Jack pointing out land-marks as we leave Queenstown behind. The landscape transforms from the rugged peaks surrounding the lake to rolling hills that gradually flatten and open into vast valleys. Madison, initially chatty, eventually dozes off in the backseat, her headphones still playing.

"This area is called the Gibbston Valley," Jack explains as we drive through a particularly picturesque stretch. "Famous for Pinot Noir grapes. The schist soil and climate are perfect for them."

"You really do know a lot about wine," I observe.

His hands tighten slightly on the steering wheel. "Grew up with it. Hard not to absorb some knowledge."

"Your family's vineyard, is it big?"

Jack clears his throat. "It's... established. Been around for generations."

Something about his tone makes me glance at him more care-fully. His shoulders have tensed, and his eyes keep darting to the side mirrors as if checking whether we are being followed.

"You okay?" I ask quietly, not wanting to wake Madison.

"Fine," he says, too quickly. "Just... been a while since I've been back."

I study his profile as he drives, noting the tightness around his jaw, the way his knuckles have whitened on the steering wheel. This is more than just normal anxiety about introducing a girlfriend to family. Something else is going on.

The GPS announces we are approaching Cromwell, and Jack's tension seems to increase with each kilometer. We round a bend, and I spot a sign by the roadside that makes my heart skip.

McKenzie Estate - Est. 1872: Award-Winning Central Otago Pinot Noir
Private Tours by Appointment Only

The sign is elegant, understated but unmistakably high-end, with a stylized 'M' logo that matches the label on the bottle of wine Jack had ordered that first night at Giuseppe's.

The $300 bottle.

My mouth goes dry, my pulse thunders in my ears as the ground I thought I knew disappears entirely.

"Jack," I say slowly, "is... is *that* your family's—"

"Yes," he cuts me off, his voice strained. "That's... ours."

Ours. The casual ownership of what is clearly a substantial operation hits me with unexpected force. I know his family owned a vineyard, but this is not some small family farm. This looks like a major commercial operation.

"I thought you said your family had a vineyard," I say carefully. "This looks more like a...winery. A big one."

His laugh is hollow. "It is. Both, actually."

We turn onto a private road that twists through acres of meticulously maintained vines stretching in every direction. The scale is overwhelming—row after row, precision-planted along gentle slopes that catch the afternoon sun.

"How big is this place?" I ask, my mind struggling to process what I am seeing.

Jack swallows visibly. "The original estate is about 300 hectares. But there are other...properties now. Parcels added over generations."

Properties. Parcels. The casual way he uses these words sends a chill through me. This is not just a vineyard; this is an empire.

We drive for several more minutes down the private road—still on McKenzie land, I realize with growing unease. Eventually, the main house comes into view, and my breath catches.

House is not the right word. It is a sprawling mansion of stone and glass, perched on a rise that commands views of the entire valley. Modern but timeless, with multiple wings and expansive terraces. Landscaped gardens surround it, and I can see a pool glittering in the distance.

Madison stirs in the backseat, pulling off her headphones. "Are we—" Her words cut off as she spots the house. "Holy *shit*."

For once, I don't correct her language.

Jack pulls up to a circular driveway where several luxury vehicles are parked. A group of people has assembled on the front steps—a welcoming committee. I recognize Jack's sisters from the photos he'd shown me, along with an elegant older couple who have to be his parents.

"Jack," I say, my voice barely above a whisper. "What, exactly, did you *not* tell me?"

He turns to me, his blue eyes filled with an emotion I couldn't quite name—fear, maybe, or resignation.

"Everything," he whispers back. "I didn't tell you everything."

Before I can respond, the front door opens, and his family starts moving toward our car.

It is too late for explanations. The moment of truth has arrived, and I am completely unprepared.

chapter
thirty

THE DRIVE to the estate feels like a slow-motion car crash I can see coming but can't prevent. Every kilometer brings us closer to the inevitable collision of my two worlds, and I am powerless to stop it.

I have rehearsed what to say a dozen times during the night, lying awake beside Sophia while she sleeps peacefully, unaware of what is coming. But when morning arrives, the words have evaporated, leaving only a hollow dread in the pit of my stomach.

Now we're here... and it's too bloody late.

My family has assembled on the front steps like a welcoming party for visiting dignitaries—Dad in his casual but unmistakably expensive weekend attire, Mum in one of her designer dresses that she probably considers "simple," my sisters arranged in what looks like a carefully choreographed tableau.

"Jack?" Sophia's voice is unnaturally steady. "Is there anything you'd like to tell me before we get out of this car and meet your family?"

I turn to her, wanting to explain everything, knowing there isn't time, knowing it is already too late.

"I'm sorry," I manage. "I should have told you sooner. I wanted to, I just—"

"Mr. McKenzie!" Mrs. Petersen, our longtime housekeeper, appears at my window, beaming. "Welcome home! Everyone's been so excited. And these must be your special guests!"

I see Sophia flinch at the "Mr. McKenzie." I'd always just been "Jack" to her, to everyone at Metro General. The formality is the first crack in the façade.

"Mrs. Petersen," I nod, forcing a smile. "Yes, this is Sophia Mitchell and her daughter, Madison."

Madison has already scrambled out of the car, her eyes wide as she takes in the estate.

"Oh my God," she breathes, turning in a slow circle. "This is like a movie set."

I watch as Sophia composes herself, squaring her shoulders in that way she does before dealing with difficult situations at the hospital. The charge nurse armor, I call it—her ability to project calm confidence regardless of her inner turmoil. But I'd never been on the receiving end of it before, and it feels like a knife in my gut.

"Sophia," I begin.

"We should greet your family," she interrupts, her voice professionally pleasant. "They're waiting."

She is right. My family has started moving toward us, my mother in the lead, her arms already outstretched in welcome.

"Jackson!" she calls, using my full name as always. "Finally! We were about to send out a search party!"

I see Sophia register the "Jackson" with a slight tightening around her eyes. Another revelation. My mother reaches us, enveloping me in a perfumed embrace before turning to Sophia.

"And you must be Sophia! We've heard so little about you, despite our constant questioning." She shoots me a pointed look before taking Sophia's hands in hers. "Helen McKenzie. Welcome to our home."

"Thank you for having us," Sophia replies with perfect composure. "Your estate is beautiful."

"Oh, this is just the main house," my mother says dismissively. "Wait until you see the rest of the property. The wine cave, the tasting rooms, and—" her eyes light up "—you absolutely must visit our kiwi conservation sanctuary. Jackson started it when he was sixteen."

Another glance from Sophia, another twist of the knife.

"A kiwi sanctuary?" Madison perks up immediately.

"Yes, dear," my mother beams. "We have a breeding colony of Tokoeka kiwis—the southern brown kiwi. Quite rare, especially outside their natural range. Jackson found an injured one when he was a boy, tramping at Milford Sound, and convinced Michael to establish a protected area."

"That's amazing!" Madison enthuses, while Sophia's expression grows more strained.

My father approaches next, shaking Sophia's hand warmly. "Michael McKenzie. Welcome to New Zealand. Jack tells us you're quite something in the medical line."

"I'm a charge nurse at Metro General Hospital," she answers. "Emergency department."

"Fascinating," my father replies, and I can tell he genuinely means it. "Much like our Jack here, always drawn to the frontlines. Though we had hoped he'd eventually return to help run the family business."

I see Charlotte wince. At least one of my sisters recognizes the disaster unfolding.

Madison has gravitated toward Emma, who is already showing her something on her phone—probably rugby highlights, knowing Em. Lily approaches Sophia with her usual gentle manner.

"We've prepared the Blue Suite for you," she says. "It has the best view of the mountains. Jack thought you'd like that."

Sophia's gaze flicks to me. "Jack did, did he?"

Lily, always perceptive, must have sensed the tension. "We can show you there now if you'd like to freshen up before the tour."

"A tour would be wonderful," Sophia says, her smile not quite reaching her eyes.

My mother claps her hands together. "Perfect! Jackson, why don't you help with the luggage while I start showing Sophia and Madison around? We'll begin with the main house, then the original vineyard, and finish at the winery complex."

Before I can object, my mother has swept Sophia and Madison toward the house, my sisters falling in alongside them. My father lingers behind, studying me with a knowing look.

"You didn't tell her, did you?" he asks quietly.

"I was going to. Today. Before we arrived." I run a hand through my hair. "I just...couldn't find the right moment."

"There is no right moment for this kind of revelation, son." He shakes his head. "She seems like quite a remarkable woman. Strong."

"She is." My voice cracks slightly. "And I may have just lost her."

My father squeezes my shoulder. "If she's as remarkable as she seems, perhaps not. But it won't be easy." He pauses, looking toward the house where my mother is already gesturing expansively as she guides Sophia through the entrance. "She'll either walk out tonight or be family forever. No in-between with that one."

I nod, not trusting my voice.

"You'll have to fight for her," he says simply. "But first, you've got some groveling to do."

As we follow the others toward the house, I can see Sophia's back —straight, tense, her head tilted slightly as she listens to my mother describe the original painting in the entryway. Madison is a few steps ahead, practically bouncing with excitement.

The contrast between them is a perfect visual representation of my dilemma. Madison, delighted by the discovery; Sophia, processing betrayal with every step.

I'd wanted so badly for her to love my home country, my family, the beautiful place where I'd grown up. But I'd failed to understand that by hiding such a fundamental part of my identity, I'd made that impossible. Because how could she love a man she didn't really know?

The realization hits me with crushing force: in my fear of being judged for my family's wealth, I'd become something far worse: a man who has systematically deceived the woman he loves.

And now I have to face the consequences.

chapter
thirty-one

THE MCKENZIE ESTATE'S main house is a masterclass in understated luxury. No gaudy displays of wealth, just the quiet confidence of people who have never questioned their place in the world. Every piece of furniture, every artwork, every subtle design choice speaks of generations of taste and privilege.

I move through the space on autopilot, nodding and making appropriate sounds of appreciation as Helen McKenzie—not the friendly "call me Helen" but the imperial "Helen McKenzie"—points out architectural features and family heirlooms.

"This painting was commissioned for Jackson's great-grandfather," she explains, gesturing to a massive landscape dominating one wall. "The artist captured the original homestead perfectly, don't you think?"

"Beautiful," I murmur, though what I really want to say is *Who the hell is Jackson?*

Madison has no such filter. "Wait, is Jack short for Jackson?" she asks, turning to Emma. "I didn't know that."

Emma's eyebrows rise slightly. "You didn't? It's always been Jackson Charles McKenzie on all the official—" She stops abruptly, catching Jack's warning look. "Sorry," she adds, not sounding sorry at all.

Jackson Charles McKenzie. Another piece of the puzzle I haven't known I was solving.

My mind is working overtime, cataloging each new revelation, mapping them against what I'd thought I knew. The "family business" is not some modest vineyard where Jack had learned about grapes as a child; it is a massive commercial operation spread across multiple properties. The "picking grapes" stories take on an entirely new context—not a boy helping with the family farm but the heir to an empire, perhaps indulging in a carefully cultivated narrative of humble beginnings.

And all those "points" for our flight upgrades? I am beginning to doubt they have anything to do with paramedic conferences.

"And this is the formal dining room," Helen continues, leading us into a space that could comfortably seat twenty. "Though we usually eat in the smaller family dining room unless we're entertaining."

Smaller. Family. Dining room. Each word a little dagger.

"You have a beautiful home, Mrs. McKenzie," I say, reverting to formality as a shield.

"Oh, Helen, please," she replies with a dismissive wave. "And this is just the homestead. Jackson has his own cottage near the wine cave, though he hasn't used it much these past few years."

His own cottage. While I'd been budgeting for a yard service to maintain my modest suburban home, the man I am falling in love with apparently owns a *cottage* on a family estate that looks like something out of a travel magazine.

As the tour continues, I find myself watching Jack as much as the surroundings. He hangs back, shoulders tense, a look of barely contained dread on his face. *Good*, a bitter part of me thinks. *At least he knows how badly he's screwed up.*

We move outside to the vineyard portion of the tour. Helen keeps up a steady stream of information about grape varieties, soil

composition, and the history of the estate. Under different circumstances, I would have found it fascinating. Now, each fact feels like
further evidence of Jack's deception.

"Of course, Jackson was always more interested in rugby than
viticulture," Helen remarks as we walk between rows of carefully
tended vines. "Though he did earn his sommelier certification before
shooting through to America to play at being a paramedic."

I stumble slightly, caught off-guard by both the casual dismissal
of Jack's career and the revelation of yet another qualification I'd
known nothing about.

Jack is at my side instantly, a hand at my elbow to steady me. I
flinch away from his touch.

"I'm fine," I say quickly. Too quickly.

The hurt in his eyes is genuine, but at that moment, I can't bring
myself to care.

"Mom," Madison calls from up ahead, where she is walking with
Lily and Emma. "Lily says we're going to see the kiwi sanctuary Jack
started! Is that true?"

"Apparently," I call back, unable to keep a hint of sharpness from
my voice.

"It's quite remarkable," Michael says, falling into step beside me.
"Not many sixteen-year-olds would convince their parents to set aside
fifty acres for endangered birds. But Jack was always... *different*. And
good on him for that."

I glance at him, surprised by his supportive tone. "Fifty acres," I
repeat. "That's... substantial."

"For the birds? Yes. For the estate? A small corner." Michael's
eyes crinkle. "Though Helen threw a fit about the location. Prime
grape-growing slopes, you see. Jack insisted it was the perfect micro-
climate for the kiwis."

I can't help but picture teenage Jack, standing up to his family
for a wounded bird. That part, at least, feels like the man I know.

Helen has moved ahead with Madison and the sisters, giving us a moment of relative privacy. Michael seems to sense the tension and discretely increases his pace, leaving Jack and me briefly alone.

"Sophia," Jack begins, his voice low and urgent. "I know this is overwhelming. I should have—"

"Yes, you should have," I cut him off. "But not here. Not now."

"When?" The naked plea in his voice almost breaks through my carefully maintained composure.

"I don't know." I look straight ahead, focusing on Madison's animated gestures as she talks with Emma. "I need time to process... all of this."

"Of course," he says, defeat evident in his tone. "Whatever you need."

The tour continues, with Helen proudly showcasing the winery operations, the temperature-controlled storage caves, the tasting rooms where visitors sample McKenzie Estate's award-winning Pinot Noir. The scale is staggering—not just a business but a small empire that has clearly been built over generations.

By the time we reach the guest house—a "simple" structure that is larger and more luxurious than any home I've ever lived in—I am emotionally exhausted from maintaining my facade of polite interest.

"We thought you and Madison would be comfortable here," Helen says, gesturing to the guest house. "It has its own kitchen, though you're expected at the main house for meals, of course. Jackson's cottage is just beyond those trees."

The assumption that we would be staying separately should have bothered me, but at that moment, I am actually grateful. I need space from Jack, from this whole situation.

"Thank you," I say. "It looks lovely."

Madison appears at my side, her eyes bright with excitement. "Mom, can I have the room with the mountain view? Emma says it's incredible!"

"Of course," I say, forcing a smile for her sake.

"I'll help you with your bags," Jack offers, clearly searching for any opportunity to speak with me alone.

"That's not necessary," I say coolly. "I'm sure one of the staff can assist us."

Hurt flashes across his face, but he nods. "Of course. Whatever you prefer."

Helen beams, oblivious to the tension. "Well! I'll leave you to it. Dinner is at seven in the family dining room. Nothing flash, just the immediate family."

As they depart—Jack lingering until I pointedly turn away—I finally allow myself a moment of vulnerability. My hands are trembling, and I clasp them tightly to hide it from Madison.

"Isn't this AMAZING?" she enthuses, spinning in a circle in the guest house's spacious living room. "Jack's family is like...I don't even know! It's like we're in a movie or something!"

I nod, not trusting my voice.

"The WiFi password is on the coffee table," she continues, already tapping at her phone. "I'm going to FaceTime Chloe. She's never going to believe this!"

As Madison disappears into her chosen bedroom, I sink onto a nearby chair, finally alone with my thoughts.

The carefully constructed image of Jack McKenzie—Jackson Charles McKenzie—I'd carried in my heart shatters into a thousand pieces. The humble paramedic with the charming accent. The man who brings me coffee. Who taught Madison to make pasta. Who looked at me like I hung the moon.

Was any of it real?

The familiar sensation of betrayal washes over me, bitter and nauseating. I'd been here before with Troy—that gradual realization that the person I'd given my heart to wasn't who I thought they were. Different circumstances, same gut-wrenching feeling of having been played for a fool.

Tears burn behind my eyes, but I refuse to let them fall. I am Sophia Mitchell, charge nurse at Metro General, who handles the worst without breaking a sweat. I'm not going to crumble.

But a small, wounded part of me whispers: You did it again. You trusted the wrong man. When will you learn?

I stare out the window at the perfectly manicured grounds, the mountains rising majestically in the distance, feeling more alone than I had in years.

And somewhere beyond those trees is Jack—Jackson—in his private cottage on his family's multi-million dollar estate, waiting for me to process a betrayal I am not sure I can forgive.

chapter
thirty-two

THE GUEST HOUSE door closes behind Sophia and Madison with a quiet finality. I stand frozen on the path, the mountain air suddenly chilling despite the afternoon sun.

She couldn't even *look* at me. Couldn't bear to be in the same room.

"Jackson."

Charlotte's voice, cold as lake water in winter, slices through my spiraling thoughts. I turn to find all three of my sisters standing in a loose semicircle behind me. Emma's face flushes with barely contained fury. Lily's eyes fill with disappointment—somehow worse than anger. Charlotte, the eldest, stands with perfect posture, her expression like carved granite.

"Not now," I say, my voice rough. "Please."

"No. *Now*." Charlotte's tone leaves no room for negotiation. She nods toward the vineyard. "Walk with us."

It's not a request. In the McKenzie family hierarchy, Charlotte has effectively replaced our father as the authority figure years ago. Even Mum defers to her on most family matters.

I follow silently as Charlotte lead us away from the homestead down a worn path between rows of Pinot Noir vines heavy with fruit. The harvest'll begin in day, *another* family tradition I'd abandoned.

When we reach a small clearing with a view of Lake Dunstan, Charlotte stops. The spot is familiar—our childhood hideaway, where we'd come to escape Mum's social gatherings or Dad's vineyard lectures. A neutral territory of sorts.

Charlotte turns to face me, her CEO mask firmly in place. "You manipulated her for months, Jack. Months." Her voice is controlled but vibrating with rage. "God, no wonder you shot through, you wanted to try out being poor for a while."

"That's... that's not what happened—"

"Oh, isn't it?" Charlotte cuts me off. "You play at being a working-class hero while knowing you have millions in the bank. Do you have any idea how insulting that is? Not just to Sophia, but to people who actually have to worry about paying bills?"

Emma steps forward, tears already streaming down her face, her anger never far from the surface. "She trusted you. Madison trusted you! She was calling you her stepdad!"

"No, she wasn't—"

"To Chloe, she was!" Emma shouts. "Your girlfriend's child was telling her friends you were going to be her stepdad someday. I saw the texts when she was showing me pictures! Do you even see what you did?"

The revelation hits me like a physical blow. Madison had been imagining a future with me in it... a future I'd now probably destroyed.

"I didn't know," I say weakly.

"Of course you didn't," Lily says, her voice quiet but cutting. "Because you were too busy playing pretend to see what was happening right in front of you." She takes a step closer, her normally gentle demeanor replaced by something harder. "This isn't just about her, Jack. It's about you never believing someone could love you for you unless you curated the version they saw. That's cowardice."

"Look, you know what happened with Vanessa," I say, my voice tight. "After what she did, how she planned to use me, use the family... I mean... I was terrified of—"

"Oh, don't you *fucking* dare," Lily cuts in, her quiet demeanor vanishing instantly. "Don't you *dare* use Vanessa as an excuse for this."

"I'm not—"

"Aren't you?" Charlotte's voice is ice. Her voice takes on a severe, mocking tone. "Poor little Jack got his heart broken by a social-climbing parasite, so naturally he had to lie to a single mother who probably hasn't had a vacation in years."

"That's not—"

"Vanessa was one woman," Emma says fiercely. "Yes, she was a manipulative cow, we all agree. But that was years ago! Are you going to let that one bad apple poison every chance you have at happiness? Did Sophia give you any indication—*any* at all—that she was like that? That she'd value your bank account over you?"

I open my mouth, then close it. "No."

"So instead of trusting the woman you claim to love," Charlotte continues relentlessly, "you decided to manipulate her reality based on your own baggage. Classic."

"You're nothing like Vanessa," Lily says, her voice gentler but no less firm. "She was calculated and cold from the start. You're just... scared. And that's almost worse, because you know better."

The comparison stings because they're right. Using Vanessa as justification is weak, and I know it.

"I was trying to protect—" I begin.

"Protect *who*?" Charlotte interrupts sharply. "Her or yourself? Because from where I'm standing, all you did was set up Sophia for maximum humiliation when she inevitably discovered the truth."

"You lied to her while she was raising a daughter alone and saving lives," Charlotte continues, her voice gaining intensity. "Who the hell do you think you are?"

"I never claimed to be—"

"You broke her trust," Emma cuts in, her voice cracking with emotion. "And what do you think this is going to do to Madison? That poor little girl's already watched her father disappoint her mother for years. She was just starting to believe in you, and now this!"

"I am NOTHING like him!" The words tear from my throat with unexpected force.

"Aren't you?" Lily asks, the quiet question somehow more devastating than Emma's shouting. "You both manipulated her reality. You both made her question her judgment. You both betrayed her trust."

I stagger back a step, the comparison to Troy like a knife between my ribs.

"She's a woman who gets spat on and punched and still shows up for the next shift," Lily continues, twisting the knife deeper. "And you didn't think she could handle you?"

"That's not fair," I manage.

"What's not fair," Charlotte says icily, "is bringing a woman and her teenage daughter to the literal opposite side of the world before revealing your little deception. Was that the plan all along? Get them so far from home they'd have no choice but to deal with it?"

"No!" I protest. "I was going to tell her before—"

"Before what?" Emma demands. "Before you arrived? Before you booked the tickets? Before you fell in love with her? There was never a good time because you were a bloody coward, you absolute fucking drongo!" Her words echo across the vineyard, startling birds from the vines.

"You think I don't know that?" I shoot back, my own anger finally surfacing. "You think I'm not painfully aware of how badly I've screwed up? I love her! I love them both! And I've probably lost them forever because I was too scared to trust that she'd see me, not the money!"

"And why wouldn't she?" Lily asks, her voice softening slightly.

"What evidence did you have that Sophia Mitchell, of all people, would care about your bank account?"

"That's the bloody irony, isn't it?" I laugh bitterly. "She wouldn't have. But I couldn't see that because I was too busy projecting my own insecurities onto her."

"Well, at least you've figured that out," Charlotte says dryly. "Only about ten hours too late."

We fall into tense silence, the only sound the rustle of leaves in the autumn breeze.

"She's gone, you know," Lily says finally. "I gave her the keys to one of the estate cars. She and Madison went to Lake Wanaka."

My head snaps up. "What? When?"

"Twenty minutes back," Lily replies. "They needed space."

"Space or a way home?" I ask, panic rising. "Are they coming back?"

"Their bags are still in the guest house," Lily assures me. "But honestly, Jack, I wouldn't blame her if she caught the first flight back to America."

"Jesus Christ." I sink down onto a stone bench, head in my hands. "What do I do?" I pull out my phone, fingers already typing a message before my brain catches up.

"No," Charlotte says firmly, snatching the phone from my hands. "Do not bombard her with texts. One message. Simple, direct, no excuses."

"Give me that—"

"I'm saving you from yourself." Charlotte holds the phone behind her back. "What were you going to say? Some long, rambling explanation about why you deceived her?"

"No, I—"

"Yes, you were," Emma cuts in. "Because that's what men always do. Try to explain away their mistakes instead of just owning them."

I glare at her. "That's not fair."

"None of this is fair," Charlotte replies. "Especially not to Sophia." She holds out my phone. "One message. Make it count."

I take the phone, staring at the blank text field. What can I possibly say that would matter now? What words can rebuild the trust I've shattered?

Finally, I type:

> I should have told you everything from the beginning. I was wrong and I'm sorry. No excuses. I understand if you need space. Just please let me know you're safe.

I show it to Charlotte, who nods once. "Better than I expected from you, to be fair."

I hit send, then immediately regret it. "What if she doesn't respond?"

"Then you respect that too," Lily says simply.

The minutes drag as we stand in silence, the weight of my mistakes pressing down on me. Just when I've convinced myself she won't answer, my phone vibrates.

> At Lake Wanaka with Madison. We're safe. Need time to think.

Relief floods through me. "They're at the lake. They're okay."

"See?" Lily's expression softens. "They haven't run for the airport. That's a good sign, eh."

I type back quickly:

> Thank you. Take all the time you need. We'll be here when you're ready.

"Now what?" I ask, pocketing my phone.

"Now," Charlotte says, "you figure out how to prove to her that the man she fell in love with is real, even if his bank account isn't what you pretended."

"And if she can't forgive the deception?" The question that has been haunting me since we arrived.

"Then you accept it," Emma says, her voice still thick with emotion. "But you don't stop trying until she explicitly tells you to. She deserves that much."

The enormity of what I stand to lose hits me all at once. Sophia's quiet strength, her sharp wit, her competence in crisis. The way she touches my face when she thinks I'm sleeping. Madison's infectious enthusiasm, her unfiltered questions, her fierce protectiveness of her mother.

My family. The family I'd chosen, who'd chosen me back.

My throat tightens painfully, and I turn away, not wanting my sisters to see the tears threatening to fall. But Lily's hand is already on my shoulder, turning me back toward them.

"It's okay," she says, her anger giving way to empathy. "We've seen you cry before, Jack."

I shake my head, fighting for control, but it is a losing battle. The tears come hot and fast, every wall I'd built crumbling under the weight of what I might have lost. "I've really fucked this up, haven't I?"

"Monumentally," Charlotte confirms, but her hand finds my other shoulder. "But if she's half the woman you think she is, she'll at least hear you out. Eventually."

"If she doesn't," Emma says, her own tears starting again, "I'll miss her. And Madison." She sniffs. "That kid has serious rugby potential."

I laugh wetly, wiping at my eyes. "God, Em."

"What? She does." Emma manages a watery smile. "Just, you know, when you grovel and beg for forgiveness, maybe mention I'd still like to coach her. If she wants."

"I'll add it to my list of desperate pleas," I promise.

Lily pulls me into a hug, and after a moment, Emma joins, her strong arms wrapping around us both. Finally, Charlotte—who rarely initiates physical contact—completes the circle.

"For what it's worth," Charlotte says against my shoulder, "I think you did find yourself in America. You're a better man than the flash prick who left here years ago."

"Even if I am a manipulative coward?" I ask, only half-joking.

"You've always been a bit of a coward," Charlotte replies. "But then you ran into burning buildings for strangers, so we forgave you that flaw."

"Sophia might too," Lily adds gently. "She'll be right, Jack. But you've got to earn it. If you're brave enough now to face the consequences and fight for her."

We stand there among the vines, the four McKenzie siblings united again, as the sun begins its descent toward the mountains. For the first time since arriving at the estate, I feel a flicker of hope.

Not that Sophia would forgive me... that's entirely her choice, one I'll have to accept whatever she decides. But hope that somehow, I can show her the truth: that despite my deception, the man she'd fallen for is real.

And he's fighting for his way back to her.

chapter
thirty-three

I STARE at the car keys in my palm, still warm from Lily's hand.

"It's just a loaner," she'd said, her kind eyes so different from Helen's assessing gaze. "Automatic transmission, so you don't have to worry about that. GPS is programmed for Lake Wanaka—it's 'bout an hour away. Beautiful spot."

"I can't just take your car," I'd protested weakly.

Lily smiles. "It's not mine. It's just one of the estate cars. We have several." She pauses, studying my face. "You look like you could use some space, Sophia. Anyone would."

I nod, grateful for her perceptiveness. "I'm going to see if Madison wants to come with me."

"Of course," Lily replies. "I was planning to show her the kiwi sanctuary, but that can wait."

I find Madison on the sprawling lawn with Emma, learning proper rugby passing technique. She looks up, flushed with exertion and excitement.

"Mom! Emma says I have natural talent! She thinks I could play wing if I practiced—"

"That's wonderful, sweetie," I interrupt gently. "How would you feel about taking a drive with me? There's a famous tree in a lake nearby that I'd love to see."

Madison's enthusiasm dims slightly. "Right now? But Emma was just about to show me how to—"

"I'd really like you to come with me, Madison," I say, my tone making it clear this wasn't really a request. "It's supposed to be beautiful, and we can take some photos for your Instagram."

She studies my face for a moment, her teenage perception catching something in my expression. "Okay, Mom. Let me just grab my phone from inside."

"I'll still be here when you get back," Emma assures Madison with an understanding smile. "Maybe we can work on your kicking technique later."

Now Madison sits beside me in the passenger seat of a luxury SUV that probably costs more than my annual salary, scrolling through her phone as I try to remember everything Lily had told me about driving in New Zealand.

"Stay left," I mutter, adjusting the mirrors. "Always left."

"This car is insane," Madison comments, running her hand over the leather dashboard. "It's like, way nicer than Mr. Cushman's BMW, and he's always bragging about it."

I say nothing, focusing on getting us safely down the long driveway that leads away from the McKenzie Estate. The windshield wipers activate when I mean to signal a turn, and I fumble with the controls, feeling incompetent on top of everything else.

"Other side, Mom," Madison says helpfully. "Everything's backward here."

"Perfect metaphor," I mutter as I finally find the correct lever.

Madison glances up from her phone. "You okay? You seem...upset."

"I'm fine," I lie, not wanting to burden her with my emotional turmoil. "Just adjusting to driving on the wrong side of the road."

She watches me for a moment longer, then returns to her phone. "This Wanaka Tree is super famous on Instagram. It grows right out of the lake. People come from all over the world to take pictures of it."

"That's what Lily said," I reply, grateful for the neutral topic.

The landscape unfolds as we drive, vineyards giving way to rolling hills that climb toward mountains. Under other circumstances, I would have been captivated by the beauty. Now it feels like another layer of deception—the perfect backdrop for the fairy tale I'd been living.

"Mom, slow down," Madison says suddenly. "You're drifting right."

I jerk the wheel, correcting our position. "Sorry. Still getting used to this."

"So..." Madison begins carefully. "Are we going to talk about Jack's family being, like, super rich?"

I tighten my grip on the steering wheel. "I didn't know you'd noticed."

She gives me her patented teenage are-you-serious look. "*Mom.* They have a mansion with staff and a wine empire. Kind of hard to miss."

"Yes, well. It was certainly a surprise."

"Did you really not know?" she asks, her voice softer now. "He never said anything?"

"No," I say, the single syllable heavy with hurt. "He never mentioned any of it."

Madison is quiet for a moment, processing. "That's weird. I mean, it's kind of a big thing to leave out."

"Yes, it is." I focus on the road, not trusting myself to say more without my voice betraying my emotions.

"But," Madison continues thoughtfully, "he's still the same Jack, right? The one who taught me to make pasta and brought you coffee and stuff?"

The question cuts straight to the heart of my confusion. "I don't know, Madison. That's what I'm trying to figure out."

A car approaches from the opposite direction, and I instinctively drift right before jerking back to the left lane, heart pounding.

"Wrong side," Madison reminds me, her hand bracing against the dashboard. "Remember where you are."

But that is exactly the problem, isn't it? I hadn't known where I was—in Jack's life, in his world, in his heart. I'd thought I was falling for a man who understood what it meant to live paycheck to paycheck, who valued the same simple things I did. Instead, I'd fallen for a billionaire playing at being ordinary.

Playing paramedic, Helen had said. As if saving lives was a diversion, not a vocation.

"Do you think that's why he became a paramedic?" Madison asks, as if reading my thoughts. "Because he's rich and wanted to try something different?"

"I don't know what to think anymore," I admit. "I just know that he wasn't honest with me."

"Like Dad wasn't honest?" Her voice is smaller now.

The comparison hits me hard. "Your father's situation was different. He... changed over time. Jack kept this from me from the beginning."

"But Dad was fake about, like, everything. Jack just didn't tell you about his family being rich." Madison pauses, considering. "Which is still messed up, but not as bad as Dad pretending to be a good person when he really wasn't."

I glance at her, surprised by her insight. "When did you get so wise?"

She shrugs. "I watch a lot of relationship TikToks."

Despite everything, I laugh. "Ah, the modern oracle."

The GPS guides us through small towns and across a mountain pass, the road twisting through valleys that open to reveal snow-capped peaks. Madison takes photos through the window, momentarily distracted by the breathtaking scenery.

"Can I ask you something, Mom?" she says after a while, her voice tentative.

"Of course."

"If Jack had told you about all this from the beginning, would you have dated him?"

The question catches me off guard. Would I have? Or would I have dismissed him as out of my league, a rich playboy slumming it in the ER?

"I honestly don't know," I answer truthfully. "I'd like to think it wouldn't have mattered, but..."

"But you might have thought he was just playing around," Madison finishes for me. "Like, not serious."

"Maybe."

"So maybe that's why he didn't tell you." She turns to look out the window. "I'm not saying it's right. Just... I get it. Kinda."

Lake Wanaka appears suddenly as we crest a hill, its vast blue expanse stretching toward distant mountains. The GPS directs us toward the town center, but a sign for "That Wanaka Tree" catches my attention.

"There it is," Madison says, pointing. "Can we go see it?"

I follow the signs, pulling into a small parking area near the lakeshore. As we walk along the stony beach, the famous lone tree growing out of the lake comes into view. It stands solitary but defiant, persisting despite being surrounded by elements that should make survival impossible. In the clear autumn air, the tree's twisted branches are perfectly reflected in the still water, mountains rising majestically behind it.

Madison immediately begins taking photos, positioning herself to get the perfect angle with the mountains in the background. I hang back, watching her, suddenly grateful for her presence. Her practical perspective has already given me something to consider that I might have missed in my hurt and anger.

"Mom, come get in this picture with me!" she calls.

I join her, putting on a smile as she holds up her phone for a selfie with the tree behind us. "Perfect Instagram material."

After she'd taken enough photos to satisfy her social media needs, we find a spot on the stony beach away from the other tourists. The early autumn air is crisp, the lake reflecting the mountains with perfect clarity.

"It's really pretty here," Madison says, skipping a stone across the water's surface. "Different from home, but nice."

"Yes, it is." I wrap my arms around myself, the wind off the water cutting through my jacket.

"Are you going to break up with Jack?" Madison asks suddenly, her stone sinking rather than skipping.

I look at her, surprised by the directness of the question. "I don't know yet. I need some time to think."

She nods, picking up another stone. "I like him, you know. Even if his mom is kind of snobby."

"You barely know him, Madison."

"I know he makes you happy. Or did, before today." She skips the stone successfully, watching it bounce three times before disappearing. "You haven't been this happy since...I don't know if I've ever seen you this happy, actually."

Her words hit me with unexpected force. She is right—Jack had brought a joy to my life I hadn't experienced before. The question is whether that joy had been built on a foundation of lies.

My phone buzzes in my pocket. I pull it out to see a message from Jack.

> I should have told you everything from the beginning. I was wrong and I'm sorry. No excuses. I understand if you need space. Just please let me know you're safe.

Simple. Direct. No justifications.

I show the message to Madison, watching her reaction.

"See?" she says after reading it. "He knows he messed up."

"Knowing and doing something about it are different things," I point out.

"True." She hands back my phone. "But at least he's not making excuses like Dad always does."

Again, the comparison to Troy gives me pause. Jack had deceived me, yes. But there is a fundamental difference in how he is handling the aftermath—with responsibility rather than deflection.

With cold fingers, I type a response:

> At Lake Wanaka with Madison. We're safe. Need time to think.

His reply comes immediately:

> Thank you. Take all the time you need. We'll be here when you're ready.

We. His family. The McKenzies. The dynasty I'd unwittingly stepped into.

"What did he say?" Madison asks, peering over my shoulder.

"That we should take all the time we need."

She nods approvingly. "That's good. Not pushy."

I tuck my phone away and stand, brushing sand from my jeans. "We should head back soon if we want to reach the estate before dark."

"Does this mean you're going to give him a chance to explain?" Madison asks, hope evident in her voice.

"It means I'm going to listen," I say carefully. "That's all I can promise right now."

She seems satisfied with that. As we walk back to the car, I feel oddly calm. The tears I'd held back in Madison's presence will have to wait, but her perspective has provided something valuable—a reminder that behind the deception is a man who has brought genuine happiness into our lives.

Jack had deceived me, yes. But is it the end? I don't know yet.

What I do know is that I won't make any decisions from a place of hurt and anger. Madison is with me. We are safe. We have time to figure out what comes next.

I start the SUV, adjust the mirrors, and remind myself once more: "Stay left. Everything's different here."

Different, but not necessarily wrong. Just a new reality I need to learn to navigate.

"Mom?" Madison says as we pull out of the parking lot. "No matter what you decide about Jack, I'm glad we came to New Zealand. It's beautiful here."

I reach over and squeeze her hand. "Me too, sweetie. Me too."

chapter
thirty-four

I **WAIT** in the entrance hall of the main house, stomach knotted with dread. The text had come thirty minutes after Sophia and Madison returned from Lake Wanaka:

> We need to talk. Alone. Meet me in the main house at 8.

The formal tone, so unlike Sophia's usual warmth, tells me everything I need to know about what is coming. But I deserve it. I will stand here and take whatever she needs to say.

The grandfather clock in the corner ticks relentlessly, each second stretching into eternity. I pace the polished floor, hands shoved deep in my pockets, rehearsing apologies I already know will be inadequate.

I hear her footsteps before I see her—measured, controlled, the same steady tread I'd come to recognize in the ER when she was facing something difficult. She appears in the doorway, still wearing the clothes from earlier, her hair pulled back in a simple ponytail. No makeup. No armor. Just Sophia, raw and real.

"Thank you for meeting me," she says, her voice eerily calm.

"Of course." I take a half-step toward her, then stop when I see her almost imperceptible flinch. "Sophia, listen, I—"

"*No.*" She holds up a hand. "I need you to listen. Just listen. Can you do that?"

I nod, throat too tight for words.

She moves further into the room but keeps her distance, positioning herself beside the massive stone fireplace. Her fingers trace the mantle absently, eyes anywhere but on me.

"I've spent the last several hours trying to understand," she begins. "Trying to make sense of what happened between us. Of who you really are."

"I'm still *me*," I say softly. "The same person you—"

"You're not, though." She cuts me off, finally meeting my eyes. "The Jack I knew didn't have a mansion with staff. Didn't own a vineyard empire. Didn't order $300 bottles of wine without blinking." Her voice remains steady, but I can see the hurt churning beneath her composed exterior. "The Jack I knew didn't lie to me for months."

"I didn't lie—"

"*Don't.*" The word cracks like a whip. "Don't you dare say you never lied. Omission is still deception, and you know it. You deliberately created a false impression. You watched me stress about money, about Madison's college fund, about yard service..." She laughs, a hollow sound that cuts me to the bone. "God, I was worried about affording yard service, and you own half a mountain."

"I wanted you to know me," I try. "Not my family's money."

"But the money is part of you, Jack. It shaped who you are. Your education, your opportunities, your choices." She crosses her arms tightly across her chest. "And you kept it from me. Why? Did you think I was so shallow I'd only want you for your money? Or so weak I couldn't handle your real life?"

"Neither," I say desperately. "I just...I wanted to be seen for who I really am, not what I come from."

"And instead you became a lie." Her eyes glisten with unshed tears. "Do you have any idea what it's like to stand in that house, with your mother looking at me like I'm some kind of curiosity, realizing that everything I thought I knew about you was carefully curated? Do you know what that does to a person? To their trust?"

I swallow hard. "I'm sorry. I should have told you. I wanted to, so many times, but—"

"But what? What possible excuse could justify bringing me and my daughter to the literal other side of the world before revealing the truth?" Her voice finally cracks, emotion bleeding through her careful control.

"There is no excuse," I admit. "I was a coward. I kept waiting for the right moment, and it never came, and then it was too late."

"It was too late the moment you decided I wasn't worthy of the truth." The first tear slips down her cheek, but she doesn't wipe it away. "Do you know what hurts the most? It's not the money. It's not even the lies. It's that you didn't trust me with who you really are."

"I trust you completely," I insist.

"No." She shakes her head slowly. "You don't. Because trust requires honesty, Jack. It requires vulnerability. You were so afraid I'd see your wealth instead of you that you never gave me the chance to prove I could see both."

Each word lands like a physical blow, because she is right. About all of it.

"I've spent years rebuilding myself after Troy," she continues, her voice dropping to near a whisper. "Learning to trust my judgment again. Believing that I deserved better than what he gave me."

She pauses, the silence heavy between us. When she speaks again, her voice has changed, becoming both stronger and more vulnerable.

"Troy used to tell me that women were 'built for sex and silence.' That the only time I had real value was when I was on my knees or on my back." Her eyes lock with mine, unflinching despite the tears now flowing freely. "And for years, I let him convince me that was normal. That being wanted meant being used."

A sickness rises in my throat. I'd known Troy was toxic, but this...

"And then you showed up," she continues. "You made me feel like I was more. Like I was worth something." Her voice breaks on the word. "You didn't just lie, Jack. You made me feel safe again. And that was worse."

The full weight of what I'd done crashes down on me with devastating clarity. I'd known about Troy's financial manipulation, his condescension, his control. But I hadn't known about this deeper degradation. And in my fear of rejection, I'd reinforced the lesson her ex had taught her—that she couldn't trust her own judgment. That the men she chose would inevitably betray her.

"Sophia," I whisper, my own tears falling now. "I never meant—"

"I know you didn't mean to hurt me," she says, wiping her cheeks with the back of her hand. "That's what makes it so painful. You did this with good intentions. You convinced yourself you were protecting me, protecting us. Just like Troy convinced himself his control was 'for my own good.'"

"I am nothing like him," I say, the words strangled with emotion.

"No, you're not," she agrees. "But the effect is the same. I trusted you. I opened myself to you. I let you into my life, into Madison's life. And now I'm standing here questioning every moment we shared, wondering what was real and what was carefully edited."

She moves toward the door, then pauses, not looking back at me. "Madison and I will stay until our return flight next week. I won't punish her by cutting this trip short. She's already excited about coming here, and Emma's rugby lessons, and I won't take that away from her."

"I understand," I manage.

"We'll stay in the guest house. You can stay... wherever you actually live here. But I need space, Jack. A lot of it."

"Of course! Of course. Whatever you need."

She nods once, still facing away. "You know what the worst part is? Despite everything, there's a part of me that still..." She takes a deep breath. "A part of me that wishes I could just forget all this and go back to how things were. How pathetic is that?"

Before I can respond, she steps through the doorway, pausing one last time. "Goodnight, *Jackson*."

The emphasis on my full name—a name she'd never used before—is the final twist of the knife. She disappears down the hallway, her footsteps fading until only silence remains.

I sink onto a nearby bench, the full weight of what I'd lost crushing the air from my lungs. The tears I'd managed to control in front of Sophia now come in earnest, my body shaking with silent sobs.

Not just for the relationship I'd destroyed with my cowardice, but for what Sophia had endured before me. For the woman who'd survived Troy's degradation only to have her hard-won trust shattered by my deception. For the chance I'd destroyed to be the man she deserved.

I dunno know how long I sat there, broken open in the entrance hall of my family home. Long enough that the tears eventually subside, leaving behind a hollow clarity. I have done this. No excuses, no justifications. Just my own fear and insecurity.

And somehow... if she'd allow it... I have to find a way to make it right.

Not to win her back. I've no right to expect that. But to show her that her judgment hadn't failed her. That the man she'd fallen for is real, even if his circumstances aren't what she'd believed.

I owe her that much. Even if it is the last thing I ever give her.

chapter
thirty-five

"GOODNIGHT, *JACKSON*."

The words hang in the air as I turn and walk away, not allowing myself to look back. I can feel his pain radiating behind me like a physical force, and a part of me... a small, vindictive part I'm not proud of... savors it. He *deserves* to hurt, at least a fraction of how much I'm hurting.

The cruelty of deliberately using his full name—that formal, unfamiliar name that represents the stranger he really was—has been calculated. I'd wanted to wound him, to pierce that smooth composure, to make him feel the rupture between us. Based on the stricken look that had flashed across his face, I'd succeeded.

I'm not proud of the impulse, but I can't deny the momentary, hollow satisfaction it had brought.

The walk back to the guest house seems endless. The night air is cool on my flushed cheeks, the sprawling estate grounds stretching before me in the darkness. So much space, so much land, so much everything. And he'd hidden it all from me, watching me struggle with bills and budget worries without saying a word.

When I finally reach the guest house, Madison is sprawled on the sofa, her phone in hand, texting rapidly.

"There you are!" she exclaims, looking up. "I was about to text you. I'm *staaaaarving*. Do you think they have, like, room service or something? Or should we go to the main house for dinner?"

The thought of facing Jack and his family over a formal dinner makes my stomach clench. "Let's see what we can find here first," I suggest, relieved to discover a fully stocked kitchen with enough provisions to feed us for a week.

"Whoa," Madison says, opening the refrigerator. "Look at all this cheese! And what's this?" She pulls out a package wrapped in butcher paper.

"Manuka ham," I read from the label. "It's a local specialty. Honey-cured, I think."

"No turkey?" Madison asks, rummaging further.

"I don't think they really do deli turkey here," I explain, finding a loaf of fresh-baked bread that looks like it had been delivered that day. "How about sandwiches? This bread looks amazing."

Madison helps me prepare a simple meal, slicing bread and arranging a platter with several kinds of cheese, the ham, and crisp apples. When I take my first bite of a sharp, aged cheddar, I involuntarily close my eyes.

"Oh my *God*," I murmur. "This is incredible."

"Right?" Madison is already assembling her second sandwich. "Everything here is, like, next-level fancy. Even the butter tastes better."

We eat in comfortable silence for a few minutes, the simple pleasure of good food providing a brief respite from the emotional turmoil.

"So," Madison finally says, wiping crumbs from her mouth, "did you talk to Jack?"

The question punctures the momentary peace. "Yes."

"And?" She watches me expectantly.

"And I told him I need time to think," I say, my tone making it clear I don't want to elaborate.

She studies me with that unnervingly perceptive teenage gaze. "Are you still mad?"

"It's complicated, Madison."

"You always say that," she sighs. "But I think you should talk to him more, y'know? He seemed really sorry in that text."

I nod, not trusting my voice.

"I'm going to FaceTime Chloe before it gets too late back home," she announces, sensing I'm not ready to discuss it further. "Is that okay?"

"Of course," I say, relieved for the reprieve. "I think I'll take a shower and head to bed early."

Madison hesitates, then gives me a quick, fierce hug. "It'll be okay, Mom. Whatever you decide about Jack... it'll be okay."

The simple assurance from my fifteen-year-old daughter nearly breaks me. "I know, baby. I know. Thank you."

"I love you," she says, squeezing me one more time before heading to her room.

"I love you, too."

The moment Madison's door clicks shut, the composure I'd been maintaining all day shatters. I make it to the bathroom just in time, closing the door behind me before the first sob tears from my throat. I fumble with the shower knobs, turning the water on full blast to mask the sounds of my breakdown.

I sink to the floor, back against the cool tile, and let the grief consume me.

Not just for this betrayal, but for what it represents—another failure of judgment. Another man who had created a careful fiction for me to fall for, hiding the reality of who he was. The shame burns hot and bitter, tears streaming down my face as I hug my knees to my chest.

I think of Troy, of all the signs I'd missed, all the red flags I'd ignored. And now Jack. Beautiful, kind, attentive Jack, who'd brought me coffee and made me laugh and looked at me like I was precious. Who'd been lying to me from the beginning.

The worst part is, I can't even dismiss him as a fraud like Troy. Jack's care for me and Madison had been genuine. The way he'd integrated himself into our lives? That had all been real.

But he'd kept this massive, fundamental truth from me. I'd trusted him with my vulnerabilities—financial, emotional, physical —while he'd carefully hidden his own reality from me. I'd let him in, let him see me, believed he was seeing me in return.

And all along, he'd been editing himself, curating the version he thought I could accept.

Another sob wrenches from my chest, this one deeper, primal. I press my fist against my mouth to muffle the sound, terrified Madison might hear.

When had I become this person? This fragile, broken thing who kept giving her trust to men who didn't deserve it?

The water runs cold, forcing me to finally move. I stand on shaky legs, turning off the shower I'd never actually stepped into. The mirror shows a stranger: eyes swollen, nose red, skin blotchy with grief. I splash cold water on my face, the shock helping to center me.

Madison is right down the hall. We're in a foreign country, thousands of miles from home. I can't afford to fall apart completely, no matter how much I want to. I *have* to keep it together, at least enough to get through the rest of this trip. For her sake, if not my own.

I change into pajamas and crawl under the luxury sheets of this guest house that was more opulent than any accommodation I've ever stayed in. The pillowcase absorbs the silent tears that continue to fall as exhaustion finally claims me.

Tomorrow'll bring more confrontations, more decisions. Tonight, I allow myself the mercy of sleep.

chapter
thirty-six

THE MCKENZIE ESTATE vineyard stretches before me, rows of carefully tended vines heavy with fruit ready for harvest. Normally, the sight would bring a sense of pride, of connection to this land that had sustained my family for generations. Today, it just reminds me of what I'd hidden from Sophia.

I'd been working since dawn, throwing myself into physical labor to escape my thoughts. My shoulders ache from pruning, my hands raw despite the gloves. The pain is welcome. It gives me something to focus on besides the memory of Sophia's face.

"You look like shit, little brother." Charlotte appears beside me, handing over a water bottle. "Though I can't say you don't deserve it."

I take the water without responding. What is there to say? She is right.

"She took Madison to see the west vineyard with Lily," Charlotte continues, watching my reaction carefully. "Avoiding you quite effectively."

"Good," I say, meaning it. "She needs space. I'm giving it to her."

"Noble." Charlotte's tone makes it clear what she thinks of that. "And your plan beyond hiding among the vines is...?"

"There is no plan," I admit. "I just...I need to respect what she asked for."

My phone vibrates in my pocket. I pull it out, heart racing stupidly at the thought it might be Sophia, then deflating when I saw Nate Crawford's name instead.

> Jack, mate. Nate Crawford here. Hope the trip's going well. Heard from Maria things might be a bit quiet on Sophia's end. Just checking in, make sure you're all showing her a good Kiwi welcome.

Christ. Even Sophia's colleagues back home have noticed something was wrong. The ripples of my deception spread further than I'd imagined.

"Bad news?" Charlotte asks, noting my expression.

"Just...reality." I type back a carefully vague response:

> Bit of a hiccup, mate. Working through it. She's seeing the sights. Thanks for checking.

"Sophia's friend from the hospital," I explain, pocketing the phone. "They've noticed something's off."

"Of course they have," Charlotte says. "That's what happens when you mess with someone people care about."

The reminder that Sophia has a support system, people who will notice if she isn't okay, hits harder than I expected. She isn't alone. If I can't fix this, she'll still have people looking out for her. The thought is simultaneously comforting and devastating.

"I really fucked this up, didn't I?" The question is rhetorical.

Charlotte's expression softens slightly. "Yes, you did. But fucking up is part of being human. The question is what you do next."

"I don't know what to do next," I admit. "I've never...I've never felt this way about anyone before. And I've never screwed up this badly, either."

"Start by being honest," Charlotte says. "Completely honest. No more curated versions of yourself. The real Jack—with all the privilege and the baggage and the family complications." She squeezes my shoulder. "If she can't love that version, then it was never going to work anyway."

I nod, watching a hawk circle over the distant hills. "I know."

"Dinner's at seven," Charlotte says, turning to leave. "Don't be late. And shower first, because you *stink*."

I manage a weak laugh. As she walks away, my phone buzzes again—another message from Nate.

> Hiccups happen. She's a tough one, our Sophia. You need anything, say the word. I've known her for years if you need advice.

The simple offer of support from a man who clearly cares about Sophia hits me hard. These are her people. The family she's built for herself at Metro General. If I want to be part of that, I need to be worthy of it.

Before I can talk myself out of it, I type:

> Actually, mate, if you've got a minute, I could really use some insight. I lied to her about something really big. If you've seen her get really angry, what worked to get back in her good graces?

The moment I hit send, I regret it. What the hell am I thinking, dumping my relationship crisis on a colleague halfway across the world?

The minutes stretch as I wait for a response, each passing second confirming I've crossed a line. Then, finally:

> What exactly did you lie about?

I stare at the question, at a loss for how to explain the magnitude of my deception without sounding like a complete asshole. How can I condense generations of family wealth, my deliberate concealment, and Sophia's justified sense of betrayal into a text message?

I finally type:

> Can't go into details. Just know it wasn't anything harmful, but it was fundamental. An omission that changed how she sees me.

Even that feels inadequate. I add:

> On a scale of 1-10, how fucked am I?

His response is immediate and brutally honest:

> 11. But not necessarily permanently fucked.

I bark out a laugh despite myself. Leave it to an ER nurse to deliver the unvarnished truth.

His follow-up hits even harder:

> Look, I'm the last guy who should give relationship advice. But I know Sophia. She doesn't do games. If you fucked up so bad it doesn't fit in a text, you better just own it and then pray as hard as you can to whatever deity will listen.

The straightforward assessment is like a splash of cold water. No platitudes, no false reassurance. Just the truth I need to hear.

> Thanks, mate. That actually helps. I can do that. I owe you.

I set the phone down, Nate's words reverberating in my head. *She doesn't do games. You better just own it.*

Wasn't that what Charlotte had just been saying, albeit less bluntly? Own it. Take responsibility. No excuses.

I look down at my dirt-streaked hands, calloused from the vineyard work my family had done for generations. No more hiding either part of myself; not the paramedic who worked with his hands, not the heir who benefited from privilege. *Both* are real. *Both* are me.

Now I just need Sophia to give me a chance to show her all of it.

I trudge back toward the main house, muscles aching from the physical labor. In my cottage, I shower away the sweat and grime, watching the dirt swirl down the drain and wishing my mistakes could be as easily washed away.

Clean and dressed in fresh clothes, I sit at my small desk and pull out a sheet of paper. If I can't speak to Sophia yet, I can at least prepare. Write down everything I need to say. Leave nothing unexamined.

Dear Sophia, I begin, then immediately cross it out. No letters. No distance. This has to be direct, raw, real.

Instead, I simply write: *What I hid and why. No excuses.*

And below it, I begin listing every instance, every moment where I'd deliberately concealed the truth about my background. Every opportunity I'd had to come clean but chose deception instead. Every rationalization I'd told myself to justify my cowardice.

By the time I've filled three pages, my hand is cramping and my eyes are burning. But I keep going, determined to unearth every buried truth, every hidden fear. If I am going to have any chance with Sophia, I need to understand myself first.

Pages later, exhausted and emotionally drained, I finally see the pattern. It isn't just fear of being valued for my money. It is deeper, a fundamental belief that I just am not enough on my own. That without the McKenzie name and fortune, I'm not worthy of someone like Sophia.

The realization hits me like a physical blow. I've projected my own insecurities onto her, assuming she would judge me the way I judge myself.

Nate was right. I am fucked. But maybe not permanently.

I folded the pages and tuck them away. Not as a script to follow, but as a reminder of the work I'd done today. The clarity I've found.

Tonight at dinner will be the first time I'll see Sophia since she'd walked away with that devastating "Goodnight, *Jackson*." I have no idea if she will even be willing to talk to me, let alone forgive me. But I will be there, respecting her space while making it clear I am not giving up.

And then, as Nate had suggested, I will pray harder than I ever have before.

Because a life without Sophia isn't a life I want to contemplate.

chapter
thirty-seven

"CAN we *please* go see the kiwi birds?" Madison pleads for the third time since dinner. "Emma says they come out at dusk, and Jack's sister Lily can take us to the sanctuary right now."

I set down my tea, carefully avoiding eye contact with Jack across the dining room. The meal has been excruciating—Helen's pointed glances, Michael's sympathetic ones, the sisters' attempts at normal conversation that only highlight the tension.

"Madison, I'm not sure tonight is—"

"Please, Mom?" Her enthusiasm is the only bright spot in this mess. "It's not like we can see kiwi birds back home. Jack says they're super rare, even in New Zealand."

At the mention of his name, I finally risk a glance at Jack. He has been quiet throughout dinner, speaking only when addressed directly. Now he looks up, his expression carefully neutral.

"Lily's an excellent guide," he says, his voice lacking its usual warmth. "I can stay behind if that would be more comfortable."

The offer hangs in the air between us. A part of me wants to accept, to avoid the pain of his presence. But Madison's pleading eyes win out.

"We'd appreciate the tour," I say finally, my voice formal. "Madison's been looking forward to it."

Relief flickers across his face. "Of course. I'll let Lily know."

Twenty minutes later, we follow a well-maintained path into a densely wooded gully. The evening air is crisp, autumn leaves crunching beneath our feet. Lily leads the way, pointing out native plants to an enthusiastic Madison. Jack hangs back, maintaining a respectful distance from me.

"The sanctuary covers about fifty acres," Lily explains, her voice carrying in the quiet evening. "Most of it's off-limits to visitors to protect the birds, but we have observation hides where we can watch without disturbing them."

"Fifty acres just for birds?" Madison sounds impressed. "That's huge!"

"It's a special place," Lily agrees. "We've had a breeding program here for nearly fifteen years now."

I watch Jack's profile in the fading light, the tension in his shoulders, the careful way he keeps his focus on Madison rather than me. Despite everything, there is something undeniably attractive about his passion for conservation, his gentle way of explaining things to my daughter.

The path opens into a small clearing with an educational display. The modern structure seems at odds with the wild setting, until I realize it was designed to blend into the environment, the wood weathered to match the surrounding trees.

"This is where we start the tours," Lily explains. "Though we don't get many visitors—just conservation groups and researchers, mostly."

Jack steps forward, gesturing Madison toward a display of footprints pressed into clay. "Kiwis have three toes instead of four like most birds," he explains. "It helps identify their tracks in the wild."

Madison kneels to examine the display, her excitement palpable. "They have massive feet for their size."

"They spend most of their time rooting around in the soil for worms and insects," Jack says, his voice softening with genuine enthusiasm. "They're the only birds with nostrils at the end of their beaks."

I hang back, watching the interaction. Jack's attention is entirely on Madison, responding to her questions with patience and detail, adjusting his explanations based on her reactions. It is so different from Troy, who'd barely listen when Madison spoke, his attention always divided between her and his phone, his responses generic when they came at all.

We continue along the path, the light dimming further. Lily hands us each a small red flashlight. "Regular light disturbs them, but they don't see red light as well."

The path eventually leads to a wooden structure built half underground, with viewing slots at ground level. We enter quietly, taking seats on benches facing the windows.

"This is the main observation hide," Jack whispers, his voice barely audible. "If we're quiet, they'll come right up to the edge of the clearing."

Madison can barely contain herself, bouncing slightly on the bench. "How many are there?"

"About five breeding pairs in the sanctuary now," Lily answers. "We've released twice that number into the wild over the years, mostly on the west coast of the South Island here."

Jack leans toward Madison. "What do you think is the number one predator of kiwis?"

Madison considers for a moment. "Hawks? Foxes?"

"No, actually, it's dogs," Jack says, surprising me. "Kiwis have no sternum—that's the breastbone that most birds have—and dogs love to smell. Kiwis have a very distinctive smell."

He grimaces slightly. "When I was at the National Hatchery in Rotorua, sometimes you'd almost wish for a big burp of sulfur from the geothermal vents because it honestly smelled better than the kiwis sometimes."

Madison giggles, and even I feel a smile tugging at my lips despite myself.

"So the dogs poke at them with their noses and kill them without even meaning to," Jack continues. "They're incredibly vulnerable."

As if on cue, a small, round shape emerges from the underbrush outside the hide. Even in the dim red light, I can make out the distinctive long beak and fuzzy, rounded body.

"There's one," Lily whispers.

Madison gasps. "They're fast! And so much bigger than I thought! It's like a fuzzy football with a stick."

Jack chuckles softly. "They're about the size of a domestic chicken, but rounder. The females are larger than the males—sometimes by almost a third."

We watch in silence as the kiwi probes the ground with its long beak, completely unaware of our presence. After a few minutes, it is joined by another, slightly smaller bird.

"A mating pair," Lily whispers. "They're monogamous, often staying together for their entire lives."

Jack nods. "We have to collect their eggs because they're not the best at taking care of them," he explains to Madison. "And when we do, they think a predator got them, but they're too lazy to build a new nest, so they just move on to one of their old nests and rotate through them."

"That doesn't sound very smart," Madison whispers back.

"They're surprisingly daft for a national icon," Jack agrees. "But extremely endangered, so we help them along."

I watch Jack's profile in the dim red light, the way he leans in to whisper explanations to Madison, pointed out behaviors, answered her questions with genuine interest. There is no performance here, no attempt to impress. Just the same authentic enthusiasm I'd seen when he'd taught her to make pasta in my kitchen.

"Jack was sixteen when he found that injured chick," Lily says quietly, glancing my way. "Convinced Dad to set aside this entire gully."

Another reminder of what wealth could accomplish. What ordinary person could convince their father to reserve fifty acres as a teenager? Who had that kind of power, that kind of privilege?

"I was a stubborn kid," Jack says, looking embarrassed.

"He spent that whole summer volunteering at the Rotorua breeding center," Lily continues, "learning everything about kiwi care. Even talked about becoming a conservationist before..."

She trails off, perhaps realizing she was venturing into territory that highlighted the deception.

"We occasionally have University of Canterbury students intern here," Jack says, smoothly changing the subject. "The estate helps pay for their accommodation and stipends."

Another casual mention of resources beyond my comprehension. I focus on the birds instead, trying to quiet the turmoil in my chest.

A smaller kiwi approaches unusually close to the viewing window, pecking curiously at the ground just feet away.

"That's Manawa," Jack says softly. "She was the first chick born in the sanctuary. She's unusually comfortable around the hides."

Without thinking, I speak directly to him for the first time since our confrontation. "What does the name mean?"

Jack looks startled, as if he hadn't expected me to engage. "Heart or spirit in Māori," he answers, his eyes meeting mine. "She was stubborn, always fighting. Smallest of her clutch, but the strongest."

Something passes between us in that moment—a flicker of the connection we'd shared before. I look away quickly, uncomfortable with how easily it had surfaced despite everything.

We watch the kiwis for another twenty minutes, Jack pointing out behaviors to Madison, who absorbs every word. As they interact, I find myself studying Jack more than the birds—the gentleness in his hands as he directed Madison's attention, the patience in his explanations, the way he gauged her interest and adjusted accordingly.

The man I see before me was the same one who'd brought me coffee in the ER, who'd taught Madison to make pasta, who'd looked at me like I hung the moon. The context has changed dramatically, but his essential nature hasn't.

That realization unsettles me more than anything else.

As we leave the hide and head back up the path, Madison chatters excitedly to Lily about everything she'd learned. Jack hangs back, keeping pace with me but maintaining a careful distance.

"Thanks for doing this," he says quietly, his voice barely audible above the crunch of leaves. "She seems to be enjoying herself."

"She is," I acknowledge. "She's been talking about seeing kiwis since before we left home."

An awkward silence falls between us. I sense he wants to say more but is restraining himself. A part of me appreciates his restraint—I'm not ready for another conversation—but another part aches at the wall between us.

Ahead of us, Lily is inviting Madison to help with the morning feeding. "If your mom's okay with it?" she adds, glancing back at me.

"Can I, Mom? Please?" Madison's enthusiasm is impossible to resist.

"If it's not an imposition," I say cautiously.

"Not at all," Lily assures me. "We'd love the help."

As we emerge from the woods back onto the estate grounds, the main house looms before us, its windows warm with light against the darkening sky. The casual opulence of it all strikes me again: the manicured gardens, the vineyard stretching into the distance, the mountains framing it all like a perfect backdrop.

This is Jack's world. The world he'd hidden from me. The world that had shaped him into the man I thought I knew.

Madison falls into step beside me as we approach the guest house. "That was amazing," she says, her eyes bright with excitement. "Did you see how close they came? And Jack knows so much about them."

"He does," I agree.

"He's different here," she observes, with that perceptive insight that sometimes catches me off guard. "But also the same, you know? Like, he still explains things the same way he did at home."

Home. The word sparks an ache in my chest. Home feels very far away right now, not just in distance but in time. The life we'd built there—the routines, the comfortable patterns, the growing relationship with Jack—seems to belong to another version of reality.

"Yes," I say finally. "He does."

Madison studies my face in the dim light. "Are you guys going to be okay?"

The simple question holds such weight. "I don't know, sweetheart." It is the most honest answer I could give. "It's complicated."

"Because he didn't tell you about all this?" She gestures vaguely at the estate around us.

"Partly."

"But it's still him," she insists. "Just with... more stuff."

And for one treacherous moment, I almost let myself think that way. *Just let it go, Sophia. He's kind. He adores your daughter.* Most women would look at this estate, at this life, and decide the lie didn't matter. That the destination justified the deception.

But I've *been* that woman. I spent years telling myself Troy's lies were just quirks, that the gaps between what he said and what he did were just misunderstandings. I swallowed *every* red flag because the alternative—admitting I'd been fooled—was too terrifying.

And Jack waited. He had *months* to tell me. Months of coffee and radio flirtations and slow, careful trust-building. And he let the truth reveal itself after I was already here, thirteen *thousand* miles from home, dependent on his family's hospitality, too deep in to walk away cleanly.

Maybe that wasn't calculated. No. It probably wasn't. But it doesn't have to be calculated to be a problem.

"There's a difference between having things and hiding things," I try to explain. "It's not about the money, Madison. It's about trust."

She nods slowly. "I guess that makes sense." After a moment, she adds, "But I still like him. Even if he should have told us."

"I'm glad." And I *am*. Whatever happens between Jack and me, I am grateful Madison hadn't been deeply hurt by his deception.

As we reach the guest house, I turn for one last look at the main estate. Jack stands on the path to his cottage, watching us from a distance. When he sees me looking, he raises a hand in the briefest of waves before turning away.

Inside, as Madison gets ready for bed, I find myself thinking about kiwis. Stubborn, improbable birds that couldn't fly but had somehow survived millions of years. Birds that moved between nests rather than building new ones when threatened.

There's a metaphor in there somewhere, but I'm too exhausted to untangle it.

chapter
thirty-eight

"MILFORD SOUND," Emma announces at breakfast, sliding a brochure across the table toward Madison. "One of the most spectacular fjords in the world. Jack's arranged a scenic flight and cruise for today."

My head snaps up. Jack hadn't mentioned this to me. He hadn't been at breakfast, his absence a heavy presence in itself.

Madison grabs the brochure eagerly. "Oh my God, Mom, look at these waterfalls! Can we go? Please?"

Emma glances my way, her expression carefully casual but her eyes watchful. "Jack thought you might appreciate seeing it before you leave. It's about a five-hour drive each way, but the flight's only forty-five minutes. Much less...confined."

I understand the subtext. Jack is adapting the original plan to respect my need for space. A short flight rather than ten hours in a car together.

"I'm going," Madison declares before I can respond. "Emma's coming too." She looks at me hopefully. "You'll come, right, Mom? It's supposed to be, like, the most beautiful place in New Zealand."

Part of me wants to refuse, to maintain the distance I'd established. But I'd come all this way. Missing Milford Sound because of personal turmoil seems stupid, especially when Jack is clearly making an effort to be considerate.

"Of course I'll come," I say, forcing a smile. "When do we leave?"

"The flight's at ten," Emma replies. "Jack will meet us at the airstrip in Queenstown."

As promised, Jack is waiting beside the small aircraft when we arrive at the Queenstown Airport. He looks tired, shadows under his eyes suggesting he'd slept as poorly as I had. He greets Madison warmly but maintains a respectful distance from me.

"It's an eight-passenger plane," he explains, gesturing to the sleek white aircraft. "But there are only six of us today, including the pilot."

Madison bounces excitedly. "I call window seat!"

"All the seats are window seats," Jack says with a ghost of his usual smile. "It's that kind of plane."

As we board, I notice how compact the cabin is, with barely enough room to crouch, seats arranged in pairs. I slide into one beside Madison, while Jack and Emma take seats further back.

The pilot, a weathered man with a salt-and-pepper beard and a thick Australian accent, turns to address us. "G'day, folks. Flight time to Milford is about forty-five minutes. It's a beautiful day for flying, but we'll have some turbulence over the mountains, and the approach into Milford is...well, let's call it 'sporty.'"

"Sporty?" Madison asks.

"It's one of the most challenging landings in commercial aviation," Jack explains from behind us. "The airstrip is surrounded by mountains on all sides. We essentially have to drop in."

My stomach tightens at the thought.

"Don't worry," Emma says, noticing my expression. "Harry here has done this run thousands of times. Isn't that right, Harry?"

"That's right! Three thousand, four hundred and sixteen," the pilot confirms cheerfully. "Haven't crashed one yet."

Madison giggles nervously. I grip the armrests as the engines roar to life, the small plane vibrating around us.

We climb steeply after takeoff, the earth falling away beneath us. Queenstown's layout becomes clear—the town nestled between lake and mountains, roads winding like ribbons through valleys. Despite my anxiety, I have to admit the view *was* spectacular.

As we approach the mountain range, the plane begins to buck and dip in air currents. Madison grabs my hand, her earlier excitement tempered by nervousness.

"It's okay," I assure her, though my own knuckles are white on the armrest. "This is normal."

The mountains rise to meet us, jagged peaks seeming impossibly close to the wingtips. The pilot banks sharply left, following a narrow valley between towering walls of rock. My stomach drops with each air pocket and turn.

"Our father, who art in heaven..." I mutter under my breath as the plane dips particularly violently.

I hear a quiet chuckle from behind me—Jack, recognizing my prayer. Our eyes meet briefly before I turn back to the window, unsettled by how easily we slip into old patterns of shared humor despite everything.

The mountains give way to even more mountains, peak after peak of snow-capped majesty stretching to the horizon. Madison had recovered her excitement, taking photos with her phone and exclaiming at each new vista.

"Look, Mom! Waterfalls!"

Indeed, thin ribbons of white cascade down sheer cliffs, some seeming to fall directly from the clouds.

"That's just the beginning," Jack says. "Wait until you see them up close on the cruise."

The approach to Milford is every bit as "sporty" as promised. The plane descends rapidly between mountain walls that seem impossibly close, the runway appearing at the last possible moment.

My breath catches as we drop the final few hundred feet, touching down with a bump that had several passengers—myself included—uttering involuntary gasps.

"Ladies and gentlemen, welcome to Milford Sound," the pilot announces cheerfully. "Local time is 10:47 AM, and the weather is, well, perfect."

Madison is out of her seat the moment we stop, pressing against the window. "The mountains go straight into the water!"

As we disembark onto the small airstrip, I'm totally struck by the scale of the landscape. Towering peaks rise directly from the dark water, their reflections making perfect mirrors. The air is cool and impossibly clear, carrying the scent of rain and vegetation.

A small bus transfers us from the airstrip to the harbor, where a sleek tour boat awaits. As we board, I notice Jack hanging back, letting Madison and Emma go ahead.

"Thank you," I say quietly as we wait our turn. "For arranging this. It was thoughtful to choose the flight instead of driving."

He looks surprised by the acknowledgment. "I thought it would be...easier. For everyone."

"It was the right call," I say simply.

We find seats on the upper deck, Madison and Emma at the rail for the best view, Jack and I in chairs behind them. A buffer of strangers separates us, which feels both a relief and oddly disappointing.

As the boat pulls away from the dock, the true scale of Milford Sound becomes apparent. Waterfalls thunder from cliffs thousands of feet high, creating rainbows in the mist where sunlight breaks through.

Unlike the fjords of Norway or Alaska, Milford's walls are carpeted with lush rainforest that clings impossibly to near-vertical rock faces. The water is so still it creates perfect mirror images of the mountains, making it difficult to tell where reality ends and reflection begins.

A tour guide begins pointing out features through a microphone. "Milford Sound is actually a fjord, carved by glaciers during the ice age. It's nearly 15 kilometers long and surrounded by peaks rising over 1,200 meters from the water..."

I try to focus on his words, on the spectacular scenery unfolding around us, but my awareness of Jack just meters away keeps intruding. The familiarity of him—the way he leans forward when something interests him, the slight tilt of his head as he listens—makes my chest ache with a confusion of feelings I wasn't ready to examine just yet.

"Look, Mom!" Madison calls, pointing to a rocky outcrop where fur seals lounge. "They're so cute!" I join her at the rail, grateful for the distraction. The boat glides deeper into the fjord, dwarfed by the sheer rock walls rising on either side.

"Ladies and gentlemen," the tour guide announces, "we'll be serving complimentary tea and coffee in the main cabin. I must apologize to our international visitors... it's American-style coffee, I'm afraid."

A collective "*awwww*" of disappointment rises from the predominantly Kiwi and Australian passengers.

I can't help but laugh. After everything I'd experienced in New Zealand, this cultural quirk finally makes perfect sense. Jack's eyes meet mine across the deck, a tentative smile pulling at his lips. I look away quickly, unsettled by how easily he could still reach me.

As Madison and Emma go below to get drinks, I notice a heavily pregnant woman sitting alone near the bow. She shifts uncomfortably, one hand pressed to her lower back, the other resting on her prominent belly. Something about her posture, the tension in her shoulders, the way she keeps checking her watch...triggers my ER nurse instincts.

I wasn't the only one who'd noticed. Jack had also spotted her, his eyes narrowing in professional assessment. Our gazes meet briefly, a moment of shared concern that transcends our personal situation.

"Third trimester," I murmur as he approaches. "Looks uncomfortable."

"Thirty-six, thirty-seven weeks at least," he agrees quietly. "Pretty remote place to be that far along."

The moment feels strangely intimate—this shared professional language, the shorthand of two people used to assessing medical situations together. For a fleeting second, we're just Sophia and Jack again, charge nurse and paramedic, partners in the work we both loved.

"I'm sure it's fine," I say, more to break the moment than from conviction. "Probably just backache from the ride here."

Emma rejoins us, Madison following with a hot chocolate. "What are you two looking so serious about?"

"Nothing important," I lie, accepting the tea she offered.

The boat continues its journey into the fjord, eventually turning around in the Tasman Sea before making its way back toward the harbor. As we round a dramatic cliff face, a pod of small dolphins suddenly appears alongside the boat, their distinctive rounded dorsal fins cutting through the dark water.

"Dusky dolphins!" the guide announces excitedly over the PA system. "A resident pod that calls Milford Sound home. They're one of the smallest dolphin species in the world and unique to New Zealand waters."

The sleek creatures race alongside us, jumping playfully in our wake, creating perfect arcs against the backdrop of towering cliffs. Passengers rush to the railings, cameras raised, as the dolphins perform what seems like choreographed acrobatics.

"They're so fat and cute!" Madison exclaims, nearly spilling her hot chocolate in her excitement. "They look like little torpedoes!"

The views are even more spectacular on the return journey, with the sun now highlighting different features of the landscape and glinting off the occasional dolphin fin as they continue to escort us. It was so beautiful that I had almost forgotten about the pregnant woman when a cry from the lower deck cuts through the guide's commentary.

"Help! Is there a doctor on board?"

Jack and I are moving before the words fully register, instinct overriding everything else. We push through passengers to find the pregnant woman on her hands and knees, face contorted in pain, a puddle of fluid beneath her.

"Her water broke," a panicked friend explains. "The contractions started suddenly, she says they're coming fast!"

I kneel beside the woman, slipping automatically into nurse mode. "I'm Sophia, I'm an ER nurse. What's your name?"

"Hannah," she gasps between quick breaths. "It's too early. It's too early! My due date's three weeks away."

Jack kneels on her other side. "I'm Jack, a paramedic. We're going to help you, Hannah. How far apart are the contractions?"

"Maybe a minute? I don't know, th-th-they came on so fast." Her face contorts as another wave hits. "Oh God, I think I need to push!"

I exchange a look with Jack. This isn't just labor—this is precipitous labor, progressing far too quickly for comfort, especially in our current situation.

"How far are we from the harbor?" Jack asks the wide-eyed crew member hovering nearby.

"Twenty minutes at least," the young man stammers. "We're going as fast as we can."

"We might not have twenty minutes," I say quietly to Jack. "Hannah, we need to check your progress. Is that okay?"

She nods desperately, gripping her friend's hand.

The crew clears the lower cabin, directing other passengers upstairs. Madison pushes forward, ignoring Emma's attempt to guide her away.

"I want to help," she insists, her eyes wide with a mixture of concern and curiosity. "What can I do?"

"Madison, sweetie, this isn't—" I begin, but am cut off by Hannah's sudden cry as another contraction hits.

"Jack, see if they have any medical supplies on board," I direct, falling into our familiar pattern without thinking. "And we need clean towels, blankets, anything you can find."

He nods, immediately moving to action. I turn my attention to Hannah, helping her into a more comfortable position as I assess her situation.

Emma tries again to guide Madison away. "Come on, let's give them space to work."

"But I want to see," Madison protests. "Maybe I could help somehow."

Jack returns moments later with a basic first aid kit and an armful of clean linens. "Not much," he says grimly, "but it's something." He rummages through the kit, examining its contents with a practiced eye.

As I examine Hannah, my worst fears are confirmed. "Baby's crowning," I say quietly to Jack. "This is happening now."

He nods, already arranging the supplies we have. "Hannah," he says calmly, "your baby is coming very quickly. We're going to deliver right here. Everything's going to be fine."

Madison has positioned herself where she can see, despite Emma's protective hand on her shoulder. Her face is a mix of fascination and growing apprehension as she realizes what is about to happen.

"On the next contraction, I need you to push," I instruct Hannah.

The next moments blur into a focused intensity. Hannah pushes with primal determination. Jack supports her while I guide the baby's head, our hands working in perfect coordination despite the months of distance and days of tension.

"I can see the head," I announce. "You're doing so great, Hannah. One more big push."

Madison's face has paled considerably, her earlier curiosity replaced with shock at the reality of childbirth. Emma notices immediately. "Madison, honey, let's step outside—"

"I'm fine, I just—" Madison starts, then suddenly claps a hand over her mouth, her face turning a sickly shade of green.

Emma reacts instantly, pulling Madison away just as she doubles over and retches. "Oooookay, that's our cue to exit," she says firmly, guiding Madison quickly toward the door.

The moment turns critical when I realize the umbilical cord is wrapped around the baby's neck. Without a word, Jack reaches for the meager supplies we had, ready with exactly what I needed before I could ask.

"Cord's around the neck," I say quietly, our heads close together over our patient.

"Can you slip it over?" he asks, his breath warm against my cheek.

"Going to try."

Our hands work together in the tight space, his steadying Hannah while mine carefully maneuvers the cord. For those critical moments, there is no wealth disparity, no betrayal, no hurt. Just two medical professionals working to bring a life safely into the world.

With a final push from Hannah and careful guidance from me, the baby slips free. A boy, small but perfect...but alarmingly silent.

"He's not crying," Hannah says, panic rising in her voice. "Why isn't he crying!?"

Jack is already moving, grabbing what looks like a saline squeeze bottle from the first aid kit. In one smooth motion, he empties the saline, cuts off the narrow tip with a pair of scissors from the kit, and creates a makeshift bulb syringe. The improvisation is quick, efficient—testament to years of emergency field work.

"He needs a little help clearing his airway," Jack explains calmly to Hannah, his tone completely reassuring despite the urgency of the situation. "This happens sometimes with fast deliveries."

I hold the newborn, slightly inclined, while Jack works rapidly, using his improvised suction to clear the baby's mouth and nose. The close quarters force us together, his body pressed against mine as we hunch over the infant. I can feel his heartbeat, rapid with adrenaline, his breath warm against my cheek.

"Come on, little one," he murmurs, his hands gentle but sure.

A moment later, the baby gives a spluttering cough, followed by a lusty, indignant cry.

"There we go," Jack says, relief evident in his voice. "Hello, mate. Welcome to Milford Sound."

Our eyes meet over the crying newborn, a moment of pure connection that transcends our personal conflict. Without words, Jack passes the baby fully to me, our hands brushing intimately in the transfer, fingers lingering a fraction longer than necessary. The touch sends electricity through me that has nothing to do with the adrenaline of the delivery.

For a heartbeat, it is not the baby in my arms that makes me feel overwhelmed—it is Jack's eyes meeting mine, full of something I don't have the strength to name.

I place the baby on Hannah's chest, guiding her to hold him skin-to-skin. "This will help regulate his temperature and breathing," I explain. "He's perfect, Hannah. You did such a good job! He just needed a little help getting started."

Jack is already wrapping clean linens around both mother and child, his movements synchronized with mine as we work to keep them warm. Again, our hands brush several times, each contact a reminder of the connection that still hums between us despite everything.

While I attend to Hannah and the baby, Jack is on his phone, arranging for medical evacuation from the harbor. "Te Whatu Ora is sending a chopper," he reports back. "They'll meet us at the harbor. Ten minutes out."

"Good," I nod, still monitoring Hannah and her newborn. "Baby's APGAR improved after the suction, but I'd feel better with a full pediatric assessment."

Jack kneels beside me again, his presence both comforting and unnerving. "You were amazing," he says softly, for my ears only. "That was... I've delivered babies before, but never with a nuchal cord, and never on a boat..."

"We were lucky," I deflect, though the praise warms me despite myself. "She did all the hard work."

"No," he insists gently. "It was you."

I meet his eyes then, really meet them for the first time since the revelation. The admiration there is genuine—the same look he'd given me in the ER when I'd handled a difficult case with calm efficiency. It wasn't about attraction or even our personal connection, but pure professional respect.

That, at least, hadn't changed.

When we dock, everything moves quickly. The evacuation helicopter is waiting, its rotors still turning. Jack handles the handover to the flight medics with practiced efficiency, providing a concise report of the delivery, the nuchal cord, his improvised suction intervention, and Hannah's current status.

Emma and Madison reappear as they are loading Hannah and the baby into the helicopter. Madison looks pale but composed, her earlier nausea under control...though sporting a conspicuously large wet spot on her shirt.

"Mom! Is she okay? The baby?" she asks, keeping a safe distance from the medical activity.

"They're both fine," I assure her, suddenly aware of how exhausted I feel. The adrenaline is wearing off, leaving me shaky.

"You guys were like...superheroes or something!" Madison says, her eyes wide with residual shock and something like awe. Then her face turns sheepish. "I threw up."

"That's okay. It's not really a front-row sport," Jack says with a tired grin.

"Perfectly normal reaction," Emma assures her. "First time I saw a calf being born on the estate, I passed out cold."

"The way you and Jack just took charge and knew exactly what to do," Madison continues, looking at me with newfound respect. "That was incredible."

Jack approaches, looking as drained as I feel. "The helicopter's taking them to Queenstown Hospital," he reports. "They'll be in good hands there."

"You guys were amazing," Emma echoes Madison's sentiment. "Talk about teamwork. The way Jack rigged up that suction device— I wouldn't have thought of that in a million years."

Jack glances at me, a question in his eyes. "Your mom did the hard part," he says to Madison, deflecting the praise.

"We did it together," I correct, the words coming before I could stop them.

Something shifts in his expression—a cautious hope quickly contained.

"Our flight back to Queenstown leaves in thirty minutes," he says. "Unless you'd rather stay longer?"

"I'm good," I say, suddenly desperate for the familiarity of our temporary home at the estate. "It's been quite a day already."

The drive to the Milford airfield is mostly silent, at least between Jack and me. Emma and Madison chat in the back seat, Emma distracting Madison with stories of the local wildlife and geography, carefully avoiding any mention of the birth we'd just witnessed.

I stare out the window, acutely aware of Jack beside me, my eyes fixed on his hands resting on the armrest of his seat. I'd felt those same hands working alongside mine minutes ago, felt the brush of his fingers as we'd transferred the struggling newborn between us. The memory of that touch—professional but undeniably intimate— lingers on my skin.

On the flight back, Madison sits with Emma, their heads together as Emma explains something about the landscape below. I find myself beside Jack, the small plane not offering many seating options.

"Thank you," he says quietly as we reach cruising altitude. "For letting me help. You could have...I would have understood if you'd pushed me away."

"That would have been unprofessional," I reply. "And stupid, given the circumstances."

"Still." His voice is soft. "It meant something. To work with you again, even briefly."

I don't answer, unsure what to say that wouldn't reveal too much of my conflicted feelings.

After a moment, he adds, "I've missed it. The work. Being a paramedic."

"You're still a paramedic, Jack," I say, surprised by the admission.

"Not here." His gaze drifts to the window. "Here I'm just Jackson McKenzie, heir to the estate. Nobody sees the rest."

The vulnerability in his voice catches me off guard. For the first time, I glimpse what it might be like for him—trapped between worlds, neither fully accepting him for all that he was.

I have no response that wouldn't open doors I'm not ready to walk through, so I remain silent for the rest of the flight.

Back at the guest house, Madison is still processing what she'd witnessed, her initial nausea replaced with thoughtful curiosity as I try to shower away the stress of the day.

"Mom?" she calls through the bathroom door. "Can I ask you something?"

I wrap myself in a towel, opening the door to find her perched anxiously on the edge of the bed. "Of course, sweetheart. What is it?"

"That was..." She hesitates, clearly struggling for words. "I had no idea it was so...intense. And gross. And kind of terrifying."

I sit beside her, water still dripping from my hair. "Childbirth is one of the most primal, powerful things a body can do. It's not always pretty."

"Is it always like that?" she asks, her voice smaller now. "So... scary? Do I have to go through that someday?"

The vulnerability in her question touches me deeply. "It's not always like that," I say carefully. "Hannah's labor was unusually fast. Most first-time mothers have hours of labor before delivery."

"That sounds worse, not better." Madison looks genuinely concerned.

"It's intense," I acknowledge. "But also...miraculous. When I had you, it was the hardest thing I'd ever done, but also the most worthwhile."

"Did it hurt? Like, really bad?"

"Yes," I say honestly. "But they have pain management options, and the moment I held you...nothing else mattered."

Madison absorbs this, her face thoughtful. "I don't think I want kids."

"That's completely fine," I assure her. "It's your choice, always. And you have many, many years to figure it out."

She nods, then changes topics with teenage abruptness. "The way Jack fixed it when the baby wasn't breathing...that was amazing. He just, like, made a thing out of nothing."

"That's what paramedics do," I say. "Especially good ones. They improvise with whatever they have."

"You guys worked together like you were reading each other's minds," she continues, studying my face. "Even when you're mad at him, you still...fit together. Like puzzle pieces."

I sigh, not ready for this particular conversation. "That's different, Madison. Professional compatibility isn't the same as personal trust."

"I know, but..." She hesitates. "You still care about him. I can tell."

"It's complicated," I say, falling back on the phrase I'd been using for days.

"Adults always say that when they don't want to talk about their feelings," she observes with surprising insight.

I can't help but laugh. "You're too good at this."

"TikTok," she replies with perfect seriousness. "Lots of relationship advice there."

"Ahhh. I should have known. The modern oracle strikes again."

Madison's expression turns serious again. "I think he deserves another chance, Mom. After seeing him today...the way he knew exactly what to do, how he didn't panic...and the way he looks at you..."

The simple statement hangs between us. I busy myself with drying my hair, avoiding her gaze.

"He lied, Madison. For months."

"I know." She kicks her feet against the bed frame. "But he also saved that baby with you today. And he cares about stupid birds that can't even fly. And he makes you laugh."

I look at her then, this remarkable person I'd raised, with her uncanny ability to cut through complexities to the heart of things.

"And," she adds quietly, "you still love him. Don't you?"

I couldn't bring myself to answer, but my silence was apparently answer enough.

"That's what I thought," Madison says, sliding off the bed. "I'm going to FaceTime Chloe before dinner, okay?"

"Go ahead," I say, grateful for the reprieve.

"I love you, Mom," Madison says, bounding back towards her room.

"I love you, too, baby," I call after her.

Alone, I stare at my reflection in the mirror. The day's events have shaken something loose inside me. Watching Jack work, his hands steady and capable, his focus absolute. The way we'd moved together without words, anticipating each other's needs in the crisis. The feeling of his fingers brushing mine as we'd transferred the struggling newborn between us.

That connection is real. It's always been real. The question is whether it is enough to rebuild what has been broken.

I'm not ready to answer that question. Not yet.

But for the first time since the revelation, I allow myself to acknowledge the possibility that Jack—the real Jack, beneath the deception—might be worth fighting for.

chapter
thirty-nine

"UGH, Dad's being so weird on Instagram again," Madison mutters from the sofa, scrolling through her phone. We've been back from Milford Sound for a few hours, and I've been pretending to read the same page of my book for the past twenty minutes, my mind still replaying the day's events.

"What's he done now?" I ask, grateful for the distraction from my thoughts about Jack.

"Just posting about his 'entrepreneurial journey' or whatever. The usual crypto stuff." Madison continues scrolling, her expression growing increasingly disgusted. "#financialfreedom #alphamindset... so cringe."

I make a noncommittal noise and pretend to return to my book. Troy's social media presence has grown increasingly bizarre since our divorce, but I stopped following him years ago. The only updates I get are Madison's occasional reports or his insufferable texts about her "nutrition plan."

"Oh my God," Madison suddenly sits bolt upright. "Mom! Look at this!"

"What?" I look up, alarmed by her tone.

She turns her phone toward me, a TikTok video already playing.

It's some kind of viral supercut where multiple creators have taken clips of Troy wearing a serious expression in a black t-shirt, talking dramatically about being "canceled by the woke mob." Each creator has added their own mocking commentary, effects, or reaction shots, transforming Troy's self-important monologue into something ridiculous.

"This is so embarrassing," Madison groans, her face flushing. "He's gone viral in the worst way possible."

I watch in horrified fascination as Troy's face contorts dramatically on screen, his voice overlaid with cartoonish sound effects while text captions mock his expressions. The original video shows him complaining about "censorship" and how "certain powerful interests" don't want men to speak the truth about "biological realities," but it's now buried under layers and layers of internet mockery.

"When did he post this?" I ask, taking the phone from her to see better.

"The original video? I don't know, a week ago? But this supercut thing is getting millions of views." Madison sinks deeper into the sofa. "I'm going to die. What if someone from school recognizes him as my dad?"

An uncomfortable knot forms in my stomach as I watch more of the supercut. "What was he 'canceled' for exactly?"

"I have no idea," Madison says, reclaiming her phone. "Probably just being his usual cringey self. But now he's the 'hostage video guy' on TikTok." She scrolls through comments. "People are saying he looks like he's being held at gunpoint while reading a ransom note."

Despite myself, I feel a surge of vicarious embarrassment. Even after everything Troy had put me through, there is something deeply uncomfortable about seeing him become an internet laughingstock. And beneath the embarrassment lurks a more troubling thought—what would have prompted Troy to make the original video in the first place?

"The comments are brutal," Madison continues, grimacing.

"Someone said he looks like 'Jordan Peterson if he ate nothing but alpha male podcasts and protein powder.'"

"Madison, maybe that's enough internet for today," I suggest, suddenly not wanting to see any more of Troy's humiliation, regardless of how deserved it might be.

She nods, looking relieved to have an excuse to stop watching. "It's just so weird. Like, I'm used to Dad being embarrassing, but not...internet famous embarrassing."

I consider whether to pursue this topic further...but looking at Madison's genuinely disturbed expression, I decide against it. Whatever Troy has done, dragging Madison further into it would only cause her pain.

"Let's forget about that," I say, rising from my chair. "We should start getting ready for dinner at the main house."

Madison looks grateful for the change of subject. "Emma says she's going to show me more rugby techniques after dinner."

"That sounds fun," I say, forcing enthusiasm I don't entirely feel. The thought of Madison engaged in a high-contact sport wasn't exactly comforting to my maternal instincts, but her excitement is infectious.

As Madison disappears into her room, I can't help but think about the irony of my situation. Here I am, still reeling from Jack's deception about his wealth, while simultaneously wondering what Troy has done that led to his "cancelation."

The universe certainly has a twisted sense of humor.

———

At the main house, Madison gravitates immediately to Emma, the two of them deep in rugby strategy by the time I arrive in the sitting room. Jack is nowhere to be seen, which is both a relief and, strangely, a disappointment.

"Red or white?" Lily asks, appearing beside me with two glasses of wine.

"Red, please," I say gratefully. After the day's events—the miraculous and terrifying childbirth on the boat, the unwelcome reminder of Troy's existence—alcohol seems necessary.

"You look preoccupied," Lily observes, her keen eyes studying my face. "Still processing the excitement from Milford Sound?"

"Partly," I admit. "It's been a...full day."

"Did Jack tell you the mum and baby are back at Queenstown and both doing splendidly?"

"He didn't mention it," I say, surprised to realize Jack hadn't texted me with the update.

"He's trying to respect your boundaries," Lily says gently. "Even when it means not sharing good news he knows you'd want to hear."

Before I can respond, Madison's voice rises above the quiet conversations. "Mom, Emma says I have natural talent for rugby. She thinks I could make a high school team back home if I wanted."

"That's wonderful, sweetie," I say, forcing enthusiasm I don't quite feel.

"Troy would hate it," Madison adds with a hint of teenage defiance. "He thinks girls should stick to 'aesthetic' sports."

Emma's eyebrows shoot up. "Did he actually say that?"

"Yeah, like last month when I mentioned wanting to try out for the football team." Madison rolls her eyes. "He said soccer was fine for girls because it was 'flowing and graceful,' but I shouldn't play anything where I might get bruises or 'look unladylike.'"

Emma's expression darkens. "Sounds like Troy has some...interesting views on women in sports."

"That's putting it mildly," I mutter, taking a sip of wine.

"Men, right?" Emma says with a significant look my way.

"Speaking of men with opinions," I say, lowering my voice as Madison becomes distracted by Lily showing her something on her phone, "Madison just showed me a viral video of Troy having a meltdown about being 'canceled by the woke mob.' Any idea what that's about?"

It is meant as a casual comment, a moment of shared exasperation between women, but Emma's reaction is anything but casual. Her face drains of color, her eyes darting toward Madison to ensure she wasn't listening.

"You...you don't know?" she asks, her voice dropping to a whisper.

"Know what?"

Emma hesitates, then sets down her wine glass. "Come with me. We should talk privately."

Alarm bells ring in my head as I follow Emma down a hallway and into what appears to be a small study. She closes the door behind us, her typically vibrant demeanor replaced by uncharacteristic seriousness.

"What's going on?" I ask, suddenly apprehensive.

Emma runs a hand through her short hair, looking deeply uncomfortable. "Look, Sophia...I don't know if now is the right time to get into this. You're already dealing with so much with Jack and—"

"Emma," I interrupt firmly. "Whatever it is, I need to know."

She sighs heavily. "Okay, but first, listen. Sophia, you're whānau now. Family. No matter what happens with Jack. Madison's incredible, and you're already part of us. That's why I'm telling you this. Not as Jack's sister. Just...as someone who's got your back."

Her uncharacteristic hesitation only increases my anxiety. "Just tell me."

"It's about Troy. His online presence." Emma meets my eyes directly. "What I'm about to tell you is going to be upsetting. Really upsetting."

"I can handle it," I say, falling back on the calm I'd cultivated through years of ER crises.

Emma takes a deep breath. "Troy has been posting truly vile, misogynistic content online for months, possibly years. Real 'redpill' stuff—demeaning women, describing them as property, objects for men to use." She pauses. "And it gets worse when he talks about daughters."

The room seems to tilt slightly. "How do you know this?"

Emma opens a drawer in the desk. "Because Jack had our security consultant document it."

She pulls out a folder and places it on the desk between us, looking deeply conflicted. "I shouldn't be showing you this. Jack would probably be furious with me. But after hearing Madison talk about Troy's attitudes toward her sports activities...I think you need to know what you're really dealing with."

"Jack was investigating Troy? When? Why?" My voice sounds distant, even to my own ears.

"After you mentioned those controlling texts about Madison's nutrition," Emma explains. "Jack was worried about Troy's influence. He asked our family security consultant—Rawiri, ex-Special Forces—to look into Troy's online presence."

With trembling fingers, I open the folder. The first page is a profile screenshot showing a gym selfie of Troy, his face partly obscured but unmistakable to me, with a bio that reads: "Unapologetic Male. Financial Dominance. Traditional Values. Escaping the Matrix."

As I flip through the pages, each screenshot is worse than the last. Post after post of Troy expounding on "female nature," how women were "built for submission," how feminism had "destroyed Western civilization." Some posts detail his sexual exploits in degrading terms. Others discuss "strategies" for manipulating women into compliance.

My stomach lurches when I reach posts specifically about ex-wives and daughters.

"...ex-wives are usable goods at best, damaged beyond repair at worst..."

"...women hit the wall at 35, their only value after that is what they've produced for you..."

Then, the worst: "Daughters are liabilities if not properly controlled. A father's primary responsibility is to instill obedience early, to prevent them from becoming unmanageable shrews incapable of attracting high-value men..."

The words blur as tears fill my eyes. "Oh my God," I whisper, my hand flying to my mouth. "He's talking about Madison. He's talking about our daughter."

"I'm so sorry, Sophia," Emma says quietly.

I can't tear my eyes from the page. Troy had written detailed "strategies" for "managing daughters" to ensure they remained "marriageable assets." He advocates restricting their independence, monitoring their appearance, and teaching them to "respect male authority unquestioningly."

The careful composure I'd maintained through countless traumas in the ER shatters. Tears stream down my face as I grip the edge of the desk to keep from collapsing.

"I tried to protect her," I gasp between sobs. "I stayed in that marriage too long because I thought it was better for Madison. I let him demean me, control me, because I thought at least Madison was safe from his toxicity." A ragged laugh escapes me. "And all this time, he saw her as nothing but a liability. A thing to be controlled."

Emma moves closer, her hand on my shoulder. "You couldn't have known, Sophia."

"I should have known," I insist, the guilt crushing me. "I'm her mother! I should have seen what he really was!"

"There's more," Emma says gently, guiding me to a chair as my legs threaten to give way. "He appeared on a podcast called 'The Alpha Male Revolution.' There's a transcript."

I flip to the transcript with shaking hands, my eyes catching horrifying phrases:

"...and that's the bottom line, fellas. Your daughters? They need to understand their place. They need to be taught to obey men, to respect male authority unquestioningly. It's for their own good, their own protection. A daughter who doesn't know how to submit to a strong man is a danger to herself and a disgrace to her father..."

A sob tears from my throat, raw and primal. "How could he say these things? How could he think this way about his own daughter? About any woman?"

Emma sits beside me, her usual brash confidence replaced by genuine compassion. "I don't know, Sophia. I really don't."

As the initial shock begins to subside, a question forms through my tears. "If this is all online, how has Madison never seen it? How has no one at school found it and told her?"

"Because it's not online anymore," Emma says quietly. "Jack made sure of that."

I look up sharply. "What do you mean?"

"After Jack saw all this, he was beyond furious. I've rarely seen my brother that angry." Emma's voice softens. "He confronted Troy directly."

"He did what?" I can't process what I'm hearing.

"About a week before you came to New Zealand," Emma explains. "He arranged to meet Troy at a coffee shop when Troy was picking up Madison."

"That day," I whisper, memory clicking into place. "Madison mentioned seeing Jack there. I thought it was just a coincidence."

"Not a coincidence," Emma confirms. "Jack showed Troy what he'd found—all the screenshots, all the evidence. And he made it crystal clear that if Madison ever found those posts— which she inevitably would as she got older—it would destroy her."

The pieces suddenly fall together. "So that's what the 'canceled by the woke mob' video was about."

"Exactly," Emma nods. "Troy took down all the vile content after Jack confronted him. But apparently he couldn't resist playing the victim with that ridiculous video."

"Why didn't Jack tell me about any of this?" I ask, still trying to comprehend the magnitude of what I'm learning.

Emma's expression grows serious. "He said it wasn't his place to come between Madison and her father. That he didn't want to be the one to tell you something that might force you to restrict Madison's contact with Troy. He just wanted the harmful content gone before she could ever see it."

"So he confronted Troy, made him take down everything, and never said a word to me." I struggle to process Jack's quiet intervention. "He protected Madison without seeking any credit."

"I was ready to fly to the States and rugby tackle that twat into next week," Emma says, her bluntness startling a wet laugh from me despite my tears. "But Jack handled it his way. I don't know exactly what he said to Troy, but all that vile stuff came down, and this whiny video is all that's left."

I wipe my eyes, trying to collect myself. "I had no idea it was this bad. I knew Troy had issues, but this...this is pure hatred."

"Are you okay?" Emma asks gently.

"No," I admit, my voice breaking. "I've spent years trying to shield Madison from the worst of Troy's influence while still allowing her to love her father. I've swallowed my own pain, my own anger, because I thought that was what good mothers do." Fresh tears well. "And all this time, he's been viewing her as a possession. A liability. Something to be controlled rather than cherished."

Emma squeezes my hand. "You're an incredible mother, Sophia. And Madison is amazing, really—strong, independent, kind. Whatever toxic garbage Troy believes, it hasn't touched her because of you."

I nod, trying to take comfort in her words. "I need to figure out how to handle this with Madison."

"If anyone can navigate that impossible situation, it's you," Emma says with surprising confidence. "Jack always said you were the strongest person he'd ever met."

The compliment, relayed secondhand, pierces through my emotional turmoil. "Where is Jack now?"

"Walking the kiwi sanctuary, I bet," Emma says. "He goes there when he needs to think. Has since he was a teenager."

I stand, decision made. "Could you keep Madison occupied for a while? I need to talk to him."

Emma's smile is knowing despite the heaviness of our conversation. "Absolutely. I've been meaning to show her some proper rugby tackling techniques anyway."

As I leave the study, my emotions are a violent storm—horror at Troy's true nature, guilt over not protecting Madison better, fear for her future relationship with her father, and overwhelming gratitude toward Jack that threatens to drown out everything else.

The wealth deception is still real. The broken trust still needs repair. But Jack's quiet protection of Madison without seeking credit or advantage reveals something essential about his character that I can't ignore.

It's time to have an honest conversation... about *everything*.

chapter
forty

DUSK SETTLES OVER THE SANCTUARY, painting the dense native bush in shades of gold and amber. Silver ferns unfurl at the edges of the path, their undersides catching what little light remains. The air carries the earthy scent of damp soil and native herbs, a primordial fragrance unique to New Zealand's ancient forests. I follow the familiar path deeper into the gully, away from the estate's manicured grounds, seeking solitude in the one place that has always brought me peace.

My mind won't stop replaying the scene from the boat—that tiny, still baby in my hands, skin bluish, umbilical cord having been wrapped around his neck. In all my years as a paramedic, few moments have terrified me more than that silent newborn, the mother's panicked question hanging in the air: "Why isn't he crying?"

I'd kept my face neutral, my hands steady, but inside I'd been screaming. The improvised bulb syringe had been pure desperation, muscle memory from similar situations, albeit with proper equipment. Those seconds between clearing the airway and hearing that first indignant cry had stretched into eternity.

We'd been lucky. *So* lucky.

I pause at the entrance to one of the observation hides, leaning against the wooden structure, allowing myself to feel the full weight of what could have happened.

It wasn't the first time I'd stood at the edge of life and death like that. Unbidden, the memory surfaces—one of my first major trauma calls as a new medic in the city. A pregnant woman, thirty-four weeks along, involved in a high-speed rollover on the Beltway. When we get there, she is unresponsive, barely a pulse. Her husband had been driving—dazed but conscious, screaming her name through the cracked windshield.

We work her in the back of the rig, hands slick with blood, compressions bouncing both mother and baby with each desperate cycle. I remember shouting vitals to the hospital over the radio, begging for a trauma bay and OB team to be standing by. I remember the smell of diesel and adrenaline. I remember her eyes—open, but gone.

They do a postmortem C-section right there in the ER trauma bay. We keep compressions going while pulled her onto the table, trying to buy them seconds. Just seconds. But it was already too late.

They deliver the baby anyway, tiny, blue, and impossibly still. I stand there, chest heaving, still wearing the blood we'd fought through to get her there. And I watch as the OB team calls time.

I draw a shaky breath, the memory still raw despite the years. Today could have gone the same way. One small deviation—a slower response, a less effective makeshift suction, a more severe complication—and that baby might not have taken his first breath.

What strikes me most, thinking back on the emergency, is Sophia's unshakable calm. She'd handled the precipitous delivery, the nuchal cord, everything with the same quiet competence she brings to the ER. Never once letting Hannah see the danger, never breaking the fiction that everything was proceeding normally, protecting that new mother from the terror of how close they'd come to tragedy.

I'd known Sophia was extraordinary from the very first time I'd dropped a patient off at Metro General, and got to see her work. Seeing her in that crisis, maintaining her composure while literally holding lives in her hands...it had only confirmed what I already knew.

She was the strongest person I'd ever met.

And I'd betrayed her trust completely.

The sanctuary is quiet around me, the kiwis not yet emerging for their nightly foraging. I move to a fallen log and sit heavily, the weight of everything—the near miss on the boat, the situation with Sophia, my own deception—crushing down on me.

From this secluded spot, I can see a slice of the main house in the distance, lights glowing warmly against the darkening sky. Sophia and Madison are in there, probably enjoying dinner with my family, while I hide in the woods like a coward.

The sound of footsteps on the path startles me. No one comes to the sanctuary at this hour except—

"Jack?"

Sophia's voice, soft in the gathering darkness. I turn to see her silhouetted against the fading light, her figure unmistakable even in shadow.

"Here," I call, my voice rougher than intended.

She approaches cautiously, picking her way along the path with careful steps. As she draws closer, I can see she'd been crying—her eyes puffy, her usually composed features drawn with emotion.

"Are you okay?" she asks, stopping a few feet away.

The simple question—her concern for me despite everything—breaks something inside me. A laugh that is more like a sob escapes my throat.

"No," I admit, scrubbing a hand over my face. "Not really."

She hesitates, then moves to sit beside me on the log, close but not touching. "What's wrong?"

I shake my head, struggling to articulate the storm inside. "That baby today...he wasn't breathing at first." My voice cracks. "All I could think about was another call, years ago. A pregnant woman in a car wreck—thirty-four weeks. We did CPR all the way to the hospital, but by the time we got there, she was gone. They tried a crash C-section, but...it was too late. We lost them both."

The words tumble out, unstoppable now. "We were so close to that today. So damn close. If the improvised suction hadn't worked, if the cord had been tighter around his neck, if you hadn't recognized the issue immediately..."

"But it did work," Sophia says softly. "You acted quickly, and the baby's fine. Hannah's fine."

"This time," I whisper. "This time we got lucky."

To my horror, I feel tears welling, the professional distance I maintain in crises crumbling now in the aftermath. I turn away, not wanting her to see this breakdown on top of everything else.

"Jack," Sophia says, her voice achingly gentle. "Jack. Look at me."

I can't. Shame and residual fear keep my gaze fixed on the ground.

Then her hand is on my arm, the first deliberate touch she'd initiated since the revelation. The simple contact shatters what remains of my control. The tears come in earnest then, my shoulders shaking with the force of them.

"I'm sorry," I gasp between ragged breaths. "I'm so sorry."

Without a word, Sophia moves closer, her arms encircling me. I stiffen in surprise before melting into her embrace, my face pressed against her shoulder as emotion overwhelms me.

We stay like that for long minutes, my tears gradually subsiding, her hand moving in slow, comforting circles on my back. When I finally pull away, embarrassed by my breakdown, her own eyes were wet with silent tears.

"I didn't mean to—" I begin.

"It's okay," she interrupts. "You don't always have to be strong, Jack. Not with me."

The simple acceptance in her voice stuns me. After everything, after my deception, she is still offering comfort, still seeing beyond the surface to what lies beneath.

"I know about Troy," she says quietly.

The abrupt change of subject catches me off-guard. "What!?"

"I know what he was posting online. What you confronted him about." Her eyes hold mine steadily despite the tears still clinging to her lashes. "Emma showed me the screenshots."

"What? How did this—" I struggle to process this unexpected turn.

"Troy apparently became the main character on the internet today. Some viral TikTok thing. Madison showed it to me." A grim smile touches her lips briefly. "One thing led to another, and...Emma told me everything."

I run a hand through my hair, mortified. "Sophia, I never meant for you to see those posts. The things he said—"

"About women. About me. About Madison." Her voice hardens on her daughter's name. "His own daughter, Jack. His own flesh and blood, and he sees her as a 'liability' to be 'controlled.'"

The raw pain in her voice makes me ache to hold her again, but I remain still, uncertain of my place. "I'm sorry, Sophia. I'm so sorry you had to see that."

"Why didn't you tell me?" she asks, the question lacking accusation, just genuine curiosity.

I choose my words carefully. "It wasn't my place to come between Madison and her father. I didn't want to be the reason you had to restrict her access to him. I just...I couldn't bear the thought of her finding those posts someday, seeing how he really views her."

"So you confronted him yourself. Made him take it all down. And never said a word to me about any of it." Her eyes search mine. "You protected Madison without seeking any credit."

I shrug uncomfortably. "It was the right thing to do."

"And by doing it quietly, you ensured Madison could still have a relationship with her father, strained as it might be." She shakes her head slowly. "That level of consideration...after everything I thought about you when I discovered your deception..."

I reach for her hand, hope flickering at this small opening. "Sophia, I never meant to—"

She pulls back suddenly, her face shifting from gratitude to something harder, more resolute. "No, Jack. My turn to talk. And you are going to listen."

She begins to pace, the carefully constructed walls around her heart starting to crumble, revealing the raw hurt beneath. "Do you have any idea what it felt like, standing in that house, meeting your mother who called you 'Jackson,' seeing the sheer scale of all this, and realizing that the man I'd let into my life, into Madison's life, was a stranger?"

She whirls back to face me. "I already told you how Troy viewed me, Jack. How he systematically tore down my confidence, my independence, my sense of self-worth until I barely recognized the woman in the mirror." Her voice breaks, but she pushes on, the words tumbling out, fueled by years of suppressed pain and fresh betrayal. "And for years—*years*—I let him convince me that was normal."

My face is a mask of anguish. I reach for her, but she recoils. "Don't."

She pauses for a moment.

"And then you showed up," she continues, her voice thick with unshed tears. "This kind, funny, attentive paramedic with a heart of gold. You made me laugh! You were good to Madison. You made me feel...seen. Cherished, even." She chokes on the word. "You made me feel safe enough to want to try again, to believe that maybe not all men were like Troy."

She takes a ragged breath. "So when I realized everything you told me about who you are, about your life, was a lie—what do you think that did to me, Jack? It wasn't just about the money. It was about the trust. The honesty. You made me a fool all over again, Jack."

Sophia's words hit me with the force of a physical blow. Each one is a perfectly aimed scalpel, slicing through my pathetic defenses, exposing the raw, ugly truth of what I'd done.

The comparison to Troy, the man whose vile online persona I'd just seen laid bare, is a stake through the heart. I'd wanted to be everything Troy wasn't for her, and instead, I'd become just another man who had betrayed her trust, who had made her question her own judgment.

Tears stream down her face now, those beautiful blue eyes filled with a pain so profound it mirrors the desolation in my own soul. I want to pull her into my arms, to hold her, to somehow absorb her hurt, but her earlier "Don't" echoes in the space between us.

"Sophia," I start, my own voice cracking. I have to make her understand, even if understanding doesn't mean forgiveness. "There are no words...no excuses for what I did. For how much I've hurt you."

She stands rigid, arms wrapped around herself, waiting.

"I was a coward," I say, the admission raw and true. "Plain and simple. I was terrified. Terrified that if you knew about...all this..." I gesture vaguely at the sprawling estate around us, "...you'd see the money, the name, and not me. That you'd think I was just another privileged tosser, or that I was slumming it, or that I couldn't possibly understand your life, your struggles."

"So you assume the worst of me?" she whispers, her voice trembling. "You didn't think I was capable of seeing past a bank account?"

"No! That's not...I was projecting my own baggage, Soph. My whole life, I've seen how people change when they find out about my family. The way they look at you differently, the assumptions they make. I just wanted...for once...to be just Jack. The paramedic. The bloke you shared coffee with, the one who made you laugh. I wanted that Jack to be enough for you, before you knew about the other one."

"But it wasn't the whole truth, was it?" she says, her voice flat. "It was a curated version. A lie of omission that went on for months. Every conversation, every shared moment...was it all calculated?"

"Never calculated," I insist, stepping closer, unable to bear the distance. "Every moment with you, with Madison, was real. The most real thing in my life. The hiding...that was my fear, my stupidity. I kept telling myself I'd find the right time, the perfect moment to explain, but it never came. And the longer I waited, the harder it got, the more I had to lose."

I finally reach her, gently taking her hands. They are cold, trembling. She doesn't pull away this time, but she doesn't respond either.

"Sophia," I whisper, my voice breaking. "And if—if there's a road back from this, if we can find our way again—then I'd give all of it up. Every cent. Every acre. All the 'legacy'. I'd take your name, Sophia. I'd be Jack Mitchell and never look back, just as long as I had you."

Silence stretches between us, filled only with the sound of our ragged breathing and the distant call of a night bird.

"You idiot," she finally says, her voice barely audible. "You already have me."

The words take a moment to register, my mind struggling to process what I'm hearing. "What?"

"You already have me," she repeats, her voice stronger now. Her hands tighten around mine. "I'm still angry. I'm still hurt. But I love you, Jack. The paramedic in America. The vineyard heir in New Zealand. All the complicated, sometimes infuriating parts that make you who you are."

Hope blooms so suddenly it's almost painful. "Sophia—"

"I'm not saying it will be easy," she continues. "We have a lot to figure out. But I don't want to lose what we've found because of fear or pride. And what you did for Madison...confronting Troy without ever seeking recognition or advantage...that tells me everything I need to know about your character, Jack McKenzie."

In the dim light of the sanctuary, Sophia leans forward, her hand cupping my cheek with infinite tenderness. "I've spent too many years being careful, keeping people at arm's length to protect myself. I don't want to do that anymore. Not with you."

Her lips find mine, hesitant at first, then with growing certainty. I respond with equal gentleness, hardly daring to believe this is happening. When we part, her forehead rests against my chest, our breath mingling in the cool evening air.

"What happens now?" I whisper.

"Now," she says, her voice stronger, "you show me your cottage. The real one, not the guest house. I want to see where Jack McKenzie actually lives when he's home."

Understanding dawns. "Are you sure? We don't have to—"

"I'm sure," she interrupts, her gaze resolute. "I want to know all of you, Jack. No more holding back. No more secrets."

I stand, pulling her gently to her feet, our hands still linked. "It's not far. Through those trees, just beyond the main path."

We walk in silence, close enough that our shoulders brush occasionally. The forest is alive around us—the rustle of nocturnal creatures, the distant call of a morepork owl, the soft whisper of wind through the trees. By the time we reach the cottage, darkness has fully descended, the path illuminated only by moonlight filtering through the canopy.

I hesitate at the door, suddenly self-conscious. "It's nothing fancy. Just a place that's...mine."

The cottage is small by McKenzie Estate standards—two bedrooms, a common area with fireplace, a kitchen, all built from local stone and native timber. I'd helped design it during my final year of high school, before I'd left for university. It had been my refuge during holidays home, the one place on the estate that feels truly separate from the family business.

I flick on the lights, watching nervously as Sophia steps inside, her eyes taking in every detail—the books scattered on the coffee table, the hiking boots by the door, the old guitar I'd had since uni propped in the corner.

"This is you," she says after a moment, turning to face me. "The real you."

"As real as I get," I admit. "This is where I hide when the family expectations get too much. Where I can just be Jack."

She moves toward me, a new determination in her expression. "No more hiding. Not from each other." Her hands find my chest, resting over my heart. "Show me who you really are, Jack McKenzie."

The invitation in her words, in her touch, is unmistakable. I gather her close, my lips finding hers in a kiss that quickly deepens from tender to desperate. Months of longing, days of separation, hours of uncertainty, all of it pours into this single point of connection.

My hands trace the familiar curves of her body, rediscovering territory I'd feared lost forever. She responds with equal fervor, fingers tangling in my hair, pulling me closer as if afraid I might disappear.

"Bedroom," she murmurs against my lips, already working at the buttons of my shirt.

"Yes, ma'am," I growl, scooping her up without hesitation.

She laughs—low, breathless, wrecked from emotion and relief—and her arms lock around my neck as I carry her, never breaking the kiss. We bump against the hallway wall once, laughing again, mouths tangling, fingers tugging and fumbling. When we make it to the bedroom, I lay her down like something sacred and immediately follow, pressing her body beneath mine.

Clothes vanish between kisses, her shirt over her head, my belt undone with shaky hands, jeans pushed down without care. She rolls me onto my back and straddles my hips, wild-eyed and panting, her hair a dark curtain around her face as she kisses her way down my chest.

"God, I missed this," she whispers, lips brushing over my skin, her fingers grazing the sharp line of my hipbones. Her touch is reverent and greedy all at once.

"I missed you," I manage, breath catching as she slides down, her hands stroking along the insides of my thighs. "I thought I'd never—Sophia—"

She returns to me in a flash, kissing me hard, devouring, like she could crawl inside my skin and stay. "I'm here now," she whispers. "I'm yours."

"Say that again," I beg, flipping us with a low growl, pinning her wrists gently above her head, our bodies perfectly aligned.

"I'm yours," she says, breathless, desperate.

I release her wrists and let my hands roam—over her ribs, the swell of her breasts, the soft dip of her waist, cradling her buttocks. She arches into me with a moan when my mouth closes around her nipple, her legs falling open beneath me. My name spills from her lips again and again, and I answer with my body, with every touch and kiss, until she is writhing and whispering, "Please. Jack. Now."

I slide into her slowly, watching her eyes—watching them go wide, watching her lips part as she gasps and arches, fitting around me like we'd never been apart.

"You're still perfect," I murmur.

"So are you," she chokes out, clinging to me like I was air.

I move slowly at first, drinking in the way she moves with me—every shift of her hips, every breathless gasp, every whispered prayer. Then we find our rhythm again—familiar, instinctive, electric—and the slow build becomes urgency.

Her nails bite into my back. I pull her forehead to mine.

"Jack," she whispers, over and over. Like it means something. Like it was everything.

I feel her begin to tighten around me and reach between us, brushing my thumb against the place where we were joined, and she shatters with a cry—head thrown back, eyes squeezed shut, legs wrapped around me so tight I saw stars.

I follow seconds later, spilling into her with a groan that shakes loose something from my chest I didn't know I'd been holding. I collapse beside her, gathering her trembling body against mine as aftershocks ripple through us both. For long minutes, we lie in silence broken only by our gradually slowing breaths, limbs entangled, hearts beating in tandem.

We lie there afterward, tangled and spent, sweat cooling on our skin. She is pressed against me, one hand on my chest, her legs still twined with mine. I can't stop touching her—running my hand along the curve of her waist, brushing her damp hair from her face, kissing her temple over and over.

"You okay?" I ask, voice rough with emotion and aftermath.

She looks up, eyes still dazed and glowing. "Better than okay."

I kiss her again, slower this time. Lingering. Intentional.

"That felt like...more than sex," she whispers.

"It was," I say. "It was you and me, choosing each other again."

"I never thought I'd have this again," Sophia says finally, her voice soft in the darkness. "You. Us."

I tighten my arms around her. "I thought I'd lost you forever when you saw the estate."

"It wasn't the money that hurt, Jack." She lifts herself onto one elbow to look down at me. "It was feeling like I didn't know who you really were. That everything we'd shared might have been based on a fiction."

"Nothing between us was ever false," I promise. "The man who brought you coffee, who taught Madison to make pasta, who fell in love with you at the first radio call—that was always me. The real me."

She smiles, tracing the line of my jaw with her fingertips. "I know that now."

Sophia's eyes suddenly widen. "Madison! I completely forgot—"

"I'm sure my sisters have it under control," I reassure her, but she is already reaching for her phone on the nightstand.

"I should at least let them know I'm not coming back to the guest house tonight." She sends a quick text, then relaxes back against me. "Emma replied immediately. Apparently Madison is having the time of her life learning rugby tackles. Emma says not to worry, they've got it covered."

"Told you," I say, pressing a kiss to her shoulder. "Those three have been conspiring since the moment you arrived."

Sophia slips from the bed, the moonlight bathing her naked form in silver as she walks to the wide window overlooking the vineyard and Lake Dunstan beyond. The full moon hangs impossibly large in the southern sky, casting ripples of light across the water.

"It's so different," she murmurs, her silhouette breathtaking against the night sky. "The moon, the stars. Everything's upside down here."

I watch her, entranced by the simple beauty of this moment—Sophia in my cottage, in my life, standing unguarded and free.

She turns slightly, catching sight of herself in the antique mirror that hangs beside the window—and me behind her, still in bed, watching her with undisguised adoration.

"You're not even looking at the view," she says, a smile in her voice.

I rise, moving to stand behind her, my arms encircling her waist, my chin resting on her shoulder. "I have the better view."

"Charmer," she whispers, leaning back against me.

In the mirror, our bodies align perfectly—her head nestled in the crook of my neck, my arms wrapped around her waist, her hands resting over mine. I hold her gaze in the reflection.

"You fit," I say softly.

"What?"

"You fit." I gesture toward our reflection. "Look. Look in the mirror. You fit right here, perfectly."

Her eyes follow mine to the mirror, taking in the way our naked bodies are intertwined—her head fitting perfectly into the space between my shoulder and chin, our bodies aligned like pieces of a puzzle.

"This is where you belong," I murmur against her ear. "This is where I belong. To you."

Tears glisten in her eyes, catching the moonlight. "To each other," she corrects softly.

A comfortable silence falls between us, the kind that only exists between people who have moved beyond the need for constant reassurance. Outside, an owl calls, its voice carrying through the night.

"I meant what I said," I tell her eventually. "About taking your name. About giving up all of this if that's what it took."

"I would never ask you to give up your family, your heritage." She kisses me softly. "But I appreciate the offer. It showed me how much you were willing to sacrifice."

"Jackson Charles Mitchell," I test the sound of it. "Has a nice ring, don't you think?"

"Hmm." She pretends to consider. "Maybe we could hyphenate. Mitchell-McKenzie."

"Or McKenzie-Mitchell?"

She laughs. "We don't have to decide tonight."

"No," I agree, pulling her closer. "We have time."

"All the time in the world," she murmurs, nestling against my chest.

As Sophia's breathing deepens into sleep, I remain awake, marveling at the miracle in my arms. The journey that brought us here—from radio flirtation to ER coffee delivery, from first dates to family revelations, from heartbreak to reconciliation—feels like both an odyssey and a homecoming.

For the first time in my life, I'm fully known. Fully accepted. Not as the McKenzie heir with his paramedic hobby, not as a rebellious rich boy playing at real life, but as the complete, complicated man I truly am.

And that, more than all the vineyards and estates in the world, feels like the greatest wealth of all.

chapter
forty-one

MORNING SUNLIGHT FILTERS through Jack's bedroom window, warming my face and gradually pulling me from sleep. For a moment, I'm disoriented—the unfamiliar room, the exceptionally comfortable bed, the solid warmth of Jack's body pressed against mine. Then memory floods back—our confrontation in the sanctuary, our reconciliation, the night we'd spent rediscovering each other.

I shift carefully, not wanting to wake him, and study his face in repose. Sleep softens his features, erasing the worry lines that had etched themselves between his brows over the past few days. This close, I can see the faint scatter of freckles across his nose, the slight stubble darkening his jaw, the tiny scar near his temple that I'd never noticed before.

Jack McKenzie. Jackson Charles McKenzie. The paramedic with the accent. The vineyard heir. The man who had broken my trust and then earned it back through quiet acts of protection and raw honesty.

As if sensing my scrutiny, his eyes flutter open, momentarily confused before focusing on me. A slow smile spreads across his face —not the careful, hesitant smile of recent days, but the full, unguarded expression I'd fallen for.

"Morning," he murmurs, voice rough with sleep. "Not a dream, then."

"Not a dream," I confirm, leaning in to press a kiss to his lips.

The kiss deepens quickly, his hand sliding beneath the sheet to trace my hip, my waist, my breast. Heat blooms wherever he touches, my body responding with embarrassing eagerness. His leg slips between mine, and I gasp at the contact, already aching for him again.

Just as things are progressing from sleepy affection to something more urgent, my stomach grows loudly, breaking the moment.

Jack laughs against my neck. "Sounds like someone needs breakfast."

"Ignore it," I mutter, pulling him back toward me.

"Can't have you fainting from hunger," he teases, nipping at my earlobe. "Besides, I smell coffee. Mum's probably had the staff preparing breakfast for hours."

That gives me pause. "The staff. Your family. They'll know I stayed here."

"Probably." His expression turns serious. "Does that bother you?"

I consider the question. Does it bother me? A few days ago, the idea of Jack's family knowing the intimate details of our relationship would have mortified me. Now..."No," I realize. "It doesn't. Though I should probably check on Madison."

"Mmm, good point." Jack reaches for his phone. "I'll text Emma."

A moment later, his phone chimes with a response. "Emma says Madison is already at breakfast with everyone. Apparently, she's been up since dawn with Lily, helping with the kiwi feeding."

"I've never seen her voluntarily wake up early," I marvel. "Your family has some kind of magic touch."

"More likely it was the promise of seeing rare nocturnal birds," Jack says, sitting up and stretching. "Speaking of magic touches..." He waggles his eyebrows suggestively.

I swat his shoulder. "Breakfast first. We're going to need our strength."

Twenty minutes later, showered and dressed in yesterday's clothes (slightly wrinkled but presentable), we make our way hand-in-hand from Jack's cottage toward the main house. The morning is crisp and clear, the mountains rising majestically against a brilliant blue sky.

"Nervous?" Jack asks as we approach the house.

"A little," I admit. "It's not every day you face your boyfriend's wealthy family the morning after reconciling from a major relationship crisis."

"Boyfriend," he repeats, smiling. "I like the sound of that. Very teenage."

"Partner? Significant other?" I offer.

"How about 'the man who adores you and plans to spend the rest of his life making you happy'?" He squeezes my hand. "Too wordy for everyday use?"

"Just a bit," I laugh, warmth spreading through my chest at the casual reference to our future together.

We enter through the kitchen door, where the delicious aroma of coffee, bacon, and freshly baked bread envelops us. A woman I recognize as Mrs. Petersen, the housekeeper Jack had mentioned, is directing two younger staff members in breakfast preparations.

"Mr. Jackson!" she exclaims, her face lighting up. "And Ms. Mitchell! Everyone's in the breakfast room. I've just sent through fresh pastries."

"Thanks, Mrs. P," Jack says warmly. "Smells amazing as always."

"Back to your old tricks already, young man," she scolds good-naturedly. "Sneaking in through my kitchen to avoid the front door."

Jack grins, unrepentant. "Some habits never die."

Mrs. Petersen turns to me, her expression softening. "Lovely to see you this morning, Ms. Mitchell. Your daughter is quite the charmer—she's been helping with the kiwi feeding since dawn."

"Please, call me Sophia," I say. "And thank you for making us feel so welcome."

She beams at me. "Off you go, now. Helen's been asking after you both."

As we continue through the house, Jack leans close. "Mrs. Petersen's approval is not given lightly. You've officially been accepted into the McKenzie inner circle."

"One down, how many to go?" I ask, only half-joking.

"Just one that truly matters," he says, pausing before the breakfast room door. "Madison. Though from the sounds of it, you've got nothing to worry about there."

He was right. As we enter the sunlit breakfast room, Madison's laugh is the first thing I hear—bright and uninhibited as she recounts something to the assembled McKenzies. "...and then Mom just took the needle and shoved it right into the guy's chest, and everyone was like, whoa!" Madison is gesturing dramatically. "Jack says it's called a needle decompression, and it saved the guy's life!"

Emma spots us first. "Speaking of the heroes," she announces, her face splitting into a knowing grin. "Look what the kiwi dragged in."

All heads turn our way. Madison's face lights up. "Mom! Jack! Where have you been? Lily took me to feed the kiwis this morning, and they're so cool! Did you know the females are bigger than the males? And they're related to ostriches? And—"

"Breathe, Madison," I laugh, crossing to kiss the top of her head. "Good morning, everyone."

Helen McKenzie's eyes are sharp as they move from me to Jack and back again, taking in our clasped hands, our slightly rumpled appearance. "Good morning, indeed," she says, her tone unreadable. "Coffee?"

"Please," I say, sliding into an empty chair beside Madison. Jack takes the seat on my other side, his hand finding mine under the table.

Michael McKenzie catches my eye from across the table and gives me a small, approving nod. "Sleep well?" he asks Jack, his tone deceptively innocent.

"Wonderfully," Jack replies, matching his father's casual delivery. "The cottage always was the most comfortable place on the property."

Charlotte snorts into her coffee. "Subtle, you two."

Throughout this exchange, Madison is watching with the keen attention of someone who knows adult subtext is flying over her head but is determined to catch as much as possible. "So," she says slowly, turning to me, "are you and Jack okay now?"

Leave it to a teenager to cut straight to the heart of the matter once again. The breakfast table falls silent, all pretense of polite morning conversation is abandoned as everyone awaits my answer.

I look at Jack, who gives me an encouraging smile, then back to Madison. "Yes," I say simply. "We're okay."

"More than okay," Jack adds, lifting our joined hands to press a kiss to my knuckles.

Madison's face breaks into a wide grin. "Good. Because Emma already promised to keep coaching me, and that would have been super awkward if you guys were still mad at each other."

Laughter breaks the tension, and conversation resumes around the table. I help myself to the gorgeous spread—fresh pastries, fruit, eggs prepared three different ways, bacon that puts American versions to shame.

"So," Helen says, setting down her teacup with deliberate precision, "what are your plans now, Jackson? Will you be extending your stay in New Zealand?"

Jack glances at me. "We haven't really discussed details yet, Mum."

"Well, you must have some idea," she presses. "The harvest begins tomorrow. Your father could use your help, even if it's just for a few days before you...return." The slight pause before "return" carries volumes of disapproval.

"Actually," Jack says, his voice steady despite the tension I can feel in his body, "I've been thinking about that."

"Oh?" Helen's eyebrows rise expectantly.

Jack takes a deep breath. "I'm going back with Sophia and Madison. To America. To my job."

Helen's teacup clatters against the saucer. "But surely now that things are...resolved," she flicks a glance at me, "you'll reconsider this paramedic phase. It's gone on long enough, Jackson. It's time to take your place here, with the family business."

"It's not a phase, Mum," Jack says firmly. "It's my career. My calling. And I'm good at it."

"Of course you're good at it," Helen dismisses. "You're a McKenzie. You'd be good at anything you put your mind to. But that doesn't mean you should waste your education, your heritage, running around in an ambulance when you could be making a real difference here."

The dismissive way she refers to Jack's work—work that saves lives daily—makes something snap inside me. Before I can think better of it, I find myself speaking. "With all due respect, Mrs. McKenzie, Jack makes a 'real difference' every single day. Just yesterday, he helped deliver a baby on a boat and saved its life when it wasn't breathing."

Helen looks startled, as if she'd forgotten I was there. "Well, yes, that's very admirable, but—"

"And last month," I continue, warming to my subject, "he recognized the signs of an aortic dissection in a patient that three other responders had missed. That man is alive today because of Jack's training and instincts."

Jack squeezes my hand in silent gratitude, but I wasn't finished. "Your son is an exceptional paramedic. He's respected by his colleagues, trusted by his patients, and absolutely vital to our community. It's not a hobby or a phase or a rebellion—it's who he is. And it's one of the many reasons I love him."

A stunned silence falls over the table. Helen's mouth opens and closes like a fish out of water. Michael is watching me with newfound respect. The sisters are exchanging glances that range from shocked (Charlotte) to delighted (Emma) to quietly proud (Lily).

Jack clears his throat. "There's something else," he says, his voice steady despite the tension crackling in the air. "When Sophia and I return to America, I'm thinking of taking her name."

Helen's coffee cup, which she'd just lifted to her lips, freezes mid-air. "What?"

"If things continue to progress between us," Jack clarifies, "and we reach that point, I'm open to becoming Jack Mitchell. Or Mitchell-McKenzie, perhaps."

The coffee cup hits the table with a splash, liquid sloshes over the rim. "YOU CANNOT BE SERIOUS," Helen exclaims, all pretense of decorum abandoned. "Give up the McKenzie name? For what? To drive an ambulance and play at being a working-class hero?"

"Helen," Michael cautions, but she isn't listening.

"*Four* generations of McKenzies have built this legacy, Jackson," she continues, her voice rising. "Your great-grandfather William came back from Gallipoli with a shattered leg, after half the Otago Battalion was lost at Chunuk Bair, and still transformed this valley into something lasting. Your grandfather James fought at Monte Cassino and El Alamein, returned home, and expanded the vineyard when everyone said it was madness. Your father took that legacy global—put the McKenzie label on the same tier as Napa and Bordeaux. And now you want to throw it all away to become...what? An *ambulance driver!?*"

"Paramedic," Jack corrects calmly. "And yes, if that's what it takes to show Sophia I'm serious about our future together."

"This is absurd," Helen declares, turning to me with flashing eyes. "Surely you're not encouraging this madness?"

All eyes swivel to me. Madison is watching the exchange with wide-eyed fascination, like a tennis match where the stakes had suddenly skyrocketed.

"Actually," I say, matching Jack's calm, "I think it's a wonderful gesture, but completely unnecessary." I turn to Jack. "You don't need to change your name to prove anything to me, Jack. McKenzie is part of who you are, part of your heritage. I would never ask you to give that up."

"But I would," he insists. "In a heartbeat."

"I know," I say softly. "That's what matters."

Helen makes a sound somewhere between a scoff and a gasp. "This is ridiculous. You barely know each other."

"I know her," Jack says with quiet intensity. "I know her character, her heart, her strength. I've seen her handle emergencies that would make most people crumble. I've watched her raise an incredible daughter while working one of the most demanding jobs in healthcare. I've seen her forgive a betrayal that many would find unforgivable." He turns to face me fully. "I know that I love her, and that I want to build a life with her, whether that's here or in America or anywhere else in the world."

"Oh, for heaven's sake," Helen mutters, but there's less heat in her voice now.

"Mom," Charlotte says firmly, "enough. This is Jack's decision."

"But he's throwing away everything—"

"He's choosing his own path," Michael interrupts, surprising everyone. "Just as you did when you defied your parents to marry me. And might I remind you, Helen, that both his great-grandfather and grandfather came back from war to serve this community in their own way. Jack has chosen a different battlefield, but he's still a McKenzie through and through." Helen's mouth snaps shut, color rising in her cheeks.

Michael turns to Jack and me, his expression softening. "The McKenzie name will always be yours, son, whatever you choose to call yourself. And the estate will always be your home, even if your life is elsewhere." He looks directly at me then. "And I hope, in time, Sophia and Madison will come to see it as home too—whether for visits or...something more permanent."

"Thank you, Mr. McKenzie," I say, genuinely touched.

"Michael, please," he corrects with a warm smile.

Madison, who had been watching this entire exchange with rapt attention, finally speaks up. "So does this mean we can come back? Because Emma promised to teach me the haka, and I really want to see the kiwis again."

The tension breaks as everyone laughs, even Helen managing a reluctant smile. "Yes," Jack assures her, "you can absolutely come back. Both of you."

"Awesome!" Madison beams. "Wait till I tell Chloe! She's going to be so jealous."

As conversation flows around us, Jack leans close to my ear. "Thank you for defending me," he whispers. "No one's ever done that before. Not with my mother."

"Get used to it," I murmur back. "That's what partners do." His eyes, warm and full of wonder, hold mine. "Partners," he repeats. "I like that."

"You okay?" I ask, noting the lingering tension in his shoulders. Standing up to his mother couldn't have been easy, especially with the weight of family expectations bearing down.

"Better than okay," he says, his expression clearing. "For the first time in my life, I feel like I'm exactly where I'm supposed to be."

As his hand finds mine again beneath the table, I can't help but agree. Despite the unlikely path that has brought us here—across oceans, through deceptions and revelations, past hurt and into forgiveness—this feels right. It feels like home. Not the estate, grand as it was. Not New Zealand, beautiful as I find it. But this—Jack's hand in mine, Madison's laughter blending with his sisters', the future stretching before us, uncertain but full of promise. This is where we belong.

Together.

Epilogue

SOPHIA

"Trauma team to Bay One. Trauma team to Bay One."

The familiar page echoes through Metro General's ER as I finish reviewing lab results for a chest pain workup. My shift is almost over, but the adrenaline kicks in automatically, my brain shifting into the focused state I'd cultivated over years of emergency medicine.

"What's coming in?" I ask Maria as I pass the central desk.

"MVC rollover. Multiple patients. First one's critical." She glances up from her computer. "Medic 402 is bringing them."

My heart does the familiar little skip it always does at the mention of Jack's unit. Three weeks since our return from New Zealand, and that reaction hasn't faded—if anything, it has intensified.

I reach Bay One just as Nathan is setting up, his movements efficient and precise. "Partial amputation, right arm," he reports. "They've got it controlled for now, but he's lost a lot of blood."

The bay doors whoosh open, and there is Jack, guiding the stretcher alongside Rodriguez. His face is set in the professional mask I recognize, but his eyes find mine immediately, a flash of warmth breaking through before he refocuses on his patient.

"Thirty-six-year-old male, ejected during rollover," Jack reports crisply as they transfer the patient. "Partial amputation, right arm at the elbow, CAT tourniquet applied. Hypotensive at scene, responding to fluids. GCS 14, alert but confused. No loss of consciousness reported."

Dr. Ward moves in immediately, already assessing the mangled arm as the trauma team swarms around the patient. Jack steps back, giving them room to work, and moves to my side.

"Hey," he says softly, just for me.

"Hey yourself," I reply, unable to suppress a smile despite the chaos around us. "Bad one?"

"Second patient's less critical. 405 is bringing her in now." He glances at the trauma team working efficiently, then back to me. "We still on for tonight?"

"Absolutely. Madison's off to Chloe's at nine." I check my watch. "I'm off at seven."

"Perfect. I'll be there at seven-thirty." His radio suddenly blares a hard series of tones, and he grimaces. "Got to go. That's dispatch."

"Be safe," I say, our ritual now.

He squeezes my hand quickly. "Always."

As he jogs back to his rig, I return my attention to the trauma in progress, the momentary distraction set aside as I focus on the patient's needs. But the warmth of Jack's brief touch lingers, a reminder of how thoroughly he'd integrated into my life since our return.

Three hours later, I'm stepping out of the shower when I hear Madison's excited voice from the kitchen, followed by Jack's deeper tones and laughter. I smile, wrapping myself in a towel. He must have let himself in with the key I'd given him last week.

When I emerge from the bedroom, dressed for our date in a simple black dress and low heels, I find them at the kitchen island. Madison is showing Jack pictures from her school project while simultaneously devouring what appears to be Thai takeout.

"I thought you were eating at Chloe's," I say, leaning against the doorframe.

Madison looks up, mouth full of pad Thai. "Change of plans.

Chloe's mom had a meeting, so I told her I'd find something here to eat instead."

"And I brought dinner because I figured someone might be hungry," Jack adds, his eyes warming as he takes in my appearance. "You look beautiful."

"Thank you." I move into the kitchen, pressing a kiss to his cheek. "This was thoughtful."

"There's green curry for you in the bag," he says. "Figured you might want something before we go out."

"Perfect." I pull out the container, the familiar spicy aroma making my stomach growl. "How was the rest of your shift?"

"Busy. That second crash victim ended up having an occult splenic laceration that didn't present until later." He shakes his head. "But she's stable now. Good catch by Dr. Ward."

"She's the best trauma attending we've got," I agree, taking a bite of curry. "How was school?" I ask Madison.

"Fine. I got an A on my geography project." She grins at Jack. "I did it on New Zealand. Ms. Garcia was super impressed that I'd actually been there."

"Used those McKenzie connections, did you?" Jack teases.

Madison rolls her eyes. "I may have mentioned that my mom's boyfriend's family owns a famous vineyard. Just a casual reference."

"Very subtle," I laugh.

"Speaking of the McKenzies," Jack says, sliding an envelope across the counter to me. "This came for you today. Express from Aotearoa."

I recognize Helen's elegant handwriting immediately. "Your mother?"

"Apparently." He looks as surprised as I feel. "Emma texted that Mum was 'up to something' but wouldn't elaborate."

I open the envelope carefully, pulling out a thick cream-colored card with the McKenzie Estate logo embossed in gold. Inside is a handwritten note in Helen's perfect penmanship:

Dear Sophia (and Madison),

Michael and I would be delighted if you would join us for the holiday season at McKenzie Estate. We understand your work schedules may make a Christmas visit challenging, but we could perhaps compromise on New Year's? The summer harvest will be in full swing, and I've taken the liberty of reserving space for you both on the estate's annual helicopter tour of the vineyards.

Emma insists that Madison's rugby training continue, and Lily has already planned several excursions to wildlife sanctuaries that she claims Madison would enjoy.

As for myself, I thought perhaps you might appreciate a tour of the Lakes District Hospital. Though quite small compared to your Metro General, I've spoken with Judith Wilson (our local MP) who assures me Te Whatu Ora would be most interested in your professional perspectives on rural emergency services. Judith mentioned they're developing an exchange program for senior emergency staff, and your experience would be most valuable.

Lily also mentioned that she would be honored if Madison might consider being a junior bridesmaid in her February wedding to Oliver. I realize this would require a second trip so soon after the holidays, but Lily has quite fallen in love with Madison's enthusiasm. As she put it, "anyone who gets that excited *about rugby and kiwi birds is clearly McKenzie material."*

Jackson, of course, is welcome as well, though I imagine that goes without saying.

Please consider the invitation. Whatever our initial misunderstandings, family is family.

Warmest regards,

Helen McKenzie

"Well," I say, passing the card to Jack. "That's unexpected."

He scans it quickly, eyebrows rising. "A helicopter tour? And my mother talking to Judith bloody Wilson?" He shakes his head in disbelief. "Do you have any idea what this means? Wilson's National Party, and my parents are staunch Labour supporters. They'd sooner drink California wine than vote National. She must be calling in every favor she has."

"She called us family," I point out, the word catching in my throat.

Jack's expression softens. "She's right. You are." He takes my hand, his thumb tracing circles on my palm. "Both of you."

Madison, who'd been reading over Jack's shoulder, lets out a piercing squeal that makes both of us jump.

"EEEEEEE! I get to be in a WEDDING? IN NEW ZEALAND?" She is practically vibrating with excitement. "Can I tell Chloe? Please? She's going to DIE."

"I think that's a yes to Lily's invitation," Jack laughs, his eyes crinkling at the corners.

"Are weddings in New Zealand different?" Madison asks, already typing furiously on her phone. "What do junior bridesmaids wear? Will there be a special dress? Does Lily like purple? Because I look amazing in purple."

I can't help but smile at her enthusiasm. "Let's start by accepting the invitation before you plan the entire wedding, sweetie."

"Say yes," Jack urges, his blue eyes alight with hope. "I want to show you everything we missed the first time. The summer harvest festival, swimming in Lake Dunstan, stargazing from the cottage roof..."

"Is that a yes?" Madison presses, her excitement palpable.

I look between them—my daughter and the man who has somehow become essential to both our lives in such a short time—and feel the last of my reservations melt away.

"Yes," I say, squeezing Jack's hand. "Let's go back to New Zealand." I pause, then add innocently, "And maybe we can take a quick flight over to Australia, too. I've always wanted to see a kangaroo."

Jack's face freezes in horror, as if I'd casually suggested drop-kicking a cocker spaniel puppy. His mouth opens and closes several times before he catches the mischievous glint in my eye.

"You!" He lunges for me, fingers finding my ribs. "You did that on purpose!"

I dissolve into laughter as he tickles me, squirming in his arms. "Your face!" I tease, breathless. "You should have seen it!"

"Aussies and Kiwis are natural enemies," he informs me with mock seriousness, still tickling mercilessly. "Like Scots and other Scots."

"Oh my God, CRINGE," Madison groans, though she is clearly fighting a smile. "Get a room, you two."

"This is a room," Jack points out, finally releasing me as I wipe tears of laughter from my eyes.

"You know what I mean," Madison rolls her eyes, already typing furiously on her phone. "Wait until I tell Chloe I'm spending New Year's in New Zealand. She's going to literally die."

Jack's smile is radiant as he pulls me close again, pressing a kiss to my temple.

"Best decision I ever made," I say honestly, then pause for a moment's consideration. "Well. I guess that'll be two weddings we're going to be at in short order-"

The doorbell rings, signaling Chloe's arrival. Madison grabs her overnight bag, pausing to hug me fiercely.

"Have fun on your date," she says. "Don't wait up."

"Text me when you get to Chloe's," I call as she heads for the door.

"I will!" She turns back briefly. "Oh, and Jack? My dad's being weird about the formal next month. Says I can't go because it's a 'breeding ground for promiscuity' or something equally stupid. Can you talk to him?"

Jack exchanges a quick glance with me, silent communication passing between us. We've been navigating the Troy situation cautiously since our return, aware of the delicate balance between protecting Madison and not alienating her father completely.

"We'll figure it out," Jack promises. "Your mom and I will talk to him together."

Madison's relief is visible. "Thanks. You guys are the best. LOVE YOU!" With a final wave, she is gone, the door slamming behind her.

"Troy's at it again?" Jack asks quietly once we were alone.

"He's been escalating since that viral video humiliation," I sigh. "I think he's trying to reassert control."

"We won't let him," Jack says simply, his hand finding mine again. "Not with Madison."

The casual "we" warms me from within. That is the difference now—I'm not facing Troy's toxicity alone anymore. I have a partner, someone who stands beside me not because he has to, but because he chooses to.

"So," I say, leaning into him. "This date. What exactly did you have planned?"

His arms encircle my waist, pulling me closer. "Well, I was thinking drinks at that new place downtown, maybe that jazz club you mentioned wanting to try..."

"Or," I suggest, my hands sliding under his shirt, "we could stay in. Make use of this empty house."

His breath catches as my fingers trace the ridges of muscle beneath his shirt. "Christ, Sophia," he murmurs, bending to capture my lips in a kiss that quickly deepens from gentle to urgent.

When we break apart, both breathless, he presses his forehead to mine. "I'm meant to be romancing you properly tonight," he says, his accent thickening as it always does when he is affected. "Flowers, wine, the works."

I smile against his lips. "Jack McKenzie, haven't you figured it out yet? All I need is you."

He lifts me suddenly, earning a surprised laugh as he carries me toward the bedroom. "You do realize this means we're completely missing our dinner reservation?"

"I'm not hungry," I say, wrapping my legs around his waist. "Not for food, anyway."

His laughter vibrates through me as he kicks the bedroom door closed behind us.

Hours later, after whispered laughter and rediscovered rhythms, we lay tangled in the sheets, my head on his chest, his fingers tracing idle patterns on my bare shoulder. The bedside clock read 11:43 PM —Madison will be home in the morning.

"I've been thinking," Jack says, his voice rumbling beneath my ear. "About New Zealand. About us."

I prop myself up on one elbow to see his face. "What about us?"

"The long-distance thing," he says, his eyes serious now. "It's not sustainable forever. Being here with you and Madison, going back for holidays...eventually we'll need a more permanent solution."

My heart quickens. "Are you suggesting...?"

"Nothing specific yet," he clarifies quickly. "Just...thinking about possibilities. What the future might look like."

"And what does it look like, in your mind?" I ask, curious.

He takes a deep breath. "Sometimes I see us here—me transferring my paramedic certification to stay permanently, building a life in your world. Other times..." He hesitates. "I wonder if you and Madison might consider New Zealand. Not immediately, but someday."

The thought sends a shiver of both excitement and apprehension through me. "That's a big change. Madison's whole life is here. My career..."

"I know," he says quickly. "It's just thoughts. Possibilities. We have time to figure it out."

"We do," I agree, settling back against him. "And for what it's worth, I'm not opposed to considering all options. Including New Zealand."

His arms tighten around me. "Really?"

"Really," I confirm. "After all, I've got connections there now. Helen mentioned the hospital..."

He laughs, the sound vibrating through his chest. "Always planning ahead, Charge Nurse Mitchell."

"Someone has to," I tease. "Paramedic McKenzie."

"Speaking of names," he says casually, though I can feel the nervous tension in his body. "My offer still stands, you know. About taking yours. If we ever...if that's something you'd want."

The vulnerability in his voice makes my heart ache. I sit up fully, meeting his gaze directly. "Jack, listen to me. I fell in love with Jack McKenzie—all of him, including his name and heritage. I would never ask you to give that up."

"But if I wanted to?"

"Then we'd discuss it," I say. "But honestly? I'm rather fond of the name McKenzie. It suits you."

His smile is slow and beautiful. "Mitchell-McKenzie has a nice ring to it too."

"It does," I agree, warmth spreading through my chest at the implication. "But we don't need to decide that tonight."

He pulls me back down beside him, pressing a kiss to my forehead. "No rush," he agrees. "We've got all the time in the world."

As I drift toward sleep in Jack's arms, I marvel at the journey that has brought us here—from those first flirtatious radio calls to reconciliation on a New Zealand estate, to this quiet certainty of building a future together. The path hasn't been straight or easy, but it has led exactly where we need to be.

Together.

Home.

No matter which side of the world we are on.

a note
from the author

DEAR READER,

Thank you for spending your time with Sophia and Jack.

I became a writer, in part, because my husband (also an ER nurse and an aspiring science fiction author) cannot write a romance scene to save his life. He's brilliant at many things, but trust me: no one wants to read his version of a love story. When he looked over my *significant* edits to the attempt in his book, he told me, jokingly, "If you're so good at this, *you* should be the one writing a book."

So I took the pen (or keyboard) and ran with it.

But the heart of this book comes from nearly two decades in emergency services. It was born from a hundred chaotic nights in the ER, whispered trauma bay confessions, and the quiet resilience of people facing impossible odds. As an EMT, firefighter, and emergency department nurse, I've spent years at the intersection of heartbreak and hope... and I wanted to write a love story that honored both.

Sophia and Jack aren't perfect. They're messy and human and deeply real to me. Sophia is exactly the kind of nurse I've been blessed to work beside throughout my career: fierce, exhausted, brilliant, and still giving everything she has to hold the world together. Jack is every medic, EMT, or firefighter who's ever cracked a joke to keep the world from falling apart.

If you're not ready to leave Metro General, the Code Blue Hearts series has more stories waiting for you. Nate, the former Navy corpsman with the color-coded lunch notes, gets his story in *No Greater Love*. Izzy Delgado—the fire lieutenant who's twice as good and getting half the respect—fights for love and her captain's chair in *Burn Notice*. And Dr. Delaney Ward, the Harvard-educated ER physician whose ice queen reputation is armor built one dismissive colleague at a time, meets her match in *Breaking Point*.

Each book stands on its own, but the characters weave through each other's lives the way real ER families do. And if you loved them and have a free moment, please consider leaving a review! For independent authors, reader reviews are the single most important way to help new readers find our books. It truly means a lot!

Thank you again for letting me share this story with you. From me, my family, and my loyal writing companion Sunny (the dog, not a metaphor), stay safe, stay stubborn, and never underestimate the power of love.

Or caffeine.

With all my heart,

Cari

available now!

NO GREATER LOVE: CODE BLUE HEARTS, BOOK 2

WHILE YOU WERE FALLING for Sophia and Jack, did you notice when Sophia's colleague desperately needed someone to watch his daughter in the break room?

That single dad was **Nathan Crawford**, and the nurse who stepped up was **Tasha Williams**.

Now discover the incredible story of a Navy Cross recipient hiding his heroism behind surgical precision and dad jokes;

A fierce Fast Track nurse who protects her heart as carefully as he protects his daughter;

An 11-year-old girl who needs a mother—and knows exactly who she wants;

A biological mother who returns years after abandoning her daughter, with lawyers, lies, and a plan to take *everything*.

That text exchange between Jack and Nate? It was just the beginning.

In Book 2, you'll discover how a simple piece of advice creates a debt that will change everything when Nathan needs it most.

"I thought nothing could top Sophia and Jack's story. I was wrong. This book destroyed me in the best way." - Early Reader

"The custody battle had me on the edge of my seat, but the found family moments made me sob happy tears." - ARC Review

Get your copy now!

Can't wait? Turn the page for a sneak peek at Chapter 1. And then, follow it up with the REST of the Code Blue Hearts series!

BURN NOTICE: Code Blue Hearts, Book 3

The good ol' boys' club has a saying: "Fire service is no place for a woman." Lieutenant Isabela Delgado has two words for them: *Watch me.* When ER nurse Jimmy Dalton writes a letter defending Izzy to her battalion chief, he thinks he's fighting for the woman he loves. Instead, he hands her enemies the ammunition they need to destroy her career.

BREAKING POINT: Code Blue Hearts, Book 4

Dr. Delaney Ward didn't claw her way through Harvard Medical School to be her father's campaign prop or anyone's idea of what a doctor should be. Her "ice queen" reputation? Armor, built one dismissive colleague at a time. Especially against Dr. Cameron Lee, whose easy swagger reminds her of every man who's ever underestimated her.

A SOUTHERN STARS CHRISTMAS: A Code Blue Hearts Novella

Do you already miss Sophia and Jack? They're back, navigating McKenzie family dinners that require diplomatic immunity, a custody threat from Troy, and a proposal that takes ten boxes to unwrap. You're gonna want to read it, no matter what time of year it is!

sneak peek for BOOK 2:

TASHA

Metro General was quiet when I arrived, the calm before the inevitable storm of a Saturday morning. I was running just late enough to be annoying, but not late enough to get called out for it. The perfect sweet spot.

I pushed through the staff entrance, my travel mug of coffee clutched tightly in one hand, mentally preparing myself for another day of bodily fluids, entitled patients, and doctors who thought "nurse" was synonymous with "personal servant." At least my scrubs were fresh, and my coffee was strong enough to strip paint. Small victories.

The break room would be packed with the day shift getting their assignments, but I needed to refill my water bottle before facing humanity. As I approached, the door burst open, and I nearly collided with Nathan Crawford—Metro General's most annoyingly punctual nurse—looking frazzled in a way I'd never seen before.

And he wasn't alone.

A girl of about eleven or twelve trailed behind him, clutching a backpack shaped like some cartoon character and a paperback book. Her dark hair was pulled back in a messy ponytail, and she had blue braces that flashed briefly when she nervously bit her lip.

Crawford's kid? Had to be. Same serious eyes, same way of standing, like she was trying to take up as little space as possible.

I stepped back, watching as Sophia immediately took control of the situation, ushering Crawford and his daughter into the charge office. Through the glass, I could see Crawford's rigid posture, the tension in his shoulders. The little girl looked small and out of place, clearly trying to be invisible.

"Babysitter drama," Maria muttered from beside me, appearing like she always did, out of nowhere. "Poor Nate!"

I took a sip of my coffee, affecting nonchalance. "Not my circus, not my monkeys."

But I kept watching. The kid...Paige. That was her name. Was fidgeting with the book in her hands. *The Giver*. I remembered that book from school. Pretty heavy stuff for a tween, but Crawford's kid was probably as serious as he was.

Wait. I remembered now. A few weeks back, Crawford had been showing around a picture Paige had drawn for a science project. Something about heart valves, way beyond what an eleven-year-old should be capable of. He'd been so damn proud, practically bursting at the seams, even though he tried to play it cool. "Just sharing some interesting anatomical information," he'd claimed, fooling absolutely no one.

I'd taken a look, more out of boredom than interest. The kid had included the interatrial septum in her analysis of heart valves. Most *adults* wouldn't catch that.

Through the glass, I could see Sophia's expression shift from stern to sympathetic. Crawford looked like he was drowning. The kid looked like she might cry any second. After a moment, they all disappeared from the break room, heading for the charge nurse's office.

"What do you think will happen?" I asked Maria, keeping my tone disinterested.

Maria shrugged. "He'll probably have to call out. With the new attendance policy, that'll be rough." She lowered her voice. "HR's been on the warpath lately."

I frowned. Crawford was a pain in the ass with his military precision and his constant "by the book" attitude, but he was also one of the few nurses who always had your back in a crisis, who never complained when shifts ran long, who took the difficult patients without whining.

And that kid. Something about her quiet determination to be

brave, the way she clutched that book like it was a lifeline...it reminded me of my cousin Alexis at that age. Scared but trying so hard not to show it.

Before I could overthink it, I found myself walking toward the charge office. I knocked once, decisively.

Three faces turned toward me as I opened the door. Crawford looked shell-shocked, Sophia looked calculating, and Paige...Paige just looked lost.

Something twisted in my chest, unfamiliar and uncomfortable.

Damn it.

"Oh my God, hiiiii, is this your daughter?" I blurted, channeling my inner enthusiastic babysitter voice. "The one who drew that heart valves picture you showed everyone!?"

Paige looked up, clearly startled. "You showed my picture to people?"

Crawford's ears reddened. "It was exceptional work."

I leaned down slightly to Paige's level, surprising myself with how genuine my interest was. "I thought it was soooooo cool how you included the interatrial septum. Most people forget that's technically a fifth distinct area."

Paige brightened visibly, sitting up straighter. "Dad helped me build a model!"

The words tumbled out before I could stop them: "If you need someone to watch her, I could stay with her in the break room. Just until you can sort something out." I shrugged, trying to look casual, like this wasn't completely out of character for me. "I'm good with kids. Got a bunch of younger cousins."

Crawford stared at me like I'd grown a second head. Sophia's eyebrows nearly hit her hairline.

"Are you sure, Tasha?" Sophia asked, her voice neutral but her eyes sharp. "You'd be responsible for her. I'd need to pull you from the floor."

"I can handle it," I replied, a defensive edge creeping into my voice. What, they thought I'd *corrupt* the kid? "For an hour or so. Give him time to make some calls."

Sophia made her decision quickly. "Okay, Tasha. Thank you. For one hour. Break room. I'll let Nathan and I handle Fast Track between us."

Crawford looked at me like I'd just thrown him a life preserver in a hurricane. "Tasha, I...thank you. Seriously. I owe you big time."

His sincerity was so unexpected it made me uncomfortable. "No worries, Crawford," I said, already turning to Paige, desperate to change the subject. I gestured to the book in her hands. "Is that '*The Giver*'?"

Paige nodded, holding it up. "For school."

"That's one of my favorites," I said, genuinely excited now. "The ending still makes me mad, though."

Paige's eyes widened. "You've read it?"

"Dystopian literature is kind of my thing," I admitted, then caught Sophia's surprised look and felt instantly defensive. "What? I read!"

Sophia raised her hands in surrender. "Never doubted it."

Crawford hesitated, then unzipped his backpack and handed Paige a smaller bag. "Your lunch. Protein bar for midmorning. Water bottle's full. Remember your inhaler's in the side pocket if you need it."

"*Dad*," Paige muttered, embarrassed. "I know."

I bit back a smile. He was so painfully earnest. It was actually kind of...sweet? No, not sweet. Thorough. Professional. Something like that.

"Want a juice box, Paige?" I asked, already steering her toward the door. "We've got apple, orange, and prune...mmmmm, we should probably skip that last one."

Paige giggled, a quiet sound, but real. My heart did a weird little flip.

Once in the break room, I settled Paige at the corner table, away from the main traffic. "So, '*The Giver*,' huh? How far are you?"

"Jonas just left the community," she said, touching the book cover. "With Gabriel."

"Oooh, the great escape," I nodded. "What do you think happens to them?"

Paige shrugged, but her eyes were alive with curiosity. "The book makes it seem like they find Elsewhere, where there's music and colors. But my friend Tyler thinks they just freeze to death."

I laughed. "Tyler sounds cheerful."

"He likes zombie movies," Paige explained solemnly.

"Of course he does," I said, grinning. "Want to know what I think?"

"What?"

"I think they make it. I think the memory of music becomes real music. I think they find people who remember how to feel things, how to see color." I leaned in conspiratorially. "And I think the sequel proves me right."

Paige's eyes widened. "There's a sequel?"

"There's four books total," I informed her. "I've got the whole set at home. Maybe I could lend them to you sometime."

Paige nodded eagerly, then hesitated. "My dad says I should only borrow books if I can return them within two weeks. He says it's respectful of other people's property."

Of course he did. "Well, maybe we can work something out," I said. "Your dad comes here pretty often, after all."

Paige smiled, a small, shy thing. "Okay."

We chatted about books for a while, and I was impressed by how articulate she was. Not just smart, but thoughtful. No wonder Crawford was so proud of her.

"Want to see a cool trick?" I asked suddenly, grabbing a tongue depressor from a supply drawer.

"Sure," Paige said, looking intrigued.

I rummaged through another drawer and found some medical tape. "When I was about your age, my mom worked night shifts at a hospital. Sometimes I'd have to hang out while she finished paper-work. One of the nurses taught me how to make these."

I folded the tongue depressor in half, securing it with tape, then cut small triangular notches on both sides. With a few more folds and twists, it resembled a butterfly. I added a few more details with a Sharpie, and voilà.

"A butterfly!" Paige exclaimed, delighted.

"Here," I said, handing it to her. "You can color it later if you want."

Just then, the break room door opened, and Crawford stuck his head in. He looked surprised to find us both smiling, Paige holding her new creation.

"Everything okay?" he asked, his eyes darting between us.

"We're good," I said, straightening up, suddenly self-conscious. "Just talking books and making butterflies. Regular stuff."

He nodded, a strange expression crossing his face. "I'm still trying to reach Mrs. Swanson. Thank you again, Tasha."

"No big deal," I said, waving him off. "Paige is cool. We're vibing."

Paige giggled at that, and Crawford's eyes softened as they landed on his daughter. For a brief moment, I glimpsed something in his expression—a fierce, protective love that was almost painful to witness.

Then he was gone, back to his calls and his patients.

"Your dad really loves you," I said without thinking.

Paige nodded, serious again. "He's the best dad ever. He tries really hard."

"I can tell," I said softly.

We spent the next half hour making more butterflies, talking about school, and comparing notes on our favorite books. When Crawford returned, announcing that Mrs. Swanson was on her way, I felt an odd pang of disappointment.

When the older woman arrived, Paige gathered her things. Then, to my complete surprise, she gave me a quick, shy hug.

I froze for a split second before awkwardly patting her shoulder. "See you around, kiddo," I managed. "Let me know what you think about the ending of that book, okay?"

As Paige left with her father and Mrs. Swanson, I found myself watching them go. Crawford's hand rested lightly on Paige's shoulder, guiding her, and she looked up at him with complete trust.

Something twisted in my chest again, that same unfamiliar feeling. It wasn't envy, exactly. Maybe...wistfulness? A strange sense of having glimpsed something precious and rare.

Then Maria appeared at my elbow, eyebrows raised suggestively. "Look at you, playing Mary Poppins."

"Shut up, Maria," I muttered, the spell broken. "The kid's not terrible. And Crawford owes me coffee for a month."

"Mmm-hmm," Maria hummed knowingly.

I grabbed my stethoscope, slinging it around my neck. "I'm going to get report. Some of us have actual work to do."

But as I headed for the nurses' station, I couldn't quite shake the image of Paige's smile when she'd held that paper butterfly, or the raw gratitude in Crawford's eyes when I'd offered to help.

It was just one weird morning, I told myself.

It didn't mean anything.

Acknowledgements

Thank you to Nora for making this book shine, it wouldn't even be here without you.

To Rain for the gorgeous art.

To my beta readers Katie, Kristen, and Paige, who caught all my mistakes and cheered me on.

To my kids for understanding when I disappeared into my writing cave.

To my husband for being there every step of the way.

To Sunny for being the best writing companion.

And to the romance community for once again welcoming a newbie with open arms.

also by cari blake

Code Blue Hearts Series

Under Southern Stars (Book 1)

No Greater Love (Book 2)

Burn Notice (Book 3) My Book

Breaking Point (Book 4)

A Southern Stars Christmas (A Code Blue Hearts Novella)

.

About the author

Cari Blake is a former EMT and firefighter turned emergency room nurse who writes romance between twelve-hour shifts. She lives with her husband (also an ER nurse), three kids (Brooklyn, Austin and Mason), and a cocker spaniel named Sunny who provides essential writing supervision. When not at the hospital or crafting happily-ever-afters, she can be found drinking dangerous amounts of coffee, working out at Burn Boot Camp, or exploring St. John, USVI.

http://www.codebluehearts.com

www.ingramcontent.com/pod-product-compliance
Lightning Source LLC
Chambersburg PA
CBHW050514110726
47899CB00005B/1460